Deathright

" 'Dev Stryker' is the pseudonym of a pair of bestselling thriller writers who have combined sales of 30 million books and 3 Edgar Awards. The talent is evident. *Deathright* is a smooth, accomplished thriller that begins with a methodical drawn-out tease and rapidly accelerates to roller coaster velocity. The action is driving and relentless.

"A highly entertaining thriller."

—*Mystery News*

End Game

"I could not put Dev Stryker's *End Game* down once I got past the first couple of pages—hell, past the first couple of paragraphs! If you're an early to bed, early to rise person, I wouldn't recommend *End Game*, because the damned book is going to keep you up nights. I really cared about Stryker's people; now I'm going to catch up on my sleep while I eagerly await the next book."

—David Hagberg
author of *Countdown*

"*End Game* is a clever and original thriller that delivers gripping suspense from first page to last."
—Thomas Chastain
past President of the Mystery Writers of America

"Dev Stryker's *End Game* has all the makings of a major bestseller. Watch for a smash movie to be made of this."

—Ed Gorman
author of *Night Kills*

DEATHRIGHT

Dev Stryker

A TOM DOHERTY ASSOCIATES BOOK
NEW YORK

This is a work of fiction. All the characters and events portrayed in this book are fictitious and any resemblance to real people or events is purely coincidental.

DEATHRIGHT

Copyright © 1993 by M.C. Murphy

Cover art by Wim van de Hulst

A Tor Book
Published by Tom Doherty Associates, Inc.
175 Fifth Avenue
New York, N.Y. 10010

Tor® is a registered trademark of Tom Doherty Associates, Inc.

ISBN: 0-812-52162-5
Library of Congress Card Catalog Number: 92-33363

First edition: January 1993
First mass market edition: August 1995

Printed in the United States of America

0 9 8 7 6 5 4 3 2 1

For Bob Meier

"He has wandered into an unknown land,
And left us wondering how very fair that land
May be, since he tarries there."

Rest in Peace.

Acknowledgments

The author wishes to acknowledge the invaluable assistance of Stephen French, who helped design the fictitious Pandora, and Dilia Mitrotti, whose family has endured the excesses of a dictatorial regime in a Caribbean nation, and seen its end.

To these individuals and others who have offered their time, advice, and support, I am grateful.

Dev Stryker

In December 1988, CIA aerial reconnaissance photographs revealed a compound in Rabta, Libya, that had been used as a research facility for the production of chemical weapons. The nature of these weapons was not known.

Prologue

Sebha, Libya

Yusef Nassif walked alone into the hot darkness of the warehouse. The place was empty, but had once been used to store grain. Now hundreds of rats swarmed in the corners, chittering angrily at the intruder.

Nassif did not like rats. *He chose this place to insult me,* he thought, feeling the sweat of his hands slick against the handle of the briefcase he carried. The rats squealed with each footfall.

"Billy Starr?" Nassif's voice echoed. There was no response.

Damn him.

He walked farther into the darkness. When he bumped into a wooden crate, the rats screamed. A pair of yellow eyes dashed past, near his foot. He froze in terror, involuntarily emitting a sharp gasp.

When the rush of blood ceased pounding in his ears, he heard laughter. It was the American's, low, mocking, a stupid sound straight from the wilderness where this creature came from.

A flashlight clicked on, and its beam shone directly into

Nassif's eyes, blinding him.

"What do you want?" the voice drawled.

"You are a difficult man to find."

"That's why I'm still alive."

You've been alive too long, Nassif thought.

Billy Starr was forty-eight years old, long past the age of most active single mercenaries. The majority of them, if they weren't killed in their twenties, retired into harmless drunks along the waterfront of Marseilles or Naples. But then, most of them did not mind retirement. They didn't need to kill the way this one did.

Nassif had argued against using the American. He was too old. Sooner or later his reflexes would fail him. And too arrogant. He never even bothered to hide his face. If Nassif's government had not given him sanctuary, a dozen Western nations would have obliterated him by now.

And he personally detested the man, this predator with no loyalties. Not to his country, not to any country. Not to any idea. Not to anyone.

The flashlight wavered for a moment, and Nassif heard the top of a flask opening, then smelled the pungent odor of whiskey as the American drank, groaning with pleasure.

An animal, Nassif thought. *No better than an animal.*

"So what's on your mind, Yusef?" the American asked, a bitter tone to his voice.

Nassif swallowed. Silently he hoisted the briefcase onto the crate and opened it. Inside lay half a million American dollars.

Starr prodded the bills with the flashlight, checking for a false bottom in the briefcase. "Looks all right," he said finally. He took another drink.

"The project is to begin in three weeks," Nassif said. "I will meet you in Panama City on the eleventh."

"What about the follow-through?"

"We have another man for that. Someone less visible than yourself," he added with distaste. "If it becomes necessary for him to contact you, it will be done through me."

Billy Starr set the flashlight on top of the money and lit a cigarette. For a moment Nassif could see the man's booze-bloated face in the glow of the match. "You're using my kid, aren't you?" Starr asked with the trace of a smile.

Nassif didn't answer.

"My, my. So the big experiment paid off. You went and made your own Frankenstein."

The Arab was nearly overcome with revulsion. Starr had murdered the boy's mother. He had intentionally waited until the boy was there to see it.

"Someone had to raise him," Nassif said tersely.

"Oh, and I'll bet you did a grand job of that." He took another drink. "Jes' grand. Is he smart?"

"He learns well."

"How many passports you got for him?"

"He speaks twelve languages."

"Good shot, too, right?"

Nassif clenched his teeth.

"Yeah, I reckon you got yourselves a real tame white boy, don't you? Bet he salutes the Libyan flag and everything."

Nassif took a step backward. "Mr. Starr, I believe our business is concluded for the moment." He left the briefcase open and walked toward the doorway.

"Nassif?"

He turned, half expecting a bullet in his brain. A bullet, and then the inevitable mutilation. Billy Starr practiced rituals unique to himself.

"What's his name?" Starr asked.

"Does that matter?"

"The girl used to call him Daniel."

The girl. The beast's mate. Nassif remembered his last sight of her, spread in parts throughout the bloodstained bedroom while the child cowered in the corner, his eyes vacant.

"He has no name," Nassif said.

Amman, Jordan

The man with no name strolled lazily through the bazaar, stopping occasionally at a booth to look at souvenirs. April was pleasant in Jordan, particularly for someone raised in the desert, as he had been.

"A relic of Jesus," the stall owner called out. "A piece of the cross."

The man shook his head.

"Guaranteed genuine. And for you only, a hundred dinars."

The man smiled politely. "No, thanks," he answered in Swedish, putting the chip of wood down.

I am a Swede, he told himself. *My name is Christiaan Franssen. I was raised in Vasterbotten. I work as the officer of protocol at the Swedish Embassy here in Amman.*

He always provided extensive backgrounds for himself. He invented a man and then became that man, crawling into his fabricated skin like a hermit crab inhabiting a shell.

I have two sisters and a brother. My parents . . .

He closed his eyes and felt himself stagger slightly. In his mind he saw a dismembered woman, her blood spreading in red blots on the satin bedspread, the walls running blood. And in front of him, standing like a giant, the long, bloody knife in his upraised hand, was his father.

That is not my father!

He wiped the back of his hand over his perspiring forehead and tried again.

My parents, Jeorg and Monica Franssen, are still alive. My father is a retired police officer. He is a big man with a belly. He still has all his hair. He has never been outside Vasterbotten.

A young Arab boy tugged at his trousers. Without losing his train of thought, "Christiaan Franssen"—whom the man truly believed he was, at this point—acknowledged the boy with a nod.

"Silver!" another stallmonger shrieked. "Beautiful, one-hundred-percent sterling silver. Guaranteed one hundred percent. Come see for yourself!"

The man walked on. The boy trailed behind him.

My name is Christiaan Franssen. Both my parents are alive.

Ahead, a heavyset Caucasian man was walking purposefully. "Christiaan Franssen" recognized him from photographs. He was Albert Neumeyer, political attaché to the American Embassy in Jordan. He was also the CIA head of station in Amman.

Albert Neumeyer had a woman whom he liked to visit at midday. Sometimes he walked through the bazaar to reach her house. "Franssen" had been waiting to see him for five days.

"Mr. Neumeyer!" he shouted, waving elaborately. The heavyset man paused, his eyes flickering automatically around the bazaar. "Christiaan Franssen," the man with no name said, extending his hand. "We met last Tuesday at the French Embassy reception. I am with the Swedish delegation." His accent was cultured but noticeable. A linguist would have pinpointed his place of origin as Vasterbotten.

"Oh. Of course." Neumeyer shook the hand dutifully. "Please to see you again, Mr. Franssen," he said, pretending to remember the man.

"This is the first opportunity I've had to take in the sights."

"Ah, good. Enjoy yourself."

Neumeyer was preparing to escape from him when the Arab boy grabbed for Franssen's wallet. Instinctively, the American shot out his hand and collared the young culprit. As he did so, Franssen ducked around comically, looking at once frightened and bewildered, and deftly deposited a small egg-sized sphere into the outside pocket of Neumeyer's jacket.

"Here you go," the American said, handing the wallet back to Franssen.

"Thank you," the Swede stammered. "Nothing like this has ever happened to me before. You are very kind."

The boy wriggled out of Neumeyer's grasp and ran away wildly. The American shrugged. "Nothing would have happened to him, anyway," he said. "Now if you'll excuse me . . ."

"Certainly. Thank you."

"You're new here?"

"Yes. I arrived just last week."

"Here's some free advice. Don't keep your wallet in your pants. The pickpockets here are like magicians."

Franssen laughed embarrassedly. "I believe you're right. Perhaps it is the early training."

"You got it." Neumeyer nodded and walked on. Franssen looked after him for a moment, then hurried away in the opposite direction.

Six, he counted. *Five, four, three, two, one . . .*

The explosion was muffled, occurring as it did against Albert Neumeyer's body, but severe enough to injure several passersby. One of the bazaar stalls collapsed when Neumeyer's bursting corpse slammed against it. The stall owner's face was lacerated by fragments of bone from the American's pulverized hip.

A shrill wail rose up almost instantly as a crowd formed around the wounded surrounding the obscenity that had once been the CIA head of station.

His killer kept walking, mentally shedding his Swedish identity with each step. Christiaan Franssen no longer existed; he had never existed.

Near the far end of the bazaar, he saw the boy, winked at him, and tossed him a ten-dinar coin. It was worth about fifteen dollars. A fair price for a life here.

"Peace be with you," the man with no name said in Arabic.

Republic of Sangre Precioso

The Caribbean

Juan Sebastapol opened his eyes at the sound of the inmate's sickness. He did not turn to look at the man who twisted over the edge of the cot, retching in dry heaves.

It was nearing dawn. Sebastapol knew the time, although there were no clocks and no windows. A decade before, when he had been locked into his first cell, he had remained awake night after night, counting the seconds endlessly until they had formed a rhythm in his brain. Now he did not need to rely on the prison schedule to give him an approximation of the time. He knew it intrinsically, almost to the minute.

Above him, a solitary guard walked over the circular metal grate that was the ceiling of the cell. The guard paused momentarily to light a cigarette, then dropped the match through the grille to the dank cement floor where Sebastapol sat.

It fizzled by his feet. Sebastapol picked it up without thinking. Nothing was wasted here.

"Doctor . . ."

Sebastapol stood up on rickety legs that ached from the dampness of the floor and went to the man. The inmate—

what was his name?—was young. He had been jailed only a few weeks before they had all been transferred to this place. His face was burning with fever and his eyes were glazed.

"I'm thirsty," the young man croaked.

"I know. We will have water soon."

The inmate nodded. His parched lips moved soundlessly. He was saying a prayer, Sebastapol guessed. The man was a priest.

Sebastapol had given the young cleric his own bed. There were only two in the large cylindrical cell, two beds for seven prisoners: Villachaise, Floria, DeMontaigne, Allartes . . .

He squeezed his eyes shut, struggling to remember their names. He had to remember, or they would all become as gray as the walls to him, as gray as time. He had to remember . . . *everything:* dates, places, names, passing conversations, smells, sensations, geometrical progressions, chess games, formulae, the feel of a woman's breasts, the molecular structure of oxaloacilic acid, the Preamble to the American Constitution, the rosary, the Dialogues of Plato, the poetry of Boris Pasternak, the taste of caramel . . . He had to remember, or he would lose his sanity.

He had spent the past ten years in this and other prisons, remembering.

During those ten years, he had received five letters from his wife. They had all come in the first year of his confinement, and had been so heavily censored that they made virtually no sense.

We will be celebrating Paolo's fifty-fifth birthday on the fifth . . .

Exactly two hundred fifty-one people attended the Music Society's annual recital. It is the seventeenth such event. How fortunate we are to have so many fine musicians living near us!

Marla. *My beautiful, brilliant woman.* She knew he would memorize the letters, would use them. Undoubtedly there had been more, scores of them, perhaps hundreds. Even though only the five had reached him, that was enough. He had understood her meaning with the first one, and was reassured after the second that he was right. The rest only made him marvel at her persistence.

They all contained the same numbers in the same sequence: 5552511768.

Oh, Marla, he thought. *Will you never give up on me? Can't you see there is no hope?*

She was giving him a telephone number.

But whose? Was it her own? A member of the underground's? Was it the number of some Western embassy? He had racked his brain over the letters, trying to decipher some message in the words between the censored holes in the sheets of paper.

And then it came, in the fifth and last letter.

Amelia is nine today.

Amelia.

He knew.

Throbbing, aching with hope, he had carried the knowledge through six more years. There had been no other letters, and Sebastapol had not seen a telephone since he had last been outside a jail, but he remembered all the same. He would use the great weapon of his mind against the men who had taken away his life. He would remember everything.

The names of the other prisoners came back. Villachaise, the publisher. Floria, and DeMontaigne. They were anti-Castro Cubans. Allartes, the Nicaraguan professor who had stopped speaking two years ago.

Allartes had been a gentle and civilized man with a droll sense of humor. But he had been beaten too often. After a year of beatings, he had retreated into his own thoughts, if he had them. His face never showed any expression, not even when the guard told him that his wife and children had been executed.

Allartes slept on the other cot in the cell. One of the newer arrivals—Castillamo, yes, that was his name—had tried to oust the vegetative professor to claim the bunk for himself, but Sebastapol had stopped him.

"I am a doctor," Juan Sebastapol had said. "As far as I know, I am the only doctor in this camp. If you take that man's bed from him, I will refuse to treat you when you are ill."

Castillamo smirked. He had been a laborer on a road-construction crew when he murdered a Sandinistan army officer whom he had found in his home, making love to Castillamo's wife.

"I won't be here long enough to get sick," Castillamo said.

The others in the cell knew better. So did Castillamo when he looked at their faces, at their long hair gone gray, at the decayed pallor of their skin, their broken fingernails, their festering sores.

"Where are you all from?" he asked quietly.

"Cuba, Panama, everywhere," Sebastapol replied. "We are all politicals, in one way or another. In some of the other cells are men from as far away as Libya and Syria. But most of us are Nicaraguans. I am from Managua."

"You're not in Nicaragua now."

"I thought not."

Sebastapol and the others had been herded into the hold of a ship three months before and brought to this place in chains and blindfolds. In the prison infirmary, he could sometimes smell the sea.

Villachaise sat up. "Where are we?" he asked, his voice hoarse with eagerness. "Do you know?"

"I know." Castillamo smiled. "The information will cost you a bunk. I don't care if it's his or yours. How about it, old man?"

In an instant the two Cubans, who had until that moment shown no interest whatever in the new prisoner or his desires, leaped up and pinned Castillamo to the bars of the cell.

"The doctor gets the bunk, understand?" one of them growled.

"All right, all right."

The Cubans let go. Castillamo spat and took a seat on the stone floor. "We're on Isla Santa Vittoria, in the old fortress on the south end of the island. The one they call El Mirador."

Sebastapol blinked slowly. "Are you sure?" he asked.

Santa Vittoria. It was almost too much to hope for.

"I'm sure. The guard told me on the way over here."

Sebastapol nodded and felt for the first time in many years the stirring of hope.

Santa Vittoria.

He had a friend on Santa Vittoria.

That had been months ago. Five months, two weeks, three days, to be exact. Juan Sebastapol remembered everything.

A short time later, the priest had arrived. He had never asked for Sebastapol's bed, but he lay in it now. He would die in it soon, the doctor knew.

Oh Lord, oh Lord, what is his name? Sebastapol rocked his head against the stone wall, pounding, harder, harder. He had to remember. His mind was his only weapon, the only weapon he had ever possessed. He could not forget. Not a scrap, not an iota, or the entire vast machinery inside his brain might become sticky and clogged and cease to function. He had to . . .

Domingo! "Father Domingo." His voice was raspy with the profound relief he felt. He had remembered. He could still remember.

He stood up and went over to the young priest. Father Domingo's lips were still moving in silent prayer. A thin stream of pink froth bubbled from his mouth.

Juan Sebastapol removed his own rag of a shirt and wiped the young man's face. "It will be soon," he said.

"*Si*, Doctor," the priest whispered. The cracked lips formed the semblance of a smile.

The bell rang.

One by one the other inmates in the cylindrical cell awoke.

"What day is it, Doctor?" Villachaise asked.

"Wednesday, July second."

One of the two Cuban counterrevolutionaries stood to relieve himself into the drain at the center of the cell. "Christ, it's already hot," he said.

Juan Sebastapol had ceased to feel the heat of the tropical climate, even in the fetid infirmary where he worked. He was an old man. Nothing could warm him any longer.

A guard slipped a tray containing mealcakes and a bowl of water through the slot at the bottom of the door. The prisoners ate, squatting. Each took a measured portion of the water. After the four healthy ones had drunk. Sebastapol carried the bowl first to Allartes, staring trancelike from his bunk, and then to the priest.

"Drink this, Father Domingo," he urged, raising the bowl to the man's lips.

The priest took a sip.

"Drink it all," the doctor said, knowing he was giving away his own portion, as he often did. "The sickness has dehydrated you."

God only knew if the priest would be given water in the infirmary. Sometimes the guards refused to provide it just to show their authority over the wizened doctor who was now their inferior.

Although lately they had not. For the past several days there had been frequent servings of water, unasked, for the patients.

Still, the guards could change their minds, and it did Sebastapol no good to complain about the conditions in the prison's so-called hospital.

The place where he worked was more a morgue than an infirmary. The few medications available were years old. Some of them were so old that they were dried to solidity inside their sealed bottles, and Sebastapol had to add water to them in order to liquefy the medicine. God only knew if they were even worth administering after the crude reconstitution, but it was the best he could do.

The infirmary was almost as filthy as the cells. Corpses remained for hours before the guards came to remove them. If patients died during the night while the doctor was locked in his cell, their bodies were left by the night guards to rot until morning.

When he was forced to operate—which he hated to do—Sebastapol had to first scrape the grime from his patients' bodies with the top of a tin can. Few survived the infirmary. Juan Sebastapol, who had once been one of the world's preeminent neurosurgeons, had become a doctor of death.

A key rattled in the door. "Out," the guard said tonelessly. No one moved except Sebastapol. He was the only one in the cell permitted to leave. Anyone else who attempted any movement would be shot. There were no penalties for killing inmates.

"That man must come to the infirmary," Sebastapol said, nodding toward the priest.

The guard looked at the sick man with suspicion.

Sebastapol suppressed the urge to shout. "You know he's dying, you bone-headed imbecile! You've seen a hundred cases just like him. There are more every day. You and the other guards are beginning to wonder about a plague, aren't you?"

But he kept his silence.

The guard was a Nicaraguan, like most of them. He called over another man in uniform, who stood at the door with his weapon aimed at the men in the cell while the first guard walked cautiously over to the priest.

He prodded the young man with his rifle. "You. Get up," he snarled. The priest did not move.

The guard kicked him. The priest raised his hands, trembling.

Suddenly Villachaise, standing at attention in a corner of the cell, clutched his stomach and spewed vomit toward the door. It came in a projectile, as if his mouth were a hose, and hit the second guard square in the chest, flecking his face with pink blood-tinged foam.

The guard gasped in surprise. There was no other sound in the room. The inmates stood rooted, not daring to breathe. Then, with calm deliberation, the guard swung around slowly and fired one bullet into Villachaise's head.

Six years, ten months, fifteen days, Juan Sebastapol recorded mechanically. That had been the length of Villachaise's incarceration.

The doctor was not particularly surprised at the man's death; everyone died in a gruesome manner here, and a bullet to the head was a better death than most. What did fascinate him was Villachaise's violent expectoration.

How long had he had the disease? Sebastapol wondered. From the others he had observed, the incubation period seemed to be very short. Symptoms began to appear soon after a meal, and worsened steadily. Death always followed, usually within three days. He had not seen any variation in the pattern. It was as if the victims had been poisoned.

His eyes snapped toward the empty meal tray.

Poisoned...

The guard who had shot Villachaise looked to each of the prisoners in turn, silently defying them to object.

The men lowered their eyes. The priest turned his blind face toward the body. He stretched out his arms to the dead man.

"Get up!" the guard near him shouted, as if suddenly springing to life. He turned to Sebastapol and gestured with his weapon. "Get him out of here."

Slowly, struggling with the young man's weight, Sebastapol got the priest into a standing position and helped him walk. "Hurry it up," the guard said as the other soldier dragged Villachaise's body out of the cell.

The sight of the infirmary filled Sebastapol, as it always did, with a sense of despair. Forty men had died during the night.

His first job of the morning was to spill the corpses off the pallets laid on the floor and pile them against a wall, from where the guards would eventually remove them. As he did this, he recorded each death in a notebook hanging from a string on a central metal pillar.

The notebook had been his idea. When the prison authorities had objected to his request for medical charts, Sebastapol argued that such documents would provide authentic proof of death. He was rewarded with a black-and-white schoolboy's notebook and a pencil.

He had almost fainted with delight at the sight of them. They would help him to remember.

In three months the notebook had been nearly filled. It was written in English, to keep the guards from prying into it. Yet if the warden or an officer of the army were to read it, he would find only medical records among the English words.

But the genius of Sebastapol's memory lay buried between them. No one here would understand that message. Perhaps only one man in the world could read it . . .

. . . the man whose telephone number Marla had given him.

Amelia is nine years old today . . .

This morning Sebastapol sat the young priest on the floor of the infirmary while he attended to the corpses. Behind the priest, the prisoners who could walk lined up, waiting for the doctor to see them. Later, the inmates who were too sick to walk would be wheeled to the infirmary in a wooden cart. *The death cart,* Sebastapol called it to himself.

Forty dead men. How many more were being removed from their cells? How many more would die before the sun set?

It *was* a plague of some kind, a poisonous plague . . .

He heard the sound of a vehicle outside the infirmary's barred window. Sebastapol was not permitted to stand near the window, but it was from here that he had smelled the sea. It was from here that he saw the small square of blue that was the sky and the high round pale disk of the sun.

A square of light fell on one of the corpses. Sebastapol moved the body and brought the priest to lie in the light. "Feel it," he said gently. "It is sun."

He looked to the window. There he saw the white truck.

He felt himself stiffen. The truck had been parked in the same spot for the past week.

It was a van, very large, with air ducts and generators bulging from its interior, and it emitted the constant whirr of an air conditioner. The day after it arrived, the first plague victims had begun to report to the infirmary.

He had recorded this event in his notebook, as well as the visit that day of the doctors who came from the van. He heard their voices as they emerged from the swollen white vehicle. They spoke in Arabic.

"What a relief to walk."

"If we're lucky, we might be able to go for a swim."

One man laughed. "No thanks."

They were silent after that.

Twice a day the Arab doctors visited the infirmary, but never to treat the patients. They only extracted vials of blood from their veins.

They never bothered with Sebastapol's notebook. He had not volunteered to give it to them. Still, he had been so delighted with the appearance of the smooth, clean men with their white coats and rubber gloves and surgical masks that he would have given up even the secrets of his notebook just to get medicine and treatment for his patients.

Doctors, real doctors! And Arabs, too, descendants of the greatest healers on earth. Surely they had come to improve conditions in the infirmary. Perhaps their suggestions to the outside world would cause reforms to be made in the prison itself.

"I am Doctor Juan Sebastapol," he said in an eager whisper when the doctors approached a patient he was treating. "I have been praying for you to come."

But the doctors had ignored him. They made gestures to brush him aside without touching him, so as not to soil themselves. They ignored his notebook, setting up their own system of charting. With a metal tool, they clamped a plastic hospital-style identification bracelet bearing a number around each patient's wrist. The numbers had nothing to do with the inmates' prison identification numbers.

The doctors conducted examinations of the prisoners, but performed no treatment and administered no medication.

Twice a day they took blood. After the patients died, the guards who collected the bodies occasionally left a corpse behind, which would later be carried separately from the infirmary. For autopsy, Sebastapol guessed. When the corpses left behind began to outnumber the ones removed, Sebastapol had assumed that the doctors were studying the effects of the plague . . .

. . . or of the poison.

* * *

The first to die were the older prisoners, the ones who were already sick and weak. They went quickly, sometimes within hours of their initial symptoms.

Soon Sebastapol had begun to notice a pattern. Most of those admitted into the infirmary with plague symptoms had come from one particular cell block or another. On Sunday, the patients were from Block A. Sebastapol had no idea of where Block A was, or of the nature of its inmates' crimes. On Monday, most of the new arrivals were from B Block.

All of those afflicted died.

This was Wednesday, and the priest from D Block, his block, was dying. Villachaise had shown symptoms of the illness before he was shot.

Juan Sebastapol wondered if this was the day when he, too, would die.

Father Domingo, the priest who was young enough to be Sebastapol's grandson, began to thrash in agony. The pink spittle frothed around his lips.

Sebastapol gave the man his hand to hold. There was nothing else he could do for him.

Suddenly the double metal doors swung open and the familiar cadre of white-coated doctors filed in. One of them gestured toward the white-faced priest.

"It's affected his nervous system," Sebastapol said, an edge of desperation in his voice as one of the doctors fitted the priest with a bracelet. A week before, he would have accepted the young priest's death. There was no hope then. But these were doctors . . .

Of course, he thought. *They don't speak Spanish. They can't understand me.* He switched to Arabic. "The symptoms are somewhat similar to those of bubonic plague," he said. "So even at this late stage, it might be possible to treat the disease with an antibiotic program . . ."

The doctors stared at him.

"Guard!" one of them yelled.

"Of course, my diagnosis—"

"Why is this man allowed in here?" the Arab doctor snapped, pointing to Sebastapol.

A lanky white man wearing civilian clothes ambled across the room. "I'll take care of him," he answered in flawless Arabic.

The offended physician turned back to the dying priest and took up a pair of tweezers and a scalpel. With a quick movement, he removed a patch of tissue from under the priest's tongue. The priest screamed. Blood poured down his chin. The medical team took a syringe of blood from his arm, then proceeded to the next patient.

Sebastapol moved toward the young cleric, but the civilian stepped in front of him. The man was obviously an American or a European. He had white-blond hair that fell across his eyes, eyes as blue as turquoises, and as lifeless.

"What's your hurry, Doctor Sebastapol?" he asked, this time in twangy, backwoods-American English.

Sebastapol blinked. "You know me?"

The man just winked as he took a silver flask from his hip pocket and drank. The fumes from the whiskey inside seemed to fill the room.

Sebastapol briefly noted the unwholesome coloring of the man's face. He would be dead of cirrhosis within two years, if his guess was right.

"If you plan to beat me, perhaps you should proceed," Sebastapol said wearily. "Otherwise, I am needed by the patients here." He gestured toward the metal double doors. Through the small pane of glass in each could be seen a long line of men, their faces gray with the sickness.

"Why do you bother, Doc?" the American asked quietly.

"You must know by now that you're all going to die. And soon, too," he added, raising his eyebrows.

Sebastapol looked to the Arab physicians. "Then . . . they're not . . ."

"They're doing tests. That's all, Doc. Just tests."

"Oh, God." He closed his eyes in despair. "It's poison, isn't it?"

The white-haired man took another drink. "Yeah. I heard you was smart as they come."

"What was used? The water?"

"Kind of makes you wish you didn't know, don't it?" He

laughed. "Well, look on the bright side. You gentlemen are taking part in one of the most important scientific tests in history."

Sebastapol felt his stomach turn. He thought he had been helping the sick by giving away most of his own water to them. Instead, he had been hastening their death.

"But why? Why us? Why here?"

"It's not meant for this pesthole, Doc," the man answered. "Once the test is over, the stuff's going to be used where it'll do the most good."

Suddenly it became clear to Sebastapol. The prison was populated by Cubans, Libyans, Nicaraguans . . . all of them political prisoners from countries whose common denominator was that they were opposed to the United States.

"America . . ." He searched the pale blue eyes of the white-haired man. "But is that not your own country?"

The man pulled a gun from behind his back. "Doc, I reckon this conversation's gone on long enough." He pointed the weapon upward and then lowered it until the barrel touched the bridge of Sebastapol's nose.

Suddenly one of the posted guards reeled drunkenly across the room and stumbled against Sebastapol. He slid slowly to the stone floor.

"Clear a bed!" another of the guards shouted, rushing over to help the fallen man. With the unconscious guard in his arms, he kicked the priest off the sunlit bed.

Sebastapol turned his face from the scene to the American who had been about to shoot him.

"Go on, git," the American said, waving the gun. "Nothing's going to keep you alive here, anyway."

Sebastapol bent over the young priest, who now lay sprawled on the floor. "Father Domingo," he whispered.

The blood on the priest's face was dry.

"He's dead," the guard said, unbuttoning the shirt of the uniformed man now occupying the bed. "Take a look at this one. That's an order, Doctor."

Sebastapol rose slowly. His eyes took in the man's bloated face, the pink froth on his lips . . .

"What can I do?" he asked quietly. "They're all dying.

Even your own kind are dying now."

The guard raised his rifle butt to strike at Sebastapol's face, then stole a glance at the American. Sebastapol noted that whoever the strange white-haired civilian was, he was not one of the Sandinistas.

"Perhaps one of the new doctors can help," Sebastapol offered. "They have medicines, instruments . . ."

The American laughed and turned away.

Sebastapol watched him walk slowly to the double doors and pass through before turning back to the guard. What he saw alarmed him.

The guard was sweating profusely. He was leaning over the cot where the other guard lay unconscious. His eyes were glassy. His mouth was open, and the cracks on his tongue were visible.

Sebastapol reached out his hand to steady the man, but the guard's weight was too much. He toppled over onto the other soldier, and the bed crashed to the floor with both of them.

From outside, Sebastapol heard the engine of the medical van start up. The shiny, white-domed roof veered around in a slow semicircle.

"Stop!" he screamed, running to the window. "It's not just the prisoners. The guards are dying too! Your damned experiment is out of control . . ."

He gasped. "Oh, good God!" he whispered.

The ground outside was littered with corpses. Surrounding the white van sprawled uniformed guards, motionless, their weapons still in their hands. The van pulled out and rolled slowly down the dirt road, waved on by the tall American.

Sebastapol gripped the bars of the window. In the distance, other vehicles were approaching, shimmering in the hot sun. This far away, his eyes were not keen enough to discern what they were, but he recognized them as military vehicles by their color.

Military vehicles on a military operation, with the United States as the ultimate target.

With the back of his hand he wiped the sweat from his

upper lip. Pink foam came away. He felt a wrenching in his bowels. The poison had begun its work on him.

But I'm dying slowly, he thought with a scientist's detachment. The guards had dropped like felled trees. If the experiment had gone out of control, if the guards had accidentally been exposed to the poison . . .

In a flush of fever, Sebastapol's senses cleared. "It was no accident," he said aloud. The guards were meant to die. Everyone here was meant to die, every living being.

Then, suddenly, Juan Sebastapol knew what he had to do, and the precise machinery of his mind forced his body into action.

Clutching his abdomen, he loped to the double metal doors and shoved them open. Before him, guards and prisoners alike lay lifeless on the floor. The arms of one guard twitched reflexively, like the limbs of an animal newly killed on the road. Sebastapol went to him. The man was dead within seconds.

Slowly Sebastapol swiveled his head. Beyond the silence of the infirmary, he could hear the shouting of inmates in their cells. And beyond that, the distant rumble of the approaching vehicles.

He took the dead guard's revolver from its holster. Then, his hands shaking, he moved slowly back into the infirmary and snapped the string holding the notebook.

He squatted there on the floor of the infirmary, writing furiously, automatically transcribing his thoughts into the code only one other man could understand. He had to stop twice to vomit. There was not much time left, he knew. He would not see the sun set on this day.

Even if he could get out, where would he go? The spit on Santa Vittoria where the prison stood was miles long. He would die before he could reach a house or a telephone.

A telephone. He could get out. He had to, for the sake of the notebook.

Sebastapol scrambled to his feet and loped toward the warden's office. There would be a telephone there.

Through his blurred vision he saw that the door was ajar,

propped open by a lifeless hand on the floor. It belonged to a guard. At her desk, the warden's secretary slumped dead. Slowly, swallowing his fear and his sickness, Sebastapol staggered past them and into the warden's inner office.

The man was on his hands and knees in front of an open safe. Sweat was pouring off his face, dropping to the floor in puddles.

"The bastards," he whispered hoarsely, looking up at the intruder.

For a moment Sebastapol stood stock still, oblivious to the gun in his hand. Then the warden shifted his huge bulk onto the doctor, trying to claw his way up Sebastapol's body. Sebastapol tried to push him off, but the warden's enormous hands wrapped around his neck.

The doctor flung his arms outward, knocking over a coffee cup on the warden's desk with the notebook he still clutched. The hot liquid splashed onto both men.

Gasping for breath, Sebastapol pulled the trigger of the revolver.

The bullet thudded through the warden's massive chest and emerged out his back, splattering the far wall with blood. The warden's eyes bulged with uncomprehending surprise. For a moment his hands retained their strong grip on the doctor's throat. Then they loosened, and a deep, rumbling sound issued from somewhere in the man's chest. He opened his mouth and expelled an eruption of bloody foam.

Shaking, Sebastapol heaved the body away, then wiped off the coffee-soaked notebook.

Remember. He lifted the receiver of the telephone.

Amelia is nine.

He dialed the number he had kept stored in his memory for ten years.

"Arthur Pierce," the voice said.

Sebastapol's eyes filled with tears at the sound of that voice, as gravelly and hard as the man himself.

"Arthur—" Sebastapol coughed and spat blood. "This is Juan Sebastapol."

He heard Pierce suck in his breath. "Where—"

"No. The phone. Meet me at the church. You understand?"

"Yes," Pierce said.

"If I am . . . gone, I will leave you a message."

"Juan—"

Sebastapol hung up and crossed himself. The call had been necessary. It had been perhaps the most important act of his life. But if the prison phone had been monitored, he had just sentenced Arthur Pierce to death.

"Go with God, my friend," he said.

He fled immediately, running as fast as his blurred vision and his worn-out canvas shoes would allow, skirting the rows of corpses littering the prison grounds.

There was no need for a fence around the old fort; any would-be escapees could easily be shot from the ramparts. The land surrounding the place was flat and bare. Not even a tree grew along the endless spit of sand.

The Church of the Sacred Heart was the only building between the town of Puerta Vittoria and the fortress on the sea. As Juan Sebastapol ran toward it, the line of military vehicles moved inexorably toward the fortress prison.

They were Jeeps. One of them veered out from the convoy and headed toward the lone man running along the barren rocks.

"Halt!" a voice on a loudspeaker rang out.

Sebastapol ignored it. They would kill him, of that he was certain. He clutched the notebook under his arm. If he was strong, he told himself, if he could run faster than he ever had in his life, if luck was with him, they would destroy only his body. His knowledge would be preserved.

Shots fired behind him, but the old doctor kept running blindly, parched with thirst. He was still not in range of their guns. But he would be soon.

Behind him, at the fort, four other Jeeps pulled up and stopped. Soldiers carrying long, heavy weapons swarmed out of the vehicles and circled the prison. Then, on a signal, flames burst out of the giant nozzles of the weapons, like the fiery breath of dragons, creating a roar like a windstorm.

The lone Jeep followed after Sebastapol.

When he reached the church, the doctor threw himself on the boarded-up doors and fell to the floor inside.

"Madre Dio," he whispered. "Thank You for letting me live this long." Crawling toward the altar, he came to a large stone at the base of three steps leading to the nave. Scrabbling, his eyes wild, he lifted the stone, threw in the notebook, then replaced the stone. With a small cry of triumph, he sank back on his knees.

Outside, he heard the Jeep come to a halt. His day had come. Sebastapol clasped his hands. "Our Father," he began, "who art in heaven . . ."

The church entryway was suddenly shadowed. Two men in suits of flameproof asbestos stood in the opening like spacemen, but the doctor did not turn around to see them. One of them raised the weapon in his hand and shot a river of fire onto Juan Sebastapol's naked back.

The old man never screamed, not as he burned, not as he died, not as the Church of the Sacred Heart blackened and crackled around him while the flames devoured it.

2

Arthur Pierce drove the Land Rover over the flat earth of the spit as if he were on a raceway. The young blond man beside him screwed the telephoto lens onto his camera and squinted into the smoke from the burning fort.

"Will you look at that!" he breathed in wonderment. "The thing's made of *stone,* for God's sake. It's burning like a bonfire. How'd they do that?" He raised the camera and began snapping.

Pierce didn't answer. He just wished that Wade Turner were not here. He wanted no company this time.

Sebastapol had said "the church." There was only one church he could have meant. The two men had gone there once, years ago, before Sebastapol disappeared into the sewer of the Central American prison system.

After hearing his friend's message, Pierce had hung up the receiver slowly, forcing himself to stay calm, and walked out from his desk toward the door. He'd met Turner in the hallway.

"El Mirador's on fire!" Turner shouted. "Let's go!" His camera bag was slung over his shoulder. He'd grabbed

Pierce's arm and pulled him along.

Pierce had had no choice but to bring Turner with him. The two men represented the entire staff of the Hyatt News Service on Santa Vittoria. This did not reflect any special importance of Santa Vittoria itself, or even of Sangre Precioso, the nation that owned the island. Instead, it reflected the location of Santa Vittoria, centered directly in the middle of the Caribbean.

From there, as bureau chief for the wire service, Pierce controlled a group of part-timers and stringers who covered the news throughout the entire Caribbean. When it was necessary, Turner could jump aboard a chartered plane and be anywhere in the area within two hours, his camera ready.

There probably were better ways to run a news service, Pierce often thought, but none that required so little in the way of manpower and budgeting. And Pierce loved Santa Vittoria, too, having settled there over a decade earlier when he had retired from his usual work back in the States.

There was another reason for the Hyatt News Service's lack of manpower on Santa Vittoria. The service just did not want anyone to look too carefully at what Pierce and Turner did for a living, because the fact was that it had been designed as a cover.

Arthur Pierce was a legitimate, experienced newsman, and Wade Turner was a good photographer, but their real work had little to do with news. Pierce had spent his entire adult life, nearly fifty years, as an undercover operative, first for the CIA, then for Hyatt. Turner was being groomed to succeed him.

Turner jolted in his seat as Pierce screeched the Land Rover to a halt outside the burned and still-smoking Church of the Sacred Heart. The main walls of the structure had caved in. Random roof rafters, blackened by fire, hung precariously from what had been the modest steeple.

"What are you doing?" Turner shouted as Pierce jumped from the Rover and ran for the chapel. "We can get closer to the fort than this."

But Pierce had already vanished into the rubble of the church.

The first thing he saw upon entering was Juan Sebastapol's charred body. His old friend's back had been fried to the bone, but his face had barely been touched by the flames. Its expression, despite the terrible pain Sebastapol must have suffered, was serene.

Pierce looked at him for a moment. "I'm sorry, my friend," he said softly, and closed Sebastapol's eyes.

Turner came in, his camera equipment clanking behind him, but stopped suddenly when he saw the body. "Jesus!" he whispered. "What did that?"

"Flamethrower, it looks like. See if you can get some shots of whoever's up at the fort."

"It's pretty far, Art . . ."

"Just do it, all right?" Pierce said irritably.

He waited until he saw the boy leave. Actually, Turner was not a boy. He was in his mid-twenties and had worked for the CIA before joining Hyatt. Besides, Davis Hyatt himself had picked Turner for the job, and Hyatt always knew what he was doing.

But the kid was as green as grass, and Pierce did not want him around while he was searching for whatever Sebastapol had left him.

Because he *had* left him something. Somewhere in this ruin there was a message that Juan Sebastapol had died to give him.

Pierce looked over the rubble, the soot-blackened walls, the pile of stones in the corner, the broken heap that had once been the altar . . .

"Of course," he muttered. The stone in front of the altar. He and Sebastapol had loosened it themselves long ago, before the church had been abandoned.

The memory of it brought him pain. He had been unable to help Juan Sebastapol then, as he had been unable to save him now.

He lifted the stone from the floor, breathed deeply when he saw the notebook, and quickly slid it in the back of his trousers, anchored by his belt.

The soles of his feet felt as if they were blistering on the graying coals of the ruined church. He would have to leave his old friend's body there, in the smoldering rubble.

Sebastapol would have understood; he had never been a sentimental man. Still, taking a last look at the charred body, Arthur Pierce felt a sadness that went beyond mourning.

When he emerged out into the road, Turner was running back toward the church. "Find anything?" the young man asked.

"No," Pierce lied. "Just a loose stone."

"There are flamethrowers up there, all right. Five of them coming out of the fort. Russian issue, looks like. What the hell's going on?"

"Guess we'd better find out," Pierce said.

Turner shot a full roll of pictures as they drove toward El Mirador. While he was changing film, Pierce stopped suddenly.

"What now?" Turner asked.

"Listen."

Above the crackle and roar of the fire, there was another sound, a hideous, skull-bursting wail like the lament of souls in hell. It was the scream of human voices.

"Oh, my God," Turner said. "They're burning the prisoners alive!"

Slowly Pierce reached for a pair of binoculars on the seat beside him. "Five, you said?"

Turner looked through his telephoto lens. "I counted five. Maybe one's gone behind the fort."

"There's nothing behind the fort except a cliff and the sea," Pierce said.

"There!" Turner swiveled to the left. "The north end. One of them is on the ground."

"That's right," Pierce said. But he wasn't looking at the body on the ground. He was following a tall figure in civilian clothes walking toward one of the asbestos-suited men holding flamethrowers. He came up behind the man, drew a pistol, and fired point-blank into the back of the man's head.

Trembling, Turner lowered his camera without a word.

"Missed a good shot, kid," Pierce said. His eyes never left

the binoculars as he watched the civilian kill the third and fourth men. The fifth saw him coming, saw the bodies of the others, and raised his flamethrower to aim at the killer. The man in civilian clothes fired into his chest before he could engage the unwieldy weapon. As he fell, a giant arc of fire shot into the sky.

"He's killed them all," Pierce said.

Turner got out of the Rover and retched.

"You okay, kid?"

Turner nodded and wiped his forearm over his face. "Just felt a little shaky for a minute. I'm all right."

The figure on the rock outcropping swiveled around suddenly to face them. Pierce felt a surge of adrenaline course through his body. Even though the man on the cliff was more than a thousand yards away, even though his image in the high-resolution binocular lenses was not perfect, Pierce knew instinctively who it was.

He threw down the binoculars and floored the gas pedal.

By the time they had driven up the long ramp leading to El Mirador, past the abandoned military vehicles and the bodies of the asbestos-suited men, the civilian was nowhere in sight.

"Wait here," Pierce said.

He stalked slowly along the wall of the fort, the heat rising in waves around him, turning his tall, slender figure into a weaving pattern. Despite his sixty-two years, Arthur Pierce still moved with the grace of an athlete, due in equal parts to good genes and long training.

The bodies of the prison guards on the ground were burned black. From the barred windows hung charred arms, their fingers splayed in pain. There was no sound now, except for the pounding of the sea and the murmur of the hot breeze.

They're all dead, Pierce thought. The prisoners, the guards, and the soldiers sent to kill the guards. Only one man was left with the secret of El Mirador.

He drew a gun, although he knew he had little chance of using it. When he arrived at the southernmost tip of the cliff, he put it away.

Hanging from the rock was a grappling hook and a length of yellow nylon rope that reached to the boulder-studded sea below. The water bore the faint traces of a wake.

"Art?" came a voice approaching from the other side of the fort. "Art? You all right?"

"I told you to stay in the car," Pierce growled.

"I was worried, that's all. There's been a freaking bloodbath. That maniac with the gun could've—"

"He's gone," Pierce said, gesturing with his chin toward the sea. "An inflatable boat, probably."

Turner went over to the grappling hook and touched it, as if trying to convince himself that what had happened was real. "He must have planned this whole thing," he said in wonderment.

Pierce grunted. He doubled back to the body of a man with a flamethrower and unzipped his asbestos suit. Beneath it was the uniform of a Sandinistan soldier. The wound in the man's chest was the size of a grapefruit.

Exploding bullets. *That fit,* Pierce thought with a mounting sense of excitement. Then he turned over the man's head, and everything was confirmed.

The corpse's left ear was missing.

Turner looked ashen. "The shooter did that?"

"It's his calling card. The arrogant bastard always takes an ear, to make sure he gets credit for the kill."

The young man turned back toward the water. "Who is he?"

"Assassin. Terrorist, mercenary, whatever he feels like, the sick son of a bitch. Got no country, no ties, nothing. Everybody in the world wants him dead, except whoever he's working for at the moment." Pierce looked out at the widening wake on the blue-green sea. Whatever had happened at El Mirador today, this was just the beginning.

"His name's Billy Starr."

3

It was the kind of coincidence that could make a man believe in God and then hate Him.

Arthur Pierce had wondered about the fate of Juan Sebastapol for ten years. Finally he had found him, on the very same island where Pierce himself lived, only to discover his friend murdered. Sebastapol would have enjoyed the irony, he thought.

But what was it that had brought Sebastapol back here?

Above, the sky was blackened by smoke still rising from the gloomy fortress that had stood on its hill for centuries like a gigantic pagan god. El Mirador, the Watcher.

It had been "El Mirador" since the sixteenth century, when the Spanish governor had built it as a first defense against attacks on the Central American coastline. Throughout the enlightened Renaissance, it had enjoyed a long and dishonorable history as a prison noted for its ingenious methods of torture.

But the fort had stood empty since the early nineteenhundreds, and when Sangre Precioso, the island nation consisting of Santa Vittoria and seven other similar islands that ran in a crescent from near Haiti toward the Panama coastline, attained its independence, the old fort became the property of the new republic.

"Never again will such a facility be needed by the free Preciosano people," said Deputy Governor Julio Rodriguez during an Independence Day celebration.

And so all believed. Until the fish began to die.

It had happened while Arthur Pierce was in Switzerland meeting with his boss at the Hyatt News Service.

Wade Turner had been left behind on the island. When Pierce returned, Turner told him about it.

"Dead fish?" Pierce had mumbled, leafing through his telephone messages.

"I heard a lot of reports, so I went up there," Turner said. "The ocean doesn't look good."

"Yeah? So?"

"So I talked to the deputy governor, Rodriguez, and he said it was some kind of oil spill from a passing U.S. Navy ship."

Pierce snorted. "Did any of the reports mention oil?"

"Nope. Even the fishermen aren't complaining about oil. Just dead fish. That's why I didn't file a story."

"Rodriguez is a lying sack of shit," Pierce had said, tossing two of the messages into the wastebasket. "He'd sell his mother to slavers for a C-note. One of the Central American countries is probably paying under the table to dump garbage on Santa Vittoria."

"That's really disgusting," Turner said. "Just because tourists don't come here, the government thinks it can get away with anything."

"Well, maybe they'll ease off now that Rodriguez knows the press is onto something."

"He said the effects would probably pass in a month or so."

"There you have it," Pierce said. "It's just as well you didn't file. Who cares about dead fish in Santa Vittoria?"

The only people who might have cared were the island's

fishermen, who made their living from the sea. But they hardly had much time to grumble, because suddenly there was money to be had elsewhere.

El Mirador had opened its doors again.

Naturally, the Sangre Precioso government had tried to keep the goings-on at the fort a secret. Just as naturally, Arthur Pierce, whose family had had ties with Santa Vittoria for almost a hundred years, had found out about it immediately.

This time Pierce had gone to the main island and talked with the deputy governor himself.

"We're going to use the fort to store old records," Rodriguez had told him with an oily smile. "By hiring the local fishermen to assist with the project, we will be helping them with their financial problems until the fish return."

Arthur Pierce had not believed it for an instant. Sangre Precioso was surely reopening as a prison, but just as no one had cared about some dead fish, no one would really care about a prison opening in some two-bit Caribbean island. So again, no story was filed.

Maybe, Pierce thought later, _if I had been a better reporter . . . or if I'd remembered more of my Agency training . . ._

But he was sixty-two years old by the time he thought these things, and the CIA had never trained him for anything like the gift Juan Sebastapol had left him.

After nine years of teaching codes and ciphers at Langley, Pierce had finally let go of the profession that had taken so much of his life and gone to work for the Hyatt News Agency. He had used Hyatt as a cover for years, posing as a journalist working around the world for the wire service, while he was involved with Agency fieldwork.

His father, Senator Frederick Pierce, who never did learn of his only son's true occupation, regarded Arthur's entry into journalism with contempt and disdain.

"A newspaperman!" he'd grunted while lighting a fat Havanna. "You, with every opportunity a young American could ask for. A veteran. A college graduate. You could have entered public service, boy. You could at least have gone into business, preserved some of your family's hard-earned assets. But the press!"

Hard-earned, my assets, Pierce had thought. Every Pierce in his family tree from the time of George III had inherited a fortune. He supposed that there was something to be said for the fact that none of them had squandered the family bundle on booze and fast women, although even that would have been more interesting than the pack of bankers, industrialists, and politicians who carried the name.

"All I've got to say is, I hope you're not planning to live the way you're accustomed to living," the elder Pierce had said with a puff of fragrant smoke. "Not on your salary as a newsman. And don't expect any handouts from me, either."

"I won't," Pierce assured him.

"You've made your bed, and now you're going to lie in it."

But Arthur was already out the door by then.

That was in nineteen fifty-four. He was twenty-six years old, had served in Army Intelligence for four years, and was on his way to Czechoslovakia on assignment for the CIA. He never saw his father again.

Pierce was a field operative, a Glory Boy in a bureaucracy bottom-heavy with pencil pushers. Fieldmen were special. They were not information gatherers, liaisons, or embassy watchers. Each of these handpicked operatives was a one-man show: a shadow, a tracker, an actor, a killer. They were experts in codes, weapons, tradecraft, and languages, as well as in "wetwork"—the Agency's euphemism for murder in its various forms—and each of these exceptional men, of whom there were less than three hundred in the world, cost the Agency hundreds of thousands of dollars to train.

When a fieldman married, there were no champagne celebrations at Langley. The operative was immediately re-called, and usually asked to resign. Since he was permitted to say nothing to prospective employers about the exact nature of his work, a cashiered fieldman often ended up as a private detective or a security guard, unless his cover profession was strong enough to support him. Glory Boys did not transfer easily into pedestrian life.

Arthur Pierce had had no intention of retiring at thirty-one, not even when he met Ludmilla Borozkova.

Ludmilla was a dancer with the Kirov Ballet. Her father, a prominent physicist, had developed a marked itch to leave the Soviet Union after having been placed under house arrest for three years. In the course of a boozy evening with some fellow scientists, Borozkov had criticized the tactics used against the Hungarians during the nineteen fifty-six uprising. One of his fellow guests had been a KGB informant.

Arthur Pierce had pulled off a blazing, shoot-'em-up rescue—in which he himself took a bullet—and managed rather miraculously to appear in West Berlin with the old man and the ballerina in tow.

After that he could hardly lie to Ludi, with whom he was falling rapidly and hopelessly in love, about his line of work. But deceiving the woman was not of paramount importance to him, anyway. Deceiving the Agency was.

His visits to the house where she lived with her father could have been explained had it become necessary, but not the burning love he felt for her. So they had kept the times they spent together a secret from everyone.

Months, and sometimes years, would go by without their seeing one another. She understood, always, though her father did not. He berated her constantly for waiting, starry-eyed, for the American spy, and beat her within an inch of her life when she could no longer keep from him the fact that she was pregnant.

As for Pierce, the long separations from the woman he loved, and their rare clandestine meetings, were agonizing. He had often told her not to wait for him, to find a life for herself, to find a husband with whom to begin a family, but she had stubbornly refused.

"You are my life," she told him. "Without you, I could not be happy. I ask for nothing, Arthur. Do not refuse to see me."

And so he had not. He had never slept with another woman after meeting Ludmilla. He risked his life to get to

Germany on the day their daughter was born, but he and Ludmilla did not marry. It was too dangerous. He knew that if he kept traveling between Prague and West Germany, sooner or later he would be followed . . . and thus lead someone from the other side to the only people in the world for whom he might betray his country.

The solution came when both of their fathers died within a month of one another. Ludmilla was suddenly free to leave Berlin. And Arthur Pierce, who had had no contact with his father for years, unexpectedly inherited the senator's entire estate.

It bought Arthur and Ludi and their daughter the safety they needed. Pierce sold everything he owned but the vacation home on the island of Santa Vittoria, where he moved Ludi and the baby. They were married quietly on the island and spent two days together before Pierce flew back to Prague.

For ten years he hid his relationship with Ludmilla from the Agency and lived his lonely life first in Prague, and then, agonizingly, in Nicaragua, where he was almost within shouting distance of his family. Yet still he rarely saw them for fear of exposing Ludi and Amelia to danger.

By nineteen seventy-three, when Pierce was forty-five years old—and the marvel of the Glory Boys for having attained such an advanced age—he had had enough. His daughter was half-grown, and barely knew him. Ludi had spent her best years alone.

He traveled to Langley, dropped the bombshell about his secret family and prepared to find a new line of work.

The Agency was properly displeased. Pierce was detained at Langley for three weeks, during which time every aspect of his personal and professional life was checked and rechecked. Ludmilla was questioned at length also, as was their daughter Amelia. Finally, begrudgingly, Pierce was given a clean bill and informed that because of his long service, it would not be necessary for him to terminate his employment with the Agency.

He was offered a teaching position at Langley, instructing recruits in the uses of codes and ciphers. It was dull work, but at last he had the yearned-for time with his family, and the years passed quickly. Amelia grew up and left home for college; Ludi tended her garden and painted scenes of the Caribbean. And Pierce accepted himself for what he now was, an aging functionary with a past that was better forgotten.

But he missed the Glory Days. Oh, how he missed them.

Ludmilla noticed it first. Arthur had taken to watching television, an activity he had always hated. He watched until the small hours of the morning, when Ludi would come down from the bedroom to turn off the set.

"Come to bed," she would say, and her husband obeyed silently.

Then would follow a week of intense agitation. Pierce would stop watching television, stop eating, stop sleeping.

"Come to bed," Ludi would say . . . until, at last, her husband refused. So one night she did not tell him to come to bed. "I want you to quit your job," she said instead.

He stared at her through hollow eyes.

"Do it. Now."

Her tone was sharp, unusual for soft, gentle Ludi.

"What are you talking about?" he asked irritably.

"I do not wish to have an old man under my foot all the time. It is like living with Papa again."

He shrugged. "Maybe that's what I am, Ludi. An old codes-and-ciphers clerk."

"Pooh! You are great journalist."

He laughed aloud.

"You laugh, yes. Because you know I am true."

"You've always been true," Pierce said, chucking her under the chin.

"Well?" Her voice had lost none of its stridency.

He was silent for a long moment. "I suppose it's a possibility," he said finally.

"Ah. Now you are talking like the man I remember."

"Actually, I've heard from Davis Hyatt. Junior." He sounded almost timid.

Ludi gasped dramatically.

He nodded. "He wanted to know if I'd be interested in working for the wire service again. He's opening an office in the Caribbean. Right on Santa Vittoria, in fact."

"I cannot believe that!" she shrieked, wide-eyed. "We could live in our old house again. Our real house, where we belong."

"Now don't get all carried away, Ludi. I haven't answered him yet."

"Why not?"

"Well, I haven't done that sort of thing for a long time. It would mean a lot of travel, and—"

"Do it, Arthur."

"Damn it, I don't know if I can. I'm not young anymore."

"Oh? Just how old are you?" she asked lasciviously, wiggling her hips.

He grinned. "Old, but still in working order."

"That is what you tell Davis Hyatt."

He stared at her. "You really think so?"

"I do."

"But I'd be gone so much."

"Good. I want to be rid of you."

"And we'd be so far from Amelia."

"Ha! You think she would notice?"

He smiled. "I guess not." He looked at her sheepishly, then suddenly kissed her full on the mouth.

"Oh, my," Ludmilla said. "Like you say, old but still in working order." She pulled him by the belt of his bathrobe. "Now you come to bed."

That night, after he was asleep, Ludi tiptoed into the den and replaced a letter she had taken from his desk. She kissed the envelope.

"Thank you, Davis Hyatt," she whispered.

So Pierce had arrived at the Geneva office of the Hyatt News Service. It had been years since he was there, and he barely remembered Davis Hyatt, Jr. He had been more than a passing acquaintance of the elder Hyatt's, the Englishman who had started the business. That Hyatt had known about

Pierce; he had even allowed him the use of the wire service as his CIA cover. He had gone so far as to save Pierce's life by providing him with an alibi on one occasion.

The Young Hyatt, who was in his late forties at the time of Pierce's visit in nineteen eighty, was every bit as gentlemanly as his father, although, Pierce thought, much less cosmopolitan than his old man.

Hyatt Senior had known virtually everyone of importance in the world. In the prime of his life he had been a relentlessly social animal, charming in a dozen languages, and his parties were legendary.

His son, on the other hand, seemed reclusive and secretive, though obviously he was bright. Stocky and pale-complected, with thinning brown hair and slightly myopic eyes, the man struck Pierce as vaguely molelike. He spoke quietly, and though he had clearly been reared in wealth and groomed for a position of power, he did not adorn himself with any of the symbols of the rich. His suit was well-fitting but worn. His only adornments were a plain Omega watch with a frayed leather band and a gold class ring.

He persisted doggedly through an obligatory quarter-hour of small talk, during which Pierce decided that he liked the man.

Finally, checking his watch to make sure enough time had elapsed, Hyatt came to the point. "We do use a number of operatives not directly associated with the news business," he said, avoiding Pierce's eyes.

Pierce grinned. "You're not going to tell me that your wire service is hooked up with the CIA, are you?"

"Why do you find that so amusing?"

"Because your father, God rest his soul, once bailed me out of a tight squeeze by insisting that I was his full-time employee and far too intelligent to ever work for such a fascist organization as the CIA. I myself thought he was overdoing it at the time, but it would be funny to know that he was having a little private joke with his friends at the Company."

"Well, Father often had private jokes," young Hyatt said.

"But no, we're not CIA." He hesitated. "That is, not precisely."

Hyatt sat down on one of the comfortable leather chairs in his enormous office, took a long cigar from a silver humidor and lit it slowly, appreciating the ritual.

"After the American Embassy in Teheran was taken last year, the security councils of several nations wisely decided to join forces against the random attacks of terrorists." He spoke slowly for an Englishman—even for one Swiss-reared—and with the casualness one would use to describe a day's fishing. "What they came up with was a temporary organization comprised of agents from various branches of the world intelligence community. These agents were to work toward the common goal of eradicating terrorism around the globe."

Pierce tried to keep from smiling. He could picture the Glory Boys from CIA, the Mossad, and the KGB working together, all the while frenziedly trying to tap one another's secrets.

"That must have been interesting," he said. "What happened to it?"

Hyatt shrugged lightly. "It works."

"There is such an organization in place now?"

"There is. It has no official designation, but we call it the Network. This is its base."

Pierce was stunned. In all his years with the CIA, he had never heard of such an organization. "How . . . how does it work?" he ventured.

"If you mean how do the agents keep out of one another's way, the fact is that they don't usually come in contact with each other. No one knows who else works for the organization."

"Except you."

"I only know the agents. My contact represents the spokesmen for the nations involved."

"Which nations are we talking about?"

"I don't know," Hyatt said. "I mentioned that this was a temporary organization. Everything is set up to disband at a moment. At the moment of my death, to be exact."

"What happens to the agents?"

"They go back to the branches from which they've been borrowed. They're all fieldmen of one sort or another. They're used to working alone. Officially, their time under me is part of their regular jobs."

Pierce nodded. "All right," he said. "Why are you telling me this?"

"I want you to be one of the agents."

Pierce didn't restrain himself from laughing this time. "I'd say I'm a little out of the age range."

"The job doesn't require youth. Just intelligence and experience. And a journalism background, for the cover. Are you interested?"

Pierce took a deep breath. "When do I start?"

"You already have," Hyatt said. "Care for a cigar?"

Pierce shook his head. "Out of sheer curiosity, Mr. Hyatt," he asked haltingly, "after what you've just told me, what would you have done if I'd refused?"

Hyatt looked at him morosely. "Why, I'd have had you killed, of course."

That had been twelve years ago.

"What did you say that guy's name was?" Turner asked as Pierce wheeled the Land Rover back onto the streets of Santa Vittoria. "The assassin, I mean."

"Billy Starr. He's been around for a while."

"Is that his real name?"

"Who knows?"

"Is he an American?"

"Oh, yes. Or was, anyway, when he was younger. People who've heard him speak say he's got an American accent. But no one knows who he really is. Just a sick killer who hires himself out to the highest bidder."

"How do you know?"

Pierce looked over at him. He'd been talking too much, remembering. It was the curse of age. "Get to be as old as me, kid, and you know everything," he said.

"Like the church?"

"What?"

"You knew there was somebody in the church."

Pierce hesitated for a moment. He looked at Turner. The kid wasn't probing. He was just curious. "I got a call," he said. "From inside."

"Inside the *prison*?"

"He was an inmate. I don't know how he got to a phone. Something happened in there."

"I'll say."

"I mean before. He knew he was going to get out."

"Why did he call you?"

Pierce shrugged. "I never found out."

"Did you know him?"

"Years ago."

"Maybe he left you something," Turner said. "Hidden in the church. A note, maybe. Something. We could go back."

"Forget about it," Pierce said. "The story I'm going to file is that a fire of unknown origin destroyed the historic landmark fortress of El Mirador, which the government of Sangre Precioso had been using as a warehouse for old documents."

Turner was aghast. "What about the dead guy in the church? What about all the dead prisoners? And Billy Starr, blowing the brains out of those soldiers?"

"Grow up, kid," Pierce advised. "When we were up at the fort, did you hear fire engines?"

"No." Turner sounded puzzled.

"That's right. The biggest fire these islands have ever seen, and not so much as a garden hose.

"That *is* weird," Turner muttered.

"No. That's Sangre Precioso. The island paradise with a payoff in every pot. If we mention it, the office will be closed in the morning, count on it. And our families will get notices that the two of us accidentally drowned on a fishing trip. No, thanks."

He pulled up alongside the shabby building where they worked.

"Go develop your pictures," he said. "I'll be in later to fax the story. Right now I've got to get home. My daughter's visiting, and it's her birthday. The ladies will kill me if I'm late."

Turner frowned as he got out of the car. "Art . . ."

"What?"

"It's just that . . . doesn't it bother you?"

"Oh, Jesus."

"I mean, there's a real story there. That guy in the church was killed trying to get to you. El Mirador was torched with God knows how many living people inside. And somewhere not far away there's this famous assassin on the loose, chopping the ears off corpses. Are you really going to sit on all that?"

"You bet your ass I am. But you feel free to go back if you want."

Turner stuck his hands in his pockets. "I'm only a photographer," he said sullenly.

"You're more than that, and you know it. And we both have more important things to do than try to get on page one of the _New York Times_."

He looked hard at Turner, nodded to himself, and drove away.

4

About a mile from his home, near the Mamba River, which wound the entire length of Santa Vittoria, Pierce pulled over and took out the notebook he had retrieved from the church. He read quickly, going through the pages front to back, then flipping backward to see if something caught his eye.

Nothing. Aside from the oddity of having been written in English, it contained nothing except the usual sort of medical notations and observations.

Patient 14562. Renal failure, diabetic coma. Complaints of headaches and frequent vomiting. Blood pressure, 365/78. Cholesterol, 2493, triglycerides, 1478, resting pulse, 143.

More case histories, more records, more numbers, but not even a name. Obviously Juan Sebastapol had been used as the prison doctor and these were his charts.

But what did they all mean? And why had Sebastapol taken the notebook with him when he'd escaped? Why had he risked his life to call Pierce, to try to meet him, to hide away the notebook . . . if it were not important?

There had to be something inside those pages. Had to be.

It was strange, Pierce thought, that Sebastapol had written the entire notebook in English. That was not his native tongue. Who knew? It was too complicated.

How did he know my telephone number?

All questions, no answers.

Pierce ran his hands over the pages. Coffee stains, still damp. On the cardboard cover were written Sebastapol's name and a number, most likely his prison ID number. 417283.

Patient 417283, Pierce thought. *Burned alive with a flame-thrower.* How did you write that in a medical report?

Pierce looked down at his hands, veiny and trembling. He started the car.

He had last seen Juan Sebastapol on this island twelve years earlier. They had loosened the stone in the church together.

"You see?" Sebastapol had shouted in triumph when the hollow space beneath the stone was revealed.

Pierce had grinned. "Now how in tarnation did you know that would be there?"

"A guess. Architects in the sixteenth and seventeenth centuries often built these island churches with secret compartments in the floor to protect the church's treasures from pirates. Since this was once a private chapel for the Lord of El Mirador, I assumed it would have one."

"Well, now I guess *you're* the Lord of El Mirador. Any plans?"

Sebastapol had smiled sadly and leaned against the old altar rail. "No, I'm not the lord of anything. Just a man whose country is being overrun and who doesn't know what to do about it."

"No one ever does," Pierce said, and then the two men had sat side by side and stared glumly out at the gathering twilight.

Sebastapol was a doctor, a brilliant neurosurgeon from Nicaragua who had studied in Vienna and still owned a large apartment there. He had been living the life of a comfortable expatriate for years before he'd returned to visit his family in Managua. What he found there shocked him.

The excesses of the American-backed Somoza dictatorship had left virtually everyone but a few wealthy families, including Sebastapol's own, in a state of desperate poverty. The seeds of revolution were already sown then, and the Communists were making veiled inroads into the consciousness of the starving people.

This was the early seventies, and Pierce was in Nicaragua, posing as a newspaper reporter. But not too many were deceived. American CIA agents were crawling all over Central America. But to Sebastapol, Pierce seemed different from the rest. The American agent seemed to understand that the battle to keep Somoza in power would ultimately be lost. The solution was to somehow force free elections in Nicaragua, to stave off the leftist revolutionaries. That was what Sebastapol had actively advocated, and Pierce took that argument to his CIA superiors.

Where it died. No one was interested in an alternative to Somoza. The old diseased regime was propped up like carrion on a stick, an invitation to the Sandinista vultures to swallow it down whole.

From time to time during the seventies, Sebastapol had visited Pierce at Santa Vittoria. The men grew close.

Sebastapol's last visit had been twelve years ago, when they had gone to the Church of the Sacred Heart together and found the small hidden vault under the altar stone. The Sandinistas had just overthrown the Somoza regime.

"What will you do?" Pierce had asked as they sat in the chapel.

"I will go back to Managua."

"Those Communist bastards will be waiting for you."

"It is still my country."

"To hell with it," Pierce said. "Go back to Vienna. Live with Marla. Be happy."

Sebastapol shook his head. "I have run long enough," he said. "I fear this may be the last time you and I will meet." The doctor replaced the altar stone.

Pierce did not answer. For he, too, sensed that this would be the last time he would see his friend.

"Give my love to Ludi. Your wife is a good woman and she will make you live long. And to Amelia."

"You remembered her name."

"I remember everything," Sebastapol said.

Six months later he had learned of Sebastapol's imprisonment. Pierce was still working at Langley then, but even the CIA's Central America desk could not help.

"Sorry, Art. The whole damned country is filled with political prisoners. We don't have a clue on how to find one Nicaraguan doctor," the head of Central American operations had told him.

He kept after them. He kept in touch with Marla Sebastapol in Vienna. But slowly hope died. There was no word from Sebastapol, no word of where he might be. And then a few years later, Pierce retired from the CIA and went to live permanently in Santa Vittoria.

When he had accepted the Caribbean post with the Hyatt News Service, he'd tried to drum up some interest in the case of missing political prisoners. But the world never seemed outraged at excesses committed by Communist governments. No one cared.

One night he had reluctantly told Marla Sebastapol over the telephone that he did not know what to do next.

"Someday he will be back. We will see him, Arthur, my dear friend."

Now I'll have to tell her to stop hoping for her husband's return.

He put the car in gear and headed toward home.

Poor bastard. His only sin was to have been born in the wrong country.

Juan Sebastapol had probably been the most brilliant man Pierce had ever met. The true Renaissance man. He had been more than a great neurosurgeon. He was also a scholar, a thinker. A master-rated chess player. A mathematician.

Once, during a reckless weekend, the two of them had gone off on a binge through St. Maarten's gambling casinos. Sebastapol had wanted to try a new system at baccarat. The mathematics, as Sebastapol explained them to him, were arcane and wildly incomprehensible . . . but the system had worked. Juan had raked in more than thirty thousand dollars. He could have broken the bank, Pierce remembered with a smile, but Sebastapol had not wanted to draw attention to himself.

Suddenly Pierce slammed on the brakes. He pulled over once again, into a junkyard, and feverishly flipped the pages of the notebook. His heart hammering, he took a pencil and a used envelope lying on the seat of the Land Rover and made a few notes of his own.

"Oh, God," he whispered.

He turned on the ignition again and peeled out of the junkyard. *Juan, You smart son of a bitch.*

5

Amelia sat on the bamboo deck of her parents' house overlooking the river. A Bloody Mary was in her hand. A pair of dragonflies coupled in iridescent silence near the rim of the glass. A tree frog sang its evening song from the swamp on the far side of the river.

She took a drink. It went down cool and peppery. "Time just stands still here, doesn't it?" she said, her eyes closed.

Her mother laughed. "Tell that to my wrinkles."

Amelia looked over at her. Ludi was standing in the kitchen, chopping fruit with an outsized knife. From the back, she could have been mistaken for a fourteen-year-old girl. The perfect carriage, the small, tight bottom, the five-foot, two-inch frame of a miniature athlete. The calves may be a little thicker, Amelia thought; they no longer needed all the muscle Ludi had given them during the years of dancing. But there was hardly a strand of gray in her ash-blonde hair, still pulled back severely, then blossoming into an elaborately braided chignon at the nape of her neck. She would always look every inch the ballerina.

Amelia, on the other hand, had inherited her father's

lanky physique. She wasn't clumsy—Ludi had trained her too carefully and too long for that—but she could never have been the dancer her mother was.

Nevertheless, she had her own style—sleek, slim, a model's glide when she walked. And she had stayed in shape, even after she'd stopped taking ballet lessons. She worked out at the New York Health & Racquet Club now, and could beat most men at most indoor sports.

Except one. The important one. Looks, 10. Sex, 0.

She took another drink from her Bloody Mary.

Now, let's not get maudlin, she told herself. Women didn't need men anymore. This was the new age, where people talked about "relationships" rather than marriages, and masturbation was condoned as a form of safe sex.

Besides, she had all sorts of other attributes that men yearned for in a woman. She could throw a baseball fifty yards. She could drive any vehicle ever made, pilot boats and single-engine aircraft. She could climb trees, read maps, make a bow and arrow from two pieces of wood and a vine, build a fire, construct an igloo (the result of a skiing accident in Gstaad, when Amelia had broken her leg on the second day of a family vacation), rappel down mountains, and fire a pistol, revolver, or rifle, all with an eighty-five-percent degree of accuracy within twenty-five meters. Things taught to an only child by a father who was trying to live out his own fantasies.

"What color is your hair?" Ludi asked, startling Amelia.

She looked at it, curling over her shoulder. "Fantasy Flame, I think," She polished off her drink, wiped the moisture from her hands onto the army-surplus fatigues she was wearing, and ambled into the kitchen to fix herself another Bloody Mary. Ludi was arranging slices of soursop on a platter of grouper ready to go into the oven.

"Is very red." Ludi batted her eyelashes. "Beautiful."

Amelia smiled wearily. "That's all right, Mom. You can say it. It looks horrible." She squeezed a big chunk of lime into her glass. "And pretentious. And out of date, too. I don't know what got into me."

"When did you do it?"

"The day after the divorce went through."

"Ah."

"Ah? Was that one of your Russian wisewoman 'ah's'?"

There was a trace of malice in her daughter's voice, but Ludmilla didn't seem to mind. She shrugged, her eyes twinkling, and held out a piece of star-shaped fruit. "Have some soursop."

Amelia took it and placed it on the plate of fish. "Oh, Mother, you don't eat *fruit* when your husband leaves you. It's got to be chocolate, or pizza, or—"

"Or liquor?"

Amelia stared at her glass. Then suddenly she giggled. "What a jerk," she said. "How can you stand me?"

Ludi laughed and put her arms around her daughter. "Little Meli," she said softly, "now is a disaster. You cry, you drink tomato vodka, you dye your hair Fancy Flame. But tomorrow you wake up and say, 'Hey! Life is not over. I am here, I am strong. And I am still young.' Yes?"

"I'm thirty."

"Happy birthday." Ludi gave her a kiss on the cheek.

"Oh, for God's sake. Doesn't anything depress you?"

"Yes," Ludi said, her eyes flashing with sudden anger. "War. Hunger. Disease. Your father's snoring, that depresses me. But not your divorce from Johnny the Dunce."

"Kadunce," Amelia corrected with a laugh. "And he insists that everyone call him Jonathan."

Ludi blurted a short, ladylike raspberry. "Is still Johnny the Dunce, even though he wear little dumb-shit eyeglasses with plain glass, for to look intelligent."

Amelia roared. "How did you know? I was always too ashamed to mention it."

"I look through them once, from behind. An' I think, this *xitrozopyj,* this deodorant-clean boy, he is like Easter egg. Painted bright on outside, but inside is nothing." Her mother's English, Amelia remembered with amusement, always disintegrated with anger. "What is it, two years you live with him?"

"Just about."

"Ptui! Too much."

Amelia pursed her lips. "Now why didn't you say all this before I married him?"

Ludi shrugged, dismissing the subject. "You would listen? Hah. Go drink. Your father will come home soon. I want to be alone in my kitchen." She shooed Amelia back onto the porch.

Outside, the river gurgled its way through the tropical garden below the deck. The sky was fading from bright pink to purple, and already a sliver of moon hung in the sky. Absently Amelia lit the citronella candles along the railing and gazed out over the darkening horizon.

No, she thought, time didn't stand still. Not here, not anywhere. Everything changed, and you had to change with it. Or you died.

She was thirty years old, senior editor of a major New York publishing house, attractive from almost anyone's point of view, intelligent, educated, broad-minded . . . and she still spent her nights alone.

What's wrong with me, anyway?

At least with Johnny the Dunce she'd had something for company besides a pile of leftover paperwork. DINKS they'd been: dual-income, no kids. No kids, no conversation, no laughs, no sex.

Who'd started that? Whose idea had it been to have a marriage in which every moment was a conscious grind? Which one of them had decided it was a good idea to live with a hostile stranger?

Jonathan had finally left her for a nineteen-year-old lingerie model. Well, she thought, at least he'd had the courage to get out, even if he'd done it less than honorably. If he'd stayed, their marriage might have gimped along forever, silent and hurting, because Amelia wouldn't have made the first move.

She would have had to be a bad guy to do that.

Instead, she'd waited, biting her nails and reading self-help bestsellers, hoping that things would get better all by themselves, trying to believe that if she cultivated a good attitude, her life would magically improve.

When Jonathan moved out, she had felt a strange kind of

relief; she hadn't had to act on her own, after all.

You could have left him two years ago, and been twenty-eight instead of thirty now, she thought. And she could have left the boyfriend before him—the lawyer who instructed her on how to fold his socks—three years before he finally gave her a black eye _(you always knew he'd do that sooner or later, didn't you?)_, and she would have been twenty-five now. And the one before that . . .

Suddenly her eyes welled with Bloody Mary tears.

You're thirty years old, and you've wasted your whole life on men you didn't even like.

Her head was splitting. She forced herself to stand up and went to get the aspirin tin from her handbag. She took two pills and washed them down with her drink.

They were not aspirin. Her pain had gone beyond aspirin a year ago. And the Valium had almost no effect on her anymore, not even when mixed with liquor, but it would have to do.

"Anybody home?" Arthur Pierce poked his head through the front door, and both women turned to face him. Ludi's face was filled with delight and surprise, as it always was when she saw her husband. Amelia, too, felt a small thrill at the sight of him.

It had always been that way. Even in the old days, when her father had worked in Europe and come home only occasionally, she had experienced a delicious feeling of security the moment he entered the room, filling it with his quiet authority.

She had never met a man with half his charm or wisdom or integrity, though God knew, she'd tried. No one could ever measure up to Daddy.

"These are for you," he said, producing an armful of red roses. "There are only a dozen there. I can't afford to match your age anymore."

"Very funny," she said, kissing him.

"What did you do to your hair?"

"Is Fancy Flame color," Ludi shouted from the kitchen. "She do it for to celebrate divorce."

"Ah," Pierce said, as if that explained everything.

Amelia rolled her eyes. Pierce patted her shoulder. "I'll be down in a minute."

He returned shortly with a small suitcase and a book.

"What's that for?" Amelia asked.

Pierce smiled. "Just an overnighter. I'll be back tomorrow afternoon."

"Oh, no, she groaned. "You're not back to running out in the middle of the night, are you?"

He shrugged. "Sometimes it can't be helped, baby."

Disappointed, she picked up the book he'd brought down. It had an old leather binding stamped in gold leaf. Pierce took it from her and set it on top of his bag.

"*Queen Hortense and the Napoleonic Wars?*" she read, making a face. "That sounds like hot reading."

"Just something I haven't looked at for a while. For the plane."

"Listen, Dad. I don't know about all this running around. You're not a kid anymore—"

"That's right," he said, interrupting her with a pat on her cheek. "So bug off."

"Men," Amelia said.

"So. What's for dinner?" he asked cheerfully.

Ludi stared back at him from the kitchen, her face expressionless. Something was wrong, she knew. She could feel it shooting out of her husband like jolts of electricity, filling the air.

Pierce walked over to her and gave her a squeeze.

"I have cooked a fish," she said, giving him her prettiest smile.

After dinner and a birthday cake that she forced everyone to eat, Ludi produced a small box wrapped in tissue. "Happy birthday, Amelia," she said.

Inside the box was a bracelet that read "Amelia" in gold letters.

It was awful. Her name! As if she were advertising her availability to any man with the slightest interest in picking her up. Her mother was beautiful, but inside her heart, Amelia knew, there was a Russian *babushka* waiting to get out. "Thank you," she said, fastening the clasp.

Her father caught her eye, laughed out loud, and she knew he understood everything.

"What is funny?" Ludi grumbled.

"Nothing," Pierce said. "Consider it a gift from both of us. I'll bring you a big box of chocolates from Geneva. Speaking of which . . ."

He took a small notebook out of his shirt pocket and scribbled a number. "This is Davis Hyatt's direct line," he said, folding the piece of paper and handing it to Amelia. "You hang on to that. Your mother would lose it in five minutes."

Amelia put it in one of the pockets of her fatigue pants. "It's safe with me, Dad," she said.

"Good. Now in case you don't hear from me by tomorrow night, you can reach Hyatt. Just hop a plane and give him a call. He'll take care of you."

Amelia and her mother looked at each other. "A plane . . . to _Geneva_?"

"Just in case anything happens to me," he said lightly. "You know I always believe in being prepared."

"Anything like what?" Ludi asked.

He took her hand. "Humor an old man, Ludi."

Amelia narrowed her eyes. There was something he was keeping from them, but she couldn't figure out why. "Dad, if there's something about your health you aren't telling us—"

"My health is just fine," he said. "Now, I wish you'd stop acting like a couple of old hens." He drank his coffee. "It's just an emergency procedure, that's all."

"Oh, one of those." Amelia smiled. During the years when she and her mother had lived alone in the Santa Vittoria house, Pierce would always have some new "emergency procedure" to drill them on when he came to visit. "Like the boat buried in the river?" she asked.

"It's a pressurized raft," Pierce corrected with a touch of grouchiness.

"You mean it's still there?"

"Not the same one you saw twenty years ago, no. But a raft is there, in the same place."

Amelia laughed. "Field maneuvers. That was when you thought Sangre Precioso was going to be the next Cuba, and the airports would be shut down."

"I thought no such thing. But banana republics are notoriously unstable governments, and you two were alone here..." He shrugged.

Amelia shook her head. "The Agency wasted you in Codes and Ciphers, Dad. You would have made a great spy."

Pierce and Ludi exchanged a look. They had never told Amelia what her father really did for a living all those years before he went to work at Langley.

"God, you two look good together," Amelia sighed.

Pierce smiled. He was looking at Ludi now and she was looking back in the secret way they had of shutting out the rest of the world. The two of them still had a raging love affair going between them that Hollywood movies couldn't begin to understand.

I wish I could find that with someone, Amelia thought. *If only for one moment* . . . "I think I'll take a walk and leave you guys alone for a while," she said.

Neither answered her. They were absorbed only with one another.

"Why are you leaving?" Ludi asked levelly.

"I have to see Hyatt. A DC-Three leaves Santa Vittoria for Caracas this evening. From there I can fly direct to Geneva. I'll be back before dinner tomorrow." He smiled distractedly.

"*If* you come back."

"Now, Ludi—"

"You would not have made such a plan with Meli if there were not some real danger."

He didn't answer.

"You still do the work, don't you?" she asked softly. "The secret work."

He held her, and felt like crying.

This was it, he thought. He would go see Hyatt, tell him about Juan Sebastapol, and then retire. He'd had his second shot at being a Glory Boy; there were no regrets anymore.

Well, almost none. He had never told Ludi that the job with the wire service was simply a cover. It was the only thing he had ever kept from her.

"You could not give it up, after all." Ludi was smiling gently.

"No," he said. "I'm sorry."

"I understand."

A wave of guilt washed over him. Ludi had always known him better than he knew himself. He had left fieldwork for her, left behind the dirty world of half-truth to give his wife and daughter a clean life with a normal man, but there was a part of him that had resented that, a part that beat against the bars of his new normalcy and waited, hoping for the danger to come again.

Did she know that? Would it have hurt her to know? "Juan Sebastapol is dead," he said.

"Juan?" Her hand went to her lips. "Where was he?"

"Here, on the island. Someone killed him today in the old Sacred Heart Chapel."

"Oh, no." Her eyes filled with tears.

"He was a prisoner at El Mirador. Right under my nose, and I never knew it. There were hundreds of them there, Ludi. Political prisoners from everywhere." He could not bring himself to tell her that they had all burned to death.

"How do you know this?"

"Juan left a message for me in code. I have to bring that to Hyatt."

"Yes. Yes, you must go right away."

"And then it'll all be over. The work, I mean. I'm going to get out, once and for all. I promise, Ludi."

She laughed and laid her head against his chest. "Pah."

Yes, this would be the last time. He would retire and live out his days with Ludmilla on this island, lazing by the tropical river with no worries except for the occasional swamp rat in the kitchen, and making love with sweet Ludi, still as wild in bed as she had been a lifetime ago.

He kissed her then, deeply, and had to fight off the urge to take her on the spot.

Ludi, Ludi, my love, he thought. *I'll make it all up to you in the years we have left. It will be different now, you'll see . . .*

But all Ludi saw, the last thing she ever saw, was the bright orange flash from an explosion in the kitchen wall less than twenty feet away. Pierce felt her disintegrate in his arms.

When he came to a moment later, he was on the other side of the house, Ludi was gone somewhere in the pall of black smoke, and a red fountain of blood was pulsing out of a stump of flesh that had once been his leg.

"Daddy!"

It was Amelia's scream, coming from somewhere outside the numb bubble of death that was encasing him. And then she was at the door leading from the deck, rushing toward him . . .

Why, she's a grown woman, he thought with surprise. *When did that happen?* Amelia was nine, she was only nine . . .

"The book," he rasped, pointing to the copy of *Queen Hortense* that still lay undisturbed on top of his overnight bag. "Get it to Davis Hyatt. You know how."

"I'm taking you to the hospital," she said, choking on sobs as she tore off part of his shirt for a tourniquet.

He grabbed her arm, dimly aware that he was hurting her but unable to control the pressure. "Amelia . . . nine . . ." he said. He could no longer hear his own words. Had he spoken? Had the sounds come out? "Remember your birthday . . . your ninth birthday . . ."

And then Ludi was standing in the smoke in front of the blown-out wall, waiting for him to come to her.

But she's real, he thought with wonder. *Maybe she hadn't died, after all. Maybe he was the only one who'd been hit. Good, good, that's the way it should be . . .*

Then something squeezed at his bowels as he realized that he wasn't seeing Ludi at all. It was a man coming at them, a man wearing a black wool ski mask and carrying a machine gun. With a strength Pierce didn't know he had, he rose up on his one leg in front of his daughter to face the blue fire of the bullets. And as they came at him, he looked into his killer's eyes and knew who he was.

6

Amelia was screaming as she crawled backward, cowering, across the deck. Her movements were unconscious; she knew only that her father was being ripped apart by bullets in front of her eyes. She hardly felt it when she toppled off the deck into the river below. It wasn't until the gunfire stopped that she realized she had to get across the river and into the swamp on the far side if she were to have any hope of staying alive.

She crossed underwater, barely thinking when she took off her shoes and swam with them in her hands. Her father had taught her to do that. He had taught her to swim toward brush, to avoid being a vulnerable target on slick mud. They had played it as a game then, her father pelting her with pebbles, Amelia howling with each sting.

"You're dead!" he had shouted, his voice heavy with disappointment. *"Might as well not even bother to get up."*

"Mama . . ."

"Scramble for it! Go for the brush, Amelia! Get behind something, quick!"

"Ow!"

"Dead again." He shook his head, zapped her with another pebble for good measure.

"Stop it, Arthur." Ludi came out, her hands on her hips. *"You're teasing her."*

"Damn it, I'm teaching her."

"Teach her other things. She is not a boy."

"Ow!"

"You're dead."

She reached the far bank at the brush. A nest of swamp rats swarmed over her arm and splashed into the water. Stifling a scream, she hoisted a leg up onto the slippery bank, fell, and slipped back down.

You're dead.

The shots crashed in a spray above her head.

The killer was a good shot. He'd aimed for her back, and missed only because she had lost her footing.

Instinctively she twisted around and scrambled up the bank, diving headfirst into the swamp before the second burst of gunfire came.

There was another hiatus, and Amelia knew that the man in the ski mask was coming into the swamp after her. She flung herself deeper into the interior, trying hard not to panic. It was nearly full dark in here, but she had to find markers to lead her back to the river. She checked her surroundings as she waded through the fetid bog, blinking against the swarms of mosquitoes, watching for rats and other animals.

Suddenly she saw that she was still clutching the book her father had given her. In her wild flight, it had become an extension of her body. Even now, she had to force her fingers off the binding. They felt stiff and throbbing as she jammed the book into the neckline of her shirt.

A boy scout is prepared, she thought inanely, and realized how close she was to cracking up.

You're dead.

Calm down, she told herself. As she wound her way silently through the swamp, listening for the sound of the river, she tried to find something that would take her mind off her fear.

Whenever she sat in a dentist's chair, she mentally recited a poem she'd written for her father when she was a child.

> *I am Saint George the dragon slayer.*
> *Sword of Truth, you are my arm . . .*

You are my arm . . .

Her eyes swam with tears.

No, she told herself. She could not afford to mourn him now. He had put his own body between her and the killer's bullets so that she might survive, and that was what she was going to do.

Something else, something else.

It was no use. She couldn't concentrate. The only words that came into her mind were from a junior-high locker-room chant:

> *Piss, shit, corruption, rot,*
> *Ninety-nine assholes tied in a knot . . .*

Well, she thought, at least she'd remembered the entire opus. It had once gone through her head constantly for two days, but she had been young then. At thirteen, words like "shit" and "asshole" possessed an almost mystical power. They were shields against girlishness. Surely one capable of uttering such vile words could not be considered helpless or juvenile. Surely the parents of such a creature could find no way of controlling their evil offspring.

Piss! Shit! She'd fairly shouted the incantation during the sixteen hours her father had left her in the Sangre Preciosan rain forest.

"Ninety-nine assholes tied in a knot, and you're the biggest, reddest, smelliest one of them all!" she'd railed into the jungle.

Her father hadn't answered. She'd been alone then . . . as she was now.

The idea for the trek through the rain forest was, of

course, Arthur Pierce's. The family had moved to Langley by then, but they returned to Santa Vittoria every summer.

"So? What do you think?" Pierce beamed as he presented Amelia with a Swiss Army knife. It was to be, he had explained, their only piece of camping equipment. The idea struck Amelia as too repulsive to acknowledge. "Well?"

"I'm working on my tan, Dad."

Amelia had spent the entire school year in Langley, longing to come back to the place her mother called their "real" home. Now that she was back, with a new bikini and a bottle of suntan oil from Paris, she was not about to leave the sunny deck of their house for a mosquito-infested hike through the primeval wilderness.

She had shifted on the chaise longue and flipped through the pages of *Glamour* magazine.

"Nonsense. It'll be wonderful fun. Just you and me."

That had done it. She had put up the pretense of continuing to struggle, but inwardly she knew she would go, would put up with whatever awful trials were in store, just to be with him.

Ever since she could remember, Arthur Pierce had been her hero, the parfit gallant knight, and Amelia wanted nothing more than to be the helpless princess he rescued from the world's dragons.

Unfortunately, he had never allowed that. To be with Arthur Pierce, Amelia had to be a gallant knight, too, even though she didn't take easily to the role.

Scared and worried, she had driven with her father to the vast jungle in the center of the island.

"If you can survive outdoors, you've got a leg up on life," he said as they left their car behind and headed up the steep hills.

"Dad, I think it's illegal to camp in the rain forest."

He laughed. "They'll have to find us first."

"Yeah," she said wistfully.

She gritted her teeth through the ordeal of the next twelve hours. They walked endlessly, pausing only occasionally when her father pointed out caves and hollow trees where it would be possible to shelter in the event of a storm, or demonstrated how to make weapons.

"Could we . . ." She hated to even say it, but she was starving. "Could we kill an animal and eat it?"

He shrugged. "No fire."

Something exploded inside her. "You didn't bring matches? What kind of camping trip is this, anyway? I'm dying of hunger. It's so dark I can't even see where I'm going. What are we supposed to sleep on?"

"Don't sleep, Amelia. Find your way out."

"What?"

"That's the point of this exercise," he said quietly. "Get out alive."

She burst into tears. "How could you do such a thing to me?" she shrilled. "This . . . this was supposed to be our vacation. I didn't want an exercise. I just wanted to be with you . . ." Her whole body shook with rage and betrayal.

"Amelia, listen. Please listen."

"No! I'm not going to listen to you anymore. You and your dumb CIA field maneuvers. What do you do for them, anyway? Codes and Ciphers! You're not even a real spy or anything. You teach fucking codes and ciphers! I wish you'd never come back! I wish you'd just left Mom and me alone!" She was shouting at the top of her lungs.

Then she realized he wasn't there anymore.

"You hear me?" she demanded, sounding a lot less sure of herself now.

Her voice echoed back to her.

"Daddy?"

It had been the most terrifying moment of her life.

For more than an hour she had screamed apologies to her father, begging him not to leave her alone, but he had not responded.

It was then that she learned how to survive.

Piss, shit, corruption, rot!

Ninety-nine assholes tied in a knot!

You bastard, you bastard.

By the time she found her way out of the rain forest, it was afternoon of the next day. She was hungry and scratched and bruised and exhausted and overridingly, indescribably, angry.

"Good job, honey."

She turned around, startled. Her father was standing behind her.

"I was with you all the way. You missed a snake about three miles back, but otherwise you passed with flying colors."

She looked at her feet. There was blood on her sneakers. Her blisters had broken hours before. She started to laugh, and the sound was bitter and thin. "Great, Dad. Glad to hear it."

"Want a lift?"

"Not with you."

"It's twenty miles to the house," he said, losing none of his cheer. "Sure your feet are up to it?"

She winced. If spending the night in the jungle hadn't killed her, the extra twenty miles would, for sure.

"No problem," she said, limping proudly past him.

Less than two miles down the road, Ludi had picked her up.

"He called me," her mother said. "Get in. I will fix your feet at home."

Amelia slid into the seat of the car and sighed. She was beyond tears now. "He's crazy," she said. "Or else he just hates me."

"Neither," Ludi said gently. "He wants to make you strong."

"For what? So I can live in the jungle?"

Her mother smiled. "Well, maybe a little bit crazy."

I am Saint George, the dragon slayer . . .

Daddy, Daddy, come back.

Her nose was running. Quickly she wiped it with the back of her hand and moved steadily westward, toward the river. She had not heard the gunman for a long time. Maybe he hadn't come into the swamp after her. Maybe he'd gone upstream, in the other direction. She could see a few dim stars above the thinning foliage of the bank. Maybe at last she was safe.

And then she saw a metal pole glinting out of the river a few hundred feet ahead.

A marker. Of course. It had to be a marker.

Emergency procedures.

She smeared herself with mud, then crawled on her belly out of the swamp to the river's edge. Fortunately, the thin sliver of moon was covered by clouds, but she wanted to take no chances. She moved as slowly as possible, swiveling her head, scanning the ground around her, listening. At the pole, she slipped into the water and began to dig in the mud.

Within a few minutes she found what she was looking for: a plastic case in which was packed a foot-square lump of gray-green rubber designed to billow into an inflatable raft. Taped to the top of the rubber square were a small collapsible oar, a repair kit, and a nozzle so that the raft could be inflated by mouth if necessary. The thought of blowing up the raft by lung power while she waited for the man in the mask to find her and kill her was too daunting to contemplate.

Please work, she thought, pulling the rip cord.

With a *whoosh,* the small bundle in her hands ballooned out of her grasp.

The noise was not loud, but in the silence of the swamp, it was earthshaking. Terrified, Amelia ducked back under the surface of the water, waiting for the shots.

There were none. When she emerged, the raft was fully inflated and bobbing on the water.

She tossed the plastic case onto the raft. Then, after a last look around, she pulled herself aboard.

She felt terribly vulnerable out on the open river and hoped the speed of the current would compensate for the temporary exposure. The sooner she could get off Santa Vittoria, the better.

Lying near the port side of the raft, nearest the protection of the swamp, she sloshed around in the bottom of the case. There was a sealed plastic packet of bills: American currency, in hundreds. She stuck the packet inside her pants pocket, next to the scrap of paper her father had given her with Davis Hyatt's telephone number on it. Then she felt another object.

It was a .38-caliber Smith & Wesson, also sealed in plastic.

A third package contained a pair of infrared goggles.

Amelia sat frozen for a moment, staring at the things Arthur Pierce had left for her. *What was my father into,* she wondered as she fitted the goggles onto her face. Through them, the black stretch of earth beyond the river seemed bathed in an eerie red light. She could see a rabbit hopping, and could make out a cluster of tall grass in the distance.

She breathed deeply. The sudden cessation of physical activity suddenly released a flow of adrenalin that made her legs tremble. She could smell the fear on her body.

Relax, she told herself. *He's probably gone by now.*

She took the oar and began to paddle downstream, constantly searching the newly red horizon beyond her goggles.

If he didn't catch you in the swamp . . .

Suddenly she pulled the oar up. She had felt something, or seen it, or heard it. She didn't know which, but she was too frightened to ignore a hunch. Picking up the gun, she slid off the raft into the water.

Within seconds the shots came from the swamp, over her left shoulder. The raft twirled crazily. Amelia flattened herself against the bank, digging her toes into the mud to steady herself. Only her head and the Smith & Wesson were above the water.

A short way downstream, the man in the mask emerged from the swamp to watch the raft sink. He looked strangely unreal, a hunched, faceless creature surrounded by red trees, standing beside a red river, with a machine gun held at high port, ready to fire.

He'll find me, he'll find me, Amelia thought wildly, her mind screaming inside her skull, but she forced her fear away from her. She would have only one shot, she knew. Concentrating with every nerve cell in her body, she managed to stop the shaking in her hands and drew the barrel of the gun up over the embankment.

He caught the movement. For a terrifying instant, the

man in the mask swiveled to face her.

She fired.

The man fell backward, spraying the night sky with machine-gun fire as he went down. Amelia watched the fireworks erupt as if in a slow-motion movie. She had heard the reports from both weapons at almost the same moment and realized that her gun had fired a split second ahead of his. Then the squawking of a million birds and the crashing of small animals through the swamp filled the silence following the din of gunfire.

Head shot, she thought numbly, feeling her bladder release.

The gun fell from her hands and sank to the bottom of the river. Amelia did not move. Tears felt hot on her face.

"Oh, Daddy," she whispered.

It was almost dawn when Amelia reached Puerto Vittoria, the island's only real city. She was caked with dried mud, her clothes hung like rags around her slim frame, her hair fell in a wild tangle. One of her shoes had lost its heel, and the loose nails had dug painfully into her foot. A mile or two outside the city, she had stopped to pound out the nails with a rock, then stuffed the shoe with grass, which now poked out, dry and bloodstained.

She didn't care. As she limped through the narrow streets, the book bobbing inside her shirt, people turned to stare, but she never noticed. She was parched, hungry, and exhausted. The unbalanced gait she'd been using since losing her heel had caused shooting pains to course up her leg. Sweat poured off her. She had walked nearly fifteen miles.

When she reached the police station, the young sergeant manning the office fairly leaped up from his desk.

"Esta buena usted?" he asked.

She nodded. "Yes, I'm all right," she answered in Spanish. The officer led her to a chair. *"Gracias,"* she said, easing into the comfort of the wooden seat.

"You are from the island, Señorita?"

"Yes. Well, no. I'm an American, but my parents . . . my parents . . ." She covered her eyes with her hand, trying to collect her thoughts. "I've killed someone," she blurted out.

"You've *what?*"

Her throat was so dry she could hardly speak. "Do you think I could have a glass of water, please?"

The policeman listened quietly while she told her story. Afterward, he sat in silence, taking notes. "You say this happened yesterday?" he asked finally.

"Yes. At around nine o'clock in the evening."

He sighed. "I'll send someone out there when I can. All my men are busy with the fire."

"Fire?"

"A fire at the old fort, Señorita," he said bitterly. "A local problem, of no concern to Americans." He put down his pen. "You will have to remain here until the deputy governor can speak with you. This is policy in matters of foul play involving foreigners."

"I am no foreigner. I was raised on this island."

He shrugged. "That is the regulation, Señorita."

She nodded wearily. "How long will it be?"

The officer took a form and began to write. "A day, maybe two." He thought about it and shrugged. "Perhaps a week."

"A week! I can't wait a week. I have to get to Switzerland . . ."

"You do not wish to identify your parents?"

"No! That is, there's nothing I can do now, not for them."

"I see. It is more important for you to travel in Europe at this time, yes?"

"That's not it. I have to get to Geneva. My father insisted . . ." She felt herself becoming hysterical.

"Miss Pierce, I'm afraid it is quite necessary that you remain here. After all, you have confessed to killing a man."

"He had a machine gun!" Amelia shrilled. "He shot at me first. It was self-defense!"

"Perhaps," the sergeant said laconically.

" 'Perhaps'? What's that supposed to mean?" She knew she was saying all the wrong things, but her mind was so clouded by exhaustion that she couldn't stop herself. "Okay. I know it's all very confusing. I don't understand what's happened myself. But someone blew up my parents' house, shot my father, and tried to kill me. I have to get out of here."

The sergeant's face was cold. "If you try, I will arrest you. Murder is a serious charge." He glared at her. "Even on this backward island," he added.

"This is an outrage!" she shouted. "I demand some sort of justice."

"Ah, yes. That is just what I would like to see you get, Miss Pierce," the policeman said with a smile.

She closed her eyes and tried to breathe deeply. *Don't fall apart,* she thought. *Not now.*

"Please," she said, her voice trembling. "I need to make a phone call."

He made a slow gesture with his head toward the black telephone on his desk. "Be my guest."

She dialed her father's office. She didn't know anyone there, but perhaps there was someone who had known her father, someone who might help her now.

"Wade Turner, Hyatt News Service," a man's voice said.

"My name is Amelia Pierce," she said as calmly as she could. "My father, Arthur Pierce, has been killed. I'm at the police station. Is there someone there who can help me?"

There was a pause. "I'll be right over," he said.

Within ten minutes a young man with tousled blond hair and eyes still blinking with sleep rushed through the doors. "Miss Pierce?" he asked gently. "I work with your father. That is . . ."

"He's dead," Amelia said. "He and my mother were killed last night by a man with a machine gun."

"Oh, my God!" Turner said. "Did you get a look at him?"

She shook her head. "I didn't see his face. He was wearing a black stocking mask, the kind skiers wear. But he chased me . . . After he shot my dad, he chased me through the swamp . . . for so long . . ."

She looked up at Turner's face. His boyish eyes were soft with compassion. "I had to kill him. I never killed anyone before."

He nodded, pretending an understanding he could not possibly feel. "That's all right," he said. "You don't have to talk about it now. Let's get out of here."

"The sergeant says I have to wait until the deputy governor gets back in a day or two."

Turner looked over at the officer, who merely shrugged.

"He says I'm under arrest."

"On what charge?" Turner demanded.

"Murder," the policeman said, his mocking eyes open wide. "She confessed."

"Where is the body?"

The policeman didn't answer.

"Is there a body?"

"I'm sending some men to the scene."

"It seems to me that without any proof of a murder, you haven't any grounds for arresting this woman," Turner said.

The policeman narrowed his eyes. "She still has to wait until the deputy governor gets back."

"Where is he?"

"Away. On business."

Turner laughed. "Rodriguez? That deputy governor? What's his urgent business? Visiting the upstairs rooms at Mama Rosa's?"

The officer almost laughed, then forced his features into a glower. "You are insulting my country, Señor."

"Oh, bullshit. Everyone knows about Rodriguez and his whores, including you. If you don't know how to reach him, I do. I'll be back."

The policeman turned his attention back to his report.

"Meanwhile," Turner continued, "you might let the lady clean up."

The officer jerked his thumb toward a rest room in the back. Amelia stood up uncertainly. Her shoe came off, and blood-soaked grass fell onto the floor.

Turner picked it up. "These look pretty well shot."

Amelia stared down at the shoes. "I've come a long way," she said. Then, suddenly, she started to cry.

Turner put his arms around her. "Listen," he said softly, "I know it must have been a nightmare, but it's going to be over soon. You just try to get some rest now. I'll be back as soon as I can."

She nodded, too confused to speak.

"And try not to think too much. We'll work all this out, believe me."

As he left, the policeman looked up from his desk. "Gringo," he muttered.

In less than an hour, Turner came back, shaved and showered. He was carrying a pair of tire-soled huaraches.

"Rodriguez is on his way," he told the police officer. "Call his office to confirm it. Meanwhile, the lady will be my responsibility until he arrives."

The sergeant raised his hands slightly, a gesture of helpless acquiescence, but his face did not change expression.

Turner held out the shoes to Amelia. "They're not very pretty, but they'll be more comfortable than the ones you're wearing."

"Thank you," she said, putting them on. "That was very kind."

He laughed. Nervously, she thought, as if her gratitude embarrassed him.

"Would you care for some breakfast?"

"Oh, yes."

"Good." He offered her his arm rather stiffly. It was the formal gesture of a man unused to being with women. Despite the ordeal she was going through, Amelia found herself feeling a sort of maternal liking for the young man. She took his arm and smiled. He smiled back, blushing fiercely.

Turner took her to an outdoor cafe, or what passed for a cafe in Puerto Vittoria. A half-dozen old tables in various stages of disrepair and some rickety chairs were spread out beneath a torn awning.

They were the only customers. The street was nearly deserted.

"Where is everyone?" Amelia asked.

"At the morgue," he said, turning visibly pale. "There was a fire at the prison yesterday. More than half the people on the island worked there. Everybody was killed."

Amelia sighed. "Then that's what the policeman was talking about. He told me I wouldn't be interested."

"He probably lost a few family members himself."

A plump, middle-aged woman came by with coffee. Turner ordered a big breakfast for both of them, but Amelia could barely force down a bite. The images of the night kept coming back, assaulting her like a recurrent nightmare.

"I can take care of the arrangements, if you like," Turner said after a long silence.

Amelia looked up, startled. She had all but forgotten his presence.

"For the funeral. I don't mean to upset you."

"The . . . of course. Thank you."

"And you're welcome to stay in my apartment until things are settled." His eyes opened wide. "I wouldn't be there, naturally. I have friends I can stay with."

She smiled. "Thanks again, but that won't be necessary. I have to leave immediately."

"Oh." He looked at her, puzzled.

"I must go to Geneva. It was my father's last request."

"He wanted you to go to Geneva?"

"It sounds crazy, doesn't it?" She lifted the book from inside her shirt. The frayed leather corners had chafed her skin to painful red welts that had begun to suppurate. "He wanted me to give this to someone."

Turner touched the sodden cover. *"Queen Hortense?"*

Amelia shook her head and leafed through the book. "The one thing I've discovered through all this is that I never really knew my father at all."

She lifted something out of the book. It was a small notebook, its cardboard cover swollen and separating into sheets. Part of the larger book had been cut out to accommodate it.

"What's that?"

"I don't know." She opened it. "It's not in Dad's handwriting."

He pulled his chair closer. "It looks like some kind of medical journal. What you can read of it."

" 'Patient 14562. Renal failure, diabetic . . .' " She squinted.

" 'Coma,' " Turner said.

"Oh. Right. 'Complains of . . .' I can't make it out."

He took the notebook from her and studied the words. "I can't either," he said finally. "Maybe once the pages dry out, it'll be easier to read." He closed the notebook and handed it back to her. "The person you're supposed to give this to . . . That wouldn't be Davis Hyatt, would it?"

She hesitated.

"All right, never mind," he added quickly. "It's just that I was with your father yesterday, and something . . . something strange happened."

"What was it?"

"He said a man called him from the prison here. An inmate your father used to know. He had escaped and wanted to meet your father in an abandoned church, but the guy was dead by the time we got there."

"Do you think he wanted to see Dad about this?" She tapped the notebook.

Turner held up his hands. "Maybe. Your dad said he wasn't going to file anything outside of the usual 'fire-of-unknown-origin' story, but he might have changed his mind and gone back to the church. I just don't know."

Amelia turned the notebook over in her hands. "A doctor's notebook. A doctor in a prison. What could it mean?"

He shook his head. "I'm not even a reporter, Amelia. I couldn't begin to guess. But if it's a story your father wanted to get to Davis Hyatt, I can send it for you. We have stuff going out every day. I could even fax it out to him, page by page. Then you could stay here until you're able to sort things out." Tentatively, he touched the gold name bracelet on her wrist.

"It's funny," Amelia said. "My mother gave that to me

yesterday. I laughed at it. Now it's all I have left of her . . . of either of them.''

"I'm sorry," he said. "I can't tell you how sorry I am."

She felt his fingers tremble slightly as he traced the letters of her name. "My parents died suddenly, too. In a car accident. It was pretty rough. Maybe I can spare you a little of what I went through."

She squeezed his hand. He was so young, she thought. So young and so lonely and so far from home. "Thank you for the offer," she said kindly, "but I think I'd better deliver it myself." She glanced up and saw the policeman still on duty watching them.

"I understand," he said. He let go of her hand and forced a smile. "Please try to eat. It'll make you feel better, really."

He was right. Even though the food had grown cold, it brought back some of her strength. Through the meal, Turner made a point of concentrating on small talk, obviously hoping she'd relax.

After the dishes were cleared away, he rose. "Please excuse me for a moment," he said. "I've got to call into the office. Right now there's only an answering machine taking messages. I'll be at the pay phone just inside. Come get me if you need me for anything."

"I'll be fine," Amelia said, smiling.

He was so eager to help, she thought. Wade Turner might be an unlikely looking knight, but he had come gallantly to her rescue.

She sat back, sipping her coffee. It was the first time she'd been able to let down in twelve hours. She thought of the young man's trembling hands, the look of hope and compassion in his eyes. It was unmistakable, that puppy-dog look. He was developing a crush on her.

He'll get over it, she thought. *He's young.*

And then the memory of the masked killer came flooding over her again, and she sat bolt upright in her chair, quaking. She forced herself to blot the horror from her mind.

He's young, but I'm not.

She felt as if she had aged a hundred years in one night.

A black Chrysler New Yorker neared the cafe, slowed

down, then stopped in front of her table. A dark-haired man in his mid-forties got out. He wore a mustache and a navy-blue silk suit.

"Miss Pierce?" he inquired politely, half bowing beside her.

She looked up.

"I have been sent by Deputy Governor Julio Rodriguez, who is waiting for you at his residence. Please come with me."

His English was accented, Amelia noticed, but the accent wasn't Spanish. He gestured to the shiny black car.

She looked back into the restaurant. "I'm here with a friend . . ."

The man exhaled with some impatience. "Madame, the deputy governor is a very busy man. He has been called away from urgent duties to see you, and I'm sure he has every intention of dispensing with your business as soon as possible."

"All right," she said. "Just one moment, please."

She stood up, feeling somewhat light-headed, and walked into the restaurant. Wade Turner was talking on the phone, taking notes. She caught his eye and gestured that her appointment had arrived. He nodded, covered the mouthpiece, and said, "Come back to the office before you leave the island if you can."

"Thank you. Thanks for everything, Wade."

She got into the backseat of the car and waved to Turner as it passed the entrance of the restaurant.

Maybe she would see him again.

8

The doors had locked as soon as Amelia entered the car. Her feet rested on something soft. She looked down and kicked aside a heavy oil-stained towel.

A telephone rang. The driver picked up the receiver and spoke into it in an unfamiliar, guttural language as Amelia watched the shabby pastel houses of the island pass by.

They were driving on a dirt road that ran parallel to the swamp. She shuddered at the memories it brought back.

Soon you'll have time to grieve, she told herself. But not now. First she had to get through the ordeal of retelling her tale to the deputy governor. If she was lucky, and with the most minimal of police investigations, he would know that she was telling the truth and would allow her to leave for Geneva. Where she would have to recount her parents' murder again to Davis Hyatt. Another stranger. There were only strangers in her life now.

But someday it would be over. Someday she might even have a life again, as far away from this place as she could get.

"Where does the deputy governor live?" she asked.

The driver hesitated. "Only a short drive from here," he said.

"No, I meant . . ." She sat back. That was strange, she thought. Everyone knew that the Precioso government officials lived on the main island, a good forty minutes' drive away. She was asking for an address; what she received was a lie.

"You're planning to go over the bridge, aren't you?" she asked.

The driver hesitated again. "Of course."

He was an Arab, she decided. Amelia had a good ear for languages, and she finally placed the accent.

Up ahead, a two-lane highway intersected the dirt road at a T.

To the right, she knew, were the docks where the freighters came, and near them, the bridge leading to the main island. But the driver did not turn right. He headed instead toward the interior of the island. There was nothing there except the vast, uninhabited expanse of rain forest.

"Where are you going?" she asked.

Her eyes met his in the rearview mirror. "Give me the book," he said.

She pressed back in her seat as if the wind had been knocked out of her.

"Now, Miss Pierce." He wiggled his fingers over his shoulder. "Give it to me now, and no harm will come to you."

"Two of them . . ." she whispered.

"Do you understand, Miss Pierce?"

Her voice, when she found it, was shrill and piercing. "Why did that man kill my parents?"

The driver reached into the left side of his jacket. At the same moment, before she could give herself time to feel afraid, she grabbed the towel from the floor and threw it over the man's head, yanking the edges so that his neck thumped against the headrest.

He pulled out a gun and waved it wildly. Slamming her body against the left rear door, she reached in front of him and pulled hard on the steering wheel.

The big Chrysler veered crazily toward the swamp, then crashed head-on into a tree. The gun fired into the roof. At the moment of impact, Amelia lost her grip on the towel, and the driver's face smashed into the steering wheel.

She herself was wedged between the driver's seat and the steel strip separating the front and rear doors. The accident left her breathless but she was able to push her way out. Then she scrambled into the front passenger seat.

How many more of them are there? she wondered. _And what's in the book that's worth killing for?_

The man beside her was still alive. A trickle of blood oozed from his forehead onto the leather-wrapped steering wheel.

Slowly Amelia lifted the gun off the floor. It was a semi-automatic Glock Nineteen Compact, fully loaded with eighteen rounds. At this range, one shot would blow the Arab's head off.

_Do it,_ she told herself. _He was going to kill you._

She sat motionless for a full minute, oblivious to the sweat pouring into her eyes. Her hands wavered, steadied, wavered again . . .

She set down the gun.

"Fuck you," she said, bracing herself against the passenger door. She kicked out with both feet until the man's inert body dropped out of the car.

She had to get off this island. Nothing else mattered now.

Edging behind the wheel, she shut off the engine, pumped the gas pedal twice, then turned the ignition key again. The Chrysler roared to life and slowly she backed the car out. Wheezing and clanking, the bumper scraping against the front wheels, it clattered down the road, heading for the docks.

"Can you give me passage to Miami?" she asked the captain of a freighter.

She could not risk the airport. Someone was bound to discover the Arab driver soon, and the airport would be the first place anyone would look for her.

The captain pursed his lips, looked her up and down, then shook his head.

"I'll pay."

He stared silently at her again. The woman had no bags. Something was stuffed into the front of her shirt, but it was not large enough to contain drugs of any significance. And the gun, of course. That would have to go.

"Not Miami. Ponce, Puerto Rico."

"How will I get off?"

He shrugged. "We will dock at night. If you are caught, I will claim you stowed away."

She swallowed. "How much?"

He sized her up. "One thousand, American."

She turned her back, pulled out the plastic packet of bills and counted its contents. One thousand dollars on the nose. She would be stone broke, and no farther than Puerto Rico.

A shudder ran through her that had nothing to do with fear. The breath in her nose felt hot and dry, yet her teeth chattered.

So tired, she thought.

"I've got to lie down."

"No bunk. The floor in the hold."

"Will you give me a blanket?"

"It is July, Señorita."

"I'm—I'm cold."

He closed his eyes in exasperation. "One thousand dollars, yes or no? I am a busy man."

She rubbed her face. It felt as if her flesh were burning. "All right," she said quietly. She handed him the bills.

"And the gun." He held out his hand.

"But . . ."

"Give me the gun," he said, beckoning impatiently.

She took the Glock out of her fatigues and gave it to him.

"You need not worry about an attack from my men, Señorita," he said gruffly. "They fear women on ships. It is bad luck. I will see that you are not found. We will dock late tonight."

The captain did give her a blanket, as well as a large and vile-smelling jacket. She wrapped herself in them like a co-

coon, yet she couldn't keep warm. She lay down on top of a large wooden crate, away from the filth and rats on the metal floor of the hold, and shivered.

It's July, she thought, *and I'm freezing.*

That was great. On top of everything else that had happened to her, she'd caught a cold. Come to the sunny Caribbean and enjoy the flu to the fullest. Ain't life grand?

Piss, shit, corruption, rot. Ninety-nine assholes tied in a knot.

It was her last truly conscious thought for the next thirty-six hours.

The man with no name stood in the black night on the ocean's shore, staring at the hundreds of dead fish at his feet. The poison, the compound known only as Z-15, was so powerful that when the prison water tower had burst from the heat of the flames, the small amount of seepage that had not vaporized had contaminated this entire part of the beach.

Fortunately, no one was permitted near the shore by the prison. The government here was easy to control, which was one of the main reasons Santa Vittoria had been selected for the experiment. That, plus its proximity to the United States.

He breathed deeply of the salt air redolent of dead fish. There was a scent in death, an underlying odor that was the same in all creatures, from the smallest egg layers to man himself. The death-smell.

He could sense it now, not only from the fish, but from the vast tomb of the sea itself. Inside its dark waters were souls, his father's among them. His father, no longer a giant, no longer holding up a silver dagger running with blood, harmless now, a part of the great unity of death.

Yes. Yes, he could smell him, too.

Let me breathe you into me, Father. Let me become you.

What had his father named his son? The boy himself had never known. He had been raised with many names, none of them real. During the years he had learned Swedish, his name had been Christiaan Franssen. As a German, he had been Walter Weibgen. He had been a Russian, a Czech, a Romanian, a Pole, an Englishman; but none of his names were real. Only the killing had been real.

He was a tool, carefully wrought, a machine. One did not, he supposed, name machines.

He had first killed a man when he was six years old. The man had been a prisoner sentenced to execution. He, the nameless boy, had been the executioner.

It had taken four bullets to kill the man. With each bad shot, the trainers had come to him, straightening his small arm, correcting his stance, ignoring the prisoner who screamed in agony a few meters away. When it was finished, they examined the wounds, nodded, and gave the boy a piece of candy.

He had improved his aim with time. He was very good now, a good machine.

But only his father had known his name, and now his father was dead.

For a moment, the death-smell turned sad in his nostrils. Then the moment passed, and the man with no name turned and walked away from the sea.

There was work to be done.

9

"Get up. Eh? Wake up. This is San Juan."

Amelia felt herself being shaken roughly awake. She felt the coldness rushing through her body again, but her eyes took a long time to open. When they did, she saw two blurred images and smelled the salty dried sweat of the freighter captain.

"The men, they leave now," he said in English, gently slapping her face. "If you get off too late, the dock patrol catch you."

She sat up slowly, fighting down a wave of nausea.

"You sick?" the captain accused. "What you sick from?"

"I think I caught the flu."

"Jesu! Then go see a doctor or something. But you no stay here. Get up." He muscled her off the crate and into a standing position. "You got to walk now."

"Okay, okay."

He shook his head as the foreign woman staggered toward the ladder, two small, trembling hands sticking out from the oversized jacket.

Poor dumb *Americana,* he thought. Who was she running

away from? Her boyfriend on vacation? He sighed. Well, it wasn't his problem. The port authorities would probably grab her within ten minutes and send her back home to the States, where she would drink a bottle of brandy and nurse her cold and tell her lady friends about her big adventure.

He ran his thumbnail along the edge of the roll of bills in his pocket and climbed up on deck, whistling.

The dock-squad policeman nudged his partner and jutted his chin toward the small figure lurching down the gangplank.

"There's a guy who needs a drink."

His partner smiled. "Somebody ought to tell him it's July. That jacket looks heavy."

The two men looked at one another silently. The next moment, they were running up the gangway.

"Tu. Pare."

Amelia never heard him. As she walked, all the sights and sounds outside the ship dissolved into a sticky, nauseating miasma. She did her best to keep moving forward, but halfway down the ramp she was seized with stomach cramps that made her double over with pain. She stumbled toward the rope railing and flailed out with both hands to catch it. Still, she felt herself slipping, going over.

"Not so fast, buddy," one of the dock policemen said and grabbed her before she went over the side. "Where do you think you're going?" He yanked her arm behind her in a hammerlock.

Then he saw the fingernail polish and the gold "Amelia" name bracelet on her wrist. Quickly he pulled the cap off her head, and her long red hair fell over her shoulders.

"What have we got here?" he asked, smiling.

The other policeman was more businesslike. He pulled the jacket off her, examined it, then tossed it aside and frisked her trousers.

Amelia shivered uncontrollably.

"Nothing—" He stepped back as she bent over, retching.

"Take it easy," the first officer said, leading her away from the mess.

"There's something in her shirt."

The policeman took out the book and flipped through it.

"Please give it back," Amelia pleaded. "I have to get to Geneva. My father's dead. They killed him, the man in the stocking mask, and the one in the car . . ."

"Americana," the patrolman gripping her said.

Amelia gave no thought to which language she was speaking. She kept babbling as the officer lifted the notebook from the cutout inside the book and looked at it curiously. *"Ingles,"* he said.

Amelia reached for it. The other patrolman jerked her hands behind her back.

"Do you have papers?" the officer holding the book asked in halting but loud English. "No papers?"

Her eyes looked up at him, blurry and unfocused.

"You will come with us, please."

At the police station Amelia listened to the sounds of words swimming around her, but she no longer made an effort to sort them out. All she knew was that she was sick . . . really, scared-to-the-bones sick.

Get the book to Davis Hyatt, her father was saying, poking her in the stomach with his blown-off leg.

But I don't have time now, Dad. I have to die first.

Do what your father tells you, Ludi's head chimed in. It was perched, bodiless, on a corner of the living-room sofa, nestled between a couple of chintz pillows. Its lips were pink and freshly made up. *You don't listen, that's your trouble, Meli. Didn't your father tell you don't get into cars with strange men? Didn't I say, "Don't marry that dumbshit Johnny the Dunce, with his phony eyeglasses?" Yes?*

Take the book to Geneva, Amelia.

Oh, Dad.

Don't sleep, Amelia. Find your way out.

"Hey! Who's the chick?"

"Stowaway on one of the freighters. Speaks English, they said. She's got no papers."

"Well, she's really sick. I think we'd better call an ambulance for her." Someone leaned close to her face. "Señora.

Señora. You hear me okay?"

"My name is Amelia Pierce," she said with great deliberation, feeling as if she were pulling out her entrails with each
word.

"*Si?* Amelia . . ."

"Pierce. Call Davis Hyatt. Tell him I have a book."

"David who?"

Give them Hyatt's phone number, honey.

Forcing herself to alertness, she could barely make out
the figure of a woman in front of her. "Wait," she croaked.

Deep in the pocket of her fatigue pants, she found the
folded square of paper her father had given her. Moving her
arm was agony, but she inched it out of the pocket, clutching the paper in her fist.

Good job, honey. I was right behind you.

"There's something in her hand," someone said, but the
voice was faint and faraway sounding, and Amelia spun off
into darkness.

She awoke in what was unmistakably a hospital room. Her
eyes slowly scanned the white walls, the slatted blinds, an
abstract pastel print, an intravenous tube connecting a plastic bag filled with clear liquid to her arm. Tentatively, she
reached over with her free hand to touch it.

From behind her, a large male hand reached over her
head and grasped her by the wrist. "Leave it alone," a deep,
raspy voice said.

He was tall and blunt-featured, with bushy dark eyebrows and a mouth that looked as if it hadn't laughed since
infancy.

"Who are you?" he demanded, his voice revealing as little
expression as his face.

Amelia felt panic rising in her. "The book . . ."

"We've got it," the man said. "Who are you?"

"My name . . ." She looked up. The bogus chauffeur had
asked too many questions, too. "Wait a minute. Who are
you?"

"Burt Sergeant," he said. "I'm with Hyatt. We got a call
from San Juan. You were brought here night before last."

She tried to see through the half-opened blinds on the far side of the room. "Where am I now?"

"This is Geneva."

Geneva. She moaned her relief. Somehow she had made it. "I have to see Davis Hyatt," she said.

Sergeant shook his head. "You'll have to give me some information first."

She sighed. "Okay, okay. My name is Amelia Pierce."

"What happened to your father?"

She rolled her head back on the pillow. "I want to see Davis Hyatt."

"What in the book did Pierce want us to see?"

Amelia didn't answer.

"Was it in code?"

"I don't know. And I wouldn't tell you if I did."

The rebuff did not seem to bother the man. "Was your father sick when he died?"

She stared at him for a moment, then burst into low, bitter laughter. "Yes," she said finally. "It was a short illness. Duration, five seconds."

"We know he was killed," Sergeant said, a note of impatience in his voice. "But we want to know if he was suffering your symptoms prior to his murder. Or if your mother was."

She closed her eyes in exasperation. "I caught the flu, for God's sake."

"Not quite."

She looked over at him.

"The doctors think it might be bubonic plague."

Amelia sat bolt upright, nearly pulling the IV out of her arm. *"What?"*

"Oh, Christ," Sergeant said, buzzing for a nurse. Fluid from the IV dripped onto the linens. "You don't have to get so excited. You're over the worst of it. They say you're suffering more from dehydration than anything else."

A nurse scurried in to replace the tube. *"Bonjour,"* she said, smiling as she worked. *"Vous vous semble beaucoup mieux aujourd'hui. Le médecin sera très content."*

"She said the doctor will be pleased that you're doing so well."

"Doctor!" Amelia said, grabbing the nurse's wrist. "I want to talk to the doctor. Please send in the doctor now."

The nurse looked with bewilderment at Sergeant. He shrugged indifferently, then gestured for the nurse to leave.

"No, don't go!" Amelia called after her. "I need to talk . . ."

The woman closed the door behind her.

"Mind telling me what that was about?" Sergeant asked blandly.

Amelia narrowed her eyes. "No, I don't mind. I plan to find out what's going on. Find someone I can trust."

"Suit yourself."

She looked at him sadly. "You're one of them, too, aren't you?" she said in a small voice.

"One of who?"

She sighed, closed her eyes, and tried to hold back tears that had already begun to slide down her face.

What did they want with her? If that ox who called himself Burt Sergeant was telling the truth, they already had the book.

For all she knew, she might still be in Puerto Rico. Or Santa Vittoria, for that matter. The journey on the freighter might have been a sham. Maybe someone had given her a drug. The coffee, with Wade Turner? Could he have been in on it, too? And the French-speaking nurse. Another setup?

Oh, and incidentally, you've also picked up a mild dose of Black Death.

She heard herself sobbing out loud. She no longer knew the difference between possibility and paranoia. It was all part of the nightmare that had begun with the murder of her parents. And she didn't know why that had happened, either.

"Miss Pierce. Miss Pierce." It was a new voice, older, gentle. She opened her eyes and saw a white-haired man in a white lab coat. "Is that your name?" he asked, smiling reassuringly.

"Ye-yes," she answered, nodding.

"I am Doctor Wolfe," he said, pronouncing it "Volf." "I

have been looking after you since you arrived. Are you feeling a little better?"

She reached up with one hand to dry her eyes. "Much better, thanks," she answered in a squeak. "Can you tell me what was wrong with me?"

"Well, I can tell you what we know . . ."

"Wait." She gestured toward Sergeant, standing near the door. "Can you get rid of him first?"

The doctor looked up at the big man. Sergeant shook his head.

"Perhaps—"

"No," Sergeant said.

Dr. Wolfe patted Amelia's hand. "Don't worry," he said, although he cast a brief glance of annoyance over at Sergeant. "First, and most important, I feel certain that you will recover fully within a few days. From what we could gather, you passed the worst phase of your illness before you were flown here."

He smiled. "You seem to have healed yourself. In fact, you may have become immune to the disease because of your contact with it. Rather like a vaccination."

"Was it bubonic plague?"

"No."

Amelia looked over at Sergeant, hatred in her eyes.

"That is, not exactly," the doctor finished. "Plague is caused by a bacillus, which is treatable with antibiotics. We have just found that your blood contains no such bacillus."

"Well, that's a relief, anyway."

"But the symptoms, except for the most obvious one, the *buboes* under the armpit, appear to be quite similar to those of plague. Plague was a starting point for us in the determination of your disease."

"A starting point?" Her sense of relief died away. "Exactly what disease do I have?"

"I must be truthful with you, Miss Pierce. We do not know. We strongly suspect a virus, but its properties are unknown to us. Perhaps once we are able to consult with other physicians—"

"How did I get it?"

"That is what we most urgently would like to know. I understand you were on a ship?"

Amelia nodded.

"Can you remember its name?"

"No . . . I'm sorry. I wasn't feeling very well."

"I understand. Where did you board this vessel?"

"In Santa Vittoria. One of the islands in Sangre Precioso. But I was there for only one day, and I didn't see anyone besides my parents. My mother, really. I saw my father only during dinner. Then they were both . . ."

He stroked her hand. "Yes, I have heard about your misfortune. It is better not to dwell on it now."

"All right."

With a squeeze, he placed her hand over her stomach. Through the thin hospital gown she could feel a wad of tape and bandages. Touching the bandages made her feel itchy.

"Strangely, the areas of greatest infection seemed to be your chest and stomach," Dr. Wolfe said. "Do you have any idea of why that would be?"

"No. Well, the book. I was carrying the book in my shirt. It chafed my skin. I had to walk for a long time."

"Book?" He looked over at Sergeant.

"Your lab's got a sample of the binding," Sergeant said curtly.

"Ah, yes. I did not know it was a book."

"Maybe the infection seeped in because my skin was broken there," Amelia offered. "I was in a swamp. I could have picked up something there."

"Very possible," the doctor said. "Our laboratories and computers are working very hard to isolate the virus, if that is what we are dealing with. So although you are feeling better, we would appreciate it if you would remain here for tests and questioning. Could you do that?"

"I guess so," she said, looking over at Sergeant. "I don't think I have much of a choice."

"Very good," Dr. Wolfe said. He stood up.

"Doctor?"

"Yes?"

"Where am I? What city?"

"You are in Geneva."

"I'd like to see for myself, if you don't mind." She tried to swing her legs over the bed, but the doctor stopped her.

"Soon you may walk around and see all you like," he said, covering her legs with the sheet. "But for now, you rest." He walked over to the window and opened the blind, revealing a vista of the city along the shore of Lake Geneva. "Can you see our famous *Jet d'Eau,* the big fountain in the lake?"

Amelia craned her neck. "Yes," she said, hope rising inside her. At least someone was telling her the truth. "Yes, I see it."

"So you believe me?"

She nodded.

"Good. Now I am sending in the nurse to change your bandages."

"Thank you, Doctor."

A few minutes after he left, a nurse entered the room, a different one this time, petite and dark-eyed. She smiled at Amelia and scowled at Sergeant.

"Outside, please," she ordered him.

Sergeant folded his arms stolidly in front of his chest.

The nurse sighed, then pulled the privacy screen all around the bed, sealing them off from the man's view.

Amelia was glad to have a barrier between herself and Burt Sergeant. She did not know for how long that awful man had been there, staring at her, looking at her sleep, watching her body, but the thought gave her the creeps.

"Thank—" She started to move her lips, but then the nurse was pressing a pillow down on her face, throwing the weight of her body on top of it, smothering her. Amelia tried to throw out her arms and legs, but the woman had her pinned.

She fought to push the pillow loose. From the corner of her eye, she caught a glint of steel. It was a knife, aimed toward her throat.

Then, close to her, so terribly close that the sound rang in her ears like a bell, came the crack of a bullet. The nurse's already distorted face seemed to explode as she fell over the bed. The IV stand crashed to the floor, ripping the needle out of Amelia's arm.

She screamed when she saw Sergeant standing next to her bed, an automatic pistol in his hand, a small tendril of smoke curling from the barrel.

"Shut up," Sergeant said through gritted teeth. He leaned down toward her and she bit his shoulder. He winced but caught her up in his arms and ran out of the room with her. A moment later he slammed through a pair of metal doors and bolted down the fire stairs.

Amelia continued to scream. She screamed with all of the rage and fear and grief she had pent up since this nightmare began. She screamed until Burt Sergeant grabbed a handful of her hair on a landing, set her down, and walked her toward another closed metal door.

"What . . . what are you . . ."

He slammed her head against the door.

10

This time when she came to, she was falling a hundred miles an hour toward earth. Her scream echoed like the wail of a banshee.

"Will you cut that out?" Sergeant said in exasperation. "I really don't like punching out women. Although with you, I could learn to like it."

"Bastard," she mumbled groggily.

"I had to do it. You were telegraphing our location to anyone with ears."

"Like the police."

Sergeant didn't answer. He was gripping a semicircular wheel. Outside, a cluster of small cottages grew larger, then disappeared. A few neat, square farms passed beneath them.

"This is an airplane!" She gasped in amazement.

"Very astute observation." He dipped the plane between two mountain peaks.

"Get me out of here!" She struggled to claw at him, then realized that she was tied firmly to the seat, her arms immobilized.

"I suppose you'd be stupid enough to kill us both up here."

"You bet I would." She spat at him.

He wiped his face with a handkerchief. "That's why I took the precaution of restraining you."

"Why didn't you just kill me in the hospital?"

"You've got it wrong, lady. Remember me? The nurse tried to kill you. I'm the one who saved your life."

"Assuming I believed you, why would she try to kill me?"

He shrugged. "Beats me."

"Wonderful. Where are we, and what are we doing here?"

He began to lower the small plane. Ahead, Amelia could see a large open field where the grass had been trimmed short.

"Never mind where we are. You'll be safe here. And what I'm trying to do is to find out who killed Arthur Pierce."

Amelia hesitated. "You don't have to do that," she said.

"Oh?"

"The man who killed him is dead. I shot him."

The plane touched down with a light bump, then circled around the field until it came to a stop near a large barn.

Sergeant kept his hands on the wheel and turned toward her. "Mind going over that again?"

She shook her head. "I'll tell Davis Hyatt. If you really work for him, then take me to him."

Sergeant got out of the plane and slammed the door.

Amelia stood on the grass, her hands still bound, while Sergeant pushed the plane into the barn. The door closed softly. Afterward there was not another sound except for the chirring of insects and the faint whistle of a breeze. There was no sign of civilization, not a house, not a telephone pole. On either side of the narrow valley rose the two snowcapped mountains she had seen from the air.

Sergeant led Amelia to a battered old Jeep, then drove for miles up the side of one of the mountains.

She said nothing during the ride.

After a half hour, he pulled up in front of a small cottage made of logs. "You'll be safe here. For a while, anyway."

"Until you kill me, you mean."

He untied her hands. Amelia immediately lunged for his face, claws out. He grabbed her, kicked open the cabin door, and threw her unceremoniously inside.

"Look, I've told you I'm not going to hurt you," he growled.

"Then why did you take my book?"

Sprawled on the floor, she looked down and saw her bare legs sticking out of the big leather jacket Sergeant had thrown over her shoulders in the car. She inched them up toward the flimsy hem of the hospital gown.

Sergeant went into another room and returned with a pair of jeans and a wrinkled cotton shirt. "Davis Hyatt's got it," he said.

Amelia scrambled to her feet. "I don't believe you."

"Suit yourself." He threw the clothes at her. "Know how to cook?"

"No," she snapped, catching the jeans in mid-air.

"That figures."

"If *you* were legitimate, you'd take me to Hyatt," she grumbled.

"If *you* were legitimate, you'd have known how to reach him yourself." Sergeant locked the front door with a key, then went into the kitchen.

Amelia looked around the room. It was rough but comfortable, with a threadbare lump of a sofa and a braided rug in front of a fireplace with a wooden beam for a mantel. On the windowsill was a small spider plant on the verge of death.

Amelia rolled the pants to a wearable length, then went into the kitchen. On an antique wood-burning stove simmered a pot of tomato sauce and another boiling with noodles. Her mouth watered. Sergeant tossed an empty can into a brown paper bag.

"Is this where you live?" she asked.

"Sometimes."

"Where are we? I mean, is this still Switzerland?"

"You don't need to know."

She sighed in exasperation. "Look, I understand that

some strange things are happening, but do you have to be quite so cloak-and-dagger about it? I mean, I'm the one everybody's trying to kill. So maybe you could at least tell me what country I'm in."

"You talk too much," Sergeant said. "But for the record, you're still in Switzerland. The area's called Appenzell."

He could be good-looking, Amelia thought, *if his face weren't perpetually twisted into a scowl.*

"Soup's on," he said, carrying two plates piled high with spaghetti to the small table. Amelia realized that she hadn't eaten any solid food since her breakfast with Wade Turner two days before.

"You can switch plates with me if you like," Sergeant said dryly. "That way you can't accuse me of trying to poison you."

She sniffed in disdain and dug in. There was no conversation. The only sound was the clink of forks against china. Her plate was clean in five minutes.

"Sure you don't want to lick it?" Sergeant asked, sipping from a water tumbler.

Amelia felt herself blushing. "I guess I was hungrier than I thought."

"Careful. Don't get too carried away. Before you know it, you may wind up thanking me, and we certainly wouldn't want that."

"Thanking you?" She was incensed. "For what? Kidnapping me? Keeping me prisoner here in the middle of nowhere?"

"It has to be this way . . . for your safety. Want some wine?"

She snatched the bottle and poured herself a glass. "Okay, maybe you're not one of them," she said. "But if you're not trying to kill me, then who do you work for, the police?"

"I told you. I work for Davis Hyatt."

"Most newspapermen don't carry guns."

He shrugged.

"Why can't I see him?" she demanded. "And don't you dare say it's because I have bubonic plague."

Sergeant smiled.

Yes, she thought disconcertedly. *Yes, he really is good-looking.*

Oh, great. Now I'm looking at murdering thugs as potential dates. Talk about desperate.

"How did you kill the man who murdered Arthur Pierce?"

"An S and W thirty-eight."

"Your gun?"

"No." She was silent for a moment. "I think it was my father's. It was sealed . . . Look, I told you I would talk. But only to Davis Hyatt."

"We'll see about that."

She felt like strangling him. "In that case, there's no reason for me to be here. I have a job in New York that I have to get back to."

"Not until the people who are trying to kill you are out of the way."

"Oh, come on. I have to call my office, at least."

"No. If whoever's behind this finds out where you are, we're both dead."

She rolled her eyes. "Then I'll send a telegram."

"I'll take care of it."

"How do you know where I work?"

"I know a lot about you. Unfortunately, so do the people who killed Pierce."

"I wish you'd stop calling him that, as if he were some associate of mine. He was my father, and . . ." She put down her glass. "Did you know him?"

After a moment, Sergeant nodded. "I knew him. He was a good man."

They drank in a silence that became oppressive. Finally Amelia said, "He used to work for the CIA. Codes and Ciphers."

Sergeant emitted a small puff of air from his nose that might have been the aborted beginning of a laugh. Then he stood up and took both plates to the kitchen.

She followed him. "I think he was doing some things I never knew about," she said.

"Like what?"

"I still don't know. But since . . . that evening, I've been thinking about a lot of things I never questioned before."

Sergeant handed her a dish and she dried it absently. "The fact that he had a gun, you mean?"

"That's part of it. He kept an inflatable raft stashed in the river near the house. The gun was in there, along with some other things. But that's not what I mean, exactly. You see, there were years when he wasn't home. I mean that literally. Years on end. My mother told me he was in Europe, but nobody ever talked about what he did there. Hell, I don't even know where in Europe he was all that time." She set down the plate. "It sounds crazy, doesn't it?"

Sergeant washed the two forks.

"And when he did come home, it seems we spent all our time together on combat maneuvers. Target practice, self-defense, survival training, that sort of thing. I used to think he was just disappointed at not having a son, but lately . . . Oh, never mind."

"I'm listening."

She peered out the small window over the sink. "Well, it almost seems as if he'd been schooling me for something. What I'm saying is that when I killed that man in the swamp, it was almost automatic. I was scared shitless, but I knew I *had* to kill him." She rubbed her arms. "It gives me the willies just to think about it."

"Sometimes it's better not to think too much," Sergeant said.

"I wish I didn't have to. But my dad's last request to me was to get the book to Davis Hyatt."

"I've told you, Hyatt's got it."

She felt her irritation rising again. "I have to know that for myself."

Sergeant sighed. "Sorry," he said. "You're not leaving this house until I say so. Period."

"I see. Macho Man has spoken."

"Oh, Jesus."

"You're treating me like a moron!" she shouted.

"Maybe you're acting like one!" he shouted back.

"You have no business keeping me here!"

"You know, maybe you're right." He lowered his voice to almost a whisper, intensifying the focus of his anger. "I shouldn't give a rat's ass whether you live another day or not. We've got samples of your blood. We've got the book. We don't really need you anymore. Plus, you're ungrateful, willful, ill-mannered, foul-tempered—"

"*I'm* foul-tempered? Listen to you! Why, you haven't said a civil word—"

"All right. All right!" He held his hands up. "You want to run out into the night right now? Fine. I don't have the time to baby-sit you twenty-four hours a day."

He took her hand, yanked her toward the door, and unlocked it. *"Bon voyage."*

She reached for the knob, then hesitated.

He opened the door for her. "Well, what are you waiting for?"

You don't even know where you are, you dumb shit. Somewhere in the middle of Switzerland. Three people have tried to kill you, and you don't have a dime for a phone call, let alone a weapon to defend yourself with. Right, Amelia. This is a great time to walk out.

She closed the door.

"There's only one bedroom," Sergeant said, walking back to the kitchen. "You can have it."

Amelia went into the bedroom and slammed the door. She could hear Sergeant laughing.

She washed with cold water in the small bathroom, then bundled back in her oversized clothes and dove into the big bed. It was comfortable beyond belief, with a thick featherbed that puffed out around her . . . yet she could not sleep.

Who is Burt Sergeant? The question loomed in her mind like a huge shadow. If he was one of the conspirators involved in the murder of her parents, she might have told him too much.

But he couldn't be, she reasoned. The others had tried to kill her on the spot. Sergeant had had plenty of opportunity to get rid of her, but he hadn't taken it. He had, in fact, despite his ungallant personality, saved her life.

Then why had he taken the book? And why did he not permit her to see Davis Hyatt? That was what she had to find out.

Slowly an idea began to take shape, then grew into a plan. It was outlandish, to be sure; something her father might have dreamed up. But it could work.

Yes, she thought. With a little effort, it would work.

She settled back into the bed, closed her eyes, and fell asleep in an instant.

The next morning when she awoke, Sergeant was gone. It was going to be easier than she'd expected.

She searched through the drawers in the kitchen. What she needed was string, but if she didn't find it, she could tear the bedsheets.

She got lucky with a ball of twine. Working in the back of the house, she carefully knotted the twine into three-inch squares until it vaguely resembled a net. Then she strung a length of twine through the rafters to suspend her creation from the ceiling. Finally she took the biggest kitchen knife she could find and lay it on the windowsill next to the locked door.

And she waited.

Sergeant returned in the late afternoon. Amelia heard the Jeep pull up near the house, but before she could run to the window to look out, she heard his heavy footsteps on the porch.

She picked up the knife and moved behind the front door, the only entrance into the cabin. Then she wiped the perspiration from her hands onto the baggy pants she wore.

The moment the door opened, she let fly the piece of string holding up her handmade mesh and watched as the net fell on Sergeant, enveloping him. Then, before he could fight, she kicked the back of his knee until it buckled, grabbing his arm in a hammerlock, threw her body on top of his, and jammed the kitchen knife up against his throat.

"Now suppose you tell me what the hell's going on," she said.

"Don't shoot! It's all right!" Sergeant bellowed.

"I'm not going to shoot you, bozo. But if you think I won't use the knife, I've got a surprise for you."

Sergeant made a noise with his tongue and looked up at her flatly. "Not you. Him."

Just then another man stepped through the doorway, a Beretta in his hand.

"Drop it, mister. I'm not kidding," Amelia said, hoping her fear didn't register in her voice.

To her relief, he complied. He tossed the gun to the floor, then looked at Sergeant with a small shrug and an expression of utter surprise.

"Jesus God," Sergeant muttered. He tried to sit up, but Amelia forced him back down.

"You can start by telling me who your friend is," she said.

"Gladly." He grunted as he swiveled his head toward the stranger. "This is Davis Hyatt."

11

The plump man in the doorway smiled and presented Amelia with a formal half-bow.

"Oh, God," she said.

"Mind taking that knife away?" Sergeant asked irritably. She did, then helped to extricate him from the tangled net. "Where'd you get this thing, anyway?"

"I made it," Amelia said.

Davis Hyatt, still standing in the doorway, lit a cigar and nodded.

"I'm sorry, really. It's just that Mr. Sergeant here didn't seem as if he were going to tell me anything, and he said I couldn't speak with you . . ."

"Yes, I see," Hyatt said. "But Burt isn't to be blamed. It's policy. I couldn't meet with you until we were certain you were who you claimed to be."

"Me!"

"Incidentally . . ." Hyatt walked into the room and pulled out a handsome leather card case containing a dozen pieces of photo identification ". . . for your own satisfaction."

She scrutinized each picture, checking them against his

face. Finally she nodded and handed the case back to him. "Well? How did you find out I'm who I say I am?"

He puffed on his cigar. "From the CIA. They had your fingerprints on file. We matched them to prints taken at the hospital."

"My fingerprints? With the CIA? But I'm not a criminal. I never—"

"When you were a child, apparently both you and your mother were questioned."

Amelia opened her mouth in surprise. "That's right!" she said. "I remember now. They wanted to know all kinds of things about my father. He was going to work for them." She looked up at Hyatt suddenly. "But why would the CIA give you my fingerprints? I mean, isn't that illegal or something, giving out a private citizen's fingerprints to a newspaper wire service?"

Hyatt walked over and sat down at the kitchen table, motioning for Amelia to sit down also. "Miss Pierce," he said, "I believe we owe you an explanation. About your father."

She took a chair. "What about him?"

"His work. Prior to his years at Langley, Arthur Pierce was one of the CIA's top field agents."

Amelia caught her breath. Suddenly, in one sentence, all of the missing pieces of her father's life came together.

"That was why he was never home," she said softly.

"He couldn't bear that part of it. He left active duty to be with you and your mother. He moved you back to the States and took the job in Codes and Ciphers. An utter waste, really, for a man of his abilities."

"Now I understand." Amelia shook her head. "I used to make fun of him about his job. The things he tried to teach me . . . I thought they were just part of some tough-guy fantasy of his." Tears of shame welled in her eyes. "Why didn't he ever tell me?"

"How could he?" Hyatt asked. "Especially since he went back to it."

"He did? When?"

"When he came to work for me."

Dumbfounded, Amelia looked to Sergeant, who only nodded.

"Then you're with the CIA?"

"No. The organization for which I work—for which you father worked—has no name. The CIA does not know we exist. Nor does your FBI, although both agencies have standing orders to cooperate with our representatives should the need arise."

His cigar had gone out. He lit it again.

"That is how we are in a position to help you now. It is apparent that your father stumbled across something on Santa Vittoria that he wasn't supposed to know about."

"The notebook."

"Most likely. Pierce went to the trouble of concealing it inside another book. And he gave it to you before he died. It must have been something of great importance to him, since he didn't even tell his partner about its existence."

"His partner?" Her brow furrowed. "You don't mean Wade Turner?"

Hyatt hesitated. "I do," he said at last. "Miss Pierce, I am giving you some very dangerous information. Information that could kill us all should you decide to divulge it." He spoke with the sour agitation of a man who was more comfortable with silence.

"I won't say anything."

He puffed on his cigar for a full thirty seconds, as if deliberating whether or not to go on. Then he spoke. "We have reason to believe that your father was right about the importance of the notebook. On its cover there's a coffee stain loaded with an unusual type of virus that the best laboratory in Switzerland does not recognize. An identical virus was isolated in a sample of your blood. Undoubtedly it was this virus, in an extremely faint concentration, that nearly caused your death."

"Do you mean I got that sick from a *coffee stain* on a notebook? A notebook that was inside another book?"

"And heavily diluted with swamp water, at that," Hyatt said. "One can only guess at its lethal potential. Now the question is, does the virus occur in nature, or was it developed for a specific purpose?"

"Like killing people?" Amelia said.

"Miss Pierce, if the preliminary lab reports are any indication, this organism could wipe out a continent. In a matter of weeks."

He squinted through the smoke curling around his face. "That is why I have been forced to tell you things you should never have known about. I must ask you to cooperate with us to the very best of your ability . . . and then forget that you ever met Mr. Sergeant, Mr. Turner, or myself."

"I understand," Amelia said softly. "Where would you like me to begin?"

Hyatt leaned back in his chair. "Give us all of it."

Amelia told Hyatt about the explosion in her parents' house that killed her mother, about the masked gunman and the flight through the swamp, about the episode at the police station, and the black car with the foreign-looking driver.

"An Arab, you said?" Hyatt asked.

"I think so. From the accent. The nurse was an Arab, too, wasn't she?"

"Possibly. She had no identification. No one at the hospital had seen her before. Was the driver killed in the accident?"

"No. I left him by the side of the road. Maybe if you checked with the hospital on Santa Vittoria . . ."

Hyatt shook his head. "Turner already has. He found the car near the docks. From its condition, he assumed there had been a problem."

"He—the driver—knew about the book," Amelia said.

Hyatt ground his teeth. "The shooter must have told him," he muttered, almost to himself.

"The shooter?"

"The man who killed your father."

Amelia shook her head emphatically. "No. He's dead. I told you, I shot him in the swamp. A head shot. He couldn't have lived."

Hyatt was quiet for a moment. Finally he said, "There's just one problem with that, Miss Pierce."

"Oh?"

"No body was found. Turner searched the area himself, after the police had gone."

"It's there, I tell you," Amelia said stubbornly.

Hyatt raised his hands slightly. "Maybe it washed downstream."

"I saw him fall. The body didn't go into the river."

Hyatt made a conciliatory gesture. Amelia went on with the rest of her story, while the two men listened.

"Did you read it? The notebook."

Amelia shook her head. "I tried to, with Wade Turner. It seemed to be some kind of medical log, but it didn't make much sense."

"Your father was an expert in codes," Hyatt said.

"A code?" She thought about it. "I suppose Dr. Sebastapol's log might have been in code, but—"

"There's no doubt about that," Hyatt said brusquely, waving away some smoke. "Our cryptologists have been trying to decipher it, but so far they haven't made any headway." He puffed silently for a few moments. "Your father must have understood the complexity of the code used. He would have wanted *someone* to know how to break it."

"Like me?" Amelia asked, faintly amused.

"Perhaps. At the end, when there was no one else . . ." He leaned forward. "Are you certain he said nothing to you before he died? Nothing that might shed some light on the message he was trying to get to me?"

Amelia swallowed. She hated having to relive those last terryifying moments at the house on Santa Vittoria. The burst of orange flame, the deafening crack of the explosion, the sight of her father staring at the bloody strings of flesh that had once been his leg . . .

"His last words were 'Remember your ninth birthday,' but—" Suddenly she stood up. "Yes!" Her voice was a whisper of triumph. "My ninth birthday! That was when he taught it to me."

"Taught what to you?"

"The code. The unbreakable code."

Hyatt put down is cigar. "Excuse me?" he said quietly.

"The unbreakable code! He was still in Europe then, and I wasn't allowed to write to him. Oh, God, it's all so clear now. He taught me the code so that we could send each other letters. I thought it was just a game, but—"

"Please explain this code to me," Hyatt said. He pulled a note pad and a pen from his heavily starched shirt.

She took them from him and began to write. "It works like this," she said as Hyatt leaned forward.

Burt Sergeant came up on the other side of her and pulled a chair close so that he could watch.

"It's not really a code. It's a cipher. Do you know the difference?" She looked at Sergeant, then at Hyatt.

"Your show, Amelia," Hyatt said.

"Okay. Well, in a code, one word—one letter even—could stand for a big, long message. Suppose the message was 'We will start bombing at nine o'clock next Tuesday night if it is not raining.' Well, you could say that the word 'red' stands for that message. So if you sent someone the word 'red,' they'd go to their codebook and look it up and see that you're bombing next Tuesday. That's a code."

"And a cipher?" Hyatt said.

"A cipher doesn't need a predetermined message. What you do with a cipher is to simply write out your message—any message—and then change it somehow so that no one else—except the person who knows the key—can read it. That's where the word 'decipher' comes from. Here, look at this."

She turned the pad around, and both men could see that she had printed, in block letters, the message:

SERGEANT IS A BASTARD.

She looked at Burt Sergeant. "Sorry. It's just the first thing that came to mind."

"Quite understandable," Hyatt said. "Please go on."

"Okay. Now, a kid's way of making a cipher would be to change every one of those letters to a number. For instance, S is the nineteenth letter of the alphabet. So instead of writing S, you would write nineteen. E is the fifth letter. So five stands for E. You just keep substituting, and so your message would look like this."

Under the letters of the message, she quickly penned in a string of numbers so that the paper read:

S E R G E A N T   I S   A   B A S T A R D.
19-5-18-8-5-1-14-20 9-19 1 2-1-19-20-1-18-4.

"See? That's a cipher. If you send off those numbers, a person could change them back to letters and read 'Sergeant is a bastard.' "

"Well of course that's much too simple," Hyatt said.

"Naturally," Amelia agreed. "So people would find ways to make the cipher more complicated." She pointed to the line of numbers. "For instance, suppose in this line of numbers—" she pointed to the cipher for "Sergeant": 19-5-18-8-5-1-14-20 "—suppose you added five to each of those numbers. Then you'd have this row of figures." She jotted them down. 24-10-23-13-10-6-19-25.

"Now, if somebody tried to transpose them back to letters, he would come up with X-J-W-M-J-F-S-Y. So now what you've done is to make your cipher that much more complicated."

She looked up.

"But still breakable, to an expert," Sergeant said.

"Not even an expert," Amelia said. "Anybody with a little knowledge and half a brain could figure it out, especially if the message is long enough. You'd look for groups of three letters that appeared frequently and then figure out that that stands for 'the.' That gives you T H E. You look for common endings. That'll give you I N G. Before you know it, you'll have enough letters that you'll be able to start building the answer. Child's play. And with a computer, you could do it all in five minutes."

"So how did your father give you an unbreakable code?" Hyatt asked.

"It's the key you use. Here, I'll show you."

She ripped out a fresh piece of paper and jotted down more numbers.

"There's our basic message. 'Sergeant is a bastard,' " she said. "Written in numbers. Now I showed that if you just add five to each number, you can complicate it . . . but it's still solvable. But you do this. You take some other message. The one we used on my birthday, for instance."

"Amelia?" Sergeant said.

She was surprised at how quickly he had understood.

"Right. 'Amelia is nine' was our key. We convert that to numbers. For now, let's just use 'Amelia,' because it will be quicker."

She wrote: A M E L I A. Then she converted each letter to its numerical place in the alphabet. 1-13-5-12-9-1.

"Now that's Amelia spelled out in number cipher. So what you do is, you add that to your original message. Remember," she said, "these numbers spell 'Sergeant is a bastard.' "

"Right," Hyatt said.

"All right. So to those numbers you add the numbers that stand for Amelia."

She wrote quickly, then turned the paper so they could see.

There were three rows of figures.

The first was 19-5-18-8-5-1-14-20-9-19-1-2-1-19-20-1-18-4, the original enciphering of "Sergeant is a bastard."

Beneath that row of figures, she had added the cipher for Amelia—1-13-5-12-9-1—over and over again. The two lines looked like this:

19-5-18-8-5-1-14-20-9-19-1-2-1-19-20-1-18-4
1-13-5-12-9-1-1-13-5-12-9-1-1-1-13-5-12-9-1

Beneath those two rows, she had drawn a horizontal line and then added the columns of numbers.

20-18-23-20-14-2-15-33-14-31-10-3-2-32-25-13-27-5

"Now you could send out that bottom cipher and the only person who could crack it would be someone who knew the key, the name Amelia. Anybody else could look forever."

"I wonder . . . in your notebook, would 'Amelia' be the key? Or maybe 'Amelia is nine'?" Sergeant asked.

"No," Amelia said with a firm shake of her head. "It wasn't my father's notebook. Nobody else would use the same old key that he and I used twenty years ago. And there I can't help you. I don't know what the key might be."

Hyatt stood up. "Thank you, Miss Pierce. You've helped a great deal."

"I hope so," she said. "I have a life somewhere. I'd like to start picking up some pieces of it."

"Yes. Yes, I know." He touched her shoulder. "We'll let you know as soon as we find anything." He gestured to Sergeant, and the two men turned to leave.

"And do try not to kill Mr. Sergeant when he returns," Hyatt said over his shoulder. "I need him."

Amelia smiled and waved good-bye as the two men drove off in the Jeep.

"Why did you tell her about the organization?" Sergeant asked, scowling. "If she's captured, she could compromise all of us."

"Come now, Burt," the Englishman said. "We can't possibly allow that woman to live."

12

An Azimut twelve-liter speedboat came to a halt on the warm Caribbean waters. The Azimut was fast, even faster than its original one hundred twenty-five horsepower engine. It was a slender steel bullet of a boat.

Its owner, Charles Lederer, fought down a wave of nausea as he lifted one end of a large burlap sack. The sack was unwieldy, containing as it did the remains of a tall man well on the way to decomposition. Tufts of the corpse's hair stuck out of the opening of the bag. Foul-smelling juices oozed through the coarse fabric, sliming Lederer's hands.

It was part of the price, he thought, willing away the urge to vomit all over his sixty-thousand-dollar Azimut, which was the last thing of value he owned. He had already lost his job with Shearson Lehman, his Jaguar XK-6, his Volkswagen Rabbit convertible, his condo in Palm Beach, and his entire stock portfolio, not to mention the 2.6-million-dollar stone-and-no-knot cedar house in Westport, Connecticut, and its furnishings, which included a fifteen-foot pink onyx table that had set him back thirty thousand dollars, four silk Bokhara rugs, and a state-of-the-art entertainment center that he had lost in the divorce, as well as his wife, two children, and a prizewinning bichon frise.

For the past three weeks he had slept either on the boat or on the rear seat of a nineteen seventy-one Ford Fairlane that he had traded for an eightball of cocaine.

Part of the price to get on my feet again, Lederer thought stoically. He swung the gunnysack in rhythm with the other man on the boat, a paying passenger named Yusef Nassif, and on the count of three, tossed it into the water.

Nassif cursed in Arabic. "You ass, you didn't tie the string properly," he growled.

The man wore an expensive suit. _Big-time Arab,_ Lederer had thought when he'd first met Nassif. A criminal, obviously—the man had offered him ten thousand dollars plus half a boatload of cocaine for the use of Lederer's boat— but rich. Nassif had money to burn, and if he needed help in disposing of six feet worth of what he termed "waste material" in exchange for a few bills, then Charles Lederer was his man. After losing career, home, and family to a cocaine habit, he no longer felt that morality was an option available to him.

Still, the sight of the body bobbing in its cloth coffin gave Lederer chills. Two long cords—the ones he had improperly tied—swayed hypnotically on the surface of the water. The Arab picked up one of the Azimut's emergency oars and tried to retrieve the gunnysack, but it sank before he could bring it back to the boat.

"Imbecile," he muttered.

Lederer felt the remnant of an emotion he used to call anger. There had been a time when he would have told off this presumptuous little man, this camel humper with his silk suit. But that time was gone, along with the corner office and the house in Westport. Now, instead, he scooped a half-inch-long fingernail into a glassine envelope of white powder and brought it, trembling, to his nose.

"It's only a body," he said, smiling brightly.

The Arab shot him a look of disgust and started the engine.

The trip toward the Florida coastline was smooth and

swift. Lederer closed his red-rimmed eyes and listened to the thrum of the blood in his veins.

"Hap-py *days* are *here* a-*gain,"* he sang silently to the raucous beating of his internal drums. He had jumped at the ten thousand. When Nassif got on board, he'd handed Lederer the money in cash, tinkered with the engine for an hour or two, and the bad times were no more. Now Lederer was out on the sparkling ocean in a vessel faster than anything the Coast Guard could afford, with a half-million dollars' worth of Colombian snow beneath the teak floorboards.

Happy days.

Nassif did not speak until they were within six miles of the Gulf Coast. "Move the boards," he said.

"Now? What if the cops—"

"If you please," the Arab said impatiently.

Lederer shrugged. "You're the one paying the bills."

"Thank you for remembering."

Always the gentleman, Lederer thought nastily as he began to unload the kilo bags onto the deck.

There were six bags. Beneath them was a large, flat box made of metal and then vacuum-sealed in plastic. "What's this?" Lederer asked, picking it up.

Nassif snatched the box out of his hands and placed it carefully under one of the seats. "Weight," the Arab said tersely.

Lederer narrowed his eyes. "What?"

"I said it was for weight. Please replace the boards."

"Weight? With the body and the two of us, we didn't have enough weight?"

"My mistake," Nassif said.

"Shit," Lederer said. "We could have carried twice the stash. You said a boatload."

"Shut up, Mr. Lederer," Nassif said, raising a pair of binoculars toward the coastline.

"You could have asked me, you know. I mean, it is my boat."

The binoculars came down. "I'm paying for it."

"And splitting the profits from the coke, remember?" Lederer was nearly shouting now, the *thrum-thrum* of his blood roaring in his ears.

"Forgive me," Nassif said quietly.

"Shit."

Lederer turned his back on him. He dug out the glassine envelope and snorted a fingernail full.

He never saw Nassif draw the automatic from his shoulder holster. He never even heard the soft report from the silenced gun. He felt only the wildest high of his life as the bullet entered his brain and the steady drumbeat of his blood shot out of his skull like liquid music.

"You were right," Nassif said, bending over Lederer's body. He extracted the ten thousand dollars from the man's hip pocket, then rolled the still-warm body over the side. "There was far too much weight on board."

Far behind them, as if coming up to watch the spectacle, a pair of sightless eyes bobbed out of a burlap bag. The body floated slowly to the surface of the water. It spun in a lazy circle, bleeding the last of its juices into the ocean, then headed south with the current.

It was going home.

13

"Give this to Amelia," Davis Hyatt said as he passed a stack of paper to Sergeant. "It's a photostatic copy of Juan Sebastapol's notebook."

Sergeant flipped through the pages. "You didn't turn up anything?"

Hyatt shook his head, frowning.

"There are five cryptologists, working in five different countries, trying to decipher this. And Pandora, of course. I've got her working almost constantly on a possible key."

Pandora was the name Hyatt had assigned to the multi-million-dollar computer that took up nearly the whole of one wall in his large office.

It was the mainframe of the international computer network that made up the organization of which Davis Hyatt was custodian.

He thought of himself as no more than that, a caretaker assigned to the massive intelligence that was Pandora, helping her to reach out with her invisible arms to the informational network of her creation.

The reports of all the field agents in the Network—which

was how Hyatt referred to the nameless organization, as if it were no more than an extension of Pandora—were synthesized and then given back to the intelligence agencies of the Network's member nations.

It was sharing on a grand scale. Israel gave a name, France a description, the Soviet Union an activity. These feeble pieces of information came to Pandora anonymously: She did not care about their source, or their accuracy. Honor was the province of men, and these unknown men, the spymasters of ideologically different, and often opposing, nations had vowed to be honorable in this one regard. They would work together, unknown to one another, to stop terrorism.

In the giant cauldron of Pandora's information banks, the small facts from here and there would merge, and Pandora would spew out something tangible and whole, another of the world's miseries, which the faceless men of the Network would try to eliminate.

Pandora listened to Davis Hyatt. She obeyed him without question. When he asked her to, she gave up her terrible treasures to him. But on this, a code learned by a nine-year-old girl, Pandora was silent.

"Without the key, the cipher can't be broken," Hyatt said wearily. "It has to be something personal—a name, a place, a sentence—between Sebastapol and Pierce." He shoved his hands into his pockets. "Two dead men."

"What makes you think the girl would know it?"

Hyatt shrugged. "Maybe she doesn't. But someone thinks she knows something. Otherwise, an attempt wouldn't have been made on her life."

"Three attempts, according to her," Sergeant said.

Hyatt sat down at his desk. "There's something you ought to know." He tossed over a glossy photograph.

It showed Arthur Pierce lying dead on the floor of his home. His eyes were open and glazed. His clothes were soaked in blood. His left ear was missing.

"Oh, Christ," Sergeant said.

"I imagine you recognize the technique."

Sergeant stared, mesmerized by the photograph. "Billy

Starr," he said in a whisper. He looked up suddenly. "The Pierce woman said she shot the man who killed her father."

Hyatt gave him a come-now look. "Then she's either demented or lying. The area was searched thoroughly. No body was found."

"It's possible she killed him. Starr wouldn't have left her alive."

"She may have wounded him, although I doubt it. The fact is, he's alive now. In Geneva."

Sergeant's forehead suddenly smoothed. "What?"

"Turner's been tailing him ever since the Pierce murder. He took the photograph before leaving Santa Vittoria."

"What about the girl's story? Could he corroborate it?"

Hyatt shrugged. "There were signs of disturbance in the swamp, but the raft she claims to have used never materialized. Nor the gun, nor the binoculars. Nor, as I've said, the body of the man she says she killed."

"Surely you don't still think she's lying."

"I don't know what to think. She may have been in on things with Starr from the beginning, in which case the notebook is a deliberate ruse to throw us off the track. Starr may want to kill Amelia to keep her from telling us what she knows about him."

"Then again, the notebook might be real and the girl's telling the truth," Sergeant said dryly.

Hyatt said nothing.

"She's a damned book editor, for God's sake. She's worked in the same place for eight years. I checked it out myself. You're dealing with a bystander, not a spy. What the hell would she be doing with Billy Starr?"

Hyatt shrugged. "She's the daughter of a CIA wildman and a Russian. She obviously knows all manner of tradecraft. You said she told you herself that she's been trained since childhood in weapons and survival skills."

"That's the point," Sergeant said. "She told me herself. And it scared her. Jesus!" He ran his hand through his hair. "You're picking at straws, Hyatt."

"Maybe you're right," Hyatt sighed. "At any rate, we'll have to go on the assumption that Starr knows the nurse in the hospital failed to kill Amelia and that he'll try to finish the job himself. The nurse, incidentally, was a Libyan. Her name was Jama Affasan. Low-level, arrested five years ago in London and released."

"I'm not surprised," Sergeant said.

"No. Starr always liked the Libyans."

"They've given him shelter," Sergeant corrected. "Billy Starr doesn't like anyone."

"Yes, of course," Hyatt said, shifting uncomfortably in his seat. Nobody knew more about Billy Starr than Burt Sergeant. "Rather like owning a pet scorpion. Starr works for whomever he pleases. Even for you Yanks at one time, so I understand."

Sergeant didn't answer. He had looked into that scorpion's very eyes. It had cost him his career once, and more. Much more.

"I say, you're all right with this, aren't you?" Hyatt asked.

"Yes."

"I can take you off—"

"I said I'm all right."

Hyatt grunted. "I want you to leave your house."

Sergeant looked up. "Why?"

"Starr must know by now that Amelia is with you. It's only a matter of time before he finds out where you fly out of Geneva. He'll learn your flight plan and come to your house. The location there is good. It's isolated. We can have men waiting for him."

"And Ame—the girl?"

Hyatt looked at him. "Miss Pierce will be inside the house, Burt. Haven't you been following this at all?"

He took a cigar from the humidor on his desk and lit it, casting a disapproving eye at Sergeant. "My guess is that it will happen within a day or two. Whatever part Amelia is playing in this, Billy Starr obviously places her death high on his list of priorities. High enough to put aside whatever plans he has for the virus to follow her halfway across the world."

He puffed contentedly. "Thank God for Amelia Pierce.

Without her, we wouldn't have the ghost of a chance to stop Billy Starr."

"And when she's done playing decoy for us—if Starr hasn't hacked her to pieces by then—we'll thank her for her help by shooting her between the eyes, is that right?"

"What is wrong with you?" Hyatt demanded, spitting out the cigar. "The woman knew enough about the Network to compromise all of us before she ever reached Geneva. What do you suggest? That we send her back to New York, so she can publish a book about us?"

"God damn it, she's a human being, not a piece of paper you stick into the shredder when you're through with it!"

"Oh, Burt—"

"She's an ordinary, decent, pain-in-the-ass lady who doesn't know what the fuck's happening to her. And you know that. All that bullshit about her being involved with Billy Starr was just your way of saying it's okay to kill her. Well, it's not okay, Hyatt. I didn't sign on with the Network to murder innocent people. Christ!"

"All right!" Hyatt spread his arms. "I didn't realize she meant so much to you."

"She doesn't mean anything to me," Sergeant said, exasperated with the man.

Hyatt had utterly no concept of human life. For him, people were as interchangeable as the names that appeared from Pandora's computer banks. As soon as one was eliminated, it was replaced with another. His thinking, Sergeant realized, was very similar to Pandora's.

It was not surprising that Hyatt had never married. Sergeant would guess that he had never even slept with a woman. He had probably never had a friend.

"She doesn't have to be in the house when Starr comes," Sergeant said.

"I suppose not," Hyatt said testily. "Look, we'll try to keep her alive."

"Until Billy Starr is caught," Sergeant finished.

"I didn't say that. Take her to Vienna."

Sergeant scowled. "Vienna? What's in Vienna?"

"Juan Sebastapol's widow. She lives on Keilgasse. Perhaps you can put the two ladies together. They might come up with something helpful about the notebook."

Sergeant nodded.

"Use the safe house on the Blumenstrasse. I'll alert Turner." He picked up his cigar and lit it again.

"Turner," Sergeant muttered under his breath.

Hyatt rolled his eyes. "*What* is bothering you now?"

"Turner doesn't know anything about Billy Starr."

Hyatt clamped his teeth around the cigar. Smoke poured out, all but obscuring his face. "And you know too much," he said quietly.

"What's that supposed to mean?" There was an edge to Sergeant's voice.

Hyatt took the cigar out of his mouth. He did not speak for a long moment. Finally he said, "Do you realize you've never spoken Amelia Pierce's name?"

A crease formed between Sergeant's eyes. He looked to either side of him, like an animal stalked by hunters with a net. "So?"

"Why is that, Burt?" Hyatt asked softly.

"I . . . I don't know. I suppose I just don't like it."

"The name?"

"Yes."

"Amelia?"

"What are you getting at?" Droplets of sweat appeared on Sergeant's forehead.

"It sounds like 'Amy,' doesn't it?" Hyatt whispered.

"That's ridiculous."

"And she resembles your wife a little, as well."

"That's even more ridiculous." He felt clammy and suddenly cold.

Amy. Amy, with the wind in your hair and our daughter in your arms . . .

"It's still too soon." Hyatt's voice seemed to come from far away at first. It pulled Sergeant up to the surface. "I don't want you to have any involvement whatever with Billy Starr."

Sergeant opened his mouth to speak, but Hyatt silenced

him with a gesture. "Turner will go after him. Not you. I hope that's clear."

Sergeant turned away.

"Is it?"

"It's clear," Sergeant said. "I'll get the girl to Vienna tonight."

14

Billy Starr. The taste of the name on his lips caused Sergeant's hands to shake as he guided the plane onto the runway and waited for clearance to take off.

He had seen Starr's work before. In nineteen eighty-one, an American student—an anti-Qaddafi sympathizer of Libyan dissidents—was murdered in Egypt. His mutilated body was found with those of two other students, both of them Libyans who had been studying in the United States. They had been vacationing together in Cairo.

The CIA was called in. Sergeant was working for the Cairo head-of-station at the time.

He had not been a Glory Boy. He had married while still a student at Northwestern, and had been raising a six-year-old daughter by the time he'd been assigned to Cairo to assist the political attaché—"Read 'head spook,'" he'd told his wife—at the American Embassy there.

Secretly, the assignment to Egypt had excited him. He had majored in Foreign Service mainly because of fantasies of intrigue and danger; but after marrying Amy, his ambitions changed.

He had loved that woman more than he had ever believed possible. She possessed a face by Botticelli, as innocent and open as a kitten's one moment, then wildly, almost wantonly, beautiful the next. She was bright and funny and practical and silly, and the best mother he had ever seen. Sometimes, when she and their daughter Rachel were playing or baking cookies or reading, Sergeant would stand by unobtrusively, just watching them. He did not need intrigue and danger. His life was complete.

The Sergeants regarded the assignment to Egypt more as an extended family outing than anything else. He was, after all, basically an administrator whose job it would be to clear up the morass of paperwork that had accumulated on the desk of the political attaché.

Amy was a registered nurse; she promptly found work at the American Hospital in Cairo. With their combined incomes, they found they were able to enjoy a lifestyle neither had ever dreamed possible, employing both a cook and a maid, and enrolling Rachel in a posh English-speaking school. The evenings were filled with embassy parties, which Amy adored and Burt hated.

He attended these gatherings, though, because his boss, a world-class drinker named Tucker Smith, with the capacity of an elephant and the ability to sort out the single grain of truth in a mountain of someone else's drunken babble, told Sergeant that his appearance at the parties was part of his duties.

As for the work itself, Sergeant figured that his job would be tolerable, if not exciting. As it turned out, it was impossible. Smith, a rotund, red-cheeked man in his early forties, was a whirlwind with a reputation at the Agency of being able to get anything done. Anything, that was, except for filing reports and going through channels before attempting one of his spectacular moves. As a result, no one back in Langley was sure of how Tucker Smith was doing anything. It was Burt Sergeant's job to fill them in.

Smith didn't take well at first to having a second snoop in the office, particularly since Sergeant's job was to catalogue

Smith's own activities, but in time he grew to like the young man.

"I'll make a deal with you," Smith had told his frustrated protégé. "You agree to work for me—that's *me,* not Langley, understand? Everything Langley knows, Congress knows. And there are enough leaks in Congress to fill a hot-air balloon. Once the press gets hold of an agent's name, he's dead. And I don't plan to let some twenty-two-year-old reporter for the *Washington Post* get me killed, get it?" He'd squinted from the smoke of a cigarette clenched between his teeth.

"Yeah, I get it," Sergeant had said.

"Good. And Langley will get everything it needs, believe me. We'll all live longer." Then he'd winked at Sergeant.

From that moment, the two men had worked as a team. By nineteen eighty-one and the discovery of the mutilated students, Sergeant knew all about Smith's operation. Langley was satisfied that the great Tucker Smith had found an able assistant, if not entirely delighted with the lack of thoroughness in Sergeant's reports.

Then, three weeks into the investigation, Tucker Smith suffered a fatal heart attack.

Langley issued orders for Sergeant to mark time until a suitable replacement for Smith could be posted to Egypt, but the wheels were already in progress. Sergeant had spoken to a number of Libyan dissidents taking refuge in Cairo, and one name had come up again and again.

Aghrab. The Scorpion.

"The Scorpion is under direct orders from Qaddafi to kill us all," one frightened schoolteacher who had fled Libya after his best friend was publicly disemboweled said. He had begged Sergeant to find him asylum in the United States, but the State Department had refused. Asylum was granted to ballet dancers and scientists, not to high school math teachers.

"Who is the Scorpion?" Sergeant had asked.

The teacher hadn't answered right away. He brought a trembling hand up to cover the tears in his eyes. "He is the wind," he whispered.

Three days later, the schoolteacher was found dismembered in his bed. The killer had strewn the corpse's body parts carefully around the bloody room: A leg hung gaily from a chandelier; a hand peeked out from behind a framed Maxfield Parrish print.

The police found no trace, not even a bloody bootprint.

Sergeant fared better. Outside the building, against the wall, were fragments of a bottle of liquor. Sergeant noticed them because he recognized a piece of the label: It was Wild Turkey, an American bourbon whiskey. In this city of Moslems, liquor itself was not commonplace, and American Wild Turkey—not a brand usually imported for use in the better restaurants and hotels—was a rarity.

He'd had it analyzed for fingerprints. There were none. Nothing to tie the broken bottle to the murder. And yet Sergeant clung to the possibility that there was a connection. It was what Tucker Smith would have done.

He knew he was right when Langley sent a telegram saying that another bottle of Wild Turkey had turned up at the scene of a similar murder/mutilation in Fez, Morocco, along with a clear fingerprint. A right thumb.

"Look for an American," he told the police.

It was a mistake. His last mistake.

The plane touched down on the grassy Swiss field, and Sergeant ran to the Jeep. Hyatt had been right about the urgency of getting the Pierce woman out of his house as soon as possible.

The Pierce woman . . . *Amelia.* The name had nothing to do with anything.

To give Hyatt credit where it was due, though, Sergeant did feel uncomfortable around her. Not because she reminded him of Amy; she did not, not in any way. Amy had been a sweet, natural beauty, buttercups and green grass. The Pierce woman was a trendy, painted women's libber, with hair colored in outer space and the disposition of a rhinoceros. But she was a woman. Burt Sergeant had not spoken with a woman in nine years.

He had slept with them, of course. There were always

women for that. But since Amy died, he had had no desire to hear a woman's troubles again. Because he could not help.

He knew that now. There was not a goddamned thing he could do to lessen the burden of anyone's sorrows. Not even his own.

Still, he had to get her out of Switzerland fast. Likable or not, Amelia Pierce was not going to die in his house . . . and it was only a matter of time before the Scorpion tracked both of them down. He had done it before.

Don't think about it, Sergeant told himself. His vision was suddenly blurred by tears. He blinked them away. *Don't. Don't . . .*

But it crashed down inside his head again, as it had done every day for nearly ten years. Still he could see his wife's face, missing an ear, wrapped in the red gauze of her blood-matted hair, her eyes staring up sightlessly from its grotesque position between her legs. The head had been severed. The limbs had been cut neatly at the joints, a butcher's work. And his daughter, his beautiful Rachel, with her blonde, braided hair. Rachel, raped and hacked apart by a sadist's hand . . .

A harsh cry escaped from Sergeant, and he swerved off the road. Gasping, acid sweat gushing through his clothes, he clutched the steering wheel until he felt its pressure against the bones of his shaking hands, and he brought the Jeep to a halt.

You're crazy, Sergeant. Crazy as a bedbug.

After a moment, he released the brake and started off again. He felt drained and small, as if he had narrowly escaped death. But this was worse than death, he knew. He had been living this nightmare for ten years, and death would have been easier to bear.

He had tried, too, or at least that was what he'd been told. The days following the discovery of Amy and Rachel's bodies had disappeared into the blackness of his insanity.

Sergeant had apparently gone to the grave site alone at night. There, the psychiatrists at Langley decided, he had cut his throat. The scar was there, an enormous, ragged ribbon snaking from ear to ear. As to whether or not the wound was self-inflicted, he never remembered. He would have to take the doctors' word for it.

He supposed they were right, if only because after his recuperation, he had tried so desperately to recall the face of the man who might have done it to him, but his mind always came up empty . . .

. . . nearly empty. At the back of things, in the recesses of his thoughts, was always the desire to do it again.

Crazy.

The Agency had already handed him his walking papers—they knew when an agent had served too long—when Davis Hyatt had approached him about his new organization.

"Why me?" Sergeant had asked bitterly in his rasp-and-cotton voice. He was living at the time in a rented apartment near Langley, considering various options in his future. He had narrowed them down to two: a bullet in the brain, or a running automobile in a closed garage.

"I thought you might like the opportunity to find your wife's killer," Hyatt said.

For a moment, Sergeant had felt a jolt of anger at the soft-looking Englishman for mentioning it. But the moment passed, and with it, a certain dread that Sergeant had been living with. Suddenly the murder of his family was a *fact*, not a forbidden secret.

He swallowed. "How would I do that?"

"I would give you access to any file from almost every intelligence agency in the world."

Briefly Sergeant had entertained the notion that Davis Hyatt might be an escaped lunatic. Then Hyatt handed over a sheaf of photographs. All of them showed victims of the same sort of postmortem mutilations he'd been investigating before Amy and Rachel's deaths. There were more than eighty photographs.

"Those pictures represent an area of some thirty thousand square miles. Nevertheless, I believe it is the work of one man. And I want to know who he is." Hyatt leaned back in the brown, plastic swivel chair where Sergeant had placed him and lit a cigar. "That, plus you're the right sort of man for this job."

"What sort is that?"

"You're experienced in research," Hyatt said mildly. "You're a good investigator. You've got no ties anymore." A cloud of smoke billowed up around him. "And you're suicidal," he said. "I can use you."

Sergeant had spent months in researching the eighty murders. They had taken place over the span of sixteen years. The killings had occurred all over the world, but they had two things in common: The first was that each of the victims was marginally political, from the wife of the Mexican political attaché in Lebanon to a smut merchant in Greece, believed to have been dealing in black-market small arms. The second was that each had been mutilated in some way.

Sergeant studied the pictures of the dead. They looked as if their killer could not bear to leave them untouched in death, as if he needed, somehow, to anoint himself with their blood.

And *killer*, singular, was the operative word. For Sergeant had felt certain that one man was responsible: the man known as the Scorpion.

He'd studied the photographs until he felt as if death and dismemberment were his constant companions. He dreamed of the bodies, saw the world through a filter of blood. In its own macabre way, Sergeant's immersion into the horror that had killed his family served to expiate his guilt about his own survival. In time, he no longer felt an urgent need to kill himself.

But he did need to kill the Scorpion. Oh, more than life and breath, he needed to find this man, to look into his eyes at the moment of death. And if his own death occurred at the same time . . . Well, he wouldn't dwell on that. It was too much to hope for.

He'd thrown himself into the investigation with fevered intensity. He personally checked every fingerprint from every known international felon even remotely associated with any of the eighty murder/mutilations against the single print found on the bottle of Wild Turkey in Cairo.

Nothing.

He learned about killing styles from the photographs, which were by now permanently engraved in his mind. At first all eighty seemed to have been committed by the same person. But after a time, Sergeant grew to see the differences in technique, as well as the development of one particular method discernable in sixty-six of the murders.

He slashed. One initial blow to the throat, before the victim could scream. Then a short stab to the heart. That probably killed the person. It had killed Amy.

(No, no, mustn't stop to go crazy now, have to think. Think. Think.)

Then the mutilations. The fun. The one constant in the more recent of the photographs was the missing left ear. Where did he put them, Sergeant wondered. Did this maniac have a room somewhere with ears mounted in groupings like pinned butterfly specimens? Was one of them Amy's? And another, a small one, pink and perfect . . .

He turned over the sheaf of photographs. A drop of perspiration splatted across the gray, fingermarked backs of the pictures. But the images were still there, inside his head. He had memorized all sixty-six of them, and he could not erase them from his mind.

Then use it, he told himself. *Do the job. Keep yourself sane long enough to find the Scorpion.*

He took a deep breath and closed his eyes. There they were, each photograph flashing through his mind in chronological order.

The Scorpion was right-handed. Sergeant could tell that from the angle of wounds in the photographs. And the print on the Wild Turkey bottle came from a right thumb. A large one. So the killer was a big man, a big right-handed man who liked a knife and drank whiskey.

Of the sixty-six killings attributable to him, a disproportionate number were Libyans.

So the Scorpion was in some way linked to Libya.

Amy, oh, Amy, why did he have to take our little girl?

(Look for an American.)

Why did he have to take you? Tears streamed down Sergeant's face.

Look for . . .

"An American," he'd told Hyatt.

"Really, Burt," the Englishman had answered with annoyance. "You've seen the dossiers on every American terrorist known to us. God knows, there aren't that many of them."

"I don't think the Scorpion's one of them," Sergeant said. "I don't think we've got anything on him. Anything at all. I want to go through military records."

"Beginning when?"

Sergeant thought for a moment. "Nineteen sixty. Maybe a few years before that."

"For God's sake, man!" Hyatt thundered. "We didn't have a terrorist problem in nineteen sixty. Besides, the fellow probably wasn't even born then."

"I think he was. I think he was trained in the military."

"So you plan to look through the records of every soldier, sailor, airman, and marine since nineteen sixty? What would you be looking for?"

"Dishonorable discharges. Courts-martial. Evidence of psychosis. The Scorpion's crazy, Hyatt. That might have shown up on his records."

Hyatt sighed. "If he's that crazy, he wouldn't have been accepted in the first place. No. You've already spent four months on this. What you're proposing will take another year." He shook his head. "I'm afraid we'll have to close the books on this one."

"I'm going to find him, Hyatt." Sergeant's voice was low, but its intensity caused Hyatt to look up with something like fear in his eyes.

"No, you're not," Hyatt said, rising to his feet. "Look, Burt, this is one we just aren't going to win. Even if you find out who the Scorpion is, you're not going to catch him. Your days in the field are over. They ended when you slit your throat over your wife's grave. Do you understand?"

Sergeant blinked, clenched his jaw. "I'm not crazy anymore, Hyatt."

"No? Listen to yourself! You're obsessed with the man—a man who could be anyone."

In a motion too swift for Hyatt to stop, Sergeant slammed him against the wall. "He's the bastard who killed my wife and daughter!" he shouted.

He let go of the smaller Englishman, his shoulders slumped.

"Oh, God, Davis," he whispered. "Just let me find out who he is. I can't do anything from here except book work anyway. But I'll put in the time, and I might come up with something." There was anguish in his voice. "Christ, it's all I've got to live for. Let me find the bastard's name."

Tentatively, Hyatt touched the younger man's shoulder. He could feel Sergeant trembling beneath his clothes. He retracted his hand. It was like touching the dead.

He looked out the window. Sergeant was broken beyond repair. It didn't matter, he knew, whether he ever found who the killer was or not. Burt Sergeant was dead.

"You have six months," Hyatt said.

At the end of five, Billy Starr's name emerged on Sergeant's computer. Starr, Willard C., Lance Corporal. Marines. Two tours in Vietnam, beginning in nineteen sixty-four. Purple Heart. Court-martialed in nineteen sixty-six on charges of murdering an officer.

The officer's body had been discovered in a brothel in Saigon. He and the prostitute he was with had been slashed across the throat, stabbed in the heart with a short knife, then hacked to bits. The madam of the brothel positively identified Billy Starr, but the case was closed and the charges against him transferred to the civilian court system after it came out during the trial that Starr was only sixteen years old.

After his discharge, Starr was sentenced to a juvenile facility in his home state of Arkansas, from which he escaped during his first week. No one in Arkansas had seen or heard from him since, although the state police did not take his name from the active file for seven more years.

The small black-and-white photograph of Starr on the

corner of his file card at the juvenile home was apparently the only one in existence. He had no family. His father had been killed in a mining accident when Billy was five years old. His mother and sister were murdered in a manner similar to that of the marine officer and the prostitute in Saigon.

Billy Starr disappeared the day before their bodies were found in the mud along a creek near West Falls, Arkansas. Four days later, he enlisted in the Marine Corps in Baton Rouge, Louisiana. He was fourteen years old then.

Burt Sergeant stared at the photograph. It showed a tall, rangy boy with a shock of white-blond hair and the irises of his eyes so pale that they were almost indistinguishable from the whites surrounding them. They were wary eyes, mocking, sly, fearless. The eyes of a psychotic.

Extreme personality disorder, the file card read. *Initial psychiatric interview indicates further tests to determine future placement.*

Starr was too crazy for the institution, and they knew it. But it wasn't their problem anymore, Sergeant thought. It hadn't been since nineteen sixty-six.

There was a set of fingerprints on the file card. It matched Billy Starr's Marine Corps prints.

And the right thumb matched the print from the bottle of Wild Turkey found in Egypt.

Two years later, after the hijacking of a Damascus Airlines plane, Muammar Qaddafi openly accepted the hijackers into Libya. One of them was a tall, white-haired man.

Now Billy Starr belonged to the world.

For his persistence in unmasking the Scorpion, Burt Sergeant had been rewarded with a promotion. Then, after the death of Davis Hyatt's assistant, Sergeant was asked to fill the man's place. Thereafter he worked as Hyatt's shadow, coming to know almost as much about the Network as Hyatt himself did. In nine years, he had become irreplaceable.

Yet in nine years, despite the size of the dossier on him, Billy Starr had not been found.

* * *

"Hello?" he called softly as he entered the cabin. "Are you here?"

He did not like the woman's name. He did not like the woman and her damned lying insistence that she had killed the murderer of her parents, and he did not like her damned, defiant feminist games. "Get out here where I can see you!" he shouted.

There was no answer.

He ran through the small house, slamming open its few closet doors. She was gone.

"You stupid bitch!" he rasped. Escaping now was asking to be killed. Walking into the Scorpion's mouth. One morning, in some innocuous hotel room, the maid would enter to make the beds and there she would be, stabbed, her throat slashed, her dismembered head between her legs.

"Amy!" Sergeant sobbed. "Amy . . ."

"What is it?"

The woman stood in the doorway, holding an armful of wildflowers. They spilled out over her white elbows. Her hair, billowing in the breeze from the open door, smelled of the sky and the earth. She had come back to him. He had awakened from the nightmare. The morning had come at last, and Amy was with him again.

"I was just picking some flowers . . . Are you all right?"

Involuntarily, he lifted a hand to touch her face. Then he saw that it was not Amy's face, could never be Amy's face . . . and he wondered how much longer his frail sanity would allow him to live.

"What did you call me, anyway?" She smiled at him and picked a straw out of her hair.

Sergeant turned away in disgust. "Get in the Jeep," he said hoarsely.

15

"There's trouble, isn't there?" Amelia asked as the taxi sped them past the monumental buildings of Vienna's Ringstrasse.

"Nothing for you to worry about," Sergeant said gruffly.

Outside, a timeless city offered itself: the huge arched expanse of the opera house; the imperial gardens of Hofburg; the intricate beauty of the parliament building, fronted by its gold-trimmed marble statue of Athena rising out of a tiered fountain—all of them lit spectacularly against the night sky. But inside the taxi the air was thick with fear. It was as if Sergeant and Amelia had carried their horrors with them.

The train ride from Sergeant's home in northeast Switzerland had been long, and neither had been talkative. Amelia ached with fatigue and tension.

"Dad always wanted me to see Vienna," she said. "He told me about the Riesenrad, the big Ferris wheel, although I can't imagine him riding it . . ."

Sergeant barked some directions to the driver.

". . . himself," she finished. She knew he wasn't listening.

She clasped her hands tightly and turned back to the window.

The house on the Blumenstrasse smelled musty and vaguely soiled. Three Players cigarette butts were crushed out in a chipped plastic ashtray near the sofa. This was where Hyatt's agents in Vienna holed up, hiding themselves or others, and the cheap anonymity of the place reflected its constantly changing tenants.

"How long will we be here?" Amelia asked.

Sergeant shook his head. "Not too long." He took the copy of the notebook out of a leather case and gave it to Amelia. "This is for you. Read it over tonight. Tomorrow we'll meet Juan Sebastapol's widow. Maybe something she says will jog your memory."

She thumbed through the papers. "Then Hyatt and his men haven't figured anything out, either."

She put the papers down, walked to the window, and lifted the dingy yellow blind. Outside, the street was as innocuous as the house.

A house for hiding in, she thought. A place for spies, informants, defectors, for all the people who had somehow slipped through the fabric of citizenship and law and found themselves, like Amelia herself, without protection.

It occurred to her that everyone who had ever come to this shabby house on this shabby street had been afraid. *How many of us are there? How many people are spending this night running from place to place like rabbits seeking shelter in a field?*

Sergeant lowered the blind. "Don't stand near the windows," he said, pushing her away. "You've got to assume a little responsibility for your own safety."

Amelia felt her anger rush to the surface and boil over. "Just what is your problem with me, mister?" she demanded.

"Oh, not again." He dismissed her with a gesture, but she grabbed his arm.

"Don't walk away from me. You obviously have some kind of chip on your shoulder about me, and I want to know what it's about." She could feel her face reddening.

Sergeant made a move to escape, disliking the touch of her fingers, but she held fast.

"All right," he rasped. "I don't know what you're up to, and I don't like the idea of risking my life to protect someone who may be working against me."

"What are you talking about?" Amelia asked, genuinely bewildered.

"Hyatt thinks you may have set up your father's murder."

Incredulous, Amelia stared at him blankly for a moment. Then her whole body seemed to tremble, as if about to fly apart right there in the middle of the room. "How dare you?" she said, her eyes glistening with tears.

Sergeant immediately regretted his words. "I don't think that's true, for what it's worth." He walked a few feet away from her; he was more comfortable with some distance between them. "And I told Hyatt that. But what we can't resolve is why you would lie about killing the murderer."

"The man in the swamp? But I did kill him. I swear it."

"He's followed you to Switzerland. Hyatt's expecting him to come to my house in Appenzell. To kill you."

Her hand flew to her mouth. "That can't be! He's dead."

"The man was spotted by a trained agent."

"Turner? But how could he have even known what the killer looked like? I never saw his face. Turner must have followed someone else."

Sergeant shook his head. "No. It's the same man. I've been studying him for nine years. His work is recognizable."

"His 'work'?" The word felt loathsome in her mouth. "He was a murderer, with a machine gun."

Sergeant didn't answer, but she would not let go. "What are you getting at? What 'work'?"

"He came back," Sergeant said quietly. "After he lost you in the swamp . . ." He made a confused gesture. "Or after whatever happened. He came back to the house and left his mark."

"Which was? Tell me, damn it!"

Sergeant looked at his hands. "He cut off your father's left ear."

A small sound rushed out between Amelia's lips. She groped for a chair and sat down.

"I'm sorry," Sergeant said.

"Who is he?" Amelia's voice was bitter.

"His name is Billy Starr." He inclined his head slightly. He did not want his pain to be visible. "He's killed more than a hundred people. My wife and daughter were two of them."

She looked up from her own grief. "Oh, my God," she breathed.

"It was a long time ago," Sergeant said lamely.

Amelia stood up and went to him. Tentatively, she touched his arm, his back: the instinctive gestures of a woman offering comfort.

Sergeant moved away from her. "I'll make some dinner," he said, shambling into the kitchen.

Amelia followed him with her eyes.

Sergeant was clattering the pots and pans. A variety of canned goods were piled on the kitchen counter.

"I'll cook," Amelia said, gently pushing him away.

"I thought you said you couldn't cook." He made a point of not looking at her.

"I lied. That was when I wasn't willing to cook you anything but strychnine."

He smiled, and somehow that made Amelia even more sad, because the smile was an imitation. Sergeant's eyes crinkled in the corners, but there was no mirth in them. It was as if the laugh lines around them had become no more than wrinkles.

"Truce?" she asked, holding out her hand.

Sergeant took it. "Truce."

"Now go amuse yourself while I get something together here."

"You didn't find strychnine, did you?"

She picked up a can of Spam. "I won't need it," she said. "This is almost as deadly. It just works slower."

There was no television in the house, so Sergeant turned on a radio. He slowly dialed from station to station, but it seemed that the radio programs in Vienna played only Strauss waltzes or earsplitting hard rock. He opted for the waltzes.

"You know the first meal I ever cooked?" Amelia called out as he settled himself into an easy chair and picked up a month-old copy of *Time* magazine.

"Let me guess. Bean-sprout cake. With carob chip frosting, festooned with alfalfa sprouts."

"Very funny. Yuppie food, you mean."

"No offense intended. I hear that some very nice people are yuppies."

She ignored him. "The first meal I ever cooked was rattlesnake-and-root stew."

"I think the strychnine sounded better."

"I was ten years old. My father took me camping on one of the uninhabited islands near Santa Vittoria. It was one of Daddy's combat holidays."

She opened a cabinet and extracted several dusty jars half-filled with spices. "We were going to stay for three days. He brought no food. He said we had to live off the land."

She sprinkled thyme and rosemary into a pot filled with green beans, sliced canned potatoes, and cubes of gelatin-covered Spam. "Phew," she said, raising her eyebrows.

"That bad?"

"Wait a minute. I think I've found the magic ingredient." She opened a box of instant rice. "Success," she called out. "Something to build this meal around."

"So tell me about the rattlesnake."

She laughed. "I was the hunter. Daddy gave me a bow and arrow and a knife and told me to go find food. I didn't get twenty feet from the tent when this evil-looking swamp adder came at me and buried its fangs in one of my boots. The only way I could get loose was to cut off its head with the knife."

Sergeant put down the magazine. "And?"

"I didn't realize it, but I must have been yelling, because

when I looked up, Daddy was there." She smiled. "I guess, now that I think about it, he was always there when I needed him."

The thought made her sad, so she covered up with talk. "It was the first time I ever wished I were a boy, because he had this look of pride on his face that you just couldn't imagine, and I knew then that that was probably something boys got from their fathers a lot more often than girls did. And he hugged me and asked me if I was all right, and then he took off my boot, made sure that none of the venom had gotten me, and said, 'Good hunting, Amelia.' "

"And then you ate the snake?" Sergeant asked wanly. "Just like that?"

"We made a stew. Daddy helped me dig up some edible roots, sort of like native potatoes, and then he showed me how to clean the snake. But I couldn't eat it. I told him that. So he just sat there next to the fire, chowing down on this pail of rattlesnake slop, and he said, 'You will if you get hungry enough.' "

"And?"

"I held out till midnight or so. Then I ate it. It wasn't bad."

"People say it tastes like chicken," Sergeant said.

"People say everything tastes like chicken. They even call tuna 'Chicken of the Sea.' " She tasted her creation, which had come to a boil. "You know, this is going to be all right."

"Does it taste like chicken?"

She tried it again. "Well, actually, it's more like rattle-snake."

They ate at the small pullout table in the corner of the living room. Sergeant wolfed down most of his portion without a word.

"Wonderful," he said when he was finished. "I'll do the dishes."

"It wasn't that wonderful. We'll both do them."

The little kitchenette was too small for the two of them, and they kept brushing by each other as they set to washing and drying the pots and plates. At another time, in another context, it might have been an occasion for harmless flirting, but they moved about leadenly, quietly, and finally Amelia realized that she was exhausted and that Sergeant was, too.

When the dishes were put away, they looked awkwardly at each other for a moment before Sergeant said, "I'll take the couch."

She thought about a pro forma protest, then decided that she was too tired to argue. Instead, she nodded and walked off toward the bedroom door.

"Amelia," he called softly. The name seemed to hang in the air for a moment like an echo.

She turned around. "Yes, Burt?"

"Your dad was proud of you. He talked about you once."

She felt suddenly breathless. "What did he say?"

"That you'd killed a rattlesnake when you were ten years old."

She smiled. Then, because she was afraid to cry in front of Burt Sergeant, she disappeared into the bedroom.

It was still dark when she woke up; she had no idea of the time. She might have slept for one hour or for five.

Then she heard a sound and realized that it was what had wakened her. It was a low rumble, sounding like the auxiliary gasoline generator they had had at their home in Santa Vittoria.

She rose from the bed, donned a dingy bathrobe that was hanging on a hook inside the door, and quietly stepped into the hall. There were no lights on in the living room, but enough light slanted in through the windows from the street that she was able to see Sergeant clearly. He was sprawled out, still dressed, on the loveseat that was much too small for him. His legs dangled over one arm of the sofa, and the sound was coming from him: a roaring, rumbling snore, punctuated by grunts as he moved from one awkward, uncomfortable position to another.

On bare feet, she moved closer and stood there for a moment looking down at him, feeling a motherly sort of pity for the man. It really would be the decent thing to do, she decided, to offer him the bed. She would fit onto the sagging couch more easily than a six-foot-tall man could.

She reached down to touch his shoulder. "Burt . . ."

Suddenly her wrist was caught in an iron clamp. Sergeant spun up off the couch and pushed a gun to her forehead.

She gasped.

In the soft, diffused light of the room, she saw his face twisted with violent anger. Then his visage softened and he exhaled a long puff of breath.

"What are you doing?" he asked, lowering the gun.

"My wrist," she said, hearing the quake in her voice.

He released his grip. "Sorry," he mumbled.

"I didn't mean to startle you. You were snoring. It woke me up. Then I saw how scrunched up you were on this couch—"

"It's all right. No big deal."

He had been afraid that someone had broken in. When Amelia realized that, everything began to fall apart. There had been too much death, too much killing, too many threats. All at once, without planning to, she buried her face against Sergeant's chest, sobbing uncontrollably. He stood there awkwardly for a moment, then tossed his gun on the sofa and put his arms around her.

"Easy, easy," he said. "It's all right."

"How do you deal with it?" she asked finally.

"With what?"

"With all of it. All the killing. Your own family . . ."

"Time takes care of things," he said, knowing it was a lie. "Don't think about it anymore. Everything's going to be all right."

But Amelia kept on sobbing. She made no effort to move from the small place of safety she had found in the comfort of Sergeant's big arms.

"It's the fear," she said, trying to bring herself under control. "I'm just so scared. I'm so damned scared all the time."

He did not respond. There was nothing he could say. All he could do was to hold her and feel her warmth against his body . . . the soft, feminine warmth he had not permitted himself for years.

"Stay with me," she said. "For a while."

She led him into the bedroom.

"Amelia—"

She kissed his mouth. "Please," she whispered.

Slowly, uncertainly, his arms circled her waist. The bathrobe slipped down, and he brushed his lips against her bare shoulders, smelling the faint perfume of her skin, and suddenly he was filled with a roaring passion, a terrible, longing hunger so strong he was sure it would kill him.

"Don't do this," he said, but it was too late by then. They went at each other in a frenzy. Their bodies slammed together as if, by their wild motions, their extravagant need for one another, they could ward off death, which lay in the shadows of the past and waited somewhere just beyond the door of this shabby house. For this moment, now, there was no fear.

16

Amelia did not hear the telephone ring. She awoke in time only to hear Sergeant say, "All right. I'll let you know."

He put down the phone and looked over at her. She was instantly wide awake, tense in his arms.

"What's the matter?" she asked.

"Starr didn't show up at my place," he said sourly.

Amelia's voice was cold. "He's never going to show up. I told you, I killed him."

"I don't want to argue it with you," he said and hugged her gently. "You say you killed him. We've got a trained operative who says he's alive and that he followed him back to Europe. I don't know who the hell it is, and I don't care. But the fact is, someone wants you dead."

He felt her tremble.

"Don't worry," he whispered. "He can't know we're here."

"Why don't we just give him the notebook?" Amelia asked shrilly. "We can't make any sense of it. . . . it probably doesn't make any sense. Let him have the damned thing."

Sergeant looked away. "He'd kill you anyway," he said softly.

"But why? I can't hurt him. I don't know anything."

"He doesn't know what you know. But he sent the nurse, and probably the phony chauffeur, too, to kill you. That means you're important to him. He'll try again."

They were silent in each other's arms for a long moment. Finally Amelia asked, "So what do we do?"

"What we came for," Sergeant said. "We go see Juan Sebastapol's widow." Suddenly he smiled. "And for the occasion, I'm going to take you shopping for some clothes. You can't go visiting in Vienna in a pair of men's dungarees."

He kissed her forehead. Then he pulled her close to his chest so she wouldn't see the worry in his eyes.

They ate a breakfast of pastry and coffee with *shlag* at a small cafe where Sergeant refused to sit outdoors, then stopped at a sprawling department store near the Karlsplatz. There Amelia picked out a conservative dark blue dress, a pair of medium-heeled dark shoes, pantyhose and underwear.

"How do I look?" she asked.

"The dungarees suited you better," Sergeant replied with a smile. He took her old clothes from her and dumped them in a garbage bin on the street. Then, while she waited in the store's entrance, he hailed a cab and hustled her quickly into the backseat.

They pulled up in front of an elegant old *Jungendstil* house in one of the city's historic residential areas. Here there were no new apartment buildings, no garden complexes, just old structures that had stood for centuries. It would have been easy, stepping from the cab, to imagine that one might see Mozart turning a corner and strolling down the center of the cobblestone street.

Sergeant twisted the lion's-head doorbell, and a white-haired, pink-skinned woman with an old-fashioned muffin bonnet on her head answered the door.

"*Ja?*"

"Mrs. Sebastapol?" Sergeant asked.

The old woman's eyes darted from his face to that of the young woman beside him.

"You have an appointment?" she asked in thickly accented English.

"No, but—"

"Frau Sebastapol ist nicht zu haus," she snapped. She began edging behind the door to close it.

Amelia stepped forward. "Please," she said. "Just tell her that Amelia Pierce is here. My father—"

"—is Arthur Pierce," another voice said.

A tall woman in her mid-sixties walked to the door. She was well dressed and moved with the effortless grace born of generations of aristocratic self-discipline. Her dark hair was pulled back into an elaborate chignon, revealing a face that had once been extraordinarily beautiful.

"Sehr gut, Eva," she said, dismissing the maid. "I am Marla Sebastapol," she told her two visitors.

Amelia spoke first. "Mrs. Sebastapol, this is Burt Sergeant. He was an associate of my father's."

"Yes, yes." The older woman's eyes were dancing. "Then you have come about my husband?"

"Yes," Sergeant said. "Although—"

"Where is he? Is he well? Is he free?" She clasped her hands, almost as if in prayer. "I must admit I had stopped hoping. For so long I thought—"

Then she saw the look in Amelia's eyes, and the light went out of her own. "You have come to tell me that Juan is dead," she said flatly.

"I'm sorry," Sergeant said. "He died six days ago."

"Six days . . ." The woman made a fist and brought it to her lips. Then she raised her patrician head and opened the door wide. "Thank you for letting me know. Please come in."

She led them into a room furnished with priceless antiques, obviously lovingly maintained, and gestured for them to sit down. "I hope you will join me for coffee," she said. "The Viennese love it almost as much as you Americans do."

"Thank you," Amelia answered.

After speaking quietly with her maid, Marla Sebastapol turned back to her guests and sat down.

"You resemble your father," she said.

"I was surprised that you knew his name."

Mrs. Sebastapol smiled. "We knew him very well, Juan and I." A look of pain momentarily crossed her face, but she brought it quickly under control. "We were friends long ago, when you were still a child. Your father showed us many photographs of his dear Amelia."

Amelia felt her throat close. She realized that as close as she had been to her father, she knew almost nothing about his early life with her mother, or about his life before he married Ludi. For her, Arthur Pierce, like Zeus, had sprung fully grown when she was ten years old. "I never knew he carried a picture of me," she said.

The older woman laughed, a lilting, cultured sound. "My dear, he adored you. He was almost killed on the day you were born. He was in Prague . . ."

She glanced over at Sergeant, and her hands trembled slightly.

She knows, Sergeant thought. *She thinks she's made a mistake, telling too much.*

"Arthur worked for a newspaper wire service there," Mrs. Sebastapol added quickly. "In order to cross the Czech border into Austria, he had to walk all night through the woods. Since guards with dogs were posted in the area, he smeared his body with animal droppings. Oh . . . can you imagine the aroma? And the worst part was that he had to go back in the same way a few hours later so no one would know that he had left." She shook her head, smiling. "Just to see a baby."

It had been a beautiful recovery. Sergeant marveled at the woman's composure. How many secrets had she kept over the years?

Still, she had almost let it slip that she'd known about Pierce's other life. She was old. She was grieving. She could not be trusted with too much knowledge.

Amelia was staring at the floor. "I never heard that story,

not even from my mother."

"Perhaps your mother did not even know," Mrs. Sebastapol said.

The maid came in with a tray holding a silver coffee service and a plate piled high with cream horns. She set the tray down on the table beside Mrs. Sebastapol, who lifted the plate and offered it to her guests.

"No, thank you," Amelia said. "We had pastry for breakfast."

The woman laughed. "In Vienna, one eats pastry at every opportunity, it seems, without ill effect. Unfortunately, I do not possess the rugged constitution of the Viennese. I keep these on hand for Eva." She translated into German for the maid, who blushed and smiled before leaving the room.

When Eva was gone, Mrs. Sebastapol served their coffee, then turned to face Sergeant. "You are a journalist?" she inquired politely.

"No," he replied. "I worked with Mr. Pierce on other matters."

"Ah," she said noncommittally, sipping at her coffee.

"He was an undercover agent for the CIA during Amelia's childhood. I think you know that."

She lowered her eyes. "And he is well?"

"Father died, Mrs. Sebastapol," Amelia said quietly. "He was killed on the same day as your husband."

The woman set down her cup with a clatter. "Oh, child," she whispered. "Were they together?"

Sergeant answered. "From what we can determine, no, although they were both on the same island of Santa Vittoria. Your husband was imprisoned there, it seems."

Mrs. Sebastapol closed her eyes as if in physical pain. "On Santa Vittoria!" she whispered. "So near to his friend."

"I don't think my father knew he was there until the end," Amelia said. "The prison caught fire. Just before Doctor Sebastapol escaped, he contacted my father."

"Juan escaped?"

"He was killed trying to," Sergeant said. "But he left something for Arthur Pierce. A coded message of some kind. That's what we assume, at any rate. We haven't been able to decipher it."

"Was this why Arthur was killed?"

"I think so," Amelia said. "My father gave me a notebook before he died. He asked me to give it to Mr. Sergeant's people. Since then, someone has been trying to kill me."

"Dio!" Mrs. Sebastapol exclaimed. "The notebook . . . it was Juan's?"

Amelia took the photostatic copy from her handbag. "We think so," she said.

She handed the pages across to the other woman, who reached behind and picked up a pair of gold-framed reading glasses from a small marble-topped table before looking quickly through the pages.

"This is Juan's writing," she said. "It is a medical journal of some kind, a series of patients' records. But it is nonsense."

"How is that?"

"These numbers. My husband writes 'blood pressure' but then there are numbers such as two, five, nine, four, and . . . here is another, eight, seven, six, two. Those numbers have nothing to do with blood pressure." She skimmed through the pages rapidly. " 'Resting pulse, one hundred forty-three.' Ridiculous. 'Triglycerides.' I doubt that a prison infirmary would even bother to check the inmates' triglyceride levels. It is a joke."

"Or a code?" Sergeant asked.

"Yes, of course. Juan would have made a code. Puzzles of this sort were his passion."

"My father's, too," Amelia said.

Mrs. Sebastapol nodded. "Just so." She looked up. "Amelia, are you also involved with your father's work?"

"No. At least I wasn't until he gave me this notebook. But he did teach me a cipher once. On my ninth birthday. Dad's last words to me were, 'Remember your ninth birthday.' "

The papers dropped from the woman's hands. "Amelia is nine."

Amelia gaped at her. "What did you say?"

"Oh, my child, forgive me. It was so many years ago. I'd

forgotten. I knew about this code. The unbreakable code."

"Yes!" Amelia said.

"I never learned how to use it. Those things were of no interest to me then. Later, after Juan was imprisoned, I came to regret my ignorance. With the code, I may have been able to help my husband." Tears sprang to her eyes.

"Please, Mrs. Sebastapol. Tell me about 'Amelia is nine.' "

"Your father taught Juan the code. It was a number code of some kind. Juan was in love with mathematics, and marveled that Arthur had come up with such a devilish thing. As Arthur was explaining it—they were right here in this room, as I recall—he kept using the phrase 'Amelia is nine' as a reference."

"That was the key he taught me," Amelia said. "But it's not the one used in the notebook. We've tried it."

"I see." She took off her glasses. "If only I had not been so stupid!" She pinched the bridge of her nose. "After Juan's arrest, I knew he could use that code to communicate from wherever he was imprisoned but that only Arthur Pierce could understand it. I tried to convey that in my letters to him. 'Amelia is nine' I wrote over and over, in all my letters. Every day, for months. Then every week. There was never any answer. Finally, after five years, I stopped writing. I was certain he was dead then. Until this morning . . . for a moment . . ."

She seemed to collapse inside herself. Suddenly the woman who had presented such a regal bearing just a few minutes before seemed too small for her chair.

Amelia went to her and took her hand. "It's hard to love someone," she said softly.

Mrs. Sebastapol squeezed Amelia's hand. "Yes," she said. "But it is harder not to love."

Sergeant had been listening in silence, his brow wrinkled in concentration as he dissected the elements of the widow's recollections. Finally he spoke.

"Mrs. Sebastapol, when was your husband arrested?"

"April fourth, nineteen eighty," she said without hesitation.

"Arthur Pierce was still working at Langley then."

"Yes. Juan had met with him once, months before, in Santa Vittoria. The Sandinistas had taken power in Nicaragua. I think Juan had hoped that Arthur could use his influence with the CIA to depose the new government. But, of course, that was impossible."

"What I'm getting at, Mrs. Sebastapol, is how you expected your husband to contact Pierce, who was living in the United States."

"No, no," she said with a little shake of her head. "My letters at first were the ordinary communications of a wife to her husband. I expected him to be released quickly, since the authorities had no evidence of any wrongdoing. In fact, Juan had done nothing more than meet with some prominent Nicaraguans from time to time."

"I understand that," Sergeant said. "But when did you begin to write 'Amelia is nine' in your letters?"

"After Arthur moved to Santa Vittoria. Wherever my husband was being held, I knew it had to be somewhere in the Caribbean. Someplace where he might be able to reach Arthur."

"You gave him Pierce's address?"

"Certainly not. I knew that Juan's mail would be read. I could not place Arthur in jeopardy with the Sandinistas. You see, if I had known the code myself—"

"But you didn't," Sergeant said impatiently. "How did you let your husband know where Arthur Pierce was?"

Mrs. Sebastapol's lips formed a small smile. "I invented a code of my own," she said. "Oh, it was very simple, nothing like this." She touched the papers on her lap. "I only repeated the same numbers again and again. You know, 'Uncle Ernesto bought fifty-five cows this morning' . . . 'I had five ladies to lunch' . . . 'Yesterday I dusted the picture frame you gave me for our twenty-fifth anniversary.' That sort of thing. But always the same numbers: 5-5-5-2-5-1-1-7-6-8."

Sergeant scowled. "And what was that?"

"Why, the telephone number. At Arthur's office."

Both Sergeant and Amelia froze. "Doctor Sebastapol

called my father from the prison," Amelia said.

She snatched up the papers. Sergeant handed her a pen, and she drew a grid on the back of the top sheet.

"What are you doing?" Mrs. Sebastapol asked.

Amelia did not answer. Nothing existed for her now except the strings of digits in the notebook. She took them through one set of grids and then another. Five minutes passed. Then ten. Then twenty. Finally she looked up. With trembling hands, she lifted the sheet of paper and read from it.

" 'I am on the island of Santa Vittoria in the basement of the fort known as El Mirador.' "

Mrs. Sebastapol moaned.

"We've found the key," Amelia said.

Sergeant took the worksheet and looked at it. "Will she be safe here for the next few hours?" he asked Mrs. Sebastapol.

"Yes, of course." She stood up. "You can work right here Amelia. Mr. Sergeant . . ." She gestured for him to leave with her.

"I have to go out for a while," he said. "Please don't let anyone in the house while I'm gone."

"I understand," Mrs. Sebastapol said.

"May I have a word alone with Amelia?"

She nodded and left the room, closing the door behind her.

Sergeant grabbed Amelia's arm. "You are not to leave this room until I get back, understand?" His tone was sharp and demanding, so different from the man who had held her through the night.

"What do you think I'm going to do? Run out into the street with a lamp shade on my head?"

"Do you understand?" He shook her.

"All right," Amelia said angrily. "You're hurting me."

He released her and turned toward the door.

Suddenly she was filled with a new fear. "Burt?" she asked quietly. "I just want to know one thing."

"What is it?" He turned back.

"Now that you know the key to the message, am I . . . dispensable?"

"Dispensable?"

"Isn't that one of the words you people use—dispense, eliminate, neutralize, sanction? Is your Network going to kill me, Burt?"

Sergeant looked at her for a moment, then turned away again, silent.

"I'm sorry," Amelia called out after him. "Really, I didn't mean that."

But he was gone.

17

The man with no name lay back naked against the bed's brass headboard. The woman—she had said her name was Elena—efficiently removed her clothes near a small vanity on which a bowl and a pitcher of water had been placed. The room was cheerful and clean, and did not resemble a bordello.

The Viennese are even wholesome about sex, the man thought as Elena smiled brightly at him. She was a big girl, melon-breasted and unselfconscious about the small roll of fat around her middle. Her red hair was long and thick, pulled up into a loose topknot. She pulled out two hairpins, turning her head in a coquettish tease. The man stared at her, expressionless.

"You are an American?" she asked, sliding next to him on the bed.

"I don't know," he said.

"Perhaps you do not wish to tell Elena. That is good enough. *Es macht nichts.*"

She took his hand and placed it on her breast. "You like? Hmmm?" She pretended to squirm with delight.

He reached up and touched her hair. "Has it always been this color?" he asked.

She laughed. *"Naturlich.* Would you like to see proof?" She giggled again.

His brow creased. "Why are you laughing at me?"

But she kept on laughing, and the red hair spilled over her eyes the way that other woman's did when the giant would make love to her. They had let him watch, the giant and the beautiful woman with red hair—the others had said she was the boy's mother—while they fondled one another and entwined their limbs. They had paid no attention to the boy as they slammed against each other, nude and sweating, making their animal sounds. And after the giant left, the red-haired woman would burn the white powder in a spoon and then suck it up into a needle that she plunged into her arm. Sometimes she vomited after that; sometimes she slept. When night came, one of the boy's uncles would carry him away to bed.

"Lover? Pretty man?" Elena said softly. He blinked. The prostitute's face came into focus. "Don't be angry with me." She pouted in mock contrition. She kissed his unresponsing lips. "We are losing time."

He reached his arm behind her bare back and stroked the silky white skin. Elena purred, then touched him with expert hands until he was stiff and throbbing. With a gasp, he thrust into her soft flesh, climaxing instantly.

Then he lay back and closed his eyes, shuddering. The giant must have felt this way, too, when he loved the woman with red hair. The mother-woman. Anxious. Unbearably expectant.

It had begun differently that night, the last night the boy saw the mother-woman alive. She had not made the animal sounds of love with the giant that night, and the air smelled different to the boy; there was a piercing, metallic odor. The red-haired woman had been frightened, and the giant sensed the fear and fed on it. He had teased the mother-woman with a knife at her throat, and she had cried. She had tried to get up off the bed, but the giant had laughed and pushed her down. He cut her nostril. The boy remembered that.

Blood had spurted from the mother-woman's nose.

It was the blood, the man with no name thought. The giant loved the blood.

"Aghrab," the giant had said. Scorpion.

It was the giant's name for himself, or at least the one he preferred. The boy had never learned another. He had never called the giant "Father," of course. That would not have been acceptable. And no one called him Aghrab to his face.

It was a Farsi word, not Arabic. Years later, after the boy's mother was long dead, he learned that an Iranian had provided the name. The giant had gone to Teheran and killed six people who had been sleeping in a single room. He did not use gas, or even a gun; he had killed all of them with a knife, with his own hands. The Iranian police inspector had referred to the killer as *aghrab,* a vicious creature that can kill again and again without tiring. It made the newspaper accounts.

The giant had been pleased. He was a boastful man. He enjoyed his power. He called himself "Aghrab" when he saw the blood of the red-haired woman in whose belly he was about to spill his seed because sex and death were very close.

He had straddled her on the bed then, his naked member huge. And the mother-woman had spoken something, a small, choked sound that exploded into a hiss as the giant's knife sliced through her throat. Her blood had sprayed him with fine red droplets, and he had ejaculated right there, on his knees, spilling himself onto the woman's blood, the silver knife held high in triumph . . .

The Swiss prostitute awakened him from his reverie with a kiss. Then she rose slowly and began to dress. The man with no name stood up also, going quietly to his clothes. He fumbled in his pockets for a moment. Elena smiled, expecting a tip. "You will come back, yes?"

The man pulled out a long blade. "Aghrab," he whispered.

She gasped then, in the split second before his hand clapped over her mouth. She was strong. On her feet, she might have broken loose from him, but he dove for the bed, pulling her with him. He wrapped his legs around hers, so that her back was pressed against his chest. She was alive now, her muscles taut and straining, the muffled screams inside her throat, the smell of fear on her. Yes, this was what he wanted. This was what his father had known. With a single smooth stroke, he pulled the knife across her neck and sighed with wonder as the blood shot out of her like a fountain. Then he turned her over, feeling the warm blood covering him. One more thrust, through the heart now, to still the body. The woman convulsed once, then went limp, motionless. It was done.

He sat back on his haunches and closed his eyes, taking in the scent of the kill. It was intoxicating. He was at peace.

Then, finally, reluctantly, he severed the woman's left ear and placed it in her mouth. A little surprise for the medical examiner, he thought. The communion wafer. A nice touch.

Sleepy and satisfied, he walked over to the vanity and poured some water from the pitcher into the bowl. He washed carefully, then dressed. He wore a specially designed, ultra-lightweight bulletproof vest under his clothes. In Europe, he reasoned, far too many irresponsible people owned guns.

Then he left the room, closing the door behind him and whistling tunelessly. He did not remember what he had done with the woman inside.

Machines don't remember.

18

When Sergeant returned to Marla Sebastapol's house, the old woman was pacing in the large drawing room. A glass of vodka was in her hand.

"Amelia is still working," she said. "Please excuse my bad manners, Mr. Sergeant. Can I get you a drink? Or something to eat, perhaps?"

Sergeant shook his head tensely.

"It is just all so exciting for me. At last, after all these years, I will know what my husband went through, what he was thinking . . ."

"You won't be privy to the information in the notebook," Sergeant said.

She halted suddenly, the drink sloshing in its glass. "But it was Juan's—"

"Your knowledge of the contents of the notebook would be dangerous for you, Mrs. Sebastapol."

Her face drained of color. "I imagine I am sufficiently mature to decide whether or not to put myself in danger," she responded coldly.

"Then let me put it this way. If whoever is after this notebook finds out about your involvement, he will get the information he needs from you."

"You underestimate me, Mr. Sergeant," she said, turning away.

"Forgive me, Mrs. Sebastapol, but you underestimate *him.* He'll break you. And then he'll kill you." He sat down heavily.

"You sound as if you know who he is."

The bitter trace of a smile touched his lips. "That I do," he said. "Too well."

Amelia appeared at the doorway to the sitting room. Her face was ashen, her eyes wild. Marla Sebastapol's head jerked up. "Amelia—"

"The Libyans are going to use the virus against the United States!" she blurted, her voice as dry as sandpaper. "There's an American working with them—"

"Shut up!" Sergeant hissed viciously. He leaped over to her in two strides and shook her by her shoulders.

"Burt—"

"I said shut up!"

Mrs. Sebastapol set her drink down. "Tell me about my husband."

"She isn't going to say anything." He shoved Amelia. "Get your things. Now."

She scrambled away from him.

Mrs. Sebastapol picked up Amelia's bag. "Please," she said softly. "I must know about Juan. I have waited for ten years."

"Sorry," Sergeant said, forcing himself between the two women. He pushed Amelia through the house toward the front door. At the entrance, Amelia yanked free and ran back to Marla Sebastapol.

"His book was filled with you," she said. "He thought of you to the end."

Sergeant grabbed her and pushed her out the door. With a last glance back, Amelia saw Marla Sebastapol standing forlornly in the doorway, looking like an old, old woman.

* * *

"Don't you ever touch me again," Amelia said, writhing against Sergeant's grip. "You had no call to be so rude to her. Or to me."

"My rudeness isn't going to kill that woman."

"What is that supposed to mean?"

"It means that if Billy Starr gets hold of her, she's dead. And he'll know everything, thanks to you and your big mouth."

"Billy Starr is dead!" she shouted.

Sergeant hailed a cab and pushed her inside.

Sergeant read Amelia's translation through for the second time. He blew out a stream of air. "It's almost unbelievable," he said.

"The guards weren't careful when they spoke around him. I suppose they assumed he was just another prisoner."

"But the plan itself. It's too . . . Are you sure you got this correctly?"

"Yes. It was my father's code. I didn't have to guess on any of the letters. Sebastapol was very careful about the code. Even at the end, when he was writing quickly, he used all the right ciphers. What a mind he must have had, to do it all in his head!"

"But he didn't say where the virus was going to be released, or when. You're sure about that?"

"I gave you an exact transcription. Sebastapol probably didn't know any more than that."

Sergeant laid the papers across his lap. "Did your father tell you?" he asked.

"Of course not. I would have remembered if he had."

"He didn't mention any location? Anywhere?"

"No! How many times do I have to tell you?"

"And the man—"

Amelia's eyes lit up. "You see? It's the same man I killed. Sebastapol mentions the tall, white-haired American."

"I thought you didn't see his hair," Sergeant said, his eyes expressionless.

"He's the one in the swamp, I tell you. The one who murdered my parents. And he's dead now."

"Aghrab," Sergeant said.

"What?"

"Aghrab. The Scorpion. It's what the Libyans call Billy Starr." He muttered to himself. "He may not make the connection to Marla Sebastapol."

"He won't be seeing Mrs. Sebastapol." Amelia's words were measured as she repeated the litany for him. "I've told you a hundred times. I saw him through the infrared goggles as he fell. The wound was in the middle of his forehead. He couldn't be alive."

Sergeant looked up at her from his chair. His eyes were as cold as a snake's. "Why are you lying to me?" he asked quietly.

"Damn it, I'm not lying!" she shouted. "The problem is, you don't *want* him to be dead! You want to save your precious Scorpion for yourself. Well, you're looking for the wrong man! While you're chasing a dead man, someone else is going to poison a reservoir somewhere in my country! And he's going to kill me while he's at it! Doesn't that mean anything to you?"

She exhaled a loud gust of breath. "Burt, the past is over," she said. "Your wife and daughter are dead. You have to accept that. And the man who killed them is dead, too. It sounds trite, but life does go on. You've got to go on, too."

Sergeant listened to her, trying to contain his fury.

"Listen, Burt. I didn't—"

He pushed her away. "I'll send the transcript to Hyatt," he said, slamming the door behind him.

He knew the Scorpion wasn't dead.

He knew the Scorpion too well.

Five hours later, he had not returned. The sun was setting over the rooftops of the ramshackle houses surrounding the safe house. Amelia threw back the faded orange curtain and picked up the living-room telephone.

After a moment, the line was picked up on the other end, in Geneva.

"Let me speak with Davis Hyatt, please. This is Amelia Pierce."

Hyatt was clearly displeased. "Why are you calling?" he asked curtly.

"Burt's been gone too long," she said. "He went out to send you the transcript—"

"The what?"

"The code. I . . . I broke it, and—"

"Don't say any more, please. A car will come for you."

"All right," she said softly. "But what about Burt?"

"Just stay where you are."

There was such a long pause that Amelia was about to hang up when Hyatt asked, "Amelia?"

"Yes?"

"Does Sergeant have the key to the code?"

"Yes."

The phone rang off.

For the next hour she wandered listlessly through the house, her confusion almost palpable.

Her mind drifted back to the night before, when she and Burt had lain in each other's arms. For a few moments, just a few, she had felt no fear.

The fear was back now. She sat on the edge of the bed where the two of them had made love, and a shiver ran through her. What if Burt Sergeant were lying dead somewhere, the victim of a killer she had insisted did not exist?

Then, in the back of her mind, she heard another voice, asking questions she herself had been afraid to entertain during the long hours of waiting. Why had Sergeant come back here to the safe house with the transcript? It would have been easier to leave immediately for Geneva and give it to Davis Hyatt directly. Apparently Hyatt had not received it yet.

Was he ever going to?

Stop it, she told herself. Her imagination was running wild.

Then why had Sergeant left her alone to translate the notebook? Where had he gone? What did he do?

And why had he taken the translation with him . . . and not returned?

Don't even think it, she told herself. *You're in over your head already. You don't know why these people act the way they do; you're not supposed to know.*

But why hadn't he come back?

Why was he so sure the Scorpion was still alive?

Why did he say that Marla Sebastapol was going to die because of her knowledge?

Oh, my God, she thought. *Marla!*

She ran out of the house and picked up a taxi on the Blumenstrasse. *"Fierzen Keilgasse,"* she told the driver. *"Und macht schnell, bitte!"*

There was no answer to the bell.

"Madame Sebastapol?" she called. She rang again, then beat on the door. "Please let me in!" she shouted. "Marla!"

The door was unlocked. She opened it cautiously.

"Marla?"

Her hands flew to her mouth. There, at her feet, lay the body of the old woman who had served as Marla Sebastapol's maid.

It was dark. Amelia fumbled along the wall for a light switch. When she found it and turned it on, she saw that the body was lying spread-eagled in a pool of blood. The woman's head had been nearly severed, and one of her ears was missing.

Amelia backed away, her legs buckling beneath her. "Marla?" she asked in a small voice, unable to take her eyes from the body in its obscene position.

The slash across the old servant's throat gaped like a fierce grin. But most of the blood—and she was covered with it—seemed to originate from her belly, although there was no wound there. The starched apron over the maid's black dress was stained bright red, but otherwise intact.

Amelia took a step closer to the body, holding out her hand as if to ward off whatever demons might fly out of it.

Something fell onto her outstretched fingers. A drop of blood, cold and bright.

Instinctively Amelia looked up, and then she heard her own scream, as if it were an entity leaping out of her.

Directly above dangled Marla Sebastapol's head, hung by her hair from the overhead light fixture.

The eyes were open and filmed, the mouth slack around a lolling tongue. Filaments of muscle and blood vessels jutted from the base like the roots of a plant, and in the back was the gray oval of the woman's severed spine.

Amelia's mind and body had turned to stone, rigid, her hand still held out in front of her as if she were expecting someone to kiss it, while the blood dropped steadily and slowly onto it, slick and red. Through it all, her scream filled the still house like a shrill, horrifying song.

One by one, the lights in the neighborhood went on. An old man, armed with a hammer, peered into the doorway.

"Mein Gott!" he said, dropping the hammer to the floor.

Others came in, curious onlookers who wandered through the elegant house in ghoulish fascination while Amelia sank against the wall, unable to tear her eyes from the grotesque images in front of her.

"The body's in there," one man said solemnly to the crowd. "It's on the dining-room table. She's been . . ." He crossed himself. "I pulled her dress down."

"I can't breathe," Amelia said, running out of the room.

"Fraulein! Come back," someone shouted after her. "The police will come soon. You must—"

But Amelia could not stop. It was too much like a scene she'd witnessed before. The victims' faces were different, but they looked the same in death, because their killer was the same.

So she had not killed him, after all.

Instead, she had let him make love to her.

She ran for more than a mile, her legs feeling as if they were made of springs. Finally, exhausted, her lungs burning, she slowed to a halt near a lamppost and rested her head against it.

Oh, Daddy, how could I have done this to you?

Sergeant had used her, just as all the other men in her life had used her. But this time it was so much worse.

She had no place to go now.

"Amelia?" She looked up, not bothering to wipe away the tears that coursed down her face.

It was Burt Sergeant.

"Get away from me!" she screamed, backing off.

"Come here, Amelia." He was deliberate, soft-spoken. His voice sounded hypnotic. "You shouldn't have left the house."

"You killed Marla Sebastapol!"

"No, I didn't, Amelia. The Scorpion did. I've been waiting for him. He'll come after you. You're in danger. Let me take you home."

Her back bumped against a brick wall, and she gasped at the impact. Burt Sergeant stopped, his arms outstretched. "Come to me, Amelia."

Her head was swimming. Once again she'd trusted a man who had hurt her. Once again she'd opened herself up to the knife. Only this time the knife was real, and her lover was a killer.

"No," she whispered. "Not this time. You killed my father, my mother, and my friend, but you won't kill me."

She turned the corner and fled down an alley. She heard the skittering of rats around her, and spotted the glint of their eyes as she tore over the slippery cobblestones, turning this way and that through a labyrinth of dark, empty passageways.

She nearly tripped over a pair of legs. After reeling into the far wall, she realized that it was only a homeless man, bundled up in newspapers for the night. Her breath came in ragged gasps. She stopped, listening. Aside from her breathing and the occasional rustling of the sleeping man, there was no sound. No footsteps. Quietly she walked past the hobo into another alley. He did not stir.

She heard a noise. She looked back, paralyzed with fear. The alley was empty.

Then two arms clamped around her from behind, covering her mouth, and Burt Sergeant spoke in a whisper. "Don't say anything. I'll explain—"

She bit his hand. For a split second, his grip on her relaxed and, whimpering, she wrenched free and ran back the way she had come.

She stumbled over the sleeping hobo. He twitched awake and grabbed for her ankle. Stifling a scream, Amelia pulled away and ran, even as the hobo lurched to his feet and stumbled after her.

Sergeant was close behind her in the maze of alleyways. She could feel him.

"Amelia?" he called. A question, as if he expected her to answer.

Sure, Burt. Right over this way. I'm easy. But then, you know all about that, don't you, Burt?

She slammed into a wall. Dead end. She spread her hands on the stones instinctively, but she knew she couldn't climb them.

Dead end.

Bang, you're dead.

She saw him. He was silhouetted against the light at the entrance to the alleyway. In the distortion of the angle, he seemed larger than life, looming, waiting for her to move. A sound like the keening of a wild animal escaped her as she felt her body fall limply to the stone pavement.

Then a single shot, muffled by a silencer, exploded in the still darkness from somewhere near her head. The figure at the mouth of the alley jolted back, its head and neck snapping from the force of the bullet.

Amelia stared, frozen in fear and confusion. Then slowly she lifted herself to her feet.

Behind her stood a slender man with a boyish face and a mop of golden hair. He put his automatic into a shoulder holster and smiled.

"It's over, Amelia," he said, hugging her.

She blinked at him.

"Wade Turner. Remember me?"

"Wade . . . yes," she said numbly. "Santa Vittoria."

"That's right. Come on. He may have friends. Let's get out of here."

He led her to a door, invisible in the darkness, that

opened into the ground-floor hallway of one of the ramshackle buildings. As the door closed, she looked back into the alley.

Burt Sergeant lay where he had fallen, a dark form in the shadows.

19

"I'm sorry we had to expose you to so much danger," Turner said. He offered her a pastry from a tray the room-service waiter had brought up.

She declined, leaning her head against the pale green brocade of the sofa.

They were in a second-story room in the rear of the Königswald Hotel. It was a marked contrast to the shabby safe house where Amelia had shared a bed with Burt Sergeant. Cut flowers filled crystal vases on top of polished rosewood tables. The mellow light from a single porcelain lamp lit the spacious room. Beyond pale blue-velvet draperies, a full moon hung in a starry sky above a fairy-tale courtyard garden bordered with lush, blooming hedges.

"Well, no use letting it go to waste," Turner said, wolfing down the pastry like a ravenous teenager. He drank a glass of milk afterward. "Excuse me, but I'm awfully hungry."

Amelia nodded wanly. She did not want to talk anymore. She did not want to listen anymore. If she'd had a home, she would have wanted only to go to it, curl up on a favorite chair, and sleep. But the only home she had now was an empty apartment in New York, three thousand miles away.

"Actually, I've been after Sergeant for some time. Mr. Hyatt suspected that he might have been a double, but we had to catch him at it. We knew he'd come after you for the key to the notebook, so we sent him here with you as a pretext, so he'd be alone with you."

"Thanks," Amelia said. "Thanks a lot."

He smiled his big, ingenuous smile. "Oh, you weren't in any real danger. I was watching the safe house on the Blumenstrasse."

"Oh."

Did he know they'd made love? Had he seen her come to Burt Sergeant with her secrets, handing him her vulnerable heart?

"But why didn't he just kill me?" Amelia asked. "He had plenty of opportunities. And he even saved my life at the hospital in Geneva. Why?"

Turner shook his head. "I don't know. Maybe Sergeant didn't know himself. From what I understand, the man had had some serious mental problems ever since his wife and daughter were killed. He tried to commit suicide, but he didn't even remember that. Frankly, I don't know why Hyatt ever took him on with the Network, but it's not my place to question the boss." He took her hand and held it.

"Anyway, that's behind you now. I just wish I could have stopped him before he reached Mrs. Sebastapol."

Amelia bolted upright. "Why couldn't you?" she demanded. "If you were following so closely, why couldn't you stop him before . . . before Marla . . ."

"I tried, Amelia," he said softly. "Really, believe me. But I didn't know where he was going, and he's very experienced. By the time I traced him back to Mrs. Sebastapol's house, it was all over. It took me all day to find him again." He shook his head. "Damn, I could kick myself. I should have guessed he'd go back there. It was so terrible, with her head hanging from the chandelier like that . . ."

"Stop it!" Amelia cried. She put her hand over her eyes. "I'm sorry. I have a terrible headache."

"I can call up for some aspirin."

"No, never mind. Just . . . please explain the rest to me. About Bu—about Sergeant."

Turner bit into another pastry. "There was one more killing not far from here," he said casually. "A whore. Happened today. All cut up, like she was ready to go in a salad." He polished off the last of the pastry. "Same style. The same as your dad."

"No," Amelia said quietly. "That wasn't Burt Sergeant."

Turner looked up. "Sure it was. I followed him from Santa Vittoria."

"It wasn't the same man," she insisted. "That's the part nobody believes."

"Try me," he said, smiling.

"I killed that man."

Turner's eyelids fluttered.

"I shot him in the forehead. I saw the bullet hole. He was probably a psycho, too, but he was a different psycho."

Turner blushed. "I wouldn't call them psychos, ma'am."

"You wouldn't?" She laughed, a high, hysterical laugh. "People who dismember their victims and then keep their ears for souvenirs?" Her laughter rose until it threatened to go out of control.

Turner threw what was left of his milk in her face.

She gasped. "What . . . what . . ."

"I'm sorry, Amelia," he said, rushing to wipe her off. "It's just that you've been through so much. You need some rest, or this thing's going to drive you crazy, if you'll forgive the expression."

"Yes . . . yes, I suppose so. Maybe if I could lie down for a while . . ."

"Yes, ma'am. Soon. But first I have to ask you some questions. Just so your mind stays fresh about things. I'm real sorry to put you through this, but Mr. Hyatt says—"

"Of course," Amelia said wearily. "I understand."

"Well, mostly it's about the key to the code in the notebook. Hyatt says you've got it."

"Yes. I just figured it out this afternoon. My father's phone number. That was the key. The code works with that."

Turner nodded. "And who has the notebook now?"

"I don't know. Burt Sergeant said he'd sent it to Hyatt. That struck me as strange, because I thought we should have gone back to Geneva as soon as I came up with the key."

Turner took a deep breath. "And what did it say? Basically, I mean."

"That the Libyans are somehow involved with this killer, Billy Starr—an American. I think he's the one I shot. And they're going to poison the water supply somewhere. Doctor Sebastapol thought it would be in America, although I don't know why he thought that."

"Okay, Sergeant knew this, then. And Mrs. Sebastapol. Anybody else?"

Amelia shrugged. "I don't think so. Maybe Hyatt's people figured it out."

"No, they haven't," Turner said. He leaned forward in his chair and grinned. "But surely you talked to somebody else. You must have called home. Friends? People in your office, maybe?"

"Nobody, I tell you. Nobody." Amelia spat out the words angrily. "I'm not a fool, you know. If I talked about any of this, I'd never go home again. I've read enough spy novels to know that."

Turner laughed. "I don't know if Davis Hyatt would go that far, but I follow you."

He relaxed and sat back. "So what else did Doctor Sebastapol have to say?"

"Nothing much. I mean as far as this is concerned. Most of the notebook was about Sebastapol's life in the prison, the atrocities committed there, all sorts of odd things he remembered. It was tragic, every word of it, but only the last couple of pages were about the poison. These Libyan doctors came to the prison to test the poison on the inmates. It was like a plague. It spread like crazy. Then the doctors left, and the wardens and guards—they were locals—got sick along with the prisoners. They all died, I guess, except for Doctor Sebastapol. Somehow he managed to escape. He wrote those last two pages while he was on the run."

"He was a brave man," Turner said.

Amelia felt tears sting her eyes. "Next to my father, the bravest man I've ever known." She sighed. "Anyway, the only thing he doesn't mention is where these jokers are going to plant the poison. If they're still planning to do it."

"If? Why do you say that?"

"Well, the man who was heading the operation is dead. That's the one I killed. And Burt Sergeant is dead. Who's left?"

"There are others," he said.

She looked up, feeling frightened. "Are you sure?"

"Oh, yes."

"Then it could happen at any time?"

"It'll be soon." He wiped some droplets of milk off Amelia's skirt, using long, languid strokes that went on down her legs.

She shifted uneasily. "How do you know that?"

He rose and walked behind her. His hands smoothed down the silky bodice of her dress and cupped her breasts.

She squirmed away, alarmed. The hands moved from her bosom to her neck.

"Aghrab," he whispered.

She saw the lash of a blade without even feeling his hands loosen their grip. In a millisecond, a thousand images rushed through her mind: her mother lying dead in the kitchen; the man in the stocking mask pumping a spray of machine-gun fire into her father's belly; Wade Turner's smiling, helpful face at the cafe in Santa Vittoria; the bullet hole in the middle of the killer's forehead; Marla Sebastapol's dismembered head hanging from the ceiling of her home; the elderly maid lying sprawled in her own blood; Burt Sergeant's body lying in a crumpled heap in an alley.

"Oh, God, no!" she whispered.

"You're beautiful, Amelia," Turner said, tightening his fingers.

Burt was trying to help me. She felt herself gagging, growing dizzy.

She hadn't trusted Burt Sergeant, even though he had risked his life for her. She had watched him die with no thought but relief. And this sick animal had killed him, just as he had killed Marla Sebastapol and her servant.

The thought enraged her. Suddenly all of the fear and self-recrimination within her crystallized into white-hot anger.

This shitheel isn't going to kill me, she thought. *My daddy didn't throw me into the woods for nothing.*

Almost reflexively, she swung both knees over her head and thudded them into Turner's chest. In the same motion, she threw her elbow into the side of his head. He staggered backward.

She remembered Turner's gun just as he reached for it. She dove behind the sofa. The bullet sank into the upholstered arm. She grabbed a lamp and yanked the cord. It pulled taut against Turner's leg, then came out of the wall socket.

The moment it took for Turner's eyes to adjust to the dim moonlight filtering into the windows was enough to make him misfire the second bullet. As it pinged off the far wall, Amelia threw the lamp, then ran after it toward Turner. It hit him squarely in the chest. The third bullet fired, making sparks in the darkness.

Behind him, Amelia braced herself, then kicked him in the middle of the back, sending him sprawling on the floor. She ground her high heel into his hand. He cried out in pain. Amelia picked up the gun.

"Stay down," she whispered hoarsely, not knowing what she would do next. Call the police? He would rush her while she was on the phone. Scream until someone came to help? Possible, but . . .

Then she saw the switchblade he had tried to kill her with—the same knife that had cut off Marla Sebastapol's head. She shuddered. It was lying on the floor near Turner's hand, glinting in the light of the moon.

She walked slowly toward it, but stopped short. He had seen it, too, and his fingers were snaking around the hilt. He got to his knees, the switchblade shining in his hand.

"I said get down," Amelia said, hearing the panic in her voice. "I don't want to have to shoot you."

Turner smiled. "You aren't going to shoot me," he said, rising to his feet. He cocked his head engagingly. "You've got some pretty good moves, Amelia. You work for Hyatt, too?"

"Drop . . . the . . . knife," she whispered. The gun was shaking in her hand.

"Man, he is one secretive guy. Ain't nobody knows what anybody else is doing in that setup. Why, he won't even give the Network a name." He took a step forward.

Amelia backed away.

"I underestimated you, lady. Yessiree. But you've got my respect now, believe me. And I'm not going to hurt you. You must know that."

He took small steps, diagonally, toward the door. "I'm just going to get my butt out of here, understand, and you won't ever have to worry about me again."

Then he made his move, leaping like a yellow cat, the knife poised at her throat.

She fired the gun.

Turner reeled backward, toward the window. Amelia fired again.

His feet slid in a dance. His arms swung wildly, still holding the knife.

She fired again.

Turner crashed backward through the window in a spray of glass.

And she kept pulling the trigger, shooting bullets into the empty air, until there was no sound except for the steady, rhythmic click of the empty chamber. She did not even notice when the door to the hotel room burst open and Burt Sergeant, along with the hotel manager and two armed policemen, came in.

Sergeant came up behind her and took the gun from her hands.

Amelia turned, saw him, and fainted.

20

"Fraulein. Fraulein, bitte."

A strange bald man was leaning over her. In the background, still fuzzy, were two uniformed men, also strangers. Beside them stood Burt Sergeant.

"Burt," she groaned.

The bald man, the manager of the hotel, looked over his shoulder at the bad-tempered American man who had insisted the door be broken down.

Sergeant nodded slightly, a gesture of dismissal. The manager helped Amelia to her feet and stood aside as she ran to Sergeant.

"Thank God you're alive," she said, embracing him.

He disentangled himself from her arms. "The killer shot a hobo in the alley. That part was accidental," he added coldly. "He thought it was me."

"Burt . . ." Amelia's face crumpled. "I didn't believe you . . ." She went to him again, needing his understanding, but he did not allow her to come near him.

"How you must hate me," she said miserably.

"Where is he?"

The policemen were gathered by the broken window, speaking in rapid German.

"I killed him," Amelia said. "I shot him with his own gun. He fell out the window."

Sergeant pushed past the two officers to look outside.

"I had no choice," she said. "I was going to call the police, but he came at me with a knife."

"Amelia," Sergeant said quietly, "there's no one there."

She rushed over to the window. The garden below was empty.

A black limousine was parked outside the hotel. The door opened, and Sergeant gestured for Amelia to get in. Davis Hyatt was waiting there, glaring at both of them. He tapped on the window to the driver's compartment, and the car pulled away.

"How did you know to find us here?" Amelia asked.

"Mr. Sergeant's message reached me on the car phone while I was on my way to Vienna. To rescue *you*," he said witheringly. "I told you to wait at the safe house."

Amelia looked down. "I thought Burt was the Scorpion. I went to Mrs. Sebastapol's house to warn her, but I was too late."

"What? Mrs. Sebastapol is dead?" Hyatt's face was shocked.

"Killed and mutilated," Sergeant said. "You'll get all the police reports. I got there after the fact, too."

"Then what were you doing all those hours before?" Amelia demanded.

"Miss Pierce, please," Hyatt said. His eyes narrowed. "Actually, she does have a point. What in blazes *were* you doing?"

Sergeant sighed. "Since the Scorpion hadn't come to my house in Appenzell, I had to assume he'd somehow followed us to Vienna. But he couldn't have known where the safe house was, or he'd have already gone after Amelia. So while Amelia was transcribing the notebook at Mrs. Sebastapol's, I went out into the city to make myself visible to him."

"So that he could kill you before he killed Miss Pierce, I suppose."

"So that I could stop him," Sergeant said quietly.

"Apparently you failed."

There was silence.

"Where is the transcription?" Hyatt asked at last.

"In the mail. That's the safest place for it."

"You say that Amelia finished it at Mrs. Sebastapol's house?"

"Yes."

"Then why, may I ask, did you return to the Blumenstrasse? You should have come back to Geneva immediately."

"Damn it, the safe house was the only place the Scorpion didn't know about!" Sergeant exploded. "I couldn't risk exposing Amelia at the train station. If I was going to keep anyone alive, I had to find Starr in Vienna."

"Despite my direct orders to the contrary," Hyatt said.

"It was my judgment to make at the time."

"Oh, was it now?"

"In my opinion, yes," Sergeant said stolidly. "I stayed at the safe house long enough to know that Starr wasn't coming there. Then I left to wait for him at Mrs. Sebastapol's. But he'd already killed her and her maid by the time I arrived."

"So you went back out into the city to be Starr's sitting duck."

"I went out to find him," Sergeant said hotly. "And I would have, if *she* hadn't gotten in the way."

Amelia thought he was going to strike her. "I'm sorry. I've told you I'm sorry," she said, but neither man even glanced in her direction.

"You simply cannot let go of the past, can you?" Hyatt asked Sergeant.

"That had nothing to do with anything!"

"The hell it didn't. You disobeyed my specific instructions not to go after Billy Starr."

"I've explained—"

"You blundered!" Hyatt's face was almost purple with

rage. "Your mental illness—"

"Stop it!" Amelia shouted.

The two men looked at her as if only now remembering her presence.

"You've got things wrong, both of you," she said.

"Oh?" Hyatt said, clearly not interested in the opinion of a meddling outsider. "And how is that?"

"The killer wasn't Billy Starr."

"You saw him?"

"I shot him."

Hyatt looked at Sergeant. "I suppose you weren't going to tell me this, either," he said.

"You haven't given me a chance," Sergeant answered sullenly.

Hyatt gave him a dirty look, then turned to Amelia. "So the man you saw was not Billy Starr."

"No," Amelia said.

"And would you mind telling me, Miss Pierce, how you know what Billy Starr looks like?"

"I don't. But I know the man who tried to kill me. It was Wade Turner."

Hyatt's mouth fell open.

"Wade Turner?" Sergeant echoed, incredulous.

Hyatt raised a hand to silence him. "Miss Pierce," he said, "Perhaps you had better tell us just exactly what happened."

Amelia told him everything, from her first visit to Marla Sebastapol to the shooting in the hotel room.

"Did you kill him?" Hyatt asked.

"No . . . I don't know. I don't think so."

"There was no body," Sergeant said.

"Oh, not again." Hyatt massaged his temples.

"Look, you didn't believe me the first time—"

"That is correct, Miss Pierce," he snapped. "And your account of things has only become more bizarre with time."

"I know it might be hard to believe. But I'm telling you what I saw."

"No doubt."

"Mr. Hyatt—"

"If you would please be quiet, Miss Pierce," he said irritably. "I've heard your story. Now I wish to have a little quiet." He bulged his eyes at her. "*If* you don't mind."

The limousine roared through the night like a black bullet. Amelia finally succumbed to exhaustion and fell asleep. When she awoke, it was daytime and they were making their way through the streets of Geneva.

She sat up. She had been leaning on Sergeant's shoulder. "I'm sorry," she said automatically. Then she added, "I fell asleep."

Sergeant didn't answer.

"Guess you're still mad at me."

"Just because you ran off with the Scorpion and left me for dead? Why should I be mad about a little thing like that?"

Amelia sighed. "I don't know what else I can say."

"Don't say anything, all right?"

Amelia folded her hands. "Whatever you want."

The car stopped in front of the Hyatt News Service building.

Sergeant turned to Hyatt. "I imagine I'm off this case."

"That is correct," Hyatt said crisply.

"Am I fired?"

"We'll discuss that later."

"Please don't fire him, Mr. Hyatt," Amelia said. "It was my fault that things went so wrong."

"Wait for me inside, Sergeant," Hyatt said.

Sergeant gave him a small mock salute.

"What about me?" Amelia asked.

"I think you're going home," Sergeant said.

"To Appenzell?"

"To New York." He opened the car door.

Amelia tugged on his sleeve. "Wait a minute. You mean I'm just . . . taking off? Just like that?"

"Yes, Miss Pierce," Hyatt said wearily.

"But he'll come after me there! Turner . . . the Scorpion . . ."

"We don't think so," Sergeant said. "Now that he knows

we understand the contents of the notebook, that whole crazy well-poisoning plan will be scrapped, if there even was such a thing in the first place. You'll be safe."

Amelia nodded, and her relief showed in her eyes, but she still held fast to Sergeant's sleeve.

"Please," she whispered. "Don't go. Not like this."

Sergeant looked at her with an expression of ineffable sadness. "This would have happened sooner or later."

"But . . ." Her eyes filled with tears. "Oh, Burt, I wanted to trust you."

"I know," he said softly. "But you were right not to. You caught on to the rules fast." He took her hand and held it. "Your father raised you well, Amelia."

He gave her hand a final squeeze. Then he let go, stepped out of the car, and closed the door.

Hyatt opened the partition to the driver's seat. "The airport, please," he said.

As the car pulled away, Amelia turned to catch a final glimpse of Burt Sergeant. He was walking briskly toward the building. He did not look back.

"What are you going to do to him?" she demanded.

"That, young lady, is none of your affair." Hyatt's voice was hoarse with anger. "I'd say you've caused quite enough damage in all this. One of my best men was almost killed because you insisted on running around the streets of Vienna at night."

"And another one of your 'best men' tried to murder me!"

"Oh, do be quiet, you little twit! The man who shot at Burt Sergeant, the man you say tried to kill you—"

"He did try, damn it! I'm sick and tired of being treated like a liar. Wade Turner—"

"Your Wade Turner is an impostor."

Amelia was stunned into silence.

"Turner—the real Turner—has been in touch with me all day. At the time of your so-called encounter at the hotel, Wade Turner was on the other side of Vienna."

Amelia blinked. "He could be lying," she said.

Hyatt half-closed his eyes.

"Did Burt confirm that he wasn't the same man?"

"Mr. Sergeant did not see his attacker."

"But he was the same man I talked to in Santa Vittoria."

Hyatt shook his head. "By the time you met the fellow on the island, Turner was already on his way here, following the man who shot your father."

"But he's dead!" Amelia fairly screamed it. "Why won't you believe me? I killed him in the swamp! Wade Turner is the man who's taken his place! My God, this is a nightmare."

The car turned into the departures lane at Geneva airport. "Your ticket is waiting for you at the Swissair counter," Hyatt said.

"Listen to me," she said urgently. "I know you don't believe me. But won't you at least check what I've said? Show me a picture of Wade Turner—the real one—and I'll tell you if it's the same man who came after me."

Hyatt almost smiled. "You're quite clever, you know."

"What are you talking about?"

"That perfectly obnoxious American innocence of yours. It's very good. The problem is, I don't know how good an actress you are."

She frowned and shook her head. "Suddenly this has gotten over my head," she said. "Could you go back a few light-years, so I can understand what you're trying to tell me?"

He sighed. "Only that, one, there is no proof that you killed anyone in a swamp on Santa Vittoria Island. No body could be found. Two, it is exceedingly possible that you may be in partnership with whoever killed your father and the—"

"You bastard," Amelia spat.

"Oh, come now, Miss Pierce. Surely even you have heard about women who've done far worse things in the name of love."

"Love? Who am I supposed to be in love with?"

"Billy Starr, perhaps?" Hyatt asked teasingly. "How does that sound?"

Amelia looked at him levelly. "It sounds like you're bending over backward to discredit me."

Hyatt shrugged. "Three. Wade Turner has been in my employ for several years. I have known you for exactly five days, and frankly, I have met more emotionally competent women in my life. If you are working with Billy Starr, I would be foolish to show you the photograph of the man who is trying to find him, wouldn't I?"

She sat back, feeling drained. "That's so twisted."

Davis Hyatt looked at his watch. "Your plane leaves in twenty minutes. You'd better hurry." He handed her an American twenty-dollar bill. "You'll need a taxi once you're in New York, I imagine."

She took the money. She knew there was no use in arguing any longer.

"Before you go, I must ask you again to keep your silence," Hyatt said. "It really is of utmost importance. Will you give me your word on that?"

"I've already given you my word," she said defiantly. "I'll keep it."

"Then this, I am pleased to say, is good-bye." He offered her his hand.

"Shouldn't I at least hang around until the notebook arrives in the mail? I mean, it might get lost on the way."

"My dear, the notebook itself is of small importance now. Sergeant gave me the key over a safe telephone. Our code men deciphered it according to your code."

"Then why did he ask me to translate it when we were in Vienna?"

"To see if you would give the true version, of course."

His words cut at Amelia. "Then . . . then he didn't trust me, either."

"Of course not."

"Of course not," she repeated dully.

Hyatt smiled at her. "You should have stayed at the safe house, Amelia."

She stepped out of the car. "Miss Pierce to you," she said and slammed the door.

* * *

Hyatt sat back in the seat of the car and sighed. He didn't like putting the Pierce woman on such a long leash. She knew far too much, and she was more resourceful than anyone had expected.

"Take me to St. Elizabeth's," he said. The limo swung out of the parking square into the lane and sped toward Geneva.

He should have known that any offspring of Arthur Pierce's would know how to take care of herself. The old man had kept his wits to the end, and had apparently taught his daughter to do the same.

She should never have been permitted to leave Europe. She would be easier to kill here; that had been his intention from the beginning.

But then, he wasn't calling the shots about her anymore.

21

The car stopped in front of a modern building with a huge chrome sculpture of an Aesculapius before it.

"I won't be long," Hyatt told the driver.

He took the elevator to the thirtieth floor. The rooms were spacious here, and lovely. The windows on the east side of the building afforded a view of Lake Geneva, with its spectacular spout. Every hour a giant spurt of water would rise out of the lake, covering the still water with ripples that caught the sun. He had watched it many times, for many hours.

He walked quietly into the room, mentally preparing himself for what he would see.

"Hello, Timothy," he said.

The young man in the bed turned his head slightly. He looked like a scarecrow. Hyatt touched his hand to the patient's hair. It had grown back long ago—at least he wasn't bandaged anymore—but the constant bed rest had rubbed his head bald in the back.

"Are you comfortable?"

The young man blinked slowly, as if it were an effort.

"They're giving you a lot of drugs now, I imagine."

The young man blinked again.

"That's best, I think," Hyatt said. He looked out the window.

"Do you remember how we used to go boating on the lake? The time we capsized, and the first boat to come along had your mother and her twenty-year-old boyfriend in it?" He laughed softly. "Do you remember, Timmy?"

The young man's eyes were blank. "Can you hear me?"

There was no response. The man's eyes only stared through Hyatt.

Five years was a long time to suffer. At least he was quiet now. There had been times when Timothy had been wild, exhibiting the strength of a gorilla, spewing gibberish. And, too, moments of perfect lucidity. A brain tumor was impossible to control. If it could not be eradicated, it could only be watched over.

Five years. It had cost Hyatt his life savings, and his heart.

"I'd do it again," he whispered as he picked up the dead-weight of his friend's hand and kissed it. "God knows, it's the only thing in my life I would choose to live over."

A nurse came in. She had been working in the hospital when Timothy had first been admitted. "He is looking quite well," she said cheerfully. "Considering."

"Yes," Hyatt said, but the word got caught in his throat. He nodded curtly to the nurse and left.

When he returned to his office, his secretary gave him a stack of letters and interoffice memos to sign. She had written them herself, in three languages, as she had done ever since Hyatt had taken over the directorship of the Network.

Mrs. Abbott knew nothing about the secret organization. She was aware only that over the years, Hyatt's work load as titular head of Hyatt News Service seemed to have vanished.

She was a good secretary, fiercely loyal to her boss, even though it had become clear to her that Hyatt had been all but formally removed from the news operation by the company's board of directors. To help him save face, Mrs. Abbott created a daily storm of paperwork that circulated Hyatt's name around the building and through the news agency's offices around the world.

Privately, though, she knew it was a vain attempt. Hyatt received few phone calls or visitors. He invited no one. He no longer attended the news service's planning meetings. Still, the redoubtable Mrs. Abbott persisted in her campaign to revitalize her employer's status.

"For your signature," she said deferentially.

"Thank you, Mrs. Abbott."

"Would you like me to hold your calls?"

Hyatt laughed and resisted the impulse to say "What calls?" Instead, he merely said, "Please do."

In his office, he dropped the papers on the corner of his desk. Slowly he walked over to the windows. They had been sealed with a substance developed for repairing interior seams on American rockets. No air escaped from the room. It was ventilated, heated, and cooled by special air ducts separate from those in the rest of the building.

There was a small door at the rear of the room that had never been opened. If it ever were, a heat-sensitive sealant would be sprayed from tiny holes along the opening. When closed again, the door would bond shut in a perfect weld.

These were fire precautions, in reverse. The point was not to prevent fire, but to maximize its damage. Each of the customized enhancements was designed to ensure that in the event of fire, the destruction of the room would be complete. Everything inside would burn, with no one on the outside even aware that a fire was taking place.

The Network would die in flames.

It was just a question of when.

Hyatt fingered the bone-colored draperies. Lovely stuff . . . light, yet textured. They were designed to combust on contact with direct flame.

Burn it now, he thought. *Before it's too late.*

He stepped away.

He could not burn it.

Not yet.

How did this happen to me?

His father had built the Hyatt News Service, all the while working closely with the CIA. His father had managed everything, plus a wife, a family, and a hobby or two. He'd even played the piano, albeit badly.

Davis Junior had never done anything badly. He had always succeeded. He had always been the most brilliant, the most promising, the most admirable son in anyone's acquaintance. He had taken his father's work and pushed it into a new dimension. He was the head of an organization that would stop terrorism before it destroyed the world. He was the silent, unknown man who would bring peace to the entire planet.

Peace. With only a few deaths. A small moral lapse.

Just a few more deaths.

He sat down, rested his arms, and wept.

In the sky over France, a stewardess offered one of the first-class passengers a glass of champagne.

"No," he said. "Please don't bother me again."

"Of course," the flight attendant said with a smile, resisting the impulse to throw the drink at him.

The man with no name settled back and closed his eyes. This would be his last chance to sleep for a while. His whole body ached. The fall from the hotel window had been a lucky one; without the hedges to break it, he would be dead. Still, he would be feeling the stiffness in his limbs for days to come.

He shifted in his seat. The bulletproof vest he wore was uncomfortable, but he dared not remove it, not even here. There were two dents in it, over his heart. The red-haired whore was a good shot.

Good enough to have killed his father.

He ground his teeth. He would not sleep. He would spend the time planning a party. A welcome-home party for Amelia Pierce.

Yes, he thought, smiling. He would give her something very special. Something she would remember to the end of her days.

22

Manuel Orinoco de Cevella took a deep breath as he pedaled his bicycle along the shore road on his way to separate two fools who had gotten into a barroom brawl in the next village.

Not that Manuel could do much on a bicycle. His squad car, a nineteen-eighty-one Buick Regal, had broken down for the third time this week. Nevertheless, the bar owner felt that a word from the police was in order, and frankly, Manuel was grateful for the chance to get away from the station.

The sky over Santa Vittoria was colored an impossibly vibrant blue, the sand sparkled as white as diamonds, and the turquoise waves of the Caribbean rolled in a soothing and endless rhythm.

My, yes, he thought, turning his face up to the warm sun. Here nothing has changed. Here one could almost forget the calamitous ruin that had befallen Santa Vittoria since the Arabs came, the ones who had arranged for El Mirador to open again as a prison.

The prison! Work! Coming after the plague and the poisoning of the sea, it meant there would again be money, food, life.

So what if there were strange goings-on at the prison? Manuel, who was a policeman with the Santa Vittoria Island Civilian Force, had heard the talk. He had heard of the boatloads of foreign men who had come to die in the crumbling fortress of El Mirador.

When the place went up in flames, Manuel had tried to be surprised. He had tried, because to feel no surprise would have meant that he shared in the blame for the death of so many. But in fact, he had felt no more surprise than he would have had he fallen off his bicycle after a black cat had crossed in front of him. El Mirador was a sacrilege, and from the beginning he knew that God would not tolerate it for long.

For all his life, and his father's, and the lives of all his ancestors for the past five hundred years, the old Spanish fortress had stood on its cliff, casting its black shadow over the valley. Before it was built, Santa Vittoria had been a simple place, a nameless paradise of sun and clean water and abundant food. After the fortress came the Spaniards with their so-called government, came the taxes and the executions, came the pirates and the wars with other nations and nobles.

And then it was gone, because God would not tolerate it.

The island was reclaimed by the sun and the sea and the people who tended the bright land. They kept it well for centuries, until another despot from yet another foreign land decided that Santa Vittoria belonged to him. And so El Mirador had opened its doors again, and once more death was set loose in paradise.

"It is an evil," Manuel's wife Floravita whispered, her rosary beads dangling between her work-callused fingers. "The strange ones will set free the evil in El Mirador."

Floravita scrubbed floors all week in exchange for a piece of goat meat. Two of their children had died in the plague, the death-spell that the island's government had decreed was the result of an oil spill. Manuel, suspended from his job during the plague, along with the rest of the civilian police force, earned what he could by digging graves.

"But the jobs, Floravita," he had reasoned. "The work at the prison will save Santa Vittoria from starvation."

"Only God can save us. El Mirador is the work of the devil."

"I suppose El Mirador poisoned the ocean," he had countered sarcastically.

But his wife had only looked at him then, and he knew he had stumbled upon the truth.

"The sea was poisoned . . . so that we would be grateful for the prison," Floravita said slowly, as if tasting the repugnant words.

"No . . . no!" Manuel snapped. "You are speaking like a foolish woman. It is probably against the law, what you say."

"Dio mio," Floravita had groaned, falling to her knees in prayer.

All of them burned, not just the foreign prisoners and the Sandinistan guards, but the warden, too, who had been a good fisherman before the evil days, as well as the cooks and cleaners and the other workers.

Manuel's brother-in-law Raffo died in that fire. In nineteen seventy-two, he had qualified for the hundred-meter dash in the Pan American Games. All of Santa Vittoria had sent Raffo off to Mexico City with a three-day feast, a suit sewn by the best seamstresses on the island, and a new pair of shoes. Raffo made love with four beautiful women on the night before he left.

He came in sixteenth in a field of twenty, but that made no difference. His tales of Mexico City and the Games were good for all the free beer he could ever drink.

Raffo was a fisherman, too, until the days of the death-spell and the opening of El Mirador. He worked as a janitor there. He burned to death, according to the report.

Oh, yes, Manuel thought, pumping the pedals of his bicycle. *We knew. We all knew it was an evil. And we were not surprised when our friends and brothers died inside the flaming belly of El Mirador.*

And then, after the fire . . . nothing. The Arabs were gone

and no one cared. Everyone involved in any way with the prison—dead or vanished. The old American newsman, too, and his Russian wife. The hot-water heater in their house blew up, according to the official police report. But of course the official report was dictated by the thieves in the Sangre Precioso government, and had nothing to do with the truth.

Manuel Orinoco de Cevella knew it wasn't anything to do with the hot-water heater. Not after seeing the old man's body. It had more bullet holes in it than the target at the police firing range. Not to mention the fact that one ear had been sliced off. These were not standard functions of any hot-water heater he had ever seen.

And the old man's daughter, the crazy gringo woman who kept insisting that she'd killed somebody. She was gone, too. Or dead. That was more likely. The body of the man she said she shot was never found, but that meant nothing here. Odds were, hers would never be found, either. The government would see to that. They watched everything, especially these days.

Manuel's job had become a hundred times more difficult since the fire. Now there were forms for everything, reports in quadruplicate, papers stacked in piles so high he could barely see the door from his desk. Thank God his people still had the good sense to bash one another in the head once in a while, or he would never have a chance to leave that stinking office with its mountain of useless paper.

But there would be more when he returned. Just filing a report on the two idiots in the bar would take up the entire afternoon. One copy would even go into a special pouch that would be picked up tomorrow by the English asshole. Manuel had gotten so used to calling him "asshole" in his thoughts that he no longer considered the term to be particularly unkind.

The English asshole was a messenger of some kind, very well-dressed and well-spoken, with credentials from the United Nations, NATO, and a dozen other international organizations. All he did was pick up the pouch containing the fourth copy of the routine police reports, yet he was so secretive about himself that he approached being ridiculous. He refused to say where he came from or where he'd been or who he worked for. He did say once that he had orders. Orders from someone else who had orders. He refused even to give his name.

Manuel shrugged. It didn't matter. "Asshole" seemed to suit him fine.

And so the bureaucracy ground on. It was the last vestige of the shadow of El Mirador. The death-spell was not over yet.

But one day it would pass. Of that, Manuel was certain.

The people of Santa Vittoria were learning. Like Manuel, they too felt the shame of their desperation and their greed. They too had come to understand that El Mirador was an abomination that God had not tolerated. They prayed now, and went back to the old ways. They no longer believed the government reports. The hunger was on them again, the lean times. But they would say nothing. And by their silence, they would cheat the death-spell of its power.

All the funerals had been held. The ashes of the fire had settled. The dead fish in the coastline surrounding El Mirador had been ground into mulch for gardens. And the sea was renewing itself. The fish were returning. The poison was gone.

Naturally, there had never been mention of poison in the official reports. El Mirador had simply caught fire because of faulty wiring. Strange how there had been no survivors in a place as big as the prison, when there hadn't been an explosion. Even crashed airplanes usually produced at least one live body.

Not El Mirador. No one, it seemed, made it outside. They were burned black, every one of them. Even Raffo the janitor, who had once run in the Pan American Games.

Silently, the islanders burned the newspapers containing the official reports, and took the corpses of the dead fish found near the ruin of El Mirador to the wise women and the elders among the fishermen.

"Was it fire that killed them?" they asked.

The old women and the fishermen examined the bloated

fish and shook their heads. "Poison."

"From the oil again?"

The more ancient of the wise women made the sign of the cross. "No," she said. "From the Devil."

And this time they listened. No one ate the plague fish. No one died. No one complained to the far-off government. They accepted their hunger, and waited for the death-spell to pass. And they knew that this time, with the destruction of El Mirador, it would leave forever.

Manuel Orinoco de Cevella smiled. Like the ocean, like the land and the sky, his people would find their way back to the grace of God.

Some fishermen waved to him. They had a net stretched between two boats. It was heavily loaded, by the look of it. The men stood waist-deep in the water. *They had to have gone miles out to sea for a catch like that,* Manuel thought. When had they left? At three in the morning? Or earlier? He waved back to them.

They continued to wave, their arms flapping over their heads in agitation, and soon Manuel saw that the look on their faces was not weariness, but alarm. One of them beckoned to him.

He pulled his bicycle over onto the sand and walked toward the group of men. The one who had beckoned to him was a friend of his uncle's, a big man who, through the years, had utterly lost his capacity for surprise.

"This catch is for you," he said in his deep, gravelly voice.

The men pulled the net closer to shore . . . and Manuel saw: Among the flopping, silver-bellied fish was the half-rotted corpse of a man. A tall white man, rendered whiter by the sea, with white hair. His eyes had been eaten away. The skin of his lips floated raggedly above his teeth. There was a hole in the center of his forehead, and when the sunlight hit it at the right angle, a compressed bullet glinted inside it.

Manuel stepped back in revulsion. The old fisherman laughed, then walked up to the body, careful not to step on the fish. From the corpse's shirt he extracted something shiny. He wiped it off, admired it, shook it next to his ear, then tossed it over to Manuel. It was a silver flask.

"For your trouble," the fisherman said with a hearty laugh. "I think you're going to need it."

Manuel went back to his office and filed his reports.

Later that day, the English asshole arrived to pick up his copy. He submitted it to his superior, who passed it on to his own superior, until it eventually printed out on the desk of Davis Hyatt.

Hyatt read the report with something akin to grief. Billy Starr was, it appeared, incontrovertibly dead.

Not that he'd liked the man. Hyatt had never met him, and it was abundantly clear from all the information on him that the Scorpion had been quite mad. A psychotic, ritual killer. He would not have made the best of friends.

Yet still, in the insulated loneliness of Hyatt's work, Billy Starr had been something familiar. A horror, to be sure, as all the felons, terrorists, and madmen that Pandora's silent intelligence offered him were horrors—but a personality known to Hyatt all the same.

He would miss Billy Starr. Not as much as Burt Sergeant would miss him, of course, if he were ever to know. But then, Sergeant's obsession was such that he would never accept the fact that the Scorpion was now no more than a water-bloated corpse.

Sergeant would go on hunting that ghost forever. And one day the ghost would kill him.

Hyatt fed the sheet of paper through the scanner that would enter the report into Pandora's memory.

Then he set fire to the paper and dropped it into the ashtray on his desk.

23

The tidy, elegant apartment on East Fifty-first Street seemed somehow alien to Amelia. Its black-and-white decor, which she had once planned and implemented joyously, now impressed her as stark, trendy, ultimately childish. *I am sophisticated!* it screamed. See the expensive silk calla-lily arrangement in its black hand-blown glass vase. Admire the LeRoy Neiman print, large and spectacular, with slashes of red to add a little drama to the room.

There was a layer of New York City dust—"grit" was more like it—coating the white windowsills. She had hired a cleaning service at one time, when she had first been given her promotion to the post of senior editor at Marquis Books. It had seemed inappropriate for a person of her station to scrub her own floors. But after a few weeks she'd found the arrangement to be not only costly, but unnecessary. With the exception of the week after her husband had walked out on her and she had somnambulated around the apartment wearing a housecoat—a chenille Dior; homey, yet chic—and strewing the place with moldy Bloody Mary glasses, Amelia was so fastidious that cleaning came as second nature to her.

Even now, bone-tired, drained numb by the events of the past week, the dirt on the windowsills nagged at her. She fixed herself a drink, picked up a clean folded rag and a bottle of Murphy's Oil Soap from beneath the kitchen sink, and wiped off the offending areas. Then she started on the small muntins between the panes of glass. After that she moved on to the bathroom and the kitchen, the really big jobs. By two o'clock in the morning, she was kneeling on the kitchen floor, still wearing pantyhose and the blue dress she had worn to visit Marla Sebastapol, surrounded by dirty rags and the antiseptic odors of various cleaning products.

"Jesus, what's wrong with me?" she asked aloud, laughing uneasily.

I'm scared, that's what's wrong. I'm here in this place by myself, and a madman who slices off people's heads and hangs them from the chandelier is on the loose.

She stood up, feeling her knees creak, and sipped at her third Bloody Mary. Her hands were trembling. She felt cold. Outside, the white drone of distant traffic filled the air with the city's substitute for silence.

He could kill me here, she thought, *and no one would even know it.*

He could cut her up and hang her from the ceiling by her toes like a kosher steer, and no one would find out about it until the rental agency decided to turn the apartment over to a new tenant.

And here, Miss Peabody, we have a terrific view of a putrescent corpse without any recognizable facial features. Now that's *something you don't find every day on the East Side.*

"Ha-ha. Funny. You're a real card, Amelia," she said, screwing on the tops to the bottles of soap and ammonia and Fantastik. She replaced them under the sink, then tossed the rags into a bucket.

Be realistic. Davis Hyatt wasn't just blowing smoke when he said that Wade Turner, or whoever he was, the killer, wasn't about to cross an ocean just to play mumblety-peg on your face. Even Burt Sergeant had said it: She would be safe here.

As far as the Scorpion was concerned, Amelia Pierce was

insignificant, unimportant, an extra in the movie of his sick
life. And now that Hyatt had the notebook, the plan to poison the water was blown. It would be scratched.

If there ever was such a plan, Sergeant had said.

He was right. It was preposterous. Poisoning America's
water. Really. At work, she rejected at least two thrillers
every month dealing with wicked Arabs poisoning America's water supply. She'd even seen a TV movie about it.
They'd started with the drinking fountains at Yankee Sta-
dium, not realizing that no one in America would mourn a
Yankee fan.

The poor Arabs. Now that the Russians weren't enemies
anymore, the only bad guys the spy novelists had to work
with were Middle East terrorists. The world was just getting
to be too damned livable.

See? she told herself. The only danger was in her own
mind. Besides, even if anyone did try to do her in, he'd have
to get past the doorman first. True, the doorman would
never see seventy again, but he was nevertheless stationed as
a guard in the building, and that ought to be worth something.

She went to a chair and sat down, her feet tucked under
her legs. It was a big, soft, black-leather easy chair that had
set her back more than a month's pay, but was worth every
cent of it. Home was becoming home again. Now that she'd
cleaned it, it again felt like hers, the black-and-white decor
not so jarring, the memories of Burt Sergeant not so painful.

She had made a mistake with him, that was all. It certainly hadn't been the first time she'd hopelessly screwed up
things with a man. That was the one thing, it seemed, that
she could do unerringly well.

Sergeant would never forgive her. She would never see
him again. End of story. There were, after all, worse things
than having a miserable love life.

Like the Scorpion with a knife to your throat.

The thought intruded on her like a sharp stick in her side.
She knew it was idiotic, paranoid. Still, it would probably
keep her awake all night. No matter how tired she was, she

would not be able to sleep with that terrible, irrational fear gnawing at her.

She sighed, resigning herself to waiting out the hours until morning.

But what about tomorrow? And the next day? The fear wouldn't go away just because she refused to sleep. It would be on her again the next night, and the next, and the next. What would she do, clean the same three rooms and bath over and over until she collapsed in a heap of dishpan hands and housemaid's knee?

I'm not going to be a fool about this, she told herself resolutely. She'd been through a shock, a series of shocks, but there was no reason for that to destroy her life.

Standing up, shoulders back, feeling the way she did when she'd made a difficult decision at work, she marched into the bathroom and swallowed a Valium. Then she went into the kitchen, opened the drawer where she kept her knives, and picked out an eight-inch blade. It was one of those twelve-for-twenty-nine-dollar deals advertised on television, where a smiling Asian in a chef's hat sawed through tin cans and sneakers with razor-sharp knives. They had been a gift from Jonathan's parents after he'd left her, along with a note admonishing her to come visit them at any time.

Sure, Mother Kadunce. I'll do that. And I'll bring along the knives, too, just in case your son comes home with his bimbo and his dirty laundry.

The knife had never been used, and its blade was pristine sharp. She wrapped it carefully in waxed paper before inserting it between the seat cushion and the arm of the chair. *If this pokes a hole in my three-thousand-dollar chair, I'll use it to kill myself,* she thought, feeling foolish.

But the Valium and the Bloody Mary's were beginning to work. Snuggling into the big chair, she curled her fingers around the hilt of the knife and allowed herself to relax.

Get to sleep, she told herself. She had things to do in the morning. Calls to make. A job to get back to.

And what did you do on your summer vacation, Amelia?

Oh, nothing much. Watched my parents get killed. Came

down with bubonic plague. Murdered a couple of people. Things like that.

Fabulous, sweetheart. Meet anybody interesting?

"Stop it," she said aloud. "It's over, damn it."

And it was. She had to make herself accept that the past week had been no more than a loop in the continuum of her life. It had been painful—monstrous—but it was over. All of it was over.

She felt herself begin to doze, a creeping, delicious sleepiness spreading upward from her legs to her belly to her chest to her face. Her eyes closed. As soon as she finished her drink, she would change into a pair of satin pajamas and crawl into bed.

Nothing to worry about. Nothing at all.

She slept dreamlessly until she began to choke. Her eyes watered; their focus was so hazy that the room seemed to be spinning around her.

I'm going to puke, she thought. She tried to lurch out of the chair, then realized that something was holding her down. Some*one.*

She felt a sick thud inside her stomach. He was here. The ridiculous notion, the foolish paranoia, the utter impossibility that she had managed to dispel from her mind . . . it was all real. A hand inside a black glove was over her mouth, and wrapped around it was a cloth soaked in chloroform.

The man who had cut off Marla Sebastapol's head and hung it on the chandelier as a joke had finally come for Amelia.

She screamed into the cloth. Then, as she fought for breath, the chloroform sent two sharp daggers from her nostrils into her brain. The effect was staggering. Amelia pinched her eyes closed, gasping. She heard a dim hum coming from somewhere inside her ears.

It was a sound she had not heard since she was twelve years old, on an operating table in Langley Valley Hospital. She was about to have her tonsils removed. The anesthetist, forbidding in a green cap and mask, had asked her to count backward from a hundred.

So easy, she had thought, beginning the count as he

placed a gauze cup over her mouth and nose. *Ninety-nine, ninety-eight* . . .

And then the hum had started, faint and distant, not the hum of machinery, but more like a low song that sang through her whole body.

Eighty-two, eighty-one . . .

There, spiraling up through the darkness behind her closed eyes, was a snake. A red snake, she remembered vividly, with black spots on its back, curving down in an unending coil, down deep into the dark, beckoning Amelia to come with it. *Come to the dark side.* Darth Vader had come to take her away.

She almost giggled. Almost, but not quite, because suddenly the four Bloody Marys and the Valium and the chloroform collided somewhere in the labyrinth of Amelia's digestive system. With a heave, she threw up, spewing liquid red vomit out her nose.

The killer's hand came away with a jerk. Amelia choked, gasped, hacked, doubling over and coughing in a sound that resembled a seal's bark.

And then she saw the hilt of her knife, stashed behind the chair cushion.

Her rational mind momentarily cut through the fog of alcohol and drugs. *This is it, kid,* she thought. *Kill him now, or die.*

She grabbed hold of the knife. Then, as the killer's hand reached down for her again, Amelia pulled out the weapon and stabbed blindly behind her.

The man screamed. She had hit him on the first try. Then, feeling as if she were moving in slow motion, she fell forward onto the floor, scrambled up, and turned to face her attacker.

It was the same man. The man she knew as Wade Turner. He was clutching his forearm, where blood was spilling from behind the torn fabric of his white shirt between his gloved fingers.

Amelia bolted out the door, screaming. She passed the elevator and ran for the fire stairs, howling with every step.

Come . . . come to the dark side, the red snake hissed from a place deep within her. She drowned it out with her own shrieking, senseless voice, running down the fire stairs until she collided with the old doorman.

"He didn't kill you!" she shouted in a shrill mixture of terror and jubilation.

"Are . . . are you all right?" the old man asked, not touching her. He was obviously petrified of the foul-smelling woman who'd come charging at him in her bare feet, screaming like a banshee.

"The police—" Amelia huffed, "Call the police. Right now."

"Yes, ma'am," he said uncertainly and began to shuffle toward the telephone in the small changing area off the lobby.

Amelia ran after him. "Take me with you," she pleaded, hanging on to his blue jacket like a child. "Hide me. Please."

The man with no name walked methodically into Amelia's bathroom and tied up the wound on his arm with some rolled gauze. The cut was not deep; she hadn't had the strength for that. Still, the knife had been a nice touch. It had made things so much more interesting.

But she had gotten away. Soon the police would come.

He replaced the gauze. Next to it, in the medicine cabinet, was an open container of mascara. It was the old-fashioned kind, a black block of solidified powder with a tiny brush beneath it. He held it to his nose.

It had a soft, dusty fragrance, a lovely scent.

Nearby were eyebrow pencils, three tubes of lipstick, a pair of false eyelashes glued to two plastic half-moons in a case. A pot of loose powder the color of Amelia's skin. He picked up a fat brush and smoothed it over his face.

Skin like silk, painted and dusted.

Here were a woman's mysteries.

His gloved fingers danced across the treasures in the cabinet: a toothbrush, a bottle of a preparation named Motrin, a prescription vial filled with Valium, a tin of Looney Tune Band-Aids, a container of hydrogen peroxide, two tampons wrapped in paper, a nail clipper . . . Ordinary things, yet they excited him terribly. He felt as if he were looking into Amelia's most secret and indispensable self, her very life.

His mother had once probably possessed a medicine cabinet just like this one, he thought. She had been an ordinary girl once, a student in London, when Yusef Nassif had persuaded her to come to Libya as Billy Starr's concubine.

One of the boy's "uncles" had told him that. When Nassif found out that the boy had been given this piece of information, the uncle had been killed.

The boy himself had pulled the trigger. One shot in each of the uncle's major joints.

Before he died, the uncle had begged Nassif's forgiveness, and Nassif had given it. "But such a small thing," the uncle had said as he lay in the blood-soaked dust.

The man had never understood the importance of a memory to a boy who was being raised as a machine. A memory could destroy everything.

Nassif had explained that to the boy many times. He was to have no mother and no father; he was to be alone, autonomous, perfect.

But he did remember them, the giant who fed on blood, and his victim, the mother-woman with her long red hair and skin like silk. Even now the memory of her scent stirred something alien and sweet within him. Her scent . . .

In the corner of the cabinet was a bottle of yellow liquid. Chanel No. 5. The man with no name reached for it. He held his breath. His mother had kept a bottle just like it on her dressing table.

She couldn't have, he thought. He had been far too young when she died; he could not remember such a thing, he who had so few memories.

Yet inexorably he opened the bottle, and immediately he knew he had remembered. His mother's scent filled the room, just as it had on the day of her death. Even the metallic smell of blood had not been able to mask it.

He closed his eyes and saw her face.

She had called his name then, at the moment of her death. With terror in her eyes, she had looked over to the small boy in the room and called his name, his real name.

For that instant alone, he had been alive.

"Mother," he whispered.

Slowly he replaced the lid and closed the mirrored door.

His reflection was there, staring at him blankly. A streak of face powder crossed one cheek. And something else, something he had never seen before: His face was wet with tears.

He made a move to touch them, and realized that he still held the bottle of cologne in his hands. He put it in his pocket, turned away from the mirror, and went to work.

He tidied everything, wiped the blood and vomit from the leather upholstery, replaced the knife in the kitchen drawer, put the chloroform in a plastic bag and tucked it into his jacket, and opened the windows to get rid of the odor.

Finally he let himself out the way he had come, up the fire stairs to the roof, and then a fairly easy jump across to the roof of the next building. There he walked calmly down the stairs into the empty lobby and let himself out, clutching the precious bottle in his pocket.

24

Two patrolmen arrived at Amelia's building within ten minutes.

"You the one who called for assistance?" one of them asked.

The doorman nodded hesitantly and gestured toward Amelia, who sat on a stool in the small changing room. The acrid odor of alcohol and vomit, combined with the pall of stale cigarette smoke that had hung in the windowless cubicle for decades, was revolting.

Amelia raised her head with an effort. She had not thrown up everything. At least two of the Bloody Marys and one Valium were still coursing through her bloodstream, and she was feeling the effect of them.

"I am," she said, her voice hoarse from screaming. "Someone tried to kill me."

The policemen looked at her red-rimmed eyes, then at each other. "I'll check the apartment," the younger of the officers said.

"Five E," the doorman offered. "I'll take you up there." He jangled the ring of keys hanging off his belt as they walked to the elevator.

Amelia blinked slowly. It was hard to focus.

"You feeling all right?" the remaining officer asked.

She nodded. "I guess I'm still a little drugged," she said, rubbing her face.

Immediately she knew it had been the wrong thing to say. "I took a Valium to calm down. I just got back to New York and . . ."

She strained to speak coherently. Where had she found the presence of mind to get away from Turner? It was all gone now. Nothing remained inside her head but a mish-mash of thoughts with the clarity of cold oatmeal.

She smacked her dry lips. ". . . and I was afraid someone was going to kill me, so I had a few drinks."

"Who, ma'am? Who was going to kill you?"

"Wa—" She swallowed. Davis Hyatt had cautioned her about keeping her silence. And besides, it wasn't Wade Turner. According to Hyatt, the killer was only using Turner's name. To tell the truth would simply get Hyatt, Burt Sergeant, and the real Turner killed, while the killer went free.

"I can't tell you," she said. "That is, I don't know."

"What'd he look like?"

Her mind raced and stumbled. Should she give the police a description of the man who had tried to kill her in Vienna and then followed her back to New York to try again? Would that help the New York police, who had no knowledge of what this man was?

"Could you pick him out from mug shots?"

"He wouldn't be in there," she said.

The policeman looked at her quizzically. "Why not?"

Because a man who cuts off a woman's head and hangs it from the chandelier because he's looking for a notebook is not exactly your garden-variety repeat offender, even in Manhattan, she thought grimly.

"I didn't see him," she said.

"How'd he get in?"

She shrugged. "I was sitting down. I guess I fell asleep. When I woke up, he was behind me. There was a rag in his hand. There was chloroform on it, I think."

"Chloroform?"

"Or ether. Something."

"Have any idea why he would do that?"

She took a deep breath. "No," she said, the question apparent in her voice. It was the first time she'd thought about that. Turner had tried to put her *under*. "I thought he'd just kill me. And when I stabbed him—"

The second officer walked lightly into the room, followed by the old doorman. The policeman questioning Amelia waved him off.

"Wait a minute. You said you never saw his face. You struggled with him?"

"I stabbed him. I had hidden a knife in the chair . . ." She covered her face with her hands, aware of how ridiculous she sounded.

It had all been foolish anyway, calling the police. Even if she told them everything she knew, they would probably never catch the man. Hyatt's organization had been after him for a week and came up with nothing. Burt Sergeant had been chasing the Scorpion for nine years.

"Nothing's up there," the young officer said quietly. "Place is clean as a whistle."

Of course he would clean up, Amelia thought numbly.

The older officer, who had been bent over to hear Amelia's mumbled account, straightened up, putting a hand to his back. "Look," he said in that professionally solicitous manner law officers reserve for the harmless but unbalanced, "you said yourself you were beat, had a few drinks, took a pill or something. Maybe if you get some sleep, you'll feel better in the morning."

Amelia stared straight ahead, trying not to cry. "He'll come back," she whispered.

The officers looked at one another. The younger one closed his eyes and almost imperceptibly shook his head. "No way," he mouthed silently.

"Well, if he does, we're right in the area. Here, I'll give you the number." The older one took out a pen, then looked to the doorman with an impatient gesture. The old man picked up a notepad from beside the telephone and handed it to him.

"This is the number of the station," he explained as he wrote. "Now, don't call nine-one-one unless it's a real emergency, okay? We need to keep that line open. Just call the desk, and they'll send somebody out."

"Probably us," the younger officer said with a smirk.

His partner's face remained impassive. "Got that, miss?" He removed the top sheet of paper and gave it to Amelia.

She accepted it without comment, and the policemen left.

"I'll take you up to your apartment, if you want," the doorman offered.

Amelia stood up. "No, it's all right. I'm sorry for your trouble." She walked over to the elevator in her stocking feet and pushed the "Up" button, feeling like the dunce of the world.

I should have thought of this first, Amelia thought as she picked up the phone and dialed Geneva. It would be morning there. The line rang, two bursts of faraway sound, followed by the voice of Davis Hyatt's secretary.

"This is Amelia Pierce," she said. "Please let me speak with Mr. Hyatt. It's an emergency."

"One moment, please."

Good. He's in.

She prepared what she was going to say. Be logical, no hysterics. *Yes, sir, he's struck again, but thanks to my handy-dandy, all-purpose Ginsu with the lifetime-guarantee stainless-steel blade, I'm alive and well. And still able to slice through a soft tomato.*

"Miss Pierce?" It was the secretary's voice again.

"Yes?"

"Would you mind telling me the nature of your call?"

"I'm afraid I have to talk with Mr. Hyatt personally."

There was a short pause on the Swiss end of the line. "Well, actually, he's very busy, Miss Pierce, and—"

"I told you this was an emergency!"

"—and Mr. Hyatt is having trouble placing your name," the secretary finished, unruffled.

Amelia sucked in a sharp breath. "Let me get this straight," she said finally. "He doesn't remember who I am?"

"That's right."

"But I just saw him yesterday! He brought me to the airport."

"I'm sorry, miss."

"There must be some mistake—"

"Perhaps if you wrote to Mr. Hyatt, he would respond."

Across the wire, Amelia heard another line ringing on the secretary's desk. "Good-bye."

"Wait!"

The connection was broken.

Slowly, her mind reeling, Amelia looked around the room. What was that all about? She had a momentary vision of herself as a character in *The Twilight Zone*, a television woman sitting in a black-and-white world inside a little electronic box, wondering why a man she had spoken with just hours before now failed to remember her name.

If it were *The Twilight Zone*, she reasoned with an insane logic, it would be because she had been propelled into a different space/time continuum, and the man who was Davis Hyatt in her former world had been transformed into, say, the garbage man, or the guy who watered the plants in the Hyatt Wire Service offices . . .

Yes, that makes sense, she thought cynically.

The fact was, Davis Hyatt didn't *want* to know her. She had come unbidden into his secret little sphere, and now that he'd gotten rid of her, he wanted her to stay out of his life.

As for the Scorpion, he was no longer of immediate interest to the organization. Hyatt had the notebook, and the plan to poison the water had been scrapped. Case closed.

Uh, just one hitch boss, Amelia thought. *The guy is still trying to kill me.*

Well, hang it all, you silly twit, you can't have everything, can you? Unfortunately, your death is of no immediate interest to the organization, either. Chin up and tallyho. See you in the morgue, Amelia old girl.

She was alone.

All bets are off, you bastard, she thought. *If you won't help me, fine. But I'll be damned if I'm going to lie down and die quietly.*

She checked the time. Three thirty. She wouldn't be able to do much until eight o'clock. Armed with a paper and pencil, she took out the telephone directory and wrote down the addresses of the *Times,* the *Post,* and the *Daily News.*

She would go to them and tell them everything: about the organization, the plot to poison the country's water supply, the Scorpion . . . The secrets would be out at last. All of them.

Being visible was her only possible protection. What she was planning would be a long shot, admittedly, but the killer who was after her might not be so quick to strike again if Amelia's face and name were known to the public.

Go ahead, Scorpion, take your shot. And smile, because twenty million people are going to be watching.

If the press believed her.

She undressed and went to bed, but could not fall asleep. *Would* anyone believe her? She swallowed, tasting a sudden sourness in her mouth. She had no proof to give the newspapers, not a shred of physical evidence.

No, she told herself as she forced her eyes closed. Someone would listen to her. Someone, somewhere, would believe her.

Someone had to.

It was her only chance to stay alive.

An ocean away, Davis Hyatt entered the thirtieth-floor room in St. Elizabeth's Hospital.

"Hello, Timothy," he said quietly.

The sunlight streamed through the slatted blinds, illuminating the patient's face. The young man did not squint or try to shield his eyes.

"Damn nurses," Hyatt said, closing the blinds. "Is that better?" He was answered by the rhythmic beep of the monitor above the patient's bed.

Slowly, lugubriously, Hyatt sat down on the bed beside

him. The sheets pulled taut around Timothy's wasted legs.

"I've come to give you something, Timmy." He lifted the patient's hand and held it. It was so fragile, its blue veins and knobby bones almost birdlike.

Hyatt slipped a ring off his finger and held it up for the unfocused eyes to see.

"It was my father's," he said. "Cambridge. I went there, too, but I never got my own ring. Odd, that. I suppose Father's things were always more special to me. He was a better man than I am." He squeezed the emaciated hand. "But you've heard all that before."

Hyatt took a handkerchief out of his pocket and wiped his nose. "I'd like you to have it." He laughed suddenly, ignoring the tears that spilled over his cheeks. "I suppose it isn't very sentimental, my father's school ring. But I have nothing else. No photograph albums, no romantic treasures. My work . . . my work does not encourage hoarding. It would make me too vulnerable."

He held the bony, weightless hand like an anchor while he shook with sobs.

Finally, he quieted. He wiped his face. He blew his nose. "The ring's for you. If I could have had a son, I would have wished him to be you."

He slid the ring on the young man's finger. It was far too big, so Hyatt closed Tim's hand into a fist.

The monitor beeped. The patient stared at nothing.

Hyatt rubbed a knuckle across his eyes, then took something from the pocket of his suit jacket: a hypodermic syringe, capped and filled with liquid.

"I'm sending you home, Timmy," he said quietly.

He leaned over the young man and eased the needle into the vein in his arm. The skin was already bruised and filled with needle marks, the result of months of hospital care. When the syringe was empty, Hyatt put it back in his pocket, extracted another just like it, and repeated the procedure.

Tim's eyes rolled back in his head. The monitor slowed. Slowed . . . then stopped.

"Good-bye, my fancy," Hyatt whispered.

He placed the young man's fist with its oversized ring on top of his sunken, still chest. Then he stood up and closed Tim's eyes.

A nurse ran in and grabbed the patient's wrist.

"Don't," Hyatt said. "He went quietly."

"Sir . . ."

Hyatt didn't hear what she was saying. He shuffled down the polished hallway, knowing that he had lived too long.

25

PLOT TO POISON AMERICA'S WATER?
NYC Woman Claims Secret Government Organization
Gave Her Arab Terrorist's Plans

It was a small article toward the back of a tabloid, nestled between a fuzzy photograph of a Bolivian flying saucer and an astrology column.

The story had very little substance. The Network was not mentioned by name. Neither was Davis Hyatt, Wade Turner, or Burt Sergeant. The American woman had chosen, apparently, to talk only about the mysterious coded notebook written by the inmate doctor and the horrible murder of his widow by a man identified as the Scorpion.

The man with no name folded the newspaper to conceal the story. He placed it on his seat, beside the attaché case he had just purchased. Absently, he pushed a half-eaten order of french-fried potatoes toward Yusef Nassif. He found their odor offensive.

They were in a small Brooklyn restaurant, a busy, dirty place with wooden booths and stained-glass light fixtures.

At six o'clock, the long bar was packed four deep with young men in suits, drinking beer and shouting above the din of rock music.

Nassif leaned forward. "It is useless," he said.

His partner shrugged in annoyance. *"Niemand sich glauben."*

"Speak English," Nassif ordered, somewhat alarmed by his protégé's use of German here. It was not the appropriate language, either for the location or the circumstance. Besides, he knew that Nassif didn't speak German.

"No one will believe her," the man with no name translated without hesitation. "Obviously no one has, or the story would not have been printed in this cartoon of a newspaper."

Nassif shook his head. "No. Too much has gone wrong. We cannot take the risk. You will come back with me today. I have made the arrangements."

The man with no name was silent. Like a machine, he was programmed for a specific task, unable to contemplate an alternative.

"Do you understand, Daniel?"

Daniel was the key. When he had an especially important message to deliver, a dictum that had to be followed, Nassif called him Daniel.

It was a special name for the boy, the one his mother had used. She had been punished for using it; Nassif and the others had planned to create a being with no sense of itself. But the woman had slipped on several occasions, calling her son by a name she remembered from her past. It had been her father's name, or her brother's. Usually the drugs to which she was addicted were enough to numb her memory. But sometimes, when she saw the little blond boy, she had wanted to hold him. And when she could not, she reached out to him with her voice.

"Daniel," she called softly. "Daniel, my baby, I won't let them hurt us. I know what they're trying to do to me, but I won't let them. I'll hold out for you, Daniel . . . as long as I can."

She had been dosed then, a shot of heroin mixed with a

little camphor so that it would burn in her bloodstream. She had screamed and bucked with the pain, and Billy Starr had gone to her, excited by the woman's uncontrollable contortions. And once in a while, before the heroin had a chance to work, she would call out the boy's name: *"Daniel! my baby . . ."*

It was a name that had not been permitted. The boy had been treated with the respect due a king—the experiment was meant to create a finely tuned killing instrument, the Stradivarius of killers, not a thug—but without a title. The boy would grow up to become anyone he chose. *Become,* truly, in his heart. And then un-become, at will. He was to be an intelligent, educated, loyal operative, utterly without scruples and possessing no identity, even to himself.

His father, of course, had spoiled things somewhat by murdering the boy's mother in front of him. Not by the killing, actually; killing was, after all, to be the central focus of the boy's adult life. But he had been unprepared for what he had seen. The boy had been only two years old. After the incident, he had stayed awake nights calling his own name.

"Daniel . . . Daniel . . ."

Often, Nassif thought, Billy Starr had been more trouble than he was worth. No one should have told him about the boy in the first place. The baby could have been removed, reported dead.

He sighed. It was too late for regrets now. That the boy suddenly began speaking in German was not a good sign, but perhaps with some rest, that kink in his personality could be ironed out. Things had been difficult for him lately. His father had been killed, and he had failed to eliminate the girl. The entire mission, Nassif reflected sadly, had in fact failed utterly. The operative sent to the hospital in Geneva was dead, and Nassif himself had suffered a nasty blow on his forehead when that stupid American woman had caused the car to crash on Santa Vittoria.

Nevertheless, he had to protect the boy. This had been the maiden voyage of a delicate and complex vessel, and had been planned more to test the boy than to carry out the mission. The idea of poisoning the population of the United

States was, after all, rather grandiose, and could wait for another day. But the operative had to be spared, recalled, adjusted.

That wasn't your directive, though, was it?

Nassif blinked. His orders, naturally, had been to kill the boy if anything went badly wrong.

But this wasn't some mutant freak who had to be destroyed to keep Nassif and his people safe. Daniel was a human being, a young man with a life, a small boy who had seen his father savagely murder his mother.

"Daniel, do you hear me?" he asked softly. He knew that the din of the music and the loud voices at the bar would not distract the boy. Distraction had been trained out of him.

"Yes," he answered. *"Ja."*

"Daniel . . ."

"Oui. Si. Hai."

Nassif turned his face to the wall. *I must be able to take him back!*

"This is over now," he said, having regained his composure.

"No, it's not," the blond man said, his voice as calm and mellifluous as the artificial, accentless voices programmed into computers. "It can't be over until I've finished my work."

"That has changed." Nassif tried to make the tone of his voice as calm as the other's. "We will go back. You need not even kill the Pierce woman."

"Amelia," he said, suddenly smiling. "That's the name she's using now."

Nassif frowned in confusion. "Now?" He shook his head rapidly. "No, no. That *is* her name, Daniel. Her real name."

The young man's eyes were indulgent. "Uncle, you never understood." He leaned forward and whispered conspiratorially, "It's *her*. My mother."

Nassif opened his mouth in outrage. "Daniel, your mother is dead."

"No." He clapped his hand over Nassif's. "I'm sure. I have proof. Look."

He took something out of his pocket and placed it lovingly on the table. It was a half-used bottle of cologne.

"What is that?"

The young man smiled shyly. "Her scent. She saved it for me."

Nassif breathed deeply. "Daniel, this is an ordinary bottle of cologne. One can buy it anywhere."

"No!" The light eyes blazed. "It's *hers*. She left it for me, so that I would recognize her."

"What?" How far astray had the boy's mind gone?

"She came back for me." His eyes shone.

Nassif felt a deep sadness spreading in his heart.

"She loved me, you know. My name was the last sound she made . . . 'Daniel.' I've remembered that. He was killing her. He stuck the knife in her heart."

His eyes spilled over with tears. "There was a lot of blood. But she looked at me. She knew she was going to die. She said 'Daniel'—"

"Stop this!" Nassif's voice was hoarse. "These . . . these memories can do you no good. You need care. We will go back to Rabta, to the desert. We will start again, make your mind strong—"

"No!" The blond man's eyes were wide with fear. "I won't let you unmake me again."

"Daniel—"

"Yes! My name is Daniel!" He rose to his feet and wiped the tears from his face. He was shouting. A few of the people at the bar turned to glance at him. "My name is Daniel, and I have a mother!"

"Good for you, Dan," one of the men at the bar said.

"I'll drink to that," chimed in another.

" 'M is for the million things she gave me,' " a voice sang, attempting an imitation of Al Jolson.

The blond man froze, his eyes darting around like loose marbles.

"Daniel, listen to me. *Listen* to me!" Nassif whispered frantically. He touched the man's hand. It was jerked away as if Nassif had branded it with a burning poker. The blond man's nostrils flared.

He's going to kill everyone here, Nassif thought, panicking.

It was time. This was twenty years of his life gone, but it was time.

"I've brought you a gift," Nassif said softly, managing a smile.

Daniel looked down with an exaggerated, almost comical expression of suspicion.

"Here it is. Look." Slowly, with infinite care, Nassif took a silver flask from his jacket. He smiled again. "You see? It's like your father's, Daniel. Just like his. It's yours now."

For a minute or more, the blond man stared at the shiny flask without moving. Finally he blinked. "What's in it?"

"Whiskey. Your father always drank whiskey."

"Whiskey is an evil."

"Only for Moslems. Some find it most refreshing. Some even claim it brings them happiness."

The blond man sat down slowly and took the flask from Nassif's hand. "Like the giant's," he said. His blue eyes welled with tears again.

"I . . . I hope you like it," Nassif said.

The blond man nodded. He opened his jacket and placed the flask inside, along with the bottle of cologne. Then, almost in the same movement, he drew an RMP Single Shot with a silencer attached and slipped it under the table.

Nassif opened his mouth to speak. His hands were spread out in front of him, as if attempting to ward off the bullet with his flesh. The shot fired, the sound drowned in the noise and the voices and the music.

Nassif slumped over, his head striking the table beside his plate. A french fry, covered with catsup, spilled over the side and adhered to his forehead.

Quietly, without a trace of emotion, the man with no name put the weapon back in his jacket, stood up, and walked away.

26

The appearance of the "news" story in the *Daily Mirror* did result in some attention for Amelia. She lost her job.

She had called in on Wednesday morning before going to the newspapers. Her boss, a beautiful, ambitious woman with the undoubtedly fabricated name of Villia St. John, had accepted the call with cold impatience.

"Look, if you wanted a little extra time off, you could have asked for it," she said. Villia had attained the office of company CEO before her fortieth birthday, and she hadn't done it, as she often boasted to the other members of the Young President's Club, by being a crying towel for her employees.

"I know," Amelia said patiently. "It couldn't be helped. I'll explain what's happened when I see you. I can come in today."

"Make it Monday. It'll make bookkeeping easier."

She's going to dock me for the extra week, Amelia thought in amazement. A senior editor, docked like an unreliable mail boy. She guessed it was supposed to teach her humility.

It also told her that she was out of favor, and when an

editor fell out of favor with the head honcho, the editor had better be prepared to meet the moving men when they came to take the paintings from her office.

The story appeared on Friday. Amelia nearly wept when she read it. The lead paragraph read:

> A New York City woman claims to have inside knowledge of an Arab plot to poison the water supply of the U.S.—but nobody will believe her!

It ended with tips on how *you* can be sure *your* water isn't tainted, including making a call to the State Health Department to arrange for a coliform bacteria test.

She hadn't even wanted to mention the part about the Libyan poison-water scheme. She had never quite believed it herself, despite the fuss over Sebastapol's notebook. At best, she had reasoned, the doctor had extrapolated a wild theory based on what little information a prisoner might hear from careless guards. At worst—and she had increasingly come to believe this version—the old man's brain had sprung somewhere between torture, nutritional deprivation, and age.

She had met several senile people. Often they remembered nearly insignificant events that had occurred sixty years before, although they could not remember something that was said within the past five minutes. Would it have been so different for a man who had spent ten years inside prisons, living in unspeakable conditions, to have invented human demons? He may have remembered the finest details of a complex code without having much of a grip on reality. Or caring to. The notebook may have been Sebastapol's hobby. For all anyone knew, it may have been a novel, written in a secret language so that the prison authorities would allow him to keep his toy.

It was the other things that concerned Amelia: the viral experiments on the prisoners in El Mirado, the murder of her father, mother, Marla Sebastapol and her maid, and, most prominent, the repeated attempts on Amelia's own life by a psychotic killer . . . still on the loose.

But the *Daily Mirror* hadn't seen things that way.

She had gone to the *Times* first. On the strength of her credentials, she had been introduced to the news editor himself. He had listened attentively while Amelia told about the death of her father, another newspaper man. The editor had even recognized Arthur Pierce's name. And he had listened when she'd related the incidents beginning with her escape from Santa Vittoria to the attempted murder in the hospital in Geneva, and finally to the terrifying encounter in her apartment.

While she spoke, the editor made notes on a long yellow pad, frowning, asking an occasional question. When she finished, he put down his pencil.

"The man came to your apartment last night?"

Amelia nodded.

"But the police found nothing?"

"Nothing."

"Not even the knife you used to stab him with?"

She shook her head. "It was back in the kitchen drawer."

"Just a moment, please."

He called the police department.

"They say there's been no complaint made about the incident," he said, hanging up the phone.

"I didn't file one. There didn't seem to be any point. Besides," Amelia said, "I thought Davis Hyatt would be better equipped to take care of things. You can't mention his name in the story, of course."

The news editor set down the pencil. "Why not?"

"The publicity would place his life in jeopardy. Hyatt's not my favorite person, but I wouldn't want him or anyone who works for him to die because of this. Besides, I gave him my word not to talk."

"Then why come to me with the story in the first place?"

"To keep myself alive," Amelia said. "This is the only thing I can think of that might scare the killer away."

The editor looked down at his notes and made a face. The story was souring on him. "I don't know," he said. "Without any names, there's not much real information here. And there's no evidence."

"What about the fire at the fort? And the murders?"

"There could be other explanations for those occurrences, Miss Pierce."

"And the notebook?" she went on doggedly. "I transcribed the cipher myself."

"Where is the transcription?"

She hung her head. "Hyatt's got it."

He tapped his pencil on the notepad. "Mind if I call Davis Hyatt to verify? I'll tell him we'd keep his name out of the story."

Amelia felt the muscles in her face tighten. "I tried calling him. He told his secretary he had never heard of me."

The editor pushed the yellow pad away. "It won't go," he said.

"But I'm telling the truth. I swear it."

"That's not the question. I can't run this story with no evidence. You understand." He smiled at her perfunctorily, his eyes seeking out a subordinate who would escort the Crazy Lady of the Week outside.

It had been the same with the other two daily papers. A sympathetic young man from the *Daily News* had actually called Davis Hyatt. He was told that Mr. Hyatt was unacquainted with any Amelia Pierce but that an American woman by that name had been pestering him on the telephone.

Undaunted and smelling a good story, the young editor had asked to be connected to the wire service morgue. He tried to verify the story of Marla Sebastapol's murder.

There was no story.

"Hyatt stopped it," Amelia said quietly.

The editor looked at her with barely concealed disgust. His expression seemed to say, *You were better than most, missy. I almost got taken in this time.* "Why would he do that?" he asked flatly.

"I don't know."

A nut is a nut.

"Well, thanks for your time, Miss . . . uh . . . "

"I'll find my own way out," Amelia said.

Finally, in desperation, she had gone to the *Mirror*. It was a rag, one of those papers that could no longer legally be classified as a newspaper, filled as it was with rumor, speculation, and outright falsehood. But people read it. One hundred seventy thousand people a day. People who might be able to stop the Scorpion from killing Amelia Pierce.

And they *did* listen to crazies. They listened to her.

The story ran on Friday. On Monday, when Amelia walked into the offices of Marquis Books, her secretary was waiting with a memo headed "From the Office of the President," with *Villia St. John* beneath it in neat italics. It had been delivered on Friday evening, after Villia's secretary had brought her a copy of the *Mirror,* which had slowly made its way through every office and cubbyhole in the company.

The memo requested Amelia's presence the first thing in the morning, which meant that she was expected to wait outside Villia's office until the woman deigned to see her. More humiliation.

"Thank you, Jody," Amelia said noncommittally to her secretary. "Anything else?"

Jody shook her head. "Welcome back." Her voice was subdued.

Jody was one of those bright, earnest girls who run to the New York publishing scene as soon as they get their degree from Radcliffe or Columbia, willing to work as secretaries—under the title of "editorial assistant"—for a salary any real secretary would regard as a joke.

Amelia had been an E.A. herself once. Seven years later, she occupied the office that had formerly belonged to her boss. Ever since, Amelia had been chary of the bright young things who sat outside her office answering the phones and reading the files.

She felt herself blushing. Who was she kidding? Jody knew as well as she did that the ax was falling.

"I guess this is about the story in the paper," she said, trying a weak smile.

Jody nodded wanly. "The Queen Bee called in an editor

from Doubleday Friday afternoon. She brought him over here to introduce me to him."

"Not good," Amelia said.

"I'll say. He asked me if I took shorthand." She cast a baleful glance at Amelia.

Amelia laughed in spite of herself. "That's the biz," she said.

She hung up her coat in her office and took a look around. A last look, she thought. Things had changed so radically in such a short time. Two weeks ago she had been, however technically, someone's wife, someone's daughter, someone's employee. Now she belonged to no one, belonged nowhere. Her entire life had been wiped away, as if it had been colored with washable crayons. Even Burt Sergeant was gone, and Marla. The only things left on the colorless, nightmare landscape of her new life were herself . . . and a nameless killer lurking somewhere behind her.

"Brought you some coffee," Jody said, placing a cup in front of Amelia. It was the first time in the two years Jody had been working there that she'd served Amelia coffee.

"Thanks," Amelia said.

Jody lingered for a moment at the door. "Did all that really happen?" she asked quietly.

"It doesn't seem to matter much whether it did or not," Amelia sighed. "No one believes me anyway."

Jody smiled sadly. "Good luck, Amelia."

There was little point in working through the rest of the day after Villia St. John informed her that a long rest was in order. A long rest away from Marquis Books. And every other publishing house in New York, she might as well have added, since the story about the yuppie editor in the final stages of burnout had undoubtedly already swept through the industry.

Amelia packed her personal belongings into a box requisitioned from Supply and walked home.

Davis Hyatt was waiting for her.

"I take it this is supposed to be a pleasant surprise," Amelia said.

"It was the best I could do." He offered to carry the box for her, but she refused.

They got on the elevator together. "The people in your office informed me that you'd be on your way home."

A wooden giraffe's head poked out from the box. It embarrassed Amelia. People didn't carry knickknacks and framed photographs home from the office in the middle of the day unless they'd been canned.

"Well, they were right," she said sullenly.

Inside the apartment, Hyatt settled himself into a chair and lit a cigar while she busied herself unloading the box, trying to ignore him.

"Are you curious about why I've come?" he asked.

"I'd like to think it was because I called you when my life was in danger. But that wouldn't be very realistic, would it?" She snatched the cigar out of his mouth. "And by the way, I hate these things." She opened a window and threw it out.

Then she poured herself a cup of cold morning coffee and reheated it in the microwave. "No, my guess is that you're here because of the story in the *Mirror*. Right?"

Hyatt smiled thinly.

"Or have you come to kill me?" Amelia sat cross-legged on the sofa opposite him and sipped her coffee. "That's what you threatened to do if I talked, isn't it?"

"Your story was laughable. No one believes you."

"Maybe not. But if I turn up dead, someone may. The right people might start asking the right questions, and the answers would lead straight to you."

Hyatt sighed. "None of that matters now. The Network has been compromised."

"What was I supposed to do? You wouldn't even take my phone call!"

"My dear Miss Pierce—"

"Don't patronize me. Your damned Scorpion attacked me in my apartment the night I got back to New York. And you wouldn't lift a finger to help me. Do you want to know what I think?"

"I can hardly wait to hear," Hyatt said.

"I think you sent me back here to set me up. You knew that maniac would come after me again, and you used me as bait."

"My, my. That would have made an exciting news story, wouldn't it? Pity you didn't think of it at the time."

"Get out."

"You're really quite pathetic, you know. By the way," Hyatt laughed, "if I *had* set you up for the Scorpion, your beloved Burt Sergeant most certainly would have known about it. He was the one who encouraged you to come to New York, as you will recall."

His words stung Amelia. The thought that Sergeant might have agreed to sacrifice her for the Scorpion had nagged at the back of her mind, but she had forced it away.

"The Scorpion has been Sergeant's obsession for the past decade. Do you really think he would give up the chance to catch this killer just to spare some silly woman who'd once satisfied a carnal itch—"

"You've made your point," Amelia snapped.

The doorbell rang. Amelia started for it, but Hyatt moved quickly to his feet and grabbed her arm.

"Actually, Sergeant never knew," he said with an indulgent smile.

"What?"

He opened the door.

Wade Turner walked in.

"Hello, Amelia," Turner said, drawing a gun. "Ready for me?"

Amelia felt a sickening rush of adrenalin shoot through her. She backed away, her hands shaking.

"There, there," Hyatt said smoothly. "This isn't really such a surprise, is it?"

"You were in on it all along," Amelia whispered. "You're one of them."

"No," Hyatt said, his face resigned. "But it would serve no purpose to defend myself to you." He motioned to Turner. "Kill her."

Before Amelia could move, before she could even react, Turner fired directly at her.

She saw the small orange spark in the gun's barrel, then felt a pinprick in her thigh a fraction of a second before she heard the muffled pop of the report.

My leg, she remembered thinking. *He aimed for my leg.*

And what she felt hadn't been a bullet, either. It was more like a bee sting, really, although her legs buckled under her almost instantly, and her brain felt as if it were filling fast with cotton candy, or the foam insulation that carpenters pumped into the walls of a new house.

While she was losing consciousness, the scene in front of her unfolded with unbearable slowness: Hyatt, turning away as Turner shot her, taking a step toward the door; then Turner, shifting balance as gracefully as a dancer, firing a second shot into Hyatt's back.

There was no blood. From what Amelia could see from her wooden, indifferent observation, the bullet had not even produced a hole. But then, she thought, she hadn't taken a bullet, either. It was just another bee sting, and the bee itself was now hanging from Hyatt's back, a tiny, slender thing . . .

A dart, she thought with amazement. Hyatt was lumbering around the room in a drunken semicircle, like some kind of drugged beast. His mouth was formed into a perfect, silent O, as if he were singing a note so high that the human ear could not hear it.

Then Turner pocketed the gun and slid a knife out from his jacket in the same movement. The blade glinted briefly as he held it above his head, nearly touching the overhead light in Amelia's low-ceilinged apartment. Turner's face was blank, but in his eyes there was a passion she would have found terrifying under other circumstances. As it was, she merely watched, like an unmanned, slow-motion camera recording the birth of an insect, or the opening of a flower, as Turner swung the blade at arm's length, cutting a neat, straight red line across Davis Hyatt's throat.

The blood poured out of the wound like water from a dam breaking. It washed over her, hot and metallic-smelling, and spattered Turner's face as well. Unconsciously, Turner's tongue darted out, licking a droplet of blood beside his mouth, and retreated.

Amelia's arms raised slightly, as if to protest, but by that time her brain was too numb from the drug inside the needle in her leg for her to feel anything. It was the last sight she remembered: Turner licking blood off his own face.

He was dying. He could feel the blood bubbling into his throat. Trying to suck in air was noisy, futile, like trying to breathe underwater from an exhausted air tank. He knew he had only moments left.

Slowly Davis Hyatt dragged himself across the white rug to the small end table where he had seen the telephone.

It had all gone bad. The Network had been hopelessly compromised. There would be no one now to stop the horror that he himself, in his foolishness, had helped to bring about.

But even though he had lived like a fool, he could die like a brave man. His eyes were clouding over now, and he yanked the telephone cord to bring the instrument down to the floor next to him. He pulled the telephone base close to his face so he could see the numbers, then reached out a trembling hand.

Slowly, carefully, because he would have no second chance, Davis Hyatt punched in the digits of the international telephone number.

For a long, agonizing second there was no sound. Had he misdialed? Had he not remembered the correct number? Then he heard the phone buzz—just once—before the line went dead.

Hyatt lay down his head. The special telephone hookup would now ring forever until Burt Sergeant answered it.

He had failed; his work was finished.

It no longer mattered if he lived or died . . . and this time he preferred death.

27

Burt Sergeant sat at his desk staring at the clean windowsill. For years he had not been able to see out that window because of the files and paperwork piled in front of it.

There had rested all the information known to man on Billy Starr, the man Sergeant had come to know as the Scorpion: his military papers, the small black-and-white photo of Starr as a teenager, the Arkansas police reports on the unsolved murder/mutilations of his mother and sister, the sixty-six glossies of his early kills, and all of Sergeant's research notes.

All of it was gone now. The Scorpion case was closed.

A flash of anger swept through Sergeant. *How could the case be closed?* Sergeant asked himself this for the thousandth time. In the past ten days there had been four killings—no, five. Word had come in about a Viennese prostitute found ripped apart, her left ear placed carefully in her mouth. Five killings, each one announcing the work of Billy Starr.

And yet Hyatt had closed the case.

And there was the matter of Amelia having been attacked

again. She had sworn that the man who broke into her New York apartment was the same man who had tried to kill her in Vienna. Hyatt himself had shown Sergeant the interview in the *Daily Mirror.*

As soon as he'd read it, Sergeant had volunteered to go to New York.

"Mr. Sergeant, you are the last individual on the planet I would consider sending," Hyatt had said. "Your participation in this matter is finished. The matter itself is finished, as far as I'm concerned."

"How can you say that?" Sergeant asked, stunned. "Billy Starr was in Amelia's apartment!"

"Someone was in her apartment." Hyatt raised an eyebrow. "Maybe. If she's telling the truth. Which I wouldn't count on." There was a long pause. "She lives in New York, Sergeant. Having one's apartment broken into is a routine part of life in that city. Besides, if it were Starr, he would have killed her, don't you think? For God's sake, she claims the man has already made four attempts on her life. Now, finally, when he has her at knife point in her apartment, he decides to use *chloroform?* What for, to pierce her ear before he cuts it off? Really, Sergeant, even in your delusionary state, you must realize that this was not the same man."

Sergeant had to agree. More than a hundred murders, all of them performed in the same ritualistic style. Amelia's attacker had had to be someone else.

And yet she had said that she recognized the man.

"I'll see her out of deference to you," Hyatt said at last. "I have some business in New York, anyway. I'll check on her. If there's any real danger, I'll set her up in a safe house. We have agents working in New York."

Sergeant had nodded and thanked Hyatt.

Yet, he had not felt easy. He still did not.

Hyatt had never asked Amelia to identify Turner, or even to describe him. Turner had apparently called in his reports, and Hyatt had simply accepted them, while rejecting Amelia's version of things altogether. Turner had been in the vicinity of each of the five recent murders. Near enough to see the Scorpion—or so he reported—but not near enough to stop him.

At the very least, Wade Turner was an incompetent agent; yet Hyatt had never spoken of replacing him.

And Amelia . . . Amelia swore she had killed the Scorpion.

Sergeant shook his head. The thoughts that were beginning to dance around in the corners of his mind were unthinkable.

Davis Hyatt could not possibly be involved with the murders. Hyatt was perhaps the most trusted man in the world. The greatest nations on earth entrusted their secrets to him.

And if Hyatt decided to sell out to the highest bidder, he could single-handedly bring about World War III.

That was absurd. There were reins on Hyatt, fail-safes to make sure that he could not use the Network for his own ends.

Hyatt had a boss, for one thing: the liaison between himself and the member nations of the Network. He had never told Sergeant who that man was, but it was probably of no real importance. He was most likely some ancient bureaucrat from a neutral nation who remained in office year after year, without fear of losing his job in an election. The fellow would probably have little to do except for attending social functions.

And one other job. Through Hyatt, he ensured that the Network maintained its secrecy. Were that secrecy ever breached, this unknown man would issue the order to kill Davis Hyatt, and then he would oversee the destruction of the Network.

Sergeant had guessed better than he knew. In fact, it had been one of the first procedures decided on by the secret committee of intelligence services that had developed the Network: planning for its demise.

The organization was a wild experiment, a stopgap measure instituted out of desperation. From the beginning, it had been decided that one man would run it, and that his death would signal its end.

The rationale had been that in the event of Davis Hyatt's

death—through accident or illness or assassination—the Network would suffer no public exposure. The essential thing was that its existence be kept secret, because the secrecy was its entire power. To protect that secrecy, the running of the Hyatt News Service had been turned over to others so that Hyatt was free to handle nothing but the inner workings of the Network.

To outsiders, Hyatt gave the impression of a man who'd been "kicked upstairs" to a large, plush penthouse office far removed from the daily operations of a flourishing business.

The office itself was a fortress, fortified with asbestos-lined walls, and sealed virtually airtight. The very air Hyatt breathed was rarified, pumped in through special heating and air-conditioning ducts.

It was all in preparation for Hyatt's death. After the order was given to disband the Network, it would be Burt Sergeant's duty to set fire to the room and then leave by the back door, which would seal fire-tight behind him.

At that moment, the Network would cease to ever have existed. And it all revolved around Davis Hyatt's death.

My suspicion alone could kill him, Sergeant thought, feeling his stomach churn.

A memo from Sergeant bringing Hyatt's loyalty into question would no doubt be enough to break the fragile thread of trust that tied Davis Hyatt to the Network. Any of the member nations dissatisfied with any aspect of the organization could eliminate it simply by killing Hyatt. An unprotected man, unarmed and lacking physical strength . . . It would be the easiest assignment any operative familiar with wetwork had ever drawn.

You're thinking like an assassin, Sergeant thought with disgust.

All right, he told himself. Hyatt hadn't conducted the matter with Amelia Pierce in a manner Sergeant approved of, but did that mean anything more than a difference in how the two men looked at things?

He answered himself reluctantly. *Yes.*

Hyatt's lack of concern for Amelia was beyond any normal cold-bloodedness necessary to the man's job. He had wanted to kill her right from the beginning. And now, after a spate of murders with the Scorpion's mark all over them, with the possibility that the Libyans were about to launch a germ-warfare attack on the United States, Hyatt closed the case.

It didn't make sense.

Unless one were willing to entertain the notion that Davis Hyatt was helping the terrorists.

Sergeant breathed deeply. No, he wasn't willing. Not that far. Hyatt had bailed Burt Sergeant out of a suicidal depression. He had given him work and another chance at life.

Why did Hyatt pick you? a voice inside him asked.

Sergeant's predecessor had been a Hungarian named Pavel Malocsay. After Malocsay's death from a sudden heart attack, another agent from the Eastern Bloc should have been selected. He could not imagine the Russians, particularly in the cold-war years before glasnost, agreeing to two CIA-trained men running the Network.

It had been a question in the back of his mind ever since he had started working for Hyatt. Like most questions Sergeant asked himself during those days, it was left unanswered and eventually forgotten. But the answer came now, clear and indisputable.

He never told them that the assistant named Malocsay had died.

He never told them about me.

Without specific information about the Hungarian's identity and position delivered to Hyatt's unknown superior, no one among the handful of spymasters who had organized the Network would have any inkling of Malocsay's death. The Network, without reporting, with no tangible hierarchy, was a labyrinth in which anything could get lost. An employee. A notebook. A case. A terrorist.

For the first time, Sergeant entertained the possibility that he had been hired not in spite of his mental instability, but because of it. A man who had been ready to end his own life would not be likely to pay much attention to whether or not his boss performed his job well.

And in truth, he hadn't cared. Not until now.

Was Davis Hyatt a traitor? A traitor not to one nation or one ideology, but to the cause of peace in general?

The thought made Sergeant so angry that he snapped a pencil between his fingers. It was idiotic, insane. Hyatt certainly wasn't a terrorist, nor did he side with terrorists. Even though he had been born into a life of luxury, he wasn't one of those radically guilt-ridden rich boys. Those types invariably went the way of Moscow, anyway, not of random Molotov cocktails at airports.

Still, Sergeant thought, the Scorpion had come so near . . . and Hyatt had let him slip away. He had not allowed Sergeant to stay in Vienna. And now, now when Billy Starr could finally be pinpointed and trapped, Hyatt had closed the case.

Billy Starr had vanished once again.

Wasn't that what Hyatt had really wanted right from the start?

And why was the man so intent on protecting Wade Turner?

Who was Wade Turner, anyway?

Sergeant had to collect himself. What he was formulating was no less than a monstrous accusation against a man who would be killed because of that accusation. There would be no trial for Hyatt; he would not even have the luxury of explaining to the invisible powers above him. The accusation would be the conviction, and the sentence would be death.

Hyatt had accepted the job fully aware of its dangers. He had relinquished his family's business and the possibility of doubling his fortune with it. He had accepted without question a life of monklike solitude in order to guard the secret with which he had been entrusted. There had to be another explanation for Hyatt's actions. Had to be.

Sergeant shook his head. He was not good at examining people's unspoken motives. Hell, he thought with some irony, he didn't even know if he had cut his own throat or not.

All he knew was that his boss was behaving very strangely. To call off the investigation, and then fly to New York to see Amelia . . .

Sergeant felt a shiver of alarm. Had Hyatt gone to kill her himself? Because of the story in the tabloid?

Impossible, he told himself. There was no point in killing Amelia. The piece in the *Daily Mirror* was so vague that no one was really implicated. It had been no more than a frightened woman's cry for help.

Maybe it hadn't been the Scorpion in her apartment after all. Maybe Amelia had come so unglued over the events since her parents' death that she was seeing ghosts.

Bullshit. She isn't crazy, and you know it.

Suddenly he felt very uncomfortable.

You're the crazy one, remember? So crazy that you refused to believe the one person who was telling you the truth.

Sergeant's fear deepened. He had never been able to accept Amelia's stubborn story that she had killed the man who had murdered her parents. He had not believed her because he had not wanted to believe her. His obsession with killing the Scorpion had blinded him to any other possibility.

But what if Amelia *had* killed Billy Starr? What if the Scorpion had been replaced?

It would be someone new, then, someone young. Someone who had inherited the Scorpion's legacy of death.

Someone in the Network itself, he thought with horror.

Oh, God, no. He felt nauseated.

Wade Turner.

Wade Turner had been entrusted with the Scorpion's mission. He had been on Santa Vittoria while the virus was tested on the inmates at El Mirador. He had tried to kill everyone with even the slightest knowledge of that virus. And he was undoubtedly in possession of it now.

All with the full knowledge of Davis Hyatt.

Amelia had known. She had told the truth every step of the way. For her truth, now, she too would be killed.

Sergeant had to help her somehow, even if it meant killing Hyatt himself and disbanding the Network.

And dying himself, for that would surely follow.

If the Network ceased to operate, Sergeant—Hyatt's right-hand man, who knew all the Network's secrets—

would never be allowed to live. Wherever he fled, the wet-work boys would find him . . . sooner or later.

The sudden ring of a telephone almost caused Sergeant to jump out of his chair. "Yes," he answered hoarsely.

A voice came over the line. It was a computer-generated voice, barely recognizable as human: "Please give your security identification number."

Sergeant looked around. It had been so long since he'd received the number that he had forgotten where it was kept. He set the phone down shakily and went to the file cabinet.

Davis Hyatt had given him the number soon after the Hungarian assistant had dropped dead. "Keep this in a safe place," he had said. "You may have to use it one day."

"For what?"

"One of Mr. Malocsay's duties was to set fire to my office," Hyatt said. "To physically destroy the Network."

Sergeant had blinked uncomprehendingly.

"He never had to discharge that particular duty," Hyatt continued. "But you may have to."

"But . . . why do I need this number for that?"

Hyatt had smiled enigmatically. "Because you won't be receiving those instructions from me. The number will identify you as my second-in-command."

Sergeant understood then. But now, when it was finally happening, he found himself woefully unprepared.

He pulled a sheet of paper out of the Procedures file. It contained only a five-digit number. There was no heading on the sheet, no means of identifying the number's purpose.

"Eight-six-one-seven-two," Sergeant said into the receiver.

There was a series of electronic clicks, followed by a long, low buzz. When the sound ended, the synthetic voice spoke again.

"Mr. Malocsay, this is an electronic message to inform you that your superior is no longer to be considered. You are aware of the procedures you are to follow. Please carry out those procedures immediately. Disband the organization. Repeat, disband the organization. This instruction overrides all other directives."

Sergeant said nothing, gazing off across the room, the phone still to his ear. There was a pause of ten seconds, and then the voice came again.

"Mister Malocsay, this is an electronic message to inform you that your superior is no longer—"

Sergeant hung up the telephone, then stared at it in disbelief.

Davis Hyatt was dead.

The Network had ceased to exist.

28

A telephone pole grew in front of her. It stretched and inflated at incredible speed, coming straight for her. Amelia gasped in panic, but was unable to move. Even her gasp, in fact, came out as an undignified snort. She could not move her head. She felt as if she had been frozen in lead, unable even to force her lower jaw to meet its upper counterpart.

Another telephone pole raced forward and then passed by, followed by another. She was on a road. She was in a car. She was alive, she realized numbly.

The next telephone pole became, in her mind, the barrel of a gun, poised to shoot. Wade Turner had leveled it at her on Hyatt's command. Hyatt himself, ever the gentleman, had offered a small smile of apology as Turner had pulled the trigger.

And then the smile had vanished as the Scorpion slit Hyatt's throat.

Amelia wanted to scream with the memory, but she could not force her vocal mechanism to work. It was like a nightmare, in which she was trapped inside her own unresponsive body, unable to call for help, unable, even, to articulate her terror.

The car turned down an exit ramp and followed a shop-lined suburban street. Turner parked behind a jewelry store and got out. A moment later he opened the passenger door and scooped up Amelia in his arms.

She looked at him and blinked once, lazily. His face was still dotted with drops of Hyatt's blood, now turned brown. His blond hair was matted with it.

"Blood," she said. It came out sounding like "buh."

He paused by another car, still holding Amelia in his arms. The he opened the door and slid her inside.

"Don't worry," he said gently, with the hint of a smile. "Just changing cars so that no one will find us."

His eyes were glassy. He reeked of blood. Amelia tried to turn away, but her muscles did not respond. All she could do was to shut her eyes to him and will him away.

He kissed her mouth.

A feeling of revulsion welled up inside her, the first emotion she'd felt since he had shot her with the dart gun in her apartment. But Turner only smiled at her and closed the door.

God help me, she thought.

Burt Sergeant closed his eyes. Someone had killed Hyatt in New York. Who? Where? The CIA? The KGB? Wade Turner? Or had it been Amelia herself? There was no one to answer any of his questions.

This instruction overrides all other directives.

He was no longer to concern himself with Davis Hyatt. Or with Amelia Pierce. His mission was simple. He had only to torch the office and leave, forgetting everything he ever knew about the Network.

That was a joke, and he knew it. If Davis Hyatt's life was so easily expendable, would any one of those spooks in their never-never land care a whit about Hyatt's assistant? All they knew was that there was one man outside their secret enclave who knew everything about the Network . . . one man who would soon be paid a visit by the boys in wetwork.

"Pavel Malocsay," Sergeant whispered. The realization struck him like a thunderbolt.

No one knew. Whoever would be sent to mop up the remains of the Network would be looking for the dead Hungarian. For Hyatt's official assistant. Not for Burt Sergeant.

Had Hyatt planned for this, too? Just how long ago had the man known he was going to die?

There were far too many questions to take in at once. And behind it all was the vision of Amelia. Was she dead, too, lying in a pool of blood beside Davis Hyatt?

One thing at a time, he told himself.

The Network was defunct.

Was it?

The international call . . . the instructions . . .

As of when did the Network cease to exist?

And then he realized that it was up to him. It would remain intact and operating until the moment Burt Sergeant set a match to it. It was as simple as that. Until then, he *was* the Network. He was Davis Hyatt.

His hands shook.

I am Davis Hyatt now.

Inside Hyatt's office, Sergeant turned on the keyboard to the great computer that filled the far wall. Instantaneously a message appeared: "Enter Access Code."

"Damn it," Sergeant snarled.

He pulled open the center drawer of Hyatt's desk. In it were a notepad, a fountain pen, a book of matches, and a crystal bottle of black ink. Nothing else.

A code . . . a code . . . He would have to find it for himself.

He tapped onto the keyboard the single word: "Network."

The screen in front of him responded: "Incorrect Access Code."

Next, Sergeant tried "The Network," but he got the same frustrating response.

He leaned back in the chair for a moment. Like the code in Dr. Sebastapol's notebook, the key to access Pandora would be something personal, something only Hyatt himself—

His breath caught. Slowly he typed in the name: "Pandora."

His fingers waited, poised above the keyboard. "Code Accepted."

He blinked at the screen, almost afraid to go on. Pandora was his now, and she would give up her foul secrets to him only.

The computer's main menu appeared on the screen: Fingerprints; Personnel; Field Reports; Pending Operations.

First he asked for the last six reports that had been entered. Almost immediately the computer began to scroll a string of messages. He froze it on the last message, the final piece of material that had been entered into Pandora's memory.

It read: "Santa Vittoria. Body found washed ashore, 7/16. 1.88 meters. 70 kg. estimated. Race: Caucasian. Hair: Light blond. Eyes: Blue. Personal effects: Silver whiskey flask. Identification: None. Cause of death: Gunshot wound to forehead. Condition of body: Advanced decomposition from exposure to sea."

"Oh, my God," Sergeant said aloud.

Billy Starr had been found at last.

And Hyatt had known.

Sergeant leaned forward, pulled the menu back onto the screen and entered the personnel file. He ordered up the data on Wade Turner.

Instantly, the computer screen reported: "No File Found."

Sergeant felt himself shivering with rage. The Scorpion had been replaced by another killer, another madman to carry the virus to the United States. Amelia had been the only one to stand in his way.

And Hyatt had known. He had known all of it.

There was no doubt anymore.

If Sergeant had thought about what he was doing, he might never have gone through with it. But he was fueled by a combination of anger and deadly fear, and he knew what he had to do.

He dialed the private number in Washington, D.C., of the director of the Federal Bureau of Investigation.

"This is Davis Hyatt, Priority Code Eleven International," he said.

He waited for the code to be verified. It happened almost immediately, and the voice came back on the phone. "What can we do for you?"

"I need to know if the body of a woman named Amelia Pierce was found at the scene of a homicide in New York City within the last twenty-four hours."

He gave what sketchy information he had, then waited for the answer.

After no more than a minute, the voice at the other end responded. "No, sir. No woman answering your description was found at the address you gave. However, there was a male victim, late forties, early fifties, no ID. Cause of death was loss of blood. His throat had been cut. A witness saw two people leaving the building at eleven o'clock this morning. Both were covered with blood, according to the witness. One male Caucasian, six feet, blond hair, blue eyes. One female Caucasian, long red hair. The man was carrying the woman. There's a bulletin out, but there have been no signs of them. That's all we have."

While Sergeant digested the information, the FBI man waited patiently. Code Eleven International was a priority of the highest order. Only one individual ever used it, and that person's identity was so secret that no one but the director himself could even access the Code Eleven material from the Bureau's mainframe.

"Is there anything else, sir?"

"Yes," Sergeant said quietly. "I need one of your best men to meet me in New York immediately. I am in Geneva, but I'll be there by military jet."

"Who are these people, sir?"

"The woman is not to be harmed," Sergeant said. "And the man is carrying enough poison to wipe out half your country. Now get moving."

He hung up without waiting for any comment. Next, he again used the Priority Eleven code to reach the French sureté. He ordered a Mirage jet to pick him up at the Geneva Airport immediately for the trip to Washington.

When that was done, he opened Hyatt's center drawer and took out a pack of matches.

If he had set fire to the office as he'd been instructed, he could have left a free man. The wetwork boys would not have found Pavel Malocsay, and by the time they realized who Hyatt's real assistant was, Sergeant would have been long gone.

That had been Davis Hyatt's gift to him. The payoff for letting the Scorpion—the new, living Scorpion—get away.

What had been Hyatt's payoff, he wondered.

None of it mattered anymore. Sergeant had chosen the path he was going to take. It would lead him to a prison cell, where someone would put a bullet in his brain before he could talk.

But maybe, just maybe, he could stop the Scorpion first.

29

WELCOME TO WEST VIRGINIA

The sign was lit by an overhead light, topped by stars in the night sky.

West Virginia?

Amelia's head was thudding. Slowly her eyes opened, and the deep thrum of her heartbeat alerted her to other sounds: the hum of the car's engine, the *shush* of tires on the road, the whistle of passing cars. The pungent odor of cigarette smoke was in the air. She turned her head toward the driver. Wade Turner grinned at her, a cigarette clenched between his teeth.

"Feeling all right, little lady?"

His accent's different, Amelia thought fuzzily. *And he hadn't smoked before.*

It came to her that Turner was somehow changing. The carefully studied Midwestern boyishness of the man she had met on Santa Vittoria was giving way to something else . . . to some*one* else.

The change had already begun in Vienna, when he had

tried to kill her. His speech had been different then, too, but the difference had been too small to be remarkable. Now, it seemed, Wade Turner had given himself over to a completely new personality.

He flicked the cigarette ash with his thumb, then turned on the radio. A country and western song was playing, and he whistled along tunelessly. "Too bad you can't see the mountains. Countryside's real pretty." He pronounced it "purdy." "My pappy always loved the mountains."

"Where are you taking me?"

"Oh, it's a ways. You just set back and enjoy the ride. I'll let you know when we get there." He reached across her to open the glove compartment. From it he took a silver flask, polished to a high gleam. "Get them pills for me, will you, Amelia?"

It was such a normal request, something a man on a long drive might casually ask of his wife. Automatically she reached for the small prescription bottle and handed it to him. He took off the lid, popped two small tablets into his mouth, then washed them down with a swig from the flask.

"Ahhh," he said with satisfaction. The odor of whiskey smelled foul inside the car.

He gave the vial back to her. "Pep pills. Don't want to fall asleep at the wheel, now." He took another drink, then set the flask on the seat between his legs. "You don't mind if I call you Amelia, do you?"

He touched the gold name bracelet on her wrist.

She twisted away from him in revulsion. In the backseat she saw a valise, a cheap, black hard-plastic case that a young junior executive might use for carrying home paperwork. And suddenly she understood everything, why Turner had tried so often to kill her, and why he had allowed her to live now. The answers were all in that black-plastic case.

"It's the poison," she said dully. "The virus Doctor Sebastapol wrote about."

"Got a nice ring to it. 'Amelia.' Old-fashioned, like. Pa'd like it."

"How much is there?"

Turner screwed up his face, as if trying to keep an unwelcome thought out of his mind. "Pa . . . my pa . . ." He sighed, blank-faced.

"How much?"

"Two liters," he said with a shrug. His new accent was gone.

"That—that doesn't seem like much."

"No. But then, it required only four milliliters to kill everyone at the prison." He smiled slyly. "Two hundred and twelve people in three days. Two liters is more than enough to decimate the population of this country."

She blinked, unable to speak.

He stroked her neck. His hand felt like a snake crawling over her skin. She pulled away violently.

"You hungry?"

She shook her head.

"Hey, come on." The Good Ol' Boy accent was back. "How about some Fritos and a Coke?"

"I'm not hungry," she said.

He veered onto the exit ramp. "Tell you what. I'm going to get some anyway. Just in case you change your mind." He winked at her.

Amelia began to shake uncontrollably. "Please let me go," she whispered.

He ignored her as he pulled into the parking lot of a 7-Eleven. There was only one other car there, a battered Chevrolet convertible surrounded by teenage boys ostentatiously drinking beer and trying to look tough for one another.

"Now you just sit tight, all righty?" He touched her hair. "I wouldn't let nothing bad happen to such a pretty little thing." He took the keys from the ignition.

As soon as Turner went inside, Amelia grabbed the valise and ran toward the boys.

"Please help me!" she cried breathlessly. "A man's trying to kill me. I've got to get away from here!"

One of the teenagers looked over at the glass doors of the convenience store. "That guy?"

"Yes. Please, hurry. Can you take me somewhere . . . any-where . . ."

Another stepped in front of her and crushed an empty can in his fist. "What's it worth to you, babe?" he drawled, casting an eye toward the audience of his peers.

Amelia shoved past him. "I don't have time for this," she said, sliding into the convertible. The keys were in the ignition. She would steal it if she had to.

"Okay, be cool," the can-crusher said. He plopped in the driver's seat, forcing her away from the wheel, and started the engine. Four other boys climbed into the car.

"Hurry," Amelia said.

"Hey, that's him!" one of the others whispered hoarsely as Turner came out of the store. His eyes traveled from his empty car to the convertible in which Amelia was trying to make herself small in the middle of the front seat.

The driver leaned over and addressed Turner. "Tough shit, sucker!" he yelled. Then, holding his middle finger aloft, he peeled out of the lot in a cloud of burning rubber.

The boys laughed raucously.

"Man, did you see his face?"

"Thought you was going to do a doughnut."

The driver preened, half-smiling as he maneuvered the gears on a turn onto a two-lane road. " 'Zat your boyfriend, or what?" he asked, slipping an arm around Amelia's shoulders.

She breathed raggedly, twisting around to look back. "His name is Wade Turner," she said, forcing herself to be calm. "He's already killed a lot of people . . ."

Suddenly two headlights turned in an arc and shone behind them.

"Don't worry about nothin'," the driver said, and goosed the Chevy's engine.

"We've got to get to the police."

"Bullshit."

"You don't understand. What I've got in this case—"

"We ain't going to no cops."

"This isn't a game of chicken!" Amelia screamed. "Don't you understand? He's going to kill me!"

The driver smiled. "Only if he can catch *me*."

Someone in the back clapped him on the shoulder. "Fuckin' A, man."

Amelia sighed. "Look, I appreciate what you're doing for me—"

"Suck my dick, man!" One of the boys in the backseat was standing up, his hands cupped around his mouth as he shouted to the car behind. "Got that, faggot?"

The others laughed. The driver gave a snort of approval.

"Please," Amelia pleaded. "You don't know—"

"I said, suck my—"

The orator's words were cut short by the report of a gun. His body arched backward, and he fell heavily over the front seat, starring the windshield with his head. Blood ran down the shattered glass.

Amelia pulled the body back. The boy had been hit with an exploding bullet. The entire top of his head had been blown away.

The driver, his lap now filling with his dead friend's blood, screamed, "Jesus! Jesus Christ, he's dead!"

He glanced over, and his face lost its childish mask of composure. Suddenly he looked just like a scared highschooler.

What have I brought on these children? Amelia thought. Their idea of evil was hot-wiring the principal's car. They stood no chance at all against a man like Turner.

The car veered crazily. Amelia grabbed the wheel. "Slow down," she ordered. The driver obeyed.

She spoke slowly and quietly. "Listen to me," she said. "What's on the other side of that hill?" She gestured to the west, where a forested ridge rose above the road.

"Not much. A couple of farms."

"Okay. I want you to let me out, right up there where he can see me. Then drive like hell to the nearest police station and tell them what's happened. My name is Amelia Pierce, from New York City. The man behind us killed somebody in my apartment and then brought me here. Got that?"

The young man nodded, white-faced.

Turner had almost caught up with them.

"Speed up for half a mile or so, so I've got a chance."

The young man looked up at the ridge. "Hey, lady—"

"Move it," Amelia said. He floored the pedal. "And no heroics. Just get to the cops. For your friend."

He nodded. A half mile up the road, near the crest of the hill, he skidded to a sudden stop. Amelia climbed over the boy and the body in the seat next to her, dragging the valise behind her.

"Go!" she screamed as she broke into a run.

Tires squealed behind her, but Amelia didn't look back. She scrambled up the ridge thinking only of where her hands and feet could make purchase, trying to keep the case from sliding back down the hillside.

If she didn't think about the circumstances, she told herself, what she was going through was no worse than climbing up the slick riverbank as a child while her father pelted her with rocks.

Only the rocks weren't bullets. And outsiders didn't get killed just for being in the way.

She thought of the boy's head starring the windshield of the car as Turner's bullets smashed into him.

How many more have to die?

Her foot slipped on a loose rock, and she grabbed wildly for an exposed root as her feet searched frantically for a hold. A cascade of small stones rolled down the hillside.

Don't think about it. Don't think about it now.

Willing herself to stay calm, she began to climb again. She had almost reached a small shale shelf when she heard the gunshots in the distance, and then the unmistakable squeal of a car careening out of control. A moment later she saw a ball of fire rising up with a *thoomp* from the valley to the north.

Amelia closed her eyes.

So they're gone, too, she thought. *Everyone I go near is destroyed.*

Then she smashed her head against the stone shelf until the pain was great enough to dispel the urge to let go and fall to the bottom.

"I'll kill you, Turner," she whispered. "One way or another, I'll kill you."

She dug her fingers into the earth and inched her way forward up the ridge.

30

"There are a lot of reservoirs in New York State," Robert Dallingwood said, unable to conceal the contempt in his eyes.

Dallingwood was an enormous, broad-shouldered black man with the majestic bearing of an African tribal chief. "Just how many do you expect us to cover?"

"Which ones supply New York City?" Sergeant asked.

"The ones along the Hudson."

"Then that's where we'll start."

"All of them?"

"Yes. All of them."

Dallingwood put his softball-sized fist on his hips. "Look, I don't know what kind of setup you've got here, mister—"

"Mr. Hyatt," a police officer shouted from the table covered with telephones that had been set up in the middle of Amelia Pierce's living room.

Sergeant drank his coffee. It was nearly midnight, and he felt drained. After the Mirage flight, during which he had been certain that he would be met by a contingent of law-enforcement personnel prepared to carry him off to jail, he had been surprised.

No, not surprised. Shocked was a better word. With the Priority Eleven access code, no one had questioned his identity or his authority. He had asked the FBI to arrange for the full cooperation of the New York City police, and he had it.

Within two hours of his arrival, the FBI sent Dallingwood to join three uniformed cops in the makeshift operation headquarters in the apartment of a woman who had been abducted by a terrorist of some kind. The agent had been instructed, as had the police officers, to take orders from a civilian, a man named Davis Hyatt, who obviously didn't know squat about any sort of criminal investigation.

To take orders, to ask no questions.

Dallingwood didn't like it, but he was too professional to complain. With the Bureau, he had been sent in to take over local police situations too many times not to recognize when the same thing was being done to him.

So he took his orders and he asked no questions, even when the civilian named Hyatt had set up shop at a blood-covered, evidence-filled murder scene. Even when the civilian named Hyatt had dismissed as unimportant the identity of the dead man found there. Even when the civilian named Hyatt had come up with the crazy-ass proposition that the terrorist was about to poison the water supply of New York City.

Shit, Dallingwood thought. The civilian named Hyatt didn't even know where the damned reservoirs were.

"Mr. *Hyatt.*"

Startled, Sergeant looked up at the young policeman. He had forgotten his new identity.

Had Dallingwood caught that? The black man was staring straight at him.

"Yes?" Sergeant asked with annoyance.

"The car's been located, about six miles north on Route Four. It's got Turner's fingerprints on it, and a couple of long red hairs. Must be from the woman."

She might be alive, Sergeant thought.

"There was a handkerchief on the seat, too, with blood on it, like he wiped himself off. He must've gotten some backwash when he cut the guy's throat."

"He changed cars," Sergeant said.

"Very good," Dallingwood said sarcastically.

Sergeant swallowed his anger. He needed the FBI man. Sergeant was not a detective. He was out of his depth here, and Dallingwood knew it.

But it was his only chance. It was Amelia's only chance. Whoever was ultimately in charge of the Network had made a serious error in exposing it to exactly the sort of runaway action Sergeant was taking now. He would be found out soon enough, he knew. He would be arrested, perhaps killed; but until then, he had a chance to find Wade Turner and stop him before he tore Amelia to pieces.

Sergeant just had to keep his wits about him.

He looked into Dallingwood's eyes. "How do we look for him now?"

Dallingwood shrugged elaborately. "You're the boss," he said.

Amelia heard her breath come in ragged gulps. Here, near the crest of the ridge, the ascent was almost straight up. With the case in one hand, she had been climbing mainly by grasping exposed tree roots with her other hand and scrambling up with her feet.

Both of her arms were aching. In the silence of the night, broken only by the occasional *whoosh* of cars below, she could hear the sloshing of the liquid in its container inside the case.

Not far . . . not far now . . .

With a great effort, she propelled herself up the remaining few feet of the hill. She crested it like a dolphin, chest-first, tossed the case out in front of her, and fell flat on the ground.

Then she looked up and groaned. There was nothing in sight but trees. More trees. No houses. No roads. Just another forest.

She lay her head on the mossy earth and accepted her disappointment, waiting for the galloping of her heartbeat to subside. Inches from her face, the poison in the black case sloshed quietly for a few moments, then stilled.

It's too quiet, she thought. No one had pursued her up the hill. At first she had been too frantic to listen and had concerned herself only with moving away from the highway as fast as she could. But later, during the long climb up, she had strained for the sounds of leaves rustling, of broken twigs. But there had been nothing. Even a man as well trained as the Scorpion could not climb through a forest mountain without making any sound at all.

The Scorpion . . . The name had once belonged to a man named Billy Starr, a man whom Burt Sergeant had chased for nine years. Amelia's parents had been Starr's final victims.

Now Billy Starr was dead. Amelia had killed him. But she had not killed the Scorpion.

Someone else had taken him over, inhabited the killer's psychotic mind the way a hermit crab inhabits a cast-off shell. Somehow between Santa Vittoria and this forest in West Virginia, Wade Turner had discarded himself to resurrect the Scorpion.

Why? What could possibly have prompted Wade Turner into making his life an exact duplicate of another's?

She stood up slowly, still listening. There was no one nearby, she was sure of that. Had he not pursued her, then? Had he gone after the boys, and then lost her trail?

She shut her eyes tight against the possibilities taking shape in her mind. She could still feel the weight of the teenager's body as it tumbled between her and the young man beside her in the car. One moment he had been alive—a bad, overgrown boy, calling out obscenities from the backseat of a convertible—and the next, he had been nothing more than a lump of bleeding flesh. His blood had coughed out onto the windshield from the hole on top of his head.

His blood . . . Davis Hyatt's blood . . . Marla Sebastapol's blood . . . Her own father's . . .

She started to run at breakneck speed, as if she could leave her thoughts behind if only she ran fast enough. Gasping, her legs pistoning, the black case pressed to her breast like a shield, she ran blindly. And then a light winked through the trees.

She stopped short. A star? It hadn't looked like a star.

It wasn't. It was a light, steady and welcoming. And beneath it would be a porch, attached to a house, where there would be a telephone.

She had made it!

Dazed, Amelia walked slowly for a few feet, the case dangling at her side. She looked down at it.

Anything could happen, she knew. She would go to the house and call the police, but the police had not believed her before. They might not believe her now. And this time, Burt Sergeant would not be there to help. If the Scorpion returned, if he found his way to her somehow, he must not be allowed to find the case.

Amelia knelt on the ground and looked for a digging stone. She found one, flat, with a spoonlike hollow, not far away. Then she fashioned a tool from three sticks and a piece of dried honeysuckle vine; it would do for removing embedded rocks.

She would bury the case here . . . and if she died before Turner was caught, it would remain buried forever.

When she was finished, the earth covering the case was barely distinguishable from the surrounding forest floor. Then, marking her passage the way her father had shown her—small traces left on trees, all of them at waist level so that the casual eye would not notice them—she made her way toward the welcoming light.

At the edge of the forest she paused, then burst through the trees and saw, only twenty feet away, a small, two-story house with a garage.

Please be home, she thought with desperation. *Please be home, so this nightmare can end.*

31

Burt Sergeant looked through the stack of metropolitan police reports that had come in over the past six hours and silently cursed the Wild West Show that urban America had become.

In a desperate stab at trying to find something he could tie to Wade Turner, Sergeant had asked for all the reports of random or senseless killings in the New York area in the past forty-eight hours that had not resulted in an arrest.

Now the heap of one-sheet reports covered most of the available space on the folding table he was using as a desk.

Dallingwood came over and, grinning, tossed another sheaf onto the pile. Sergeant sighed. Dutifully, he picked up the new batch and began to slog his way through them.

Nothing. Drug-related . . . Drug-related . . . Gang war . . . He leafed through the reports, his dismay mounting. Like Billy Starr, it seemed, Turner left no trace of himself unless he wanted to.

He was about to despair when he read one of the last reports in the pile. This one was a homicide, occurring just after six P.M. the previous day in Brooklyn. Two gunshots to the abdomen at close range. Victim possessed no ID. The shooting occurred during a meal in a restaurant, after which the killer had walked out.

He showed the report to Dallingwood.

"Mob rub-out," the FBI man said, handing it back.

Sergeant was about to add it to the discard pile when something caught his eye. It was the word "blond." He drew the paper closer and read it carefully. "Witnesses attest to the presence of a blond male Caucasion, 6', blue eyes, with whom the victim was apparently having an argument. The homicide was discovered by the waitress after the suspect left the scene."

"Can you get me fingerprints from this body?" Sergeant asked.

Dallingwood shrugged. "What do you want to match them to? Felons statewide? Nationwide? That'd take time."

"I've got some files."

Dallingwood raised an eyebrow. "Your own files?"

"Yes. Excuse me." He went into the empty bedroom, picked up Amelia's private telephone, and dialed the number of Hyatt's office in Geneva.

Mrs. Abbot answered. "Mr. Sergeant," she said breathlessly. "Thank God, it's you! A man from the Bundesrat has been calling all day, asking for Mr. Malocsay!" Her voice sounded frantic.

Of course it would be the Bundesrat, Sergeant thought. *Some old Swiss bureaucrat from the Federal Council who's held the same office for thirty years.*

Somehow the man must have gotten wind of the message to terminate the Network and undoubtedly wanted to know what was going on.

"I didn't tell him anything, sir, not even that Mr. Malocsay is dead. I just thought it wasn't my business, and it wasn't anyone else's either," she said snippily. "Mr. Hyatt always says if there's anything to be said, he'll say it."

"Good," Sergeant said. "Keep stalling him. Now listen carefully. I want you to go into Hy—the office and transmit the entire fingerprint file to me."

He gave her the access code and a telephone number that

would connect Pandora with one of the NYPD computers set up in Amelia's apartment. "When you're finished, get back on this line."

He put down the phone and went out into the living room. "Did you get the prints from the dead man in the Brooklyn restaurant?"

"They just came in from the morgue," Dallingwood said. He held up a sheet of paper showing an enlargement of a set of prints, its unusual characteristics marked by miniscule numbers. "A loop pattern. Also, the guy's uncircumcised. The M.E. says he might be an Arab."

"Good. Now listen. You have to tell me how to do this. I've got some fingerprints coming in from a computer in Europe. Can we transmit them over phone lines to your mainframe at the Bureau in Washington?"

"Sure. No problem. But what makes you think we don't have them already?"

Sergeant tightened his lips. "Can you do it?"

The big man inhaled sharply. "I can." He began to walk away, and Sergeant called him back. No point, he thought, in having an enemy when you can have a teammate.

The FBI man turned and raised an eyebrow.

"You're probably right about an Arab," Sergeant said, trying to soften his tone of voice. "I think we're looking for a Libyan national. That should narrow things down."

Dallingwood looked as if he were going to laugh out loud. "And you're going to send us prints of some Libyans?"

"Yeah."

"How many sets do you have?"

"About thirty thousand," Sergeant said.

The FBI man stared at him for a moment, then turned and picked up another phone. He gestured to Sergeant to wait.

He mumbled into the telephone, then scribbled a number on a piece of paper, and handed it to Sergeant.

"Here," he said. "Have your contact in Europe wait ten minutes—that will give them a chance to get ready in Washington—and then call this number. Use my name as a password. The computer boys will tell your man what to do."

Sergeant took the paper and said, "Good." He paused. "Thanks. This may be important."

"You got it," Dallingwood said.

Sergeant went back into the bedroom and whispered into the phone, "Mrs. Abbott?"

"I'm still here, sir."

He explained to her what she should do with the fingerprint file.

"Do you understand?" he asked.

"I think so. Mr. Sergeant?"

"Yes?"

"I just found this disc that fits into the computer. I was sitting here and I thought I would clean out Mr. Hyatt's cigar humidor while I was waiting. Mr. Hyatt knows I clean it, of course. I do it every day."

Sergeant frowned. "It's software for the computer?"

"That's what it looks like. I found in underneath the cigars." She laughed briefly, a birdlike chirp. "Mr. Hyatt must have put it there by accident, and now he might be looking for it. So would you mind telling him that I've located it?"

Sergeant's heartbeat quickened. "Is the disc labeled?"

"I wouldn't presume to read it, Mr. Sergeant," she said primly.

"Well, read it now."

"Very well. On your orders, Mr. Sergeant. It says, 'Not Transferred.' "

Not transferred? A grim idea was growing at the back of his mind. "All right," he said, forcing his voice to sound casual. "What I want you to do is this. After you send the fingerprint file to the FBI, transmit everything in that disc over here, using the number I gave you before."

"But Mr. Hyatt might—"

"He's here in New York," Sergeant said blandly.

"Oh, I see. Then he did need it."

"Very much," Sergeant said. "Mark it 'Private, Davis Hyatt's Eyes Only.' "

"Yes, sir," Mrs. Abbott said, her sense of urgent efficiency restored.

Thirty minutes later he was called into the corner of the living room, where fax machines and three small computers were pulling in reports from all over the metropolitan area.

One of the New York police computer men said, "This just started coming in, Mr. Hyatt. It's marked for your eyes only."

"Thanks," Sergeant said. "Why don't you get some coffee? I'll monitor this one for a while."

The first thing that appeared was a compendium of Sergeant's own recent reports on the search for Billy Starr.

Not transferred, he thought. *The bastard never sent any of it to the member nations of the Network.*

Only the police report on Billy Starr's death had been made known, so that Wade Turner could work unfettered and free. The information had gone into Pandora's massive mind and remained there, a secret between Hyatt and his machine.

He scrolled past it to the translation of Juan Sebastapol's notebook.

Not transferred.

So there was no report on the virus. No report on an antidote.

There was nothing, Sergeant realized, except a car somewhere in the continental United States carrying a disease that would make the Black Plague seem like an outbreak of chicken pox.

Oh, Amelia, he thought. *That maniac will kill you first. And then the rest of us will die. Every one of us.*

His hands clutching the tabletop, he closed his eyes. Hyatt had done this. Somehow, for some reason, the most trusted man in the world had given an assassin permission to destroy a continent.

"You all right?" Dallingwood was looking at him, his black face as impassive as an ebony mask.

Sergeant rubbed his eyes and glanced up. "I'm fine."

"Looks like a letter," Dallingwood said, gesturing toward the monitor with his chin.

Sergeant pulled the long sheet of paper being fed out of the printer toward him so that the FBI man could not see it. Dallingwood took the hint and walked away.

Sergeant began to read.

> Dear Burt,
>
> I've left this letter on a disc where Mrs. Abbott is sure to find it. If you are reading it, then I am already dead and no longer need to keep any secrets from you.
>
> I've gone to New York to kill Amelia Pierce. Or, rather, to make this request of Wade Turner, who will be glad to oblige. Her death is inevitable anyway; whatever happens, someone from the Network will eliminate her for her knowledge. Her ludicrous account in the American tabloid was enough to ensure that.
>
> But my hope is that by engaging the homicidal Mr. Turner in his favorite activity, I may be able to kill him as well. That would go a long way toward solving the terrible problems that I have helped to cause. It will be my atonement.
>
> But of course, if you are reading this, then I have failed. For that I can only apologize. The Scorpion is with you still.
>
> I knew about Wade Turner long before Amelia Pierce appeared in Geneva. His name is not Turner, by the way. He has no name, and has never had one.
>
> Curious, I think—a child reared without a name. Billy Starr left his son nothing but the ability to kill.

Sergeant leaned back in his chair.

"His son," he whispered.

"You want something" Dallingwood asked, walking toward him.

"No . . . nothing." Sergeant waved him away.

But I have called him Turner, even to his face, and he answers to it. He became, you see, rather a friend of mine.

Oh, "friend" is surely not the right word for a psychotic killer who, in all probability, has already been responsible for my death. But I did spend some time with the man, and for that time, I did not feel friendless. Indeed, I felt almost as if I were having a series of conversations with the Grim Reaper, who came to take me but decided to stay for tea and a little chat before stopping my heart with his cold hand. And so I will refer to him here as Wade Turner, to give a name to death.

He came into my life a little more than a year ago. I had spoken with Carl Eberhardt, the CIA head of station in Amman, asking for his feelings about a young agent named Wade Turner who was in his employ. I was looking for someone to replace Arthur Pierce after his retirement. I needed a man who was fluent in Spanish and had adequate credentials as a photographer to legitimately work for a wire service while serving as the Network's agent in the Caribbean. I told Eberhardt only about the photography job; he knew my background, and my father's, well enough not to ask questions about the rest.

To be honest, I could have had Turner transferred to the Network without ever speaking to Eberhardt, but I couldn't resist the impulse to speak with Carl, who was an old friend.

I was lonely, I suppose. I wanted to hear a voice I remembered. As I have learned, even an enemy's voice can be a welcome sound to one who has been forced into friendlessness for all his life. Loneliness was my vice, Burt. It has perhaps caused the fall of our civilization. One moment, when an old man wanted to hear the sound of a friend's voice . . .

Five days after I received a glowing letter of recommendation detailing Turner's credentials, Eberhardt was captured by a group identifying itself as a splinter of the Islamic Jihad.

They were really Libyans, of course. The Libyans are probably the most effective terrorists in the world, because they do not rely on passionate amateurs willing to immolate themselves for a spot on the evening news. They kill to eliminate those threatening to them, then give credit to whomever seems to want it most.

The Libyans' techniques of interrogation are by far superior to any others. They are patient, intelligent, thorough, and ruthless. It took Abu Nidal's Hezbollah two years to force Bill Buckley to talk. They ended up with an impressive report, more than two hundred pages, but most of it was dross, worthless except for the publicity it generated.

The Libyans are far more efficient. Eberhardt was killed within three weeks, and when he died, he had been drained of every pertinent bit of information his brain had ever come across. Including, I am sure, our discussions concerning Wade Turner.

How many times I've blamed myself for the death of so many people in the past weeks! If I hadn't called, if we hadn't discussed a letter, if he'd never written it, would he have even remembered Turner's name?

The real Wade Turner was killed, of course. And Billy Starr's son—the man with no name— quietly replaced him.

To make the seal complete, Eberhardt's successor, a long-standing associate named Albert Neumeyer, who might have been able to identify the "new" Turner as a fake somewhere down the road, was blown up by a bomb in an Amman bazaar.

But I ramble now. To catalogue every death is futile. It is all futile now, I'm afraid.

The boy is very bright. Turner's CIA records included a photograph, but I never saw Wade Turner in person before his transfer to Santa Vittoria, so I was not able to see that a switch had been made.

While on the island, he worked to keep Arthur Pierce from finding out about the viral experiments that the Libyans were conducting on the prisoners there. These inmates were political prisoners from totalitarian regimes around the globe, men whose deaths would never be reported or acted on. It was just a sad irony that Pierce's old friend, Juan Sebastapol, happened to be among them.

I suppose the plan called for Pierce eventually to be killed unobtrusively, perhaps as part of the holocaust at El Mirador when the fort was set afire, but Arthur saw to it that things didn't go smoothly for his killers. He had Sebastapol's notebook detailing exactly what had been going on, and he knew what to do with it.

He was getting old. In his Glory Boy days, Arthur never would have stopped to see his family before fleeing a hostile situation. Most probably he was trying to warn Amelia and her mother.

He would have been proud of his daughter, I think. She not only escaped, but carried out his dying wish to bring the notebook back to me.

It could have stopped there. If I had been deserving of the trust men like Arthur Pierce placed in me, I would not now be writing of the end of the world.

The boy, Turner, did not attempt to kill Amelia himself then. He arranged for someone disguised as a chauffeur for the deputy governor of the island to take the notebook and finish her off, but the attempt failed.

By the time Amelia arrived in Geneva, Turner was already panicking. He had the Libyans send someone to kill her in the hospital.

That was the nurse you shot.

And so now Turner had no choice but to halt his plans and dispose of Amelia himself.

That was where I came in. Because, for all of the care he took to cover his tracks, Turner had never counted on Amelia's reaching me with the notebook.

He never mentioned Amelia Pierce in his report of the Pierce murders. He said nothing about a notebook.

As soon as Amelia told us about her meeting with Turner on the island, I knew that the Network had been infiltrated.

My instructions were clear: In the event of an occurrence like this, I was to disband the Network immediately. I did not follow these instructions because I was afraid.

I've had no illusions about this, Burt. The Network was designed to be temporary, but my role in it was for life. Once the office burned, no trace was to be left of it.

No trace.

I told myself that I needed time . . . to catch the impostor, to set things right before they got out of control. Of course there was no way of doing that, since I had no idea where "Turner" was at the time. I did not even know what the man looked like.

Still, I did not disband the organization.

Oh, I suppose I would have, in time. Perhaps even an hour would have been enough for me to work up the courage to burn the files and kill myself. Or wait the day or two it would take to have me killed. It was not my fear of death so much as the anguish I felt at the injustice of having to pay such a grave price for so small an error.

And there was another reason. I have a friend. Or did; I killed him the day before yesterday. He hardly responded when I put the needle filled with morphine into his arm.

His name was Timothy Langthorpe. He knew nothing about the Network. We met thirteen years ago, and for most of those years he shared my bed. I don't believe this will be particularly shocking to you, Burt, or to anyone at the Network. But it was private, the only part of me I kept to myself. The best part.

Five years ago Timothy developed a brain tumor. Because of its location, it was inoperable. I admitted him to St. Elizabeth's Hospital in May. He had been dying by inches since then.

I did not know at the time of my moral crisis that I would kill my lover. In fact, his life was more important to me than anything in my existence. Before ending the Network and my life, I wished to say good-bye to Timothy.

And so I sat in my office with my head in my hands, doing nothing, when Mrs. Abbott buzzed through on the intercom.

"A man to see you, sir. He says it's quite urgent."

That must have been amusing to Mrs. Abbott. She believes me to be a has-been publisher, kicked upstairs on the charitable sufferance of the wire service's Board of Directors. I have not had a caller to my office in five years.

"He says his name is Wade Turner."

He says. What an interesting choice of words! Sometimes I believe the good Mrs. Abbott to be psychic.

"Do allow him to come in," I answered expansively, turning on a tape recorder I sometimes use to clarify thoughts to myself. "And please alert two security guards to come up at once and station themselves outside my door."

I was still in charge, you see.

So Mrs. Abbott escorted Wade Turner into my office.

When he came in, I shook hands with him and climbed onto the back of a tiger.

I have been riding it ever since, though the beast has long ago destroyed me.

32

"Ah, Turner," Hyatt said, rising and extending his hand. "Good to meet you at last."

Turner hesitated for a moment, then smiled broadly and shook the older man's hand.

"Somehow I pictured you as being darker in coloring," Hyatt went on. "The dossier the Agency sent me on you didn't include a photograph, I'm afraid—"

"Good try, Hyatt," Turner said softly. "Turn off the recorder, please."

Hyatt's eyebrows rose. "I'm sure I don't know what you're talking about."

The young man looked directly into his eyes. "Then let me help you," he said. "I am not Wade Turner. You must be aware of that, unless you're stupid. I don't believe you're stupid." He smiled, and Hyatt felt a curious mixture of superiority and warmth in that smile. "Not entirely, anyway."

Hyatt sat down and took out a cigar. "Suppose you go on."

"This is for the benefit of the tape recorder, no doubt," the visitor said softly. "All right. You know, unfortunately, of the existence of Amelia Pierce. That, in a nutshell, is why I'm here."

"Who tried to kill her in the hospital?"

"A fool I hired. Although by then it was already too late. My mistake. I should never have let her leave Santa Vittoria. Her being alive has caused a great deal of trouble, Mr. Hyatt. More than you know."

Hyatt smiled graciously. "I'm willing to listen."

"And I'm prepared to tell you," Turner said. "But first, you tell me something."

Hyatt raised his eyebrows.

"I'm pretty certain that Miss Pierce brought something here with her. Tell me what it was, and I'll go on."

Hyatt smoked his cigar unhurriedly.

This impostor may know nothing about the Network, he thought. *Whistling in the dark.*

"So long, Mr. Hyatt." Turner rose to leave.

Hyatt could barely contain his mirth. "One moment, please, Mr. Turner, or whatever your name is. Do you suppose you can come in here, announce that you've taken over the identity of one of my employees, tried to murder someone . . . and then just walk out?"

"I'm sure I have much less to tell the police—and the press—than you do." The two men faced each other for a long moment. "Verify the object, and I'll continue."

"I can have you killed."

"Of course you can. And then you'd know nothing at all about me." He cocked an eyebrow teasingly. "No? Won't do it? No complicity with the enemy?" He shrugged. "Then you are stupid, after all. Too bad." His hand touched the doorknob.

"It's a notebook," Hyatt said.

Turner's shoulders slumped noticeably. Slowly he walked back to his original position, then sprawled in one of the leather chairs. "I don't suppose you've got it translated yet?"

"Some cryptographers are working on it. It may be news," he added.

"Right. Davis Hyatt, newsman first and foremost. You

really can stop this pretense with me, you know."

Hyatt tasted fear inside his mouth. *How much does this man know?*

"Who are you?"

The blond man folded his hands in his lap. A meek gesture, Hyatt thought, and indeed, the young man's manner reminded him of a deflated balloon. "Who I am at the moment is Wade Turner. I became this person at the instant of his death. When I cease to be Wade Turner, I will become someone else whose identity I will have borrowed, or invented. At no time have I been, or will I be, a unique individual with a name and a history of his own." He sighed languidly. "If that is your question."

Hyatt decided to accept it for the time being, because for one thing, he had not really expected the man to tell the truth. For another, he had neither the time nor the expertise to force the truth out of him. And also, for some reason Hyatt could not fathom, this strange account sounded as if it might actually *be* the truth.

"All right," he said. "What do you want?"

"It's a matter of poison." Turner smiled unexpectedly. "Currently, it is being called Z-Fifteen. Rather a silly name, don't you think? My employers are almost childishly in love with tradecraft.

"At any rate, there is only a very small quantity of this substance available. Just enough for, say, Iraq to seriously thin out the military personnel in Iran. Or vice versa. My people plan to offer it to both."

"And who are your people?"

Turner smiled. "The manufacturers of Z-Fifteen."

"The Rabta chemical weapons plant?"

Turner made a small gesture of compliance.

"You're not a Libyan."

"I don't know what nationality I am, Mr. Hyatt."

Hyatt smoked his cigar thoughtfully. "Are you telling me you want to work as a double?"

"Not at all. I simply want to proceed with a plan that, since Amelia Pierce is alive and in your custody, might have to be scrapped. Unless I get your cooperation."

Hyatt was blankly amazed. "My *cooperation*?" Smoke sheeted out of his mouth. "You must be insane."

Turner shrugged.

"All right," Hyatt said accommodatingly. "This . . . poison. What connection does it have with Santa Vittoria?"

"The experiments were conducted on the inmates at El Mirador."

"Ah. And then the place was torched to get rid of the evidence."

"Exactly. Unfortunately, one of the prisoners escaped. He somehow passed a notebook to your man Pierce."

"Whom you also killed."

"No, I didn't. I would have, although I liked the man. But that job was left to someone else. To my father, in fact."

Hyatt stared silently at the young man, suddenly recognizing the features on his face. "Good Lord," he said finally. "Billy Starr . . . is your *father*?"

"He's dead now. Amelia Pierce killed him."

Hyatt sat bolt upright in his chair. "Billy Starr is dead?"

Turner nodded impassively. "The body has been disposed of. The Pierce woman's story can't be proved."

"Then why are you telling me?"

Turner opened his hand, palm up, as if he were releasing a bird. "Why not? You'll know most of it soon enough. Amelia will tell you about me, if she hasn't already. And I made the mistake of not mentioning her to you in my report about Pierce's death."

"Or the notebook," Hyatt said.

"Or the notebook. Which may be worthless, by the way. I don't know what's in it, either. But the author seemed to feel it worth his life to give it to Pierce. At any rate, even without the notebook, you'd have enough to force the Libyans not to sell the poison. It has been quite expensive to produce. They would hate to take that loss."

"Hence, my cooperation," Hyatt said smoothly. He had it all now, a recorded confession, and two security guards waiting to take this bedbug into custody.

"Yes. Oh, before you refuse, I'd like to offer you some money."

Hyatt laughed aloud. "Thank you, but I believe I'm beyond the age for bribery."

"Really? I was under the impression that you haven't managed your inheritance well. Some bad business ventures forced you to transfer ownership of the wire service to a new board. You made very little profit on that."

"I get by," Hyatt said with as much of a sarcastic edge as he could muster.

"And rumor has it that what resources you had have been depleted dramatically in recent years." He thought for a moment. "The past five years, more or less. Is that right?"

Hyatt felt his throat go dry.

"Your, ah, friend, Mr. Langthorpe. He had no insurance when his brain tumor was discovered, did he? Just another gay boy without a care—"

"Shut up," Hyatt hissed.

"Forgive me," Turner said. "I have no doubt that Timothy Langthorpe's life is worth the expense it has cost you, but the fact remains that you're broke."

He took out an envelope and placed it on the desk in front of Hyatt. "Here is a hundred thousand pounds sterling. There will be a second payment of equal amount when this is over—that is, when the poison has changed hands through proper channels. And, of course, your friend's medical expenses will be paid."

"Take that away," Hyatt said.

"Don't be an ass, Hyatt. It's a lot of money, considering that you don't have to do anything for it. All I want is for you not to report the information I've just given you."

Hyatt's lips formed a thin line. He shook his head.

"He'll be tortured," Turner said quietly.

The color drained from Hyatt's face. "Timothy's dying."

"Yes. He might be lucky and die before the pain gets to be too bad."

"You bastard," Hyatt whispered.

"I have more to offer."

Hyatt turned away.

"We'll give you sanctuary."

"From what?" Hyatt said angrily.

"From the Network."

"Oh, God." Hyatt reached over and shut off the tape recorder.

"That's better."

"What do you know about it?"

"No dramatics, please. What I know is that it's secret. Carl Eberhardt was a CIA head of station, and he knew nothing about it. He sent a man to work for you on Santa Vittoria believing that it was some sort of special duty for the Agency. Do you really think any organization so obsessed with anonymity would allow you—its main operative—to live after a fuckup of this magnitude?" He laughed lightly. "You're up to your balls already, Mr. Hyatt. I can't make things any worse for you."

Hyatt sat in silence. The last curls of smoke from his cigar wafted up toward the ceiling and disappeared. He set the cigar down.

"Look on the bright side," Turner said. "You probably won't even need sanctuary. Most likely this will all pass quietly. But if it doesn't, if for any reason your life is ever in danger, you would be most welcome in Libya."

"What a comforting thought," Hyatt said dryly.

Turner laughed. "It's not so bad. Two hundred thousand pounds will go a long way there. You can even bring your friend, if he's still alive. All your needs will be met for the rest of your life. No imprisonment, no torture . . . Oh, you'll probably be called upon for a little advice here and there, a few recollections from your past. As a consultant."

"As a traitor," Hyatt said.

"I don't think this is the place to argue semantics."

I can get him, Hyatt thought frantically. *First I can go along . . . for Timothy . . . and then I can take care of him.*

The Network was airtight. Whatever Turner might have guessed, he still had no idea of how the organization functioned, or of what was in its files. No agent knew those things, not even Arthur Pierce. The only way the Libyans would find out would be through Hyatt himself, and Hyatt had no intention of living long enough to let them.

It can be done. I swear it can.

"Get the notebook to me," Turner said.

Hyatt looked up. "And then?"

"And then we'll kill the woman."

Hyatt nodded.

He would make a copy of the notebook, of course. And get everything out of Amelia Pierce before she was killed. He would follow Turner in everything he did. And when Turner led him to his control, the Network would close in on the lot of them like a giant fist.

"Agreed," Hyatt said.

Turner opened the office door, nodded to the two security guards, and left.

Hyatt placed his hand over the envelope on his desk.

So, Burt, I sold out every civilized nation in the world for less money than it would cost to build a decent house.

Not that it ever occurred to me at the time. There was a new Scorpion, and I was going to catch him alone, from inside.

And if I didn't, I reasoned, if I failed, what real harm would be done? There was no reason to report anything about any poison to the Network. After all, I had only one man's word for Z-Fifteen's existence, and that man might well be a lunatic.

At worst, a few Arabs would be poisoned, probably erasing a number of terrorists' names from the Network's files, and the episode would be forgotten.

And Timothy would die in peace.

I was wrong, of course, unforgivable wrong. The "poison"—a lethal, contagious virus—was never intended for the Middle East. The notebook proved that. Most likely the reason Santa Vittoria was chosen as a site for its final experiments was the island's proximity to the United States.

But my friend Timothy did die without violence.

The Scorpion cannot harm him now.

I have left you three gifts. The first is this letter, so that you may understand the truth of the events that are leading to the Great Plague of the Twentieth Century. If there is a hell, I am certain to burn in it for my part in this horror. Even so, I can no longer do anything to stop what is to come.

My second gift to you is the identity of Pavel Malocsay. The fact that he, and not you, is the officer of record may save your life. For a while.

The third gift is an alteration of your past. You were never aware of precisely what happened after the death of your wife and daughter. The fact is that you did not attempt suicide in Egypt. It was Billy Starr who tried to kill you. I'm quite sure he would have finished the job in his own inimitable way, but he was interrupted by thieves who were using the cemetery as a hiding place.

One of them knew you, apparently, from your investigations. He claimed to have been a doctor before the Scorpion murdered his family. He patched you up as best he could and summoned the ambulance.

This information was withheld from your superiors. To safeguard the anonymity of the Network, I chose to let all concerned believe that you had cut your own throat.

The man who saved your life was hung without trial the next day.

I come to the end of my confession. It is not without regret, because now there is nothing more for me to do than kill again, and die.

Have I explained? Do you understand how I managed to turn myself inside out, from a man of ideals and dedication into a stooge for a monster?

No, probably not. I don't expect you to understand. But perhaps by the mere act of reading this letter, you have shown yourself to be not so very far removed from my weakness. Because you were never to have read it. You were to have destroyed everything relating to the Network without question.

But you couldn't do that, could you, Burt?

You had to open Pandora's box, even though you knew it to be filled with demons.

So did I. So have we all, back to the days of the Garden of Eden.

Dallingwood rubbed the back of his neck. "What the hell is this?" he asked hoarsely.

Sergeant continued to stare at the printout for a moment, then tore it off. "A letter to someone."

"No one you know, I suppose."

A young police officer approached them. "Here's the report on the fingerprints, sir. The dead man's name was Yusef Nassif. One of Qaddafi's advisers."

Dallingwood's head snapped up.

"Thank you," Sergeant said. He took the report from the officer and handed him the massive printout from Geneva. "Burn this."

Dallingwood's big hand reached out to take the sheets, but stopped as his eyes met Sergeant's.

"You're in charge, I guess," he said, withdrawing his hand.

The young policeman hustled off with the papers. Sergeant sighed.

"That's some scar on your neck," Dallingwood said.

Sergeant looked at the FBI man levelly. "I cut myself shaving."

Dallingwood let out a grim snort. "I'll get us some coffee," he said.

33

A radio was playing inside the farmhouse. Amelia brushed the dirt off her hands and dress.

Don't be hysterical, she told herself. *You don't want them to think you're a nut. Just ask to use the phone, then call the police. Tell them someone kidnapped you. Tell them about the car with the boys . . .*

She choked back a sob.

It's never going to end.

She swept a grimy hand over her eyes. "Yes, it is," she whispered fiercely. It was going to end here, in this white frame house with the yellow mosquito light on the front porch. She would call the police, and they would come for her, and they would stop Wade Turner on the road. And it would be over.

Don't panic now, she told herself.

She knocked on the door. The radio clicked off. "It's open," a voice called softly.

Amelia opened it . . . just wide enough to see inside.

The sight made her legs buckle under her.

Oh, no. Oh, God, no!

Two elderly women were lying on the floor, their throats cut. The left side of each head, where the ear had been, was clotted with blood. The ears themselves were floating in a goldfish bowl, where two guppies swam in a sphere of lurid red water.

Two children—a boy perhaps eight years old, and a curly haired girl of no more than four, with a large bruise on her cheek—were tied to kitchen chairs, facing the bodies of the dead like an audience in a theater.

The girl was crying softly, her voice a hoarse and monotonous low wail. His eyes wide, the boy stared into space. Turner was behind him, holding a bloody butcher knife to the boy's throat.

"Welcome, Amelia," he said.

She clutched the doorknob for support. Her instinct was to run, to run back into the woods, back to the highway, flag down a truck, run *away*. But she knew that if she did, Turner's first act, probably performed without a moment's thought, would be to kill the child.

"Where's the case?" he asked softly.

She swallowed.

"Really," he said, shaking his head like a father speaking to a naughty but endearing daughter. He pulled the blade across the boy's throat.

Amelia screamed.

Turned laughed, holding up the clean knife. He had skewed the angle so that he'd only wiped the blood from the dead adults onto the boy's skin. "Kind of brings out the maternal instinct in you, doesn't it?"

He returned the knife to the boy's throat. "Now. Shall I try it again?"

"It's in the woods," she said quickly. "I'll take you to it."

"That's better." He set the knife on a table beside him, where a big-barreled .44 Magnum lay. Amelia remembered the *thump* of the teenager's body against the windshield in the car.

He shot him with that, she thought.

Turner grabbed her elbow and pushed her out the door. "I don't have to remind you, do I, that if you run away from me, I'll come back and kill those charming little tykes?" His voice was even, controlled, terrifying.

"I won't run," Amelia said.

She led him into the woods as slowly as he permitted.

Time. She needed time. Sooner or later the police would find the wreckage of the teenagers' car. They might come by. A truck with a CB might come. A passerby. Someone, anyone, who could take the two children to safety.

"I think it was around here."

He slapped her with the back of his hand, knocking her to the ground. "You're lying, Amelia," he said softly, his eyes twinkling in the moonlight. He held the barrel of the forty-four to her temple. "I'll give you five minutes. If you haven't found the case by then, I'm going to have to hit you."

Her chin raised, trembling almost imperceptibly, in defiance.

"You'll be unconscious for a time," he said. "And when you wake up, the children will be dead. You don't want that to happen, do you?"

"Damn you," Amelia groaned, scrambling to her feet. She glanced at the trees, looking for her markers.

"You marked a path!" Turner said, impressed. "I'll bet you were a Girl Scout."

She found the spot and began scooping up handfuls of dirt.

"Self-sufficiency. I like that in a woman." He leaned against a tree and took a drink from the silver flask. "As a matter of fact, I like you, Amelia. Very much. You remind me a little of my mother."

With a yank on the handle, she pulled the case free and threw it at his feet.

"You carry it, please," he said. "I'd like to keep my hands free."

She picked it up. "They'll find you," she said.

"Who will, Amelia?" he asked pleasantly. "The *Daily Mirror?* I think they're busy this week looking for aliens."

They walked back to the house, the gun at her back.

"Where is your car?" she asked sullenly.

"In the garage. But we'll stop here first."

A cold shiver ran down her back. "Why?"

He put the gun in his jacket pocket and touched her hair. "You didn't really think I'd leave those two as witnesses, did you?"

For a terrible moment, she was frozen. Then she lunged at him, screaming.

The expression on Turner's face changed. The perversely tender affection was erased, replaced by the black countenance of a machine. He twined his fingers in Amelia's hair and slowly walked up the wooden steps leading to the porch, dragging her along behind him. She clawed at him, but he seemed to have forgotten her presence. Finally she threw herself forward and bit his leg.

He yanked her away so suddenly that her body twisted beneath her. When he released his grip on her hair, her face scraped against the splintered floorboards of the porch. By the time she could focus again, Turner was already walking through the door.

"No!" she screamed. With a final desperate effort, Amelia reached out and grabbed a leg of his trousers. "Don't kill them! Please! I'm begging you . . ."

He stopped.

She looked up. Past the corpses of the two women, the ladderback chairs were empty and askew. The butcher knife was on the floor, next to frayed pieces of rope.

The children were gone.

Amelia let go of Turner's leg and for a moment laughed hysterically with relief as he ran searching through the rooms. Then, suddenly aware of her own opportunity for escape, she crawled backward through the door and fled.

He had said the car was in the garage. If the keys were in it *(oh, please let the keys be there),* she could get away. If not, she would run back to the woods. He hadn't seen the marking on the trees; he was no woodsman. She at least had a chance against him there. But the car was better. The car . . .

The keys were in it.

She jumped inside and started the engine. Through the side window she could see Turner running down the porch steps. *I just might do it,* she thought, her heart hammering. *If he doesn't shoot out the tires, I can make it to a town. I can do it,* she told herself as she began to pull out of the garage. *I think I can, I think I can . . .*

Two pairs of eyes peeked out from behind a tractor next to the blue Ford.

Amelia's breath caught. It was the children. There wasn't time to get them in the car with her. And if she left them here, Turner would find them and kill them.

When she exhaled, her last hope disappeared into the air. Turner was almost at the garage now.

"Amelia Pierce, New York City," she whispered.

The boy nodded gravely.

"Get down." The eyes disappeared.

Tires screeching, Amelia backed up. Turner was holding the black case in one hand, the gun in the other, its barrel trained directly on her face.

She rested her head on the steering wheel and sobbed.

Turner climbed in beside her.

"Thank you for waiting," he said.

34

At daybreak they crossed the Tennessee border and headed west. By mid-afternoon they had traversed most of the state.

"Not far now, missy," Turner said eagerly. He had gone back to his hillbilly voice, acting as if nothing had happened since their stop at the convenience store. He patted her leg. "Them hills are something, ain't they? Folks got a saying about the Ozarks. They say the mountains ain't high, but the valleys sure are deep."

"Where are we going?" Amelia asked wearily.

He looked at her as if she had gone crazy. "Why, home, darlin'. We're going home, you and me."

"But the reservoir . . . I thought . . . New York . . ."

Turner laughed. "Now, what with your little newspaper story and everything, that's just where people are going to be looking, isn't that right? That is, if anybody even knows you're missing. A feller can up and die in whatever little rabbit hole he lives in and nobody's the wiser until the body starts to stink." He shook his head sadly. "That's life in the city. You're damn lucky I took you out of there."

"Yeah. Lucky," Amelia said.

Turner popped two more pills and took another drink. "There's other folks going to be up there, too, I reckon."

He opened the car window and spat, then rubbed his sleeve across his forehead. "Hot," he said in a whisper. "But they'll just have to wait . . . just till I get home for a while."

His eyes half closed. The car veered onto the shoulder of the road. Amelia screamed as it scraped against the guardrail.

"It's all right, darlin'," Turner rasped, pulling the car back onto the road.

"Look, you've got to stop somewhere. You're drunk."

"I will, I will." He nodded, smiling, speaking in a singsong.

Turner's face was white and glistening with sweat, and his body was giving off a rank, unwholesome odor that had nothing to do with sweat or liquor. It was the smell of sickness.

Of death, Amelia thought.

"Will you let me drive?" she asked.

"Noooo," he crooned, smiling.

"Then . . . then get to a gas station. You're on empty."

"Oh. Why, thank you, little lady. You're right about that." Looping widely, he turned off the interstate.

They passed by a McDonald's and an EconoLodge motel, as well as a Texaco station with six pumps.

"You missed it," Amelia said as they headed off on a winding country road.

"I can't trust you, darlin'," he said sadly. "Oh, I will, don't you worry. You just need a little time. Then you won't want to run away." His voice was so faint that he could hardly be heard. "_She_ wanted to go away at first, too. She wanted to leave my pa. But after a while she stayed . . ."

Amelia grabbed the steering wheel to keep the car on the road. "There's a place. Up ahead."

Turner drove into it, slowing down only a few feet from the gas pump; a cloud of dust rose up from the car.

An old man sitting on a bench outside with a cup of coffee glared at them and shook his head. Slowly he put down his cup and got up, shuffling toward them with an arthritic gait.

"Fill 'er up, friend," Turner said, getting out of the car. "And give me two extra gallons for the road."

"You got cash?" the old geezer asked, adjusting his dentures.

Turner reached inside his jacket.

Oh, God, he's going to shoot him, Amelia thought, but Turner only pulled out a wallet and brandished some bills.

Amelia got out. "May I use your rest room, please?" she asked the attendant.

The old man nodded and extracted a key from a large ring. Before Amelia could take it, Turner snatched it out of the man's hand and grasped her arm.

The attendant gave her a quick, concerned glance. She wanted to scream for help, but she knew that nothing would come of that except the old man's death. No other buildings were nearby; a gunshot, even from a Magnum, would not be heard by anyone else. The old man would die in his own blood, and no one would know why.

She blinked the tears from her eyes and allowed Turner to drag her, weaving wildly, toward the back of the station.

At the rest room he threw open the door and leaned against it. "I'll wait here," he said, grinning as she walked in.

She turned. "Can't I even close the door?"

"Nope."

"Look, there's only one exit. And I don't even have a pocketbook, so I can't write a message on the mirror with lipstick or anything like that."

Turner took a swig from the flask. "You could kill yourself," he said.

Amelia pushed past him and stepped back outside. "Never mind."

The old man was replacing the hose into the gas pump when they came out front. He wiped his hands on a rag. "You all right?" he asked, not looking at her.

"What do I owe you, Pops?" Turner asked, sauntering past Amelia.

"Twelve dollars."

Turner fished out his wallet again, and as he was counting

out the money, the old man looked at Amelia.

He wants to help me, she thought. *And he's smart enough to keep from getting killed.*

She hooked her thumb around the gold bracelet with her name on it and quietly slipped it off, letting it thud dully on the soft dirt by the old man's mud-caked boot. He did not give it even a glance, but only stared steadily at Amelia's eyes, like an old turtle who does nothing in a rush. Finally he blinked once, slowly.

He understood.

Turner paid him, and they left. In the sideview mirror, Amelia saw the old man bend over and pick up an object that glinted gold in the late afternoon sun.

"Here's something in from West Virginia," Dallingwood said. "Double murder. There was an eyewitness, a ten-year-old kid. Says a man answering the description of the perp killed his grandmother and a neighbor. Hacked off their ears."

Sergeant grabbed the report. Amelia's name was on it.

"Town called Meridian. I've already spoken with the cops down there. The kid told them to contact New York. It's what the Pierce woman asked him to do, apparently."

"She's alive," Sergeant said, feeling the blood rush to his head.

"As of midnight, anyway," Dallingwood added dubiously.

"They're moving south."

"Looks that way. I might as well call my men off the Hudson reservoirs."

"Do that," Sergeant agreed. "We'll need them elsewhere." He unrolled a map of the United States. "Meridian, West Virginia, you said?"

"Right. Looks like the nearest Interstate would be Route Seventy-five. Chances are, they got back on after the stop in Meridian."

But where are they going? Sergeant asked himself. He traced down Route 75 with his finger. South from West Virginia into . . . where? North Carolina? Tennessee?

"The damned thing is, we don't know what we're looking for. The kid remembers a blue car, old model, maybe a Ford, isn't sure. Didn't get the license number."

And then where? Alabama? South Carolina? Georgia? Florida? Panama? Where? And why?

"Meanwhile, the Bureau's files don't have a damned thing on Wade Turner, and you haven't got so much as a photograph. If you ask me—"

"Excuse me, Mr. Dallingwood," a patrolman said. "We just got a call from Ichabod, Tennessee. A gas-station attendant spotted a guy answering the description of the perp with a red-haired woman in a blue Ford sedan off Interstate Forty. Said the woman looked like she was in trouble. She dropped a bracelet with the name 'Amelia' written on it."

"Route Forty out of Tennessee," Sergeant said, turning to the map.

"Did he get a license number?" Dallingwood asked.

"Sure did." He gave him a piece of paper with the number written on it. "They're faxing in the report now."

Sergeant found Ichabod on the map. It was far to the west, less than thirty miles from the Arkansas border.

Arkansas.

Where the Scorpion learned to kill, he thought. Five days after Billy Starr joined the Marines, the mutilated bodies of his mother and sister were found in the Buffalo River. In Arkansas.

"Get the Ichabod police on the phone again," Dallingwood said. "I want to talk to the witness myself."

"West Falls," Sergeant said quietly.

"What's that?"

"West Falls, Arkansas. That's where they're headed."

Dallingwood's eyes narrowed. "Mind telling me how you figured that out?"

"I'll explain later. Can you get me a plane?"

"I'll get some men there, if you want. And the local police."

"Fine. And me."

"It's too far. You couldn't do any good there, anyway."

"I'm going, Dallingwood. And you're still under orders to accommodate me."

The black man worked his jaw. Finally he spoke. "Whatever you say."

35

Amelia was awakened out of a deep, dreamless sleep by the loud wail of a siren.

Her heart skipped and thudded. Behind them, on an otherwise deserted road, a pair of bright red and blue flashers was lighting up the darkening sky.

"Police," she said. Her throat closed with tears of relief as Turner pulled off the road.

The police knew. It was over at last.

"Get out of the car, and keep your hands where I can see them." The patrolman was young, in his mid-twenties. And he was alone. County cop, probably on traffic duty.

He held his police revolver with both hands as Turner slowly emerged from the blue Ford.

"Hands on the roof. Do it!"

The young cop was scared. Amelia could hear it in his voice, see it in the bright cast to his eyes.

You're no match for him, she thought, suddenly afraid again.

Still, the cop might be able to handle Turner. He had a gun, and he had probably called for some backup.

Just be careful. You can live if you're careful. We all can.

Turner faced the car, his hands in the air, his face was benign, almost smiling.

The patrolman frisked him clumsily. When he found the Magnum and drew it out, Turner whirled around—*just like a dancer,* Amelia thought as she watched in horror—and snapped open a switchblade that had seemingly materialized out of the air.

It was in his sleeve, of course. He'd made sure of that when he first saw the flashing lights. Did you really believe he'd let a child policeman put him in handcuffs and take him to jail like an ordinary criminal?

In a single motion, Turner sliced through the young man's throat.

The patrolman staggered backward, his eyes wide with surprise. Turner took the Magnum from him.

"Thank ye kindly," he said, then shot him through the head.

Amelia slumped in her seat, unable to move, listening to the silent scream inside her.

Get up.

She squeezed her eyes shut. She didn't want it to be happening, not again. *Will it never end?*

Get up.

There would be a radio in the patrol car. A radio, to call for help.

She forced herself out of the lethargy of her horror and ran to the cruiser. The squawk box was broadcasting some sort of rapid, unintelligible message. Amelia picked up the radio and pressed what she hoped was the transmit button.

"Help, please! There's a policeman shot here. My name is Amelia Pierce. I don't know where we are . . ." She looked around frantically for some identifying landmark. There was none. In the gray twilit sky, even the background hills were barely visible.

"Give me the number of the vehicle," a voice called over the radio.

"The number. All right . . ."

It had to be outside, in plain sight. She tumbled out the

door, still holding the small metal box of the radio.

"The number—"

Turner took the radio from her. He ripped the wires out of the dashboard. "Move over," he said.

His eyes were as flat and dead as a shark's. Spittle ran from one corner of his mouth. It was stained pink.

Holding on to the collar of her dress with one hand, he maneuvered the police cruiser back on the road and floored the gas pedal.

Turner pulled over less than a half hour later, in a woody clearing off a dirt road, behind a mountain of trash.

"We'll walk from here," he said.

His accent was gone. He blinked slowly, his mouth hanging open. His skin was sheened with sweat. His hand was clasped in a viselike grip around Amelia's arm, and she felt that if he let go, he would crumple to the floor like a rag doll. The valise hung from his left arm, a deadweight. His fingers were white around its handle.

"Don't try to run away," he said wearily. "At this point, I'll just shoot you." He stumbled and slammed into Amelia. "Keep going. It's here somewhere."

"What is?"

"The place. Home." He turned aside and vomited a long projectile of bright blood. Amelia stepped back in horror. "I said keep going!" he rasped, clinging to her viciously.

Maneuvering the valise under his arm, he took the silver flask from his pocket and drained it. Then he stood stock still, oblivious to the death grip he held on Amelia, and stared at the shining object in his hand.

"The poison," he whispered in wonderment. He suddenly burst out laughing, roaring so loudly that his whole body shook. Tears streamed out of his eyes.

"He gave me a present," he shouted. "The first present I ever got." He lifted the silver flask so that it flashed in the late-afternoon sunlight. "And he filled it with poison!"

A fit of coughing wracked him then. When it subsided, he was weeping. "Move on," he said hoarsely.

They walked along a nearly overgrown dirt path that

wound up a hill at the side of the dirt road, trudging through the forest, scratching and bruising themselves on branches and thorns.

Finally Turner spoke. "There it is." He smiled.

Amelia looked around. There was nothing in view except for a weird formation of rock.

"Peccary cave," he said. "Forty years ago some archaeologists dug out the bones of prehistoric pigs from this cave. They found some Indian skeletons, too. The peccaries must have brought the Indians into the cave to eat them."

"Did you grow up here?"

Turner shook his head. "I've never been here before. This was my father's home. It was important to me to know the area. I've listened to hundreds of hours of tape about it." He coughed. "My father didn't like it much, this place. He hated being poor."

He stopped walking. "He killed his family to get away," Turner said quietly. "Or maybe he killed them just because he wanted to. He killed almost everyone he knew." He took a deep breath. "God, I wish he'd killed me."

He smiled sadly at Amelia. "I can smell the river. Would you like to see it?"

Amelia expected him to jerk her in another direction, but instead he slid his hand down her arm and entwined his fingers in hers. "I'm sorry I've frightened you so badly. Please come with me."

He walked her through the woods, oblivious to the branches that cut his face. He breathed deeply, then shivered as if in ecstasy.

They arrived at a bluff nearly a thousand feet above a winding river.

"That's the Buffalo," Turner said. The river snaked beneath them, far, far below the sand-colored cliffs or sheer rock, spreading out its fingers toward a massive lake filigreed between tree-covered peaks in the distance.

"Table Mountain Reservoir." He reached into his jacket and pulled out the Magnum.

Amelia backed away, shielding her face with her hands, but he made no attempt to threaten her. Instead, he threw the gun over the cliff.

"We won't need that now," he said. "We've got something much better."

Amelia looked down at the black case. The journey was over. He had come home to kill for the last time.

Her eyes flooded. Her father had entrusted her with a mission to save the world, and she had failed.

"You don't have to use the poison," she whispered.

"Yes, I do."

"Why?" She turned to him suddenly, grabbed him by the front of his shirt, and shook him. "Tell me why!"

He closed his eyes. His head dropped, as if its weight were too heavy to carry. "Because this is my legacy," he said slowly. "Billy Starr sired a son to destroy the world. It is the entire reason for my existence."

Amelia let go. "Billy . . . Starr. Your father?"

"Didn't you know his name?" he asked gently. "I didn't either. Not for years and years. I just thought of him as the giant. The giant with his great sword, coming to kill you . . ."

She looked up at him, terrified. His sick mind was involving her in part of his past, something that had to do with Billy Starr.

"Wade," she whispered.

"You can call me Daniel," he said, his eyes lighting up. "It's safe here. He'll never harm you again. After I'm finished, no one will ever harm you again." He touched her hair, watching its color dance in the light. "I always loved your hair, Mother."

"Wade . . . Daniel," she said quietly, "I'm not your mother."

Turner smiled. "You don't have to pretend anymore, Mother. They wouldn't let you hold me, but you wanted to. I know that. You called my name. Before he cut you in pieces, you called my name."

He reached and held her close. "I've come back for you, Mother. And I will protect you. Always."

Amelia bit her lip. It had been easier to hate him. Now, listening to his pathetic madness, she felt only pity for this man who had been driven by horrors beyond her imagining to become a beast whose only purpose in life was to kill.

He stepped back and lifted her chin. "I'll never hurt you," he said, his blue eyes fierce with love. "I promise you that."

Then he pulled her gently back to the trail. "Come with me," he said. "It's not far now."

They found the house a few hundred yards farther. It was no more than an unpainted shack set on a patch of packed dirt. Weeds had overrun the place, and thick vines twined around the one-room shanty as if about to squeeze it like a fist around a paper carton.

Turner looked on it with wonder. He could barely lift his head, but a smile of pure joy lit up his face. "Home," he croaked. "We're home."

Gently he opened the door. There was no lock, and it creaked open to a room where sunlight shone into the darkness through the broken slats of the roof.

There was a bed with a rusted metal headboard, the stained mattress covered with paper-thin gray rags where squirrels had nested for generations. In the corner was a potbellied stove. As he walked—slowly, respectfully, as if he were entering a crypt—thick dust swirled up from the floor to dance in the shafts of slowly reddening sunlight.

It's probably just the way it was the day Billy Starr killed his mother and sister, Amelia thought.

A wooden crate with a kerosene lamp on top sat beside the bed. On the floor beside the crate lay a movie magazine with Brigitte Bardot's picture on the cover, its contents torn and scattered by the animals who had been inhabiting the place. She picked it up. The date on the corner was April, nineteen fifty-seven.

Turner took it out of her hands and pulled her gently onto the bed. "Lie with me, Mother," he said. He pulled her onto the filthy cotton cover and wound his arms around her. He was burning with fever.

"In my jacket," he said. "Take it out."

"Take what out?" She rummaged in his pockets and found the bottle of cologne. "Is this what you want?"

"Yes," he said. "Put some of it on. Please."

Amelia unscrewed the cap and splashed the scent on herself.

Turner smiled. "Thank you. I remembered, you know. All these years . . ."

He held her closer. "I'm so tired. I've waited so long to bring you here."

"I know," Amelia whispered.

"Everything will be fine now, you'll see. Fine . . ."

He dozed, his arms tight around her . . . and Amelia thought of the black case on the floor.

36

The plane was waiting when Dallingwood and Sergeant arrived at Kennedy Airport. Sergeant had never seen such an aircraft before. It was military-silver and had the rough shape of an Air Force fighter, but it was bigger through the belly, obviously having been designed for carrying VIPs who were in a hurry.

"Your private Piper Cub?" Sergeant asked.

"Fastest thing the Bureau's got. Just for us."

"I said I'd go alone," Sergeant said.

"No way." The black man shouldered the heavy bag of protective apparel borrowed from the NYPD Toxic Substances Unit and led the way to the plane.

They scrambled up a rickety ladder, and Dallingwood tossed the bag behind the seat. The plane would have held six passengers in comfort. The two men sat side by side behind the pilot.

"Take us up," Dallingwood shouted.

The pilot, young and fuzzy-cheeked, nodded and pushed the throttle. Obviously clearance had already been arranged, because without waiting the pilot barreled down the runway, lifted the nose of the plane, and the craft took off like a bullet.

"How long will this take?" Sergeant asked.

Dallingwood looked at his watch. "Less than an hour."

"An hour? Arkansas is more than a thousand miles away."

"Oh, didn't I tell you?" Dallingwood said innocently. "We're not going to Arkansas, Mr. Hyatt." He pronounced the name with mocking emphasis. "That is the name you're using today, isn't it?"

Sergeant glared at him, then leaned forward to shout to the pilot. "Set a course for West Falls, Arkansas."

"Sit down." Dallingwood swatted him back into his seat. "This bird is under my command. And you're going straight to Washington." He slapped a handcuff ring around Sergeant's left wrist. "You have the right to remain silent. You have the right to an—"

"For Christ's sake, Dallingwood!"

"Your game is up, mister. Do you understand me?" Dallingwood bellowed.

"Look. I've explained—"

"You explained shit." The big black man's eyes bulged angrily. "You smelled wrong the minute I saw you. So when you said don't bother trying to identify the stiff we found in the girl's apartment, I went down to the morgue to get his prints. And guess what? You're not Davis Hyatt, because Davis Hyatt's lying on a slab with his throat cut. We had his prints on file down at the Bureau. Did you do it?"

"Kill Hyatt?" Sergeant shook his head. "No. His death is the reason I'm here."

"Save it for the boys in Washington," Dallingwood said. "They'll want to know how you pulled off this masquerade. Davis Hyatt's got a file with the FBI, did you know that? A real special file, too confidential for me to look at, or practically anybody else. 'Bureau Director's Eyes Only.' That's how it's listed in the computer."

Sergeant looked out the window.

"And when the director got my message about who the stiff is, he was real interested, believe me. Real interested."

"I can imagine," Sergeant said blandly.

So the director of the FBI knew, he thought. The Network was unraveling already.

"What about Amelia Pierce?"

"West Falls is covered. Just in case you were telling the truth about something."

"They'll kill her."

Dallingwood's eyes narrowed. "Who's 'they'? I thought this supergeek Turner of yours was working alone."

Sergeant looked over at him slowly. "One of your guys will kill her. Probably a sharpshooter. On orders from your boss."

The FBI man started to turn away in disgust, but something in Sergeant's voice made him hesitate. "Mind explaining that?" he asked.

"Dallingwood, there are people in the world who can do anything. Oh, they're not evil people. As individuals, I'm certain they're absolutely committed to law and justice. But they're not working as individuals here."

"Who are you talking about?"

"I'm talking about an entity. A gestalt creature made up of the most powerful men on earth: the heads of the FBI, CIA, KGB, the Mossad, MI-Five . . . I don't know how many of them there are. They got together twelve years ago to form a cooperative intelligence network to combat terrorism. Davis Hyatt ran it."

"You got to be shitting me," Dallingwood said.

"That's what's in the file you aren't allowed to read. In fact, I've already told you enough to get you killed."

"Well, if this thing is so damn secret, how do you know about it?"

"I was Hyatt's assistant. We were in the middle of this case when he was killed."

"And all you want to do is to close the case, I suppose," Dallingwood said sarcastically.

"I want to save Amelia Pierce."

"Yeah, well, you can leave that to the team that's down there. They'll catch Turner."

"Maybe. If he doesn't kill her first. And once he's caught,

a stray bullet's going to find its way to Amelia. Because she won't be permitted to talk to you. There's too much at stake. That's why I've got to be there, Dallingwood. If I can keep her alive at the scene, if I can keep the Network's sharpshooter away from her, she might make it."

"How's that?" Dallingwood asked flatly. "If what you're saying is true—and I don't believe any of it for a minute— then she's going to buy it anyway, on the scene or off."

"No. She's left too big a trail. The boy in West Virginia, the gas-station attendant in Tennessee who found her bracelet, all the cops and neighbors they've talked to since then . . . Even the Network can't kill them all. Amelia's already been to a newspaper, maybe more than one. If she's not 'accidentally' killed today, there are going to be some newsmen interested in what happens to her. The Network will have to let her live."

Dallingwood eyed Sergeant carefully. He had met a lot of lunatics in his career. What this man was saying was off the wall, but there was something about it that had the ring of truth.

"You worked for this Hyatt guy, you said."

Sergeant nodded.

Dallingwood raised his chin until he looked like a colossus staring down at the mortal below him. "Then, if the woman is going to get her ticket punched just for knowing about your Network . . . how come *you're* still alive?"

"Hyatt didn't inform the Network about some things," he said, aware of the understatement. "One of them was my name. The Network enforcers are looking for someone else."

"You could have walked?"

"I suppose so."

"What *is* your name?"

Sergeant shook his head. "I can't give you that."

Dallingwood grunted and settled back in his seat. "Well, you can forget about walking now, Mr. No-name," he said. "You won't be getting out of this one."

"I know that. But maybe Amelia Pierce will."

Sergeant looked the man straight in the eye. Then, in one

twisting, shaking motion, he caught Dallingwood's head in a hammerlock and pulled the big man's automatic from his shoulder holster.

The pilot turned to face the two men in the rear, his handgun drawn. Sergeant was behind Dallingwood now, the barrel of the automatic pressed against the black man's temple.

"You can kill me yourself when this is over," he whispered to Dallingwood. "Just get me to West Falls."

"You're in a lot of trouble, boy," Dallingwood said.

Sergeant jabbed him with the gun. "So are you. Change course."

Dallingwood stared at the pilot, who stared back.

"I'll kill you if I have to," Sergeant warned.

The FBI man sighed. "Change course," he ordered the pilot. "West Falls, Arkansas."

The plane swooped in a low arc, picked up altitude, and sped south.

"You'll be shot when we land, you know," Dallingwood said.

"No. Not in Arkansas. The Network will want to find out what I know about Hyatt first. They'll kill me later."

"You got that wrong, sport. I'm going to off you myself. You promised."

Sergeant smiled. "Sorry, I forgot."

"Shit," Dallingwood said. "All right, I believe you."

Sergeant looked into his eyes. "What?"

"I said I believe you. Once we're in West Falls, there will be a hundred law-enforcement officials to see that you don't get away. Now get that gun out of my face."

Slowly, Sergeant lowered the weapon. Dallingwood made no move to take it. Sergeant dropped it into the FBI man's lap.

Dallingwood replaced the gun in his shoulder holster. "But the cuffs stay on, you crazy motherfucker."

The pilot turned around, saw Sergeant sitting quiet and unarmed, and did a double take. "Back to D.C., Mr. Dallingwood?" he asked.

The black man's eyes never left Sergeant's face. "Stay on course," he replied at last. "We're going to Arkansas."

37

Turner stirred. He moved his lips, and blood trickled out between them. Amelia fought the feeling of revulsion rising inside her. The man seemed to be melting before her eyes.

This is what we'll all be like, she thought. Once Turner released the virus into the river, it would flow downstream, into reservoirs, into wells. It could infect the population of three states. And it would be used in other places, too. No one ever willingly stopped using a weapon.

How long would it take to strip the population of North America, of Europe, of Asia?

Turner was dying. He smelled of death. How different he looked from the young man who had taken her to breakfast on Santa Vittoria two weeks before.

Silently, moving only a fraction of an inch at a time, Amelia worked her way out of his embrace. He didn't move. He had gone without sleep for two days, she reminded herself. And he was sick. He might die. He might never awaken from this bloody, dreamless sleep.

He might die.

Oh, please, God, let him die. Take him now, so that I won't have to go through this anymore.

She inched away. One foot touched the floor. She crouched so that she would not disturb the bed, and slid off slowly. She was free.

The case was on a rickety table near the window. She crept toward it. When her fingers touched the black plastic, they slid over it, leaving trails of perspiration.

How far can you get? she wondered in despair. *You don't even know where you are.*

She pushed the thought out of her mind. She would run as far as she could, for as long as she could. And if she was lucky, she might live through it.

She opened the door slowly, careful that the bright sunlight did not reach to the bed.

Then she stopped cold. There was a small paring knife, rusted with disuse, on the dusty stone mantel of the fireplace across the room.

Billy Starr's knife, she thought, envisioning the young boy slashing through his own mother and sister.

It made her shudder. And then she had another thought: *I could kill him.* Kill Turner now, before he had a chance to kill her. Slash his throat the way he had murdered Marla Sebastapol and Davis Hyatt and the policeman and God only knew how many others.

Kill a sick man in his sleep?

But he wasn't a man. He was a monster.

He moved slightly on the bed. His hair was matted with sweat. He was shivering.

"I'll never harm you. I promise you that."

She stepped out the door and ran.

Amelia's first thought was to throw the case over the bluff. But it was a long way down. The case did not seem particularly sturdy; one good bounce on a rock could easily open it. She did not know what material the virus was contained in. What if it were glass?

Her only hope was the woods. She had a good sense of direction. She knew the way to the police cruiser. She looked up at the sun, already well in the west. The car was far away; it would take her most of the afternoon to reach it, but when she did she would be clear.

She headed off at a run, slowing down slightly when she entered the woods. The trail was easy to find, and she loped along steadily, pacing herself for the long haul.

In time, the sense of danger began to fall away. With the even sound of her footfalls and the rhythmic beating of her heart, Amelia's mind cleared of everything but the run itself. The black case slapped against her leg in repetitive motion, and she grew not to notice its weight. Ahead, she saw the outcropping of rock that was the entrance to the peccary cave.

Two hours, she thought. *Ninety minutes, if I'm fast. Ninety minutes . . .*

"Amelia!"

The sound was like the cry of a wounded animal. Hoarse, anguished, filled with the hurt of betrayal. Turner had come after her.

And he was close.

His voice jolted her out of her run. Her heart suddenly thudded. Her bowels felt loose.

Why hadn't she taken the knife?

She cursed herself. She had put her life in jeopardy because of a moment's sentiment.

But he wasn't supposed to follow me. He was supposed to die there, in that room.

"Amelia?"

She twisted her head around and lost her footing. Instinctively her arms flailed out for balance. The black case smashed against the sharp ledge of rock surrounding the peccary cave and opened at once with a crack.

Amelia stifled a scream as a formless, jellylike blob fell to the ground beside her.

It was a heat-sealed pouch of clear plastic encasing a yellow-brown liquid. For a moment she could only stare at the bubbling waves of fluid inside the bag. It did not appear to be leaking. In time, its motion subsided. It lay on the ground like leftover soup saved in an oversized Ziploc bag.

Leaving it, she walked over to the case. Her ankle had

twisted badly. She would not be able to run, she knew.

The case was beyond repair. One of the locks had snapped completely off, and the lid had sprung from its hinges.

Amelia glanced at the cave. If she were trapped inside there, she would never get out.

"Amelia!"

Turner's voice came harsh and loud now. He was very near.

Amelia put the broken case under one arm and then gingerly picked up a corner of the plastic bag containing the poison. She looked behind her once more before hurrying into the cave.

The entrance was so small that she had to crouch to walk through it, and so narrow that the unwieldy, hinge-sprung case was barely manageable.

I'm in a grave, she thought. *I'm in a grave, and he'll kill me here.*

She was nearly ready to turn back when suddenly the space opened up and she was able to stand. It was pitch dark here, but she heard the screech of bats overhead in the distance.

A big cave. Maybe big enough to get lost in?

She hoped so.

She moved sideways, feeling for a wall. When she found one, she dropped the case and kept on moving.

The plastic bag felt slick in her hands. She held it more firmly, in the center. It was like a limp, dead animal, still warm with life.

What she wanted was a grotto of some kind, a recess in the damp, cold wall, where she could hide.

Like a rat in a hole, she thought, fear shaking her body. She had no other chance to live. All of her plans and dreams and fantasies had played themselves out. There was nothing left but to hide. And so she groped blindly in the dark, listening for the sound of footfalls behind her.

Instead, she heard water.

She clung to the wall, but it was becoming more slippery,

and she could smell the earth-mist of underground water. The passageway was very long. Amelia guessed she had walked more than a thousand feet when she felt a sudden break in the wall and then another mass of stone, fashioned at an angle, that met it.

This was once a river, she thought with wonder. An underground river that had long ago lost the water that formed it. She followed the bend to the smaller tributary, which wound lazily for a hundred yards or more, then narrowed into a steep, high corridor. From here, the sound of water was loud.

She stepped through the corridor as if it were a threshold. When she emerged, she was in a massive cavern. By touch she found stalactites, as large as trees, growing in her way, and massive round boulders that jutted up from the ground. The stone floor here was oddly shaped and bumpy, unlike the smooth, almost paved surface of the long riverway, and every inch of it was coated with a film of water.

This had been a lake. No doubt a larger lake had existed off in the other direction, from which the river took most of its water. But this one had joined the larger one over the course of millennia. It had let out its precious water slowly, yet still retained some of it thousands—perhaps millions—of years later.

Even now she heard the drip of falling water, and she followed the sound, moving carefully because every step was difficult and hazardous. She knew that if she broke a leg here, she would be done for, even if Turner never found her.

But she had gone far enough, and soon she would stop . . . if she found the right place.

In the dark, she could feel mist rising. There must be a ledge above her, she reasoned, where ground water dripped in a cascade. She held out her hand. The water was steady and cold. It did not possess the strength of a waterfall, exactly; it was more like the splash of a pump shower. Still, its mist felt cool and soft on her face. She clutched the plastic bag tightly, feeling with her feet for purchase on the slippery rock.

The ground was softer here; solid stone had given way to

mounds of tiny pebbles. Amelia tried to stand upright, but the pebbles moved like sand beneath her. Bending her knees, half-sitting to avoid a pratfall, she slid down a distance of eight feet or more, directly into the spill of the waterfall. She landed in an awkward sprawl a few feet behind it.

With a gasp, she scrambled upright and slowly began to search the area around her. It was about twelve feet long and five feet deep, an anteroom, a cave within a cave. In front, the steady flow of the thin waterfall provided a curtain between her and anything that might be in the cavern. Here she would be safe from bats and other rodents. Large animals wandering in would probably not scent her here.

And she would be hidden from Wade Turner.

With a sigh of relief, she sat down and listened to the music of the falling water.

Maybe I have a chance, Daddy. Maybe I'll make it after all.

She waited quietly, patiently, the plastic bag filled with deadly virus cradled like a baby in her arms. Her stay, she knew, was going to be a long one.

In the dark quiet of the cave, she allowed herself at last to think of Burt Sergeant.

It could have been something fine, she thought. She had had a chance to love, once, if she had been willing to trust herself.

But she hadn't been. Instead of believing in Sergeant's love, she had chosen to believe in his betrayal. It had been easier that way. And now he was gone, along with everyone else in her life who had mattered . . . because she had not dared to hope.

"Oh, Burt," she whispered, and the tears she had stored for so long poured out in bitter silence. She cried for a long time, until there were no tears left to cry.

She felt cold. Her hair and clothing were soaking wet; they would have little chance to dry here. She began to rub her bare arms, and realized she was still clutching the bag. It was as if the plastic had been coated with bubble gum. It pulled away in strings. It felt light. Frantically she held it up, feeling a terrible pounding in her chest.

The bag was empty.

She moaned, with a horror so deep that the sound did not seem human even to herself. The poison had been encased in gel, not in plastic. It had melted, and she had received its entire contents on her body.

She curled up into a ball and rocked back and forth, staring blankly into the darkness. She did not see Wade Turner's hand thrust through the spill of water, but when he touched her, she did not resist him.

"Come with me," he said gently.

His arms folded around her. It was the cold embrace of death itself, Amelia knew. Her time had come, and she finally accepted him.

"We'll die in the light," he said.

She took his hand and followed him.

38

The closest airport where the jet could land was at Little Rock. Dallingwood radioed ahead, and a military helicopter was waiting for them when they touched down.

A few minutes later, the helicopter was approaching the Ozarks.

"A highway cop was killed," the pilot shouted back at them. "I just got it over the radio. The local police spotted his cruiser near here."

Dallingwood leaped up. "Put me through to FBI headquarters," he said. "I'm calling out a SWAT team."

Sergeant sat up in his seat, his handcuffed hands in his lap. SWAT had a chance against Turner. A hell of a better chance than Amelia would ever have alone.

She might still be alive, he told himself. *She might still make it.*

If he could just keep the Network away from her . . .

He remembered their night in Vienna, the feel of her arms around him, the softness of her skin, the fear they had shared and somehow, through the touch of their bodies, overcome for a night.

And there were unspoken things, too.

He was not crazy. He had not tried to kill himself and then conveniently forgotten the attempt. In truth, he had been so angry with Amelia when she had thought he was the Scorpion, because in some well-hidden valley of his mind, he had been afraid that she might be right, that the man he had been looking for for nine years might be himself.

Hyatt's letter had exonerated him from that fear. Billy Starr had cut Sergeant's throat, and Billy Starr was dead, as dead as his victims. As dead as Sergeant's wife and daughter.

He could let them rest now.

But he had to keep Amelia alive.

Somehow, in the mass of law officers who had been called out to West Falls, Sergeant had to spot the sharpshooter who had been assigned to kill Amelia.

He had no doubt that the attempt would be made. Without Amelia Pierce, the Network could disband and the men in power would never speak of it again.

There is to be no trace, Hyatt had said.

In time, the sharpshooter himself would be killed. Dallingwood, too.

No trace.

When does it stop? Sergeant wondered wearily. The Network had been formed to do good. But in the end, was it any more moral or humane than the terrorists it was fighting?

Dallingwood sat back down, frowning.

"What's up?" Sergeant asked.

"A SWAT team's already been called in," the FBI man said. "Director's orders."

"That's the shooter," Sergeant said quietly.

Dallingwood took off the handcuffs. "I don't know what's going down, but there's no point keeping you in these."

"Thanks."

"By the way, an ambulance chopper from the Centers for Disease Control in Atlanta is on its way to pick up the poison. You're lady's going to come out of this just fine."

"Yeah," Sergeant said.

If I don't fuck up.

A few minutes later, they spotted the cruiser. A small army of police beat its way in twos over the wooded hillside, weapons drawn. The SWAT team hadn't arrived yet. If it had, the local cops would have been herded out of the way.

Sergeant's pulse quickened. Without the SWAT sharp-shooter, he might be able to get away with Amelia. Not for long, of course; there were too many police. But perhaps long enough to tell her what he needed to say. Long enough to say good-bye.

It was the only hope he had.

"There's the house," Dallingwood said. "Set down in the clear . . . Jesus Christ! I see them!"

Turner and Amelia were walking out of the woods to-ward the bluff. He was leaning heavily on her, and they moved in a leaden, weaving pattern.

"You're alive," Sergeant whispered.

Then he saw the SWAT helicopter coming toward them.

Amelia squinted against the bright sunlight.

"It's not far," Turner said, gasping.

In the light she could see the yellow-brown stain that covered the entire front of her dress.

"Is it bad?" she asked in a whisper. "The sickness?"

Turner touched her face. His own looked like a ghoul's, and his eyes shone with pain. "Yes," he said. "It's bad." He smiled. "But you won't have to worry about that. We're fine now. Everything will be fine."

A helicopter buzzed overhead.

Amelia stared at it blankly at first, not understanding why it would be there, flying so low in the sky above the cliff.

Then she realized that it had come for her.

"They've found us," she said, then laughed with such bit-terness that tears came to her eyes. "Now they've come."

"Help me, Amelia. I don't want them to shoot me before we reach the bluff."

She propped him up in her arms. "Daniel . . ." The name came automatically to her now.

His eyelids fluttered. "I'm all right. Please hurry."

"I'll take you to the house. You can rest in your bed."

"No, Amelia," he said gently. "We're going to jump."

Her breath caught. She tried to back away from him, but he held fast, his fingers digging into the flesh of her arm.

"Don't you see? It's the only way now. Our bodies are filled with the virus. It's in our skin, in our blood. *We're* the weapon now."

"Let go of me!" she shrieked.

Another helicopter swooped overhead. It lowered into a clearing a hundred yards from where they stood. Six men with rifles jumped out, moving toward them.

"Hurry!" With a new strength that caused his wasted face to contort in agony, Turner dragged her toward the sharp drop of the cliff's edge.

"Amelia!" A man was running down the hillside toward them. With a sob, she recognized Burt Sergeant.

"Stay away!" she screamed. "The poison's been opened. I'm . . . I'm infected."

Sergeant loped along for a few more strides, as if his legs had continued to move despite what his ears were hearing. Then he stopped. He stood there on the grassy bank and slowly covered his face with his hands.

Turner put his arm around her shoulder. "Let's go," he said.

The police and the SWAT men surrounded them in a wide semicircle. An enormous black man with a bullhorn was shouting at Turner to give up his hostage, but Turner paid no attention to him.

"We have to do it now, darling," he said. He touched her face and smiled. "Don't be afraid. It was inevitable that we be here together, you and I." He winced in pain. "You're part of my father's legacy to me. You and the poison and our death, here in the place of his birth. Now, at last, it can end."

Amelia jerked away from him violently. "Tell those men to shoot!" she shouted at Sergeant. "He's going to jump!"

The expression on Turner's face was confused, stricken.

"Why did you tell them that?" His raw voice was filled with hurt. "Why would you want them to shoot me?"

"Daniel, listen to me. You can't do this!"

His mouth set bitterly. In one quick motion he reached into his sleeve and pulled out the shining switchblade he had used to kill the patrolman. Before Amelia could move away, Turner had it at her throat.

"Hold your fire!" Burt Sergeant shouted.

Amelia looked around wildly. Sergeant stood frozen on the hillside. The riflemen, assembled around the black man with the bullhorn, held their weapons to their shoulders.

"Hold your fire," the black man repeated.

"I'm sorry," Turner said. "There's no alternative now. Don't be afraid." He picked her up in his arms, careful to keep her between himself and the police, and stumbled backward toward the edge of the cliff. "I'll help you."

Amelia screamed.

"Forgive me, Mother," he said.

In that instant she lurched forward and bit his forearm. As he gasped, she grabbed the knife jutting out of Turner's fist, oblivious to the pain as the steel edge cut into her hand. His fingers had loosened reflexively. Amelia yanked the knife free and, not daring to think about what she was doing, thrust it into his neck.

Turner staggered. His eyes widened, amazement in their pain.

"Mother . . ." he said. Blood rose in his mouth.

Then, with all the strength in her body, Amelia drew the blade across his neck.

He dropped her. As she scrambled to her feet, his gaze fell to his chest, watching the cascade of blood pour out of him. Slowly he slid to his knees and wrapped his arms around Amelia's legs.

He looked up at her.

"I forgive you, Daniel," she whispered.

His eyes glazed over. His arms dropped. Only his face remained staring upward, angelic in its peacefulness.

The Scorpion was dead.

A thousand feet below, the Buffalo River roared on.

Amelia looked at the bloody knife in her hand.

Were we so different? she thought numbly. In his insanity,

Turner had spoken the truth. It had been inevitable that they had come here to die together, for Amelia had been left a legacy every bit as powerful as Turner's own. Her, father, too, had taught her to kill. Her memories, too, had brought her inexorably to this place of death.

Now, with the silent men and their guns surrounding her, and the plague poison bursting in her body, she was alone.

"Kill me now!" she shouted in a ragged screech. She raised her arms. "Shoot me and seal my body, before I kill you all!"

A sharpshooter from the SWAT team knelt, his rifle raised.

Burt Sergeant saw the motion and ran toward him. He threw himself on the rifleman a split second before the weapon fired into the air.

"You son of a bitch," Sergeant snarled, wrapping his hands around the man's throat. Gasping and writhing beneath him, the sharpshooter pounded the rifle butt into Sergeant's back.

Sergeant never flinched. In a moment, he knew, a dozen weapons would take aim at him; he was already marked for death. But he would kill this man first. For Amelia. For all she had suffered and was about to suffer. For his own rage and helplessness. For the world that was no longer going to die because one woman would die in its place.

"Back off!" Dallingwood's voice boomed like a cannon. He held an automatic rifle in his hands. "Back off, or I'll shoot your woman myself, damn it!"

Two police officers pulled Sergeant off the SWAT man, who sat up slowly, groaning.

A third helicopter, painted white, touched down, blowing up a storm of leaves and wind. Two figures dressed like spacemen, with helmets and breathing apparatus, descended from it carrying a large stretcher covered with a clear plastic bubble in which an oxygen tank and a mask had been placed.

Dallingwood spoke to the men on a radio. They moved toward Amelia cautiously. She was crouched next to Turner's body.

When the paramedics were within ten feet of her, they opened the bubble and gestured for her to come to them.

She stood up slowly, the knife still in her hand.

"I don't think so," she said. Her voice was quiet, but in the tense stillness, every man present heard her.

She raised the knife to her chest and closed her other hand around the hilt.

"Amelia!" Sergeant roared, shattering the silence as he ran toward her.

She looked at him in alarm. "Get away!" she called. "Burt, no . . ."

"Put down that knife, or by God, you'd better be ready to use it on me!"

"You don't understand!"

"I know that I love you," he shouted. "And I don't care about anything else. Don't die, Amelia." His voice cracked with anguish. "Oh, God, please don't die!"

She watched him come closer, past the paramedics in their spacesuits, running toward death with his arms outstretched . . .

She threw away the knife. "Stop!" she commanded.

Sergeant stopped. He was sobbing.

Dallingwood talked quietly into his radio. One of the paramedics sprinted back to the ambulance chopper and came out with a large roll of gauze.

Her sad eyes locked on Sergeant, Amelia walked to the covered stretcher and got in.

The paramedics bandaged her hand quickly, then sealed the seam of the plastic bubble. They carried her away like a corpse.

Sergeant caught up. The stretcher-bearers tried to wave him away, but he ignored them.

"Amelia," he whispered.

Above the oxygen mask she wore, Amelia's eyes shone with pain and joy and heartbreak. There was no hope left now . . . only the memory of one night.

But then, sometimes memories were all that mattered.

She blinked, nodded, and raised her hand to the plastic

bubble. Blood was already seeping through the thick bandage.

Through the clear casket, Sergeant pressed her hand with his own.

Then the paramedics deposited her in the chopper before returning for Turner's body.

Sergeant watched the helicopter lift off and roar away until it was a small dragonfly in the sky. She was gone.

A pair of steel handcuffs clicked over his wrists.

"Ready?" Dallingwood asked quietly.

Sergeant nodded.

"You ran a good operation," the black man said.

Sergeant looked up at the sky. The dragonfly had vanished.

39

There were no windows in Sergeant's cell, and no bars. Just four cement walls that did not allow for the passage of time.

His days began and ended with interrogators, five different men who saw him in shifts of several hours each. When he failed to answer their questions, he was beaten.

He would answer to no one. He was beaten often. He was not permitted to sleep for more than three hours at a stretch, or to eat more than once a day.

He chose not to eat, just as he chose not to talk, though the interrogators promised that his cooperation would buy him time.

He already had far too much time. Time to think of his wife and daughter, slaughtered in his place. Of Arthur Pierce's wife Ludi, killed because she was married to an agent. Of Marla Sebastapol, murdered for her husband's knowledge. And of Amelia, dying in agony because she trusted the Network. They had never embraced the secret that killed them. They had never been the Glory Boys. But they had died all the same.

No, he did not wish to prolong his life by one moment.

Was Amelia dead yet? He could not remember how much time had passed.

He imagined that she was. None of the patients Dr. Sebastapol observed had lived for more than three days. He had to have been in this place for longer than three days.

Had she died from the poison? Or had she been beaten, too?

The thought drove him almost to tears, but he refused to shed them. The interrogators would think they were succeeding.

He looked around the room. He was alone. They would be coming back soon, but he was alone now.

Perhaps she had been killed quickly, by a merciful assassin. She deserved that much, at least, for carrying out the Network's mission. She had saved at least a million lives. A quick death was not too much to ask.

Then again, she might still be dying. Amelia was stubborn. She had a terrible will to live.

"Amelia," he whispered, doubling over into a corner.

He didn't hear the knock on the door. The interrogators were not in the habit of knocking before they entered. When Sergeant saw the shiny black shoes beside him, he wiped his nose on his sleeve and straightened up.

"What have they done to you?" came Dallingwood's booming accusation.

Sergeant took a deep breath and blinked. "Have you come to kill me?"

The black man saw the hope in his eyes. "No," he said softly. He handed him a handkerchief. "Here, pull yourself together. Jesus Christ!"

He put his hands on his hips and surveyed the cold cement room. The chain from the naked light bulb brushed against his face. He swatted it away and the light swayed, casting weirdly moving shadows on the walls. "In the fucking Federal Building," he said with disgust. "This is illegal as shit." His anger seemed to emanate from him in waves. "Where'd you get those bruises?"

Sergeant blew his nose. "Take a wild guess."

"I can't believe it. The fucking Federal Building," Dallingwood repeated. "Well, I'm going to see to it that ass gets kicked around here."

"Don't waste your time, Dallingwood." Sergeant stood up. He held out his hand.

Dallingwood shook it. "It's good to see you again."

"Same here. Thanks for getting me to Arkansas."

"It almost cost me my job."

It's going to cost you more than that, Sergeant thought sadly as he studied the enormous black face with its compassionate eyes. *No trace.* The Network would allow no trace.

Dallingwood seemed to have read his mind. "I never reported what you told me in the chopper," he said quietly. "About the Network."

Sergeant's chin snapped up. "Why not?"

"When the SWAT sharpshooter took a bead on the woman, I knew you'd been telling me the truth. So I held off for a day."

"And then?"

Dallingwood stuck his hands in his pockets. "And then the sharpshooter got himself run over by a truck. *That night.* Pronounced dead at the scene."

"Yeah," Sergeant said bitterly. "He couldn't have been allowed to testify that he'd been ordered to shoot an innocent woman."

"From now on, you can call me Colonel Klink. Ve know nussing."

"Good for you. I hope you have a long and happy life."

He turned away. After a long silence, he spoke again. "When did Amelia go?" He spoke to the wall.

"She's alive, baby."

Sergeant spun around. Dallingwood's face was split by a big, happy grin.

"What?"

"You heard me. No symptoms, aside from a gash in her hand and a twisted ankle. But her clothes were covered with some pretty nasty stuff. The guys from Toxic Substances have been swarming all over that cave for a week, excavating down to bedrock. There was some groundwater seepage, but not much. Amelia absorbed most of it herself."

"How long has it been?" Sergeant asked, incredulous.

"Eight days. They're ready to release her down in Atlanta. The lab analysts think she must have had some kind of natural immunity."

Sergeant remembered the first time he'd met Amelia, in the hospital. "She does," he said slowly. "She'd been exposed to it before."

"Well, it saved her life. And the lab's already come up with a neutralizer, in case the Libyans have some more of that crap stashed away. They say it's a strain of bubonic plague. The folks at CDC have been studying plague for twenty years. Piece of cake for them."

Dallingwood cleared his throat. "Listen, Burt. Your name *is* Burt, isn't it? I mean that letter that came over the computer from Switzerland had to be for you."

Sergeant thought for a moment, then nodded. There was nothing he could say that would lengthen his life by one millisecond now. "It's Burt. Burt Sergeant."

"I don't want to know any more about you, believe me. But I've got to tell you something. The letter . . . and the rest of the printout. They were never burned. The NYPD had standing orders from me to save every piece of paper that came out of that command station. So when the director got curious about who you were, I sent the whole kaboodle to him. 'Director's Eyes Only.' " He shrugged. "I'm sorry, Burt."

"It doesn't matter anymore," Sergeant said. "Thanks for coming." He looked down at his hands. "Have you seen Amelia?"

"Yes." He grinned. "She won't talk. That is, she's given every detail of her trip with Turner, even drew a map of the cave. But she won't say how she got involved with the guy, where she met him, anything. She says to get the information from you." He laughed.

"She's trying to keep me alive," Sergeant said.

"Hell of a woman. I'd say you were pretty lucky."

Sergeant looked up at him. "Would you?"

There was a long silence. "No, I guess not," Dallingwood said at last.

He straightened up to his full, awesome stature. "You've got a visitor, Burt. I was sent to take you to him."

"Who is it?"

"I don't know. He came straight from the director's office. Are you up to that?"

Sergeant froze for a moment. This, then, was to be the moment of his execution. Quietly. Quickly. It could have been worse.

"Let's go," he said.

Dallingwood led him through a maze of corridors and elevators until they reached a room whose doors were guarded by men in plain dark business suits. Dallingwood showed them his identification and written orders from the Office of the Director, and the guards unlocked the doors.

Inside the large chamber there was a clear lucite cube the size of an ordinary room into which a table and two chairs had been placed. An elderly man, white-haired and impeccably dressed, sat in one of the chairs, his hands folded on top of the table. His bony, elegant face was a mask of infinite patience.

Dallingwood walked Sergeant to the cube and opened a clear plastic door fitted with a lucite handle.

"There are no electric or electronic devices of any kind in this room, gentlemen," he said formally. "When you have finished, please let yourselves out and knock on the outer door."

"Thank you." Sergeant faced the black man. "Goodbye."

Dallingwood swallowed, then turned and walked away. The heavy doors closed and locked behind him.

"Sit down, Mr. Sergeant," the old man said with the trace of a European accent. "My name is Dieter Borsen. I represent the Network."

"I thought you might."

"You've done a good job."

"If I had, I wouldn't be here. And you wouldn't know my name."

Borsen smiled graciously, inclining his head.

"Perhaps. You made one error, but it was unavoidable under the circumstances."

"Not burning the documents myself?"

The old man's bushy eyebrows raised. "No, goodness no. Those were what saved you. Without Mr. Hyatt's letter to you, we would have had no knowledge of the entire Wade Turner affair."

"What, then?"

He shrugged slightly. "You did not arrange for Mr. Hyatt's secretary to be silenced."

"Mrs. Abbot? She didn't even know what was in the files she transmitted."

"She knew your name. She gave it to me."

"Is she dead now?"

Borsen nodded.

No trace.

"Suppose you tell me why you're here," Sergeant said quietly, trying to subdue his hatred of this man and what he represented.

The old man raised his head, showing his patrician profile. "I was Davis Hyatt's superior," he said. "When the Network was formed, I was its first director. I was already an old man then, but the organization was to be disbanded within a year. We believed that terrorism was a passing scourge run by amateurs, and that a consortium of powerful intelligence agencies working together would obliterate it within months."

He smiled. "We know now, of course, that we were overly optimistic. However, the incidence of terrorism has declined sharply, largely due to the efforts of the Network. But it has taken time, and it will take more time. We knew that before my year was half spent. What we did not know was that the man appointed as my successor would fail so miserably and betray us all."

Two deep, angry furrows formed between Borsen's bushy eyebrows. "Fortunately, you were able to reverse much of the damage Davis Hyatt had done." He placed his hands on the table. "That, Mr. Sergeant, is why I am here. The Network, as you may know, was to have been disbanded upon Hyatt's death."

"Yes."

"At first, the members were concerned that this matter hadn't been carried out. But on reflection—after the documents you ordered burned were examined—they decided to continue the work. With a new director. I've come to offer that position to you."

Sergeant clasped the edge of the table. He could not believe what he was hearing. *"What?"*

Borsen chuckled. "You shouldn't be so surprised. You've had ample opportunity to tell what you knew, but you chose silence. That is a good sign."

Sergeant looked down at his bruised arms. "You mean that I was beaten for a week as a test?"

"Of your character. Yes."

It was almost too much to bear. He threw back his head to laugh, but only a high, bitter cry came out.

"Your health will be restored quickly. You have a marvelous future ahead of you."

Sergeant covered his face with his hands, steadying himself. "What if I had talked?" he asked.

"I beg your pardon?"

"What if I'd spilled everything I knew about the Network? Who would have been killed, besides me? Everyone who tortured me? Everyone who read their reports?"

"Come, come. You were hardly tortured. A small discomfort, for a short time. Any prisoner of war—"

"I am not a prisoner of war!" Sergeant hissed.

The old man blinked. "I was merely pointing out that the pressure on you was not extreme. As for your questioners, you saw only one at a time, and their reports were routed directly to the Bureau director. If it had been necessary, only one other person would have been eliminated."

"One FBI agent. And Mrs. Abbot. And the SWAT sharpshooter. And, of course, Amelia Pierce."

"These things are necessary. Surely you must understand that, Mr. Sergeant."

Sergeant looked up at the ceiling and sighed. "Yes, I do,"

he said finally. "I understand more than I ever wanted to."

The old man rose and placed a hand on his shoulder. "You'll make a fine director," he said. "Incidentally, the Pierce woman hasn't died."

Sergeant carefully kept his face a blank. Dallingwood's life depended on it. "Oh?"

"There's no trace of the virus in her body. Remarkable. A pity, really. Since she's already gone to the press, the newspapers will be interested in her death."

His face registered distaste, as if he had smelled a bad odor. "We could arrange something like a mugging, I suppose," he sighed.

"And then see that the mugger is killed."

"Yes. Yes, I imagine that would do." Borsen walked slowly toward the plastic door.

"I have one condition to accepting your offer," Sergeant said.

Borsen raised his eyebrows. There had never been any question of Sergeant's accepting or rejecting anything. If the directorship were refused, the candidate would be killed. "Yes?" the old man asked politely.

"Let me kill the Pierce woman. Enough of our people have been sacrificed. I'd like to seal this matter myself."

The bushy eyebrows lowered, and Borsen smiled. "I think that's a wise decision. You can have her released into your custody at any time."

"I'll take care of her on my way to Geneva."

They walked the length of the long room together. On the far side of the heavy doors, Sergeant was a free man.

40

Sergeant walked into the office that had once belonged to Davis Hyatt. A new secretary sat in Mrs. Abbott's place. She quickly set aside a paperback book she was reading and smiled at him apologetically.

"I'm sorry, Mr. Sergeant, but the mail has not yet come, and—"

"I know." He looked at her in what he hoped was a reassuring way. "There isn't much to do here."

Except die, once your life becomes inconvenient for someone more important than you.

He went into the office and closed the door. It locked automatically behind him.

At the desk, he dictated a long tape, which he enclosed in an envelope along with a letter addressed to Robert Dallingwood.

Then he wrote another, shorter note.

Mr. Borsen:
This will serve to terminate my association with the Network.

Every pertinent piece of information that I know regarding this organization has been recorded and stored for safekeeping, along with instructions to reveal this information to the press in the event of my untimely death, or that of Amelia Pierce.

I promise you our silence, and ask only for peace.

Burt Sergeant

"Mail these immediately," he told his secretary.

"Yes, sir. Can I get you some coffee?"

"No. No coffee, Miss . . ."

"Tippe," she said with a smile.

"Miss Tippe. Do something for me."

"Certainly, sir. What would you like?"

"Go out and get your hair done."

"My hair?" She touched her hands to her gray coif. "Something is wrong with my hair?"

"Nothing. But go."

"Ah . . ." She looked around, bobbing her head like a chicken for a moment. Then she found her handbag, shrugged, and hung it on the crook of her arm. "Very well, I go."

"Have a nice day," Sergeant said.

Then he went back into the office and set fire to the draperies.

They went up like paper. Flames licked across the ceiling moldings and flew along the floor. The papers on the desk curled and blackened. The bank of computer tapes melted into a solid mass before his eyes. When the room was completely engulfed in fire, Sergeant opened the small panel at the rear of the office and walked out. It sealed behind him with a sizzle.

Amelia was waiting for him on the street below. The air was unseasonably cool, even for Switzerland, with a hint of autumn chill. She wore a light sweater over her white dress.

Her hair was brown.

Sergeant put his arms around her and kissed her. "Will you marry me?" he asked.

"That's what I'm here for."

"I'll buy you some flowers on the way." They walked arm in arm down the street. Behind them, four windows on the west wall of the Hyatt Wire Service building blackened with smoke, but nothing escaped.

Not a trace.

"Burt?" Amelia asked.

He turned and smiled at her. It was hard to believe how beautiful she was.

"Is it really over?"

"I think so," he said. "We may have to live quietly for a while."

"With no one except each other?"

"Something like that."

"I think I'll like that fine," Amelia said. They turned a corner, and the building was gone from sight. "Just fine."

Epilogue

Three months later, the chemical weapons compound in Rabta, Libya, was destroyed in an explosion of unknown origin.

Libyan leader Muammar Qaddafi publicly blamed the Israeli Mossad for the bombing. Israeli officials denied the charge.

The CIA had no comment.

Nor did the FBI, the KGB, MI-5, or the French Sureté.